SEEKERS OF WONDER

Seekers of Wonder

WOMEN WRITING FOLK AND FAIRY TALES IN NINETEENTH-CENTURY ITALY AND IRELAND

ELENA EMMA SOTTILOTTA

PRINCETON UNIVERSITY PRESS
PRINCETON & OXFORD

Copyright © 2025 by Princeton University Press

Princeton University Press is committed to the protection of copyright and the intellectual property our authors entrust to us. Copyright promotes the progress and integrity of knowledge created by humans. Thank you for supporting free speech and the global exchange of ideas by purchasing an authorized edition of this book. If you wish to reproduce or distribute any part of it in any form, please obtain permission.

Requests for permission to reproduce material from this work should be sent to permissions@press.princeton.edu

Published by Princeton University Press
41 William Street, Princeton, New Jersey 08540
99 Banbury Road, Oxford OX2 6JX

press.princeton.edu

All Rights Reserved

ISBN 9780691263830
ISBN (pbk.) 9780691263847
ISBN (e-book) 9780691263854

British Library Cataloging-in-Publication Data is available

Editorial: Anne Savarese and James Collier
Production Editorial: Sara Lerner
Cover Design: Chris Ferrante
Production: Lauren Reese
Publicity: William Pagdatoon and Charlotte Coyne
Copyeditor: Daniel Simon

Cover images from Walter Cicchetti / Alamy Stock Photo, Shutterstock, iStock, Adobe Stock, and Project Gutenberg

This book has been composed in Arno

10 9 8 7 6 5 4 3 2 1

To my grandparents,
Angelo and Emma

CONTENTS

List of Illustrations ix
Acknowledgments xi
List of Abbreviations xv
Note to the Reader xvii

Introduction: On De-Isolating Islands 1

1 The Collection of Folklore in Italy and Ireland: Women's Perspectives 21
   The Nineteenth-Century Transnational Interest in Folklore 23
   Between the Margins and the Center: Folklore Studies in Italy and Ireland 27
   Women and Folklore in Post-Unification Italy 42
   Women and Folklore in Ireland in the Long Nineteenth Century 65

2 Identity Matters: Framing the Positionalities of Four Women Folklorists 86
   Laura Gonzenbach: A Pioneering Collector in Sicily 88
   Grazia Deledda: A "Novice Folklorist" in Sardinia 106
   Jane Wilde: A "Gifted Compiler" of Irish Folklore 126
   Augusta Gregory: A Visionary Collector in the West of Ireland 147
   The "Inbetweenness" of the Folklorist: Strategies and Compromises 161

3 Women's Folklore: Reclaiming Voices and Figures in Insular Traditions 170
   The Italian and the Irish Cauldrons of Stories and Their Cooks 171
   "Fairy Justice": Women-Oriented Gazes and Narratives of Subversion 181

*Resisting Evil: Helpers and Healers between Pagan and
Christian Beliefs*   208

*Creatures "from the Outside": Magical Femininity
in Insular Folklore*   215

Epilogue: On Memory and Oblivion beyond Islandness   236

Bibliography   243

Index   279

ILLUSTRATIONS

1.1. A Gaelic League leaflet	36
1.2. Illustration of Beatrice di Pian degli Ontani, *Roadside Songs of Tuscany*	57
1.3. Beatrice di Pian degli Ontani in old age, *L'Illustrazione Italiana*, "La pastorella poetessa"	58
1.4. Illustration of Regina Marcucci by Carlo Chiostri, *Le novelle della nonna: fiabe fantastiche*, I	60
1.5. Illustration of Regina Marcucci by Carlo Chiostri, *Le novelle della nonna: fiabe fantastiche*, II	61
1.6. An Irish family around the fireside in *Ireland: Its Scenery, Character and History*	73
1.7. "Field Group Raking Hay"	81
1.8. "Stocking Corn—Harvest"	81
1.9. Peig Sayers, photograph by Caoimhín Ó Danachair	84
2.1. Grazia Deledda's postcard to Angelo De Gubernatis	117
2.2. Grazia Deledda's letter to Angelo De Gubernatis	122
2.3. Jane Francesca "Speranza" Wilde, supplement to *The Irish Fireside*	128
2.4. Augusta Gregory's postcard to Mario Manlio Rossi	153
3.1. Portrait of Dorothea Viehmann, by Ludwig Emil Grimm	176
3.2. Caterina Certo, *Sicilianische Märchen*	183
3.3. Francesca Crialese, *Sicilianische Märchen*	184
3.4. "Contadina di Monforte," *Costumi siciliani delle province di Messina e di Palermo*	185
3.5. Grazia Deledda's "Leggende Sarde," *Natura ed Arte*	188
3.6. "Donne di Barbagia," *Nuova Antologia*, "Tipi e paesaggi sardi"	191
3.7. An old Irishwoman at her spinning wheel, *The Living Races of Mankind*	196

ACKNOWLEDGMENTS

"DUE MONDI—e io vengo dall'altro" (Campo 1991 [1977]:45).[1] This evocative line from Cristina Campo's poem "Diario bizantino" resonates with the liminal lives of the real and imagined figures who populate the pages of this book. In many ways, I have also found myself standing on the threshold between different worlds as this manuscript was taking shape. The journey that led to the making of this volume has had its marvels but also its challenges, and it is now time to thank those who helped me along the way.

My first heartfelt thanks go to Helena Sanson and Paul Russell, who supported me with their invaluable academic expertise over the course of my research at the University of Cambridge. My warmest thanks also go to Gigliola Sulis and Margo Griffin-Wilson for their precious scholarly insights. I would like to extend my gratitude to the staff of the Faculty of Modern and Medieval Languages and Linguistics, the Italian Section, and the Department of Anglo-Saxon, Norse and Celtic at the University of Cambridge. The research that lies at the core of this book would have not been possible without the financial support of the Arts and Humanities Research Council and the Vice-Chancellor's Award from the Cambridge Trust. I started my studies at St. Catharine's College and completed this manuscript during my research fellowship at Murray Edwards College: I am grateful to the staff of both colleges for providing such conducive research environments, and in particular to the Modern and Medieval Languages Fellows at Murray Edwards College for their warm welcome in the college community.

I am endlessly thankful to Jack Zipes and Cristina Bacchilega. It is through their scholarly works that my views on folk and fairy tales have formed over the years. Their encouragement and intellectual generosity have greatly inspired me in pursuing this project. I also wish to express my sincere gratitude to Princeton University Press, in particular to Anne Savarese, James Collier, and Sara Lerner. It was a pleasure to work under their kind and meticulous guidance. My manuscript also benefited from the helpful feedback of the

---

1. "Two worlds—and I come from the other."

anonymous readers and from the great care of copyeditor Daniel Simon. I thank them all deeply for such professional teamwork.

This book has taken shape at the University of Cambridge, but its seeds were planted during my stays at other universities, including University College Dublin, the University of Sheffield, the University of St. Thomas in St. Paul, Minnesota, and Alma Mater Studiorum—Università di Bologna. The Erasmus Mundus *Crossways in Cultural Narratives* and the Fulbright program have been especially important in the development of my scholarly perspectives. I would like to take this opportunity to thank several supportive scholars and colleagues whom I was lucky to encounter along my path: Nancy Isenberg, David McCallam, Michael Perraudin, Sophie Watt, Alexis Easley, Shannon Scott, Ursula Fanning, Lara Michelacci, Elena Musiani, and Sara Delmedico.

I also wish to express my appreciation for various institutions and associations that supported me over the years, enabling me to carry out essential fieldwork and to participate in inspiring international conferences: the Folklore Society in London, the Women's Section of the American Folklore Society, the British Comparative Literature Association, the European Society of Comparative Literature, the Women's Studies Caucus of the American Association for Italian Studies, the London-based Italian cultural association "Il Circolo," the New Directions in the Humanities Research Network, and the Gladys Krieble Delmas Foundation. During my fieldwork, I have encountered supportive people in several locations: I am particularly thankful to Franco Mottoi, director of the Coro "Grazia Deledda" in Nuoro, and to the librarians Salvatore Audino from the Biblioteca Etnografica "Giuseppe Pitrè" in Palermo, David Speranzi from the Biblioteca Nazionale Centrale in Florence, and Teresa Leo from the Fondazione Biblioteca "Benedetto Croce" in Naples.

I am grateful to the staff of the following institutions who supported me during my research, provided me with reproductions when mobility restrictions did not allow travel, or assisted me in obtaining permissions to include the illustrations in this book: the Biblioteca "Sebastiano Satta" in Nuoro, the Biblioteca Universitaria in Cagliari, the Biblioteca Centrale della Regione Siciliana "Alberto Bombace" in Palermo, the Biblioteca Regionale Universitaria in Messina, the Biblioteca "Antonio Panizzi" in Reggio Emilia, the Archivio Contemporaneo "Alessandro Bonsanti," the Archivio Storico Giunti Editore and the Biblioteca Marucelliana in Florence, the Biblioteca Comunale Rilli-Vettori in Poppi, the Biblioteca Comunale Centrale "Palazzo Sormani" in Milan, the Biblioteca Casa Carducci, the Biblioteca Italiana delle Donne and the Biblioteca Comunale dell'Archiginnasio in Bologna, the Biblioteca dell'Ateneo Veneto, the Biblioteca Nazionale Marciana and the Biblioteca del Museo di Storia Naturale in Venice, the Biblioteca Civica Bertoliana in

Vicenza, the UCD National Folklore Collection, the National Library of Ireland, the Ulster Folk Museum, the Henry W. and Albert A. Berg Collection in the New York Public Library, and the Cambridge University Library.

Over the last few years, I had the chance to take part in academic, cultural, and public engagement initiatives that allowed me to develop creative and critical insights on folklore, fairy tales, children's literature, popular culture, and the art of storytelling. I would like to thank some of the organizers and attendees of these stimulating events, in particular Joan Hill, Elaine McDevitt, Gypsy Thornton, Annie Randall, Giovanna Summerfield, Alessandro Cabiati, Lewis Seifert, Laura Tosi, Pablo a Marca, Vanessa Joosen, Michelle Anya Anjirbag, Alice Parrinello, Nicolò Salmaso, Luca Sarti, Ludovico Nolfi, Francesco Marzella, and Silvia Giannini. I am also thankful to the Brilliant Club Scholars Programme and the University Council for Languages for the possibility to lead enriching outreach experiences aimed at sharing my research beyond academia.

Last but not least, my deepest gratitude goes to those who accompanied me with their friendship and love during this journey in other worlds, especially Alexandra, Giulia, Iveta, Roberta, and Antonio. My greatest love goes to my family for being the spring of inspiration for all my endeavors: Mamma, Papà, Cecilia, and my dearest grandparents, Angelo and Emma, whose cherished stories and values will always stay with me. I dedicate this book to them.

ABBREVIATIONS

The following abbreviations refer to sources frequently cited in this book.

Archives and Libraries

BEGP   Biblioteca Etnografica "Giuseppe Pitrè," Palermo
BNCF   Biblioteca Nazionale Centrale, Florence

Books and Journals

Ancient Cures   *Ancient Cures, Charms, and Usages of Ireland*
Ancient Legends   *Ancient Legends, Mystic Charms, and Superstitions of Ireland*
ASTP   *Archivio per lo studio delle tradizioni popolari*
RTPI   *Rivista delle tradizioni popolari italiane*
TPN   *Tradizioni popolari di Nuoro*
Visions and Beliefs   *Visions and Beliefs in the West of Ireland*

NOTE TO THE READER

THE MANUSCRIPT materials cited in this book have been transcribed as they were written in the original sources, adopting conservative criteria and maintaining the original emphases. When typos were present in the original sources, I signaled them with [*sic*]. Whenever such details were available or could be deduced, I reported the date and the number of the letters, followed by the number of the letter's page in which the quotation appears. Unless otherwise indicated, all translations into English are mine.

SEEKERS OF WONDER

INTRODUCTION

On De-Isolating Islands

The fairy tale does not have any limits, and consequently, it is also not without limits. It does not want to understand anything, and consequently, there is nothing that it doesn't understand. Its wide sea also has its distant shore, and consequently, it is also not a lonely island.

—BÉLA BALÁZS, *THE CLOAK OF DREAMS*
(2010:20, TRANS. JACK ZIPES)

THIS BOOK investigates how the cultural phenomenon of collecting and compiling folklore and fairy tales was influenced by nineteenth-century ideologies, national identities, and linguistic thought, with a focus on women's engagement with popular traditions in Italy and Ireland. The contributions of women writers and collectors to the preservation of folklore and fairy tales in these two cultural contexts shed light on their efforts as perpetuators of cultural heritage and crucial intermediaries between different social circuits. Folk and fairy-tale writings transcribed, compiled, and reelaborated by women can thus be approached as texts that crystallized on the written page ideologically laden viewpoints. These perspectives reflect both centuries-old societal constructs and nineteenth-century conceptions of gender, language, class, and ethnicity.

In this volume, I bring to the fore the impact that issues of identity exerted on the collection and compilation of folk and fairy-tale writings by exploring the lives and works of different female folklorists. Many of these women were seeking to find the extraordinary in the ordinary, turning their gazes to the margins of society to draw attention to the wondrous tales and traditions of the lower classes. The roles that women played in the gathering and publication of folklore in the nineteenth century can offer an alternative perspective on this phenomenon from the standpoint of a group that, despite frequently belonging to a higher social class and thus being more privileged than the common people they were interacting with, was still partially marginalized on a societal level due to gender. Intersecting power imbalances are therefore at work in the practice of collecting folklore. In the process of writing these narratives, it is not only power that is at stake but also women's intellectual commitment to cultural endeavors and immersion in rural communities, with the aim to preserve, assemble, and give shape—and a future—to tradition.

Folk and fairy-tale narratives "contribute to a so-called minor history" (Zipes 2012:123), a view that encapsulates the understanding of history of Giuseppe Pitrè (1841–1916), Sicilian medical doctor turned prominent folklorist, not as "un elenco di uomini, dove si registrano le date delle loro strepitose azioni, ma la rivelazione delle idee, delle passioni, dei costumi e degli interessi civili, insomma della vita di un popolo, di una nazione" (Pitrè 1864:149).[1] Starting from this conception of "minor" and yet no less significant history, this book ultimately seeks to reappraise women's influence on the perpetuation of folkloric narratives in Italy and Ireland, by relocating several female figures within a broader transcultural and transnational framework. This volume therefore proposes new connections between these cultural traditions by encompassing the fields of women's studies, history of folklore, and fairy-tale studies.

In this journey into Italian and Irish folklore and fairy tales, I draw particular attention to four women who were inspired by insular contexts: Laura Gonzenbach (1842–1878), author of *Sicilianische Märchen* (1870), a collection of Sicilian oral tales first published in German, then translated into Italian by Luisa Rubini with a rereading by Vincenzo Consolo, and into English by Jack Zipes; Grazia Deledda (1871–1936), whose Sardinian ethnographic sketches, legends, and fairy tales circulated in late nineteenth-century Italian and Sardinian journals;[2] Jane Wilde (1821–1896), who published two assemblages of folkloric narratives, *Ancient Legends, Mystic Charms, and Superstitions of Ireland* (1887) and *Ancient Cures, Charms, and Usages of Ireland* (1890); and Augusta Gregory (1852–1932), who collected traditional Irish narratives from County Mayo, County Galway, and the Aran Islands and published various collections, including *Visions and Beliefs in the West of Ireland* (1920).

By focusing on Italian and Irish contexts in the historical period ranging from 1870 to 1920 (the dates of publication of the first and the last folklore

---

1. "a list of men and the dates of their significant actions; rather, it should be a revelation of ideas, passions, customs and civil interests. In short, it should be the revelation of the life of a people, of a nation" (Pitrè in Cocchiara, trans. John N. McDaniel, 1981b:356). On Pitrè's contribution as a folklorist, see Cocchiara (1951), Zipes (2012:109–34), Bellantonio (2017), Perricone (2017), and Ferraro (2022).

2. By "ethnographic sketches," I mean concise articles with descriptions of uses and customs that aimed to portray local culture.

collection by the main subjects under investigation), I foreground the conceptions of "the folk" underpinning these women's folkloric writings, the use they make of the material at their disposal, and their attitudes toward vernacular languages. I therefore investigate the peculiarities as well as the commonalities between folk imaginations from dissimilar islands and retrace the trajectories through which oral narratives transcribed and/or rearranged by women emerged in the second half of the nineteenth century. Such a parallel approach aims to create an intertextual dialogue between diverse patrimonies of European popular traditions that have been mostly studied in isolation and helps to shed light on the role of folklore through a gender perspective, during a crucial historical phase when the process of nation-building was taking shape.

By concentrating on Gonzenbach, Deledda, Wilde, and Gregory, I explore how these seekers of wonder located themselves between the "stories" of common people and the "histories" of their respective nations, and how this nexus is constructed and reflected in their folkloric works. As Cristina Bacchilega eloquently writes, fairy tales, also known as wonder tales, "can invite us to dwell in astonishment and explore new possibilities, to engage in *wondering* and *wandering*" (Bacchilega 2013:5).[3] Wonder, in Marina Warner's words, conjures "the marvel, the prodigy, the surprise as well as the responses they excite, of fascination and inquiry; it conveys the active motion towards experience and the passive stance of enrapturement" (Warner 1996:3). Emphasizing its active predisposition, Pauline Greenhill and Jennifer Orme remind us that wonder can be seen "as a force not only for personal transformation in an individual's moment of awe, but for collective power as well" (Greenhill and Orme 2024:4). In their distinctive ways, Gonzenbach, Deledda, Wilde, Gregory, and several other women folklorists that will be explored in this book, were on a quest for wonder not only as an intellectual pursuit but also as a cultural, social, and political act aimed at reevaluating local culture—an act that more often than not has been obfuscated.

Mapping the contributions of sidelined female figures onto the discipline of folkloristics entails withdrawing from a traditionally male-dominated historiographical outlook. Questions of gender, language, class, and ethnicity are thus central in the process of recovering the memory of women folklorists' lives and works. Hence, through the critical framework of intersectionality

---

3. The term "wonder tale," or tale of magic, is frequently used to refer to folk and fairy tales. Echoing the German term *Wundermärchen*, this designation liberates "this kind of story from the miniaturised whimsy of fairyland to breathe the wilder air of the marvellous" (Warner 1996:4). For a detailed definition of wonder tale, which encapsulates the "fundamental imperative of orality," see Conrad (2008:1041–42).

(Crenshaw et al. 1995; Hancock 2016), the positionalities of these women and the circulation and reception of their works are analyzed. To this end, I consider both the paratextual features of their writings—such as prefaces, dedications, postfaces, and editorial notes—and their extratextual dimension, including biographies of the collectors, reviews of their works, and epistolary exchanges they interlaced with other relevant figures. Throughout this volume, I highlight the varying degrees of neglect that these very different figures endured. I do not force comparisons between them nor suggest that their contributions to folklore and fairy-tale studies were equally strong. My intention is rather to understand and reconstruct why these figures decided to turn their attention to popular traditions in different corners of Europe, how they approached the emerging discipline of folklore studies, and what their legacy was in this field. I will therefore not shy away from highlighting the shortcomings of their folkloric writings. Yet an awareness of these flaws does not imply that we should dismiss their works altogether. On the contrary, their contributions are emblematic of specific ways of conceiving popular traditions at the turn of the century and allow for a reflection on the role that gender plays in the practice of collecting folklore. This study is therefore not merely biographical: the trajectories of these figures are reread through the lens of the different contributions they made to folklore and fairy-tale studies in their respective sociocultural milieus, and this specific aspect of their lives—which has often been slighted or undervalued—is purposefully highlighted.

Both Irish and Italian insular contexts in the nineteenth century were by and large still untouched by the literacy processes that would drastically change the cultural landscape of the two countries. These areas were reservoirs of what Walter Ong classified as primary oral cultures, that is, "cultures with no knowledge at all of writing" (Ong 2002 [1982]:1). Bearing in mind the omnipresence of markers of insular identity in the corpus under investigation, it is worth noting the instances in which the concept of "islandness," lying at the core of the interdisciplinary academic field of *island studies* (Baldacchino 2004; Conkling 2007), finds concrete expression in these folkloric writings.[4] Islandness is not shaped according to objective geographical conditions: it is rather a constantly changing human construct, endowed with a strong "ambivalenza simbolica" (Cavallo 2013:191).[5] "Le isole sono posti particolari,"[6] claimed

---

4. The more common term "insularity" has often been used derogatorily due to its "semantic baggage of separation and backwardness" (Baldacchino 2004:272). I resort to the term "islandness" in this book to describe the complex sense of belonging to an island culture and the mutable sensory, geographical, and existential conditions of living on an island.

5. "symbolic ambivalence."

6. "Islands are special places" (Matvejević, trans. Michael Henry Heim, 1999:16).

Predrag Matvejević (2004 [1987]:30) in his seminal treatise *Breviario Mediterraneo*. Whether located in the Mediterranean Sea, in the Atlantic Ocean, or elsewhere in the real or imagined world, island cultures share a similar fluctuating sense of openness and closure, of seclusion and exposure. Yet islands are not identical: as French historian Lucien Febvre (1878–1956) observed, the islands "lost in the ocean spaces" tend to be marked by a stronger sense of isolation, while other islands "situated on the great routes of the globe" turn into crossroads of cultures (Febvre 1996 [1922]:219–20). If the Irish insular contexts lean toward Febvre's classification of "prison-isles," Sicily tends to be historically and culturally framed as an "island at the cross-roads" (Febvre 1996 [1922]:221), whereas Sardinia leans toward the classification of "prison-island," albeit paradoxically retaining features of both. Across the centuries, islands and their inhabitants have been portrayed in literary and historical discourses as alluring and threatening, as utopian and nightmarish, as proudly independent and yet constantly in danger of being colonized.[7] Alternatively represented as remote and desolate, as exotic and flourishing, the ambivalent marginality of these insular contexts and the richness of their popular cultures captivated the imagination of nineteenth-century folklorists.

When examining the folkloric traditions of these contexts, the first traits to emerge are their extreme variety on a local level and a shared sense of difference from the mainland. The frequent emphasis on specific insular mores and tropes, accompanied by an explicit and at times implicit sense of cultural difference and geographical separation, goes hand in hand with a process of "otherization" and "mythification" of these insular contexts in light of the peculiarities of the popular traditions that folklorists sought to safeguard against external influences. The European orientalizing narratives of the East (Said 1977) thus find a pertinent application within Europe itself: as Nelson Moe argues, "European identity is itself inconsistent and fractured, its boundaries fluid and variable" (Moe 2002:6). As cultural manifestations of European peripheries, nineteenth-century folkloric writings from Sicily, Sardinia, and Ireland are symptomatic of this fragmented notion of identity, suspended between a localized "other" and an outsider "self." As will be illustrated in detail in chapter 1, Ireland as a whole, and not only the outlying Irish islands, has been studied through postcolonial lenses and constructed in cultural discourses as a marginal country, ideologically closer to the so-called "Global Souths" of the world than to northern European countries. In a convergence of real and mythical spaces, the Emerald Isle has

---

7. Islands have also been frequently feminized, not only in accounts of real-life insular experiences but also on a mythopoetic level, as in the case of Tír inna mBan, the otherworldly Land of Women where several Irish heroes sojourned (Bitel 1998:164).

been evocatively associated to Atlantis, "il continente scomparso alla memoria e alla coscienza europea" (De Petris and Stella 2001:13).[8] Sardinian and Sicilian cultures, and Italian southern regional cultures more broadly, share a similar status of marginality. Nineteenth-century representations of insular spaces and their traditions as remote, backward, and primitive make the affinities between these different cultural contexts palpable. This parallel study of women who showed a keen interest in popular narratives in Italy and Ireland is thus built on this cross-cultural critical stance.

Engaging in an investigation into different cultural traditions, with the underlying hierarchical assumptions that a comparative act entails, is always a challenge: as Susan Stanford Friedman puts it, "the reasons *not* to compare are legion, centering in ways in which comparison presumes a normative standard of measure by which the other is known and often judged" (Friedman 2013:34; original emphasis). Yet the act itself of not comparing carries political implications and inevitably confines the investigation of a cultural phenomenon to a single context. Any cultural phenomenon does not occur in a limbo of sorts but rather takes place in a dynamic system of cross-cultural resonances, multilingual interactions, and transnational exchanges. Bearing in mind the self-versus-other framework imbricated in the act of comparing, I strive to avoid replicating dynamics of dominance by highlighting the importance of the local dimensions and of the specificities of the cultures hereby investigated. In doing so, I embrace Friedman's invitation to develop "a comparative methodology that is juxtapositional, contrapuntal, and reciprocal, thus opening the possibility for a progressive politics of comparison" (Friedman 2013:40). In line with contemporary trends in comparative studies, my critical perspective thus emphasizes the conceptual model of juxtaposition, rather than the broader category of comparison, in an effort to acknowledge cultural diversity and undertake a more nuanced exploration of affinities and differences in these contexts. Through this act of meaningful juxtaposition, shared resemblances come into sharper focus alongside cultural distinctions.

The twofold investigation into Italy and Ireland facilitates recognition of the historical and cultural similarities between two emerging nations that faced radical political and social changes toward the end of the nineteenth century, a period when questions of identity and nationhood assumed a crucial dimension in European intellectual circles and cultural debates. Furthermore, both countries underwent a complex process of negotiation and standardization between minor and dominant languages as part of a wider attempt to construct a sense of political unity. Italy became a unified state in

---

8. "the continent that disappeared from European memory and conscience."

the second half of the nineteenth century as a result of the political and sociocultural process of the Risorgimento, yet its regional fragmentation sailed against a feeling of national belonging. Consequently, the unity of this newborn political entity needed to be promoted by centralized cultural and linguistic interventions (De Mauro 1963:15–50; Sanson 2013a:276–80), with often partial and ineffective results, especially in southern regions.

Ireland's pervasive sense of cultural distinctiveness was on the rise in the mid-nineteenth century despite its enduring subjugation by the British Empire and the catastrophic consequences of the Great Famine.[9] In an in-depth historical study that takes into account the role of folklore both in Italy and Ireland within a global perspective, Diarmuid Ó Giolláin notes that "[a]s with the Italian south, the incomplete assimilation of Ireland's population was to be explained in evolutionary or racial terms, and Ireland became one of the many small European countries that sought independence in a struggle shaped by cultural nationalism" (Ó Giolláin 2022:332). In this historical phase, it was to the remote shores and islands of the Gaeltacht, the Irish-speaking areas concentrated in the western and southern coasts of Ireland, that folklorists, linguists, and antiquarians turned to assert the roots of "authentic" Irishness, fostering the Irish Renaissance (Foster 1977:264; O'Leary 2006:226–69).[10] These areas, and in particular the Aran Islands, were represented as the "uncorrupted heart of Ireland" (Robinson 1992:xvii). If the Italian nineteenth-century ethnonationalistic tendencies can be interpreted as an instance of "nationalism of unification," the Irish case can rather be regarded as an example of "secessionist nationalism" (O'Mahony and Delanty 1998:48). Whether pushing toward an all-embracing feeling of cultural belonging or toward a marked spirit of national distinctiveness, these wider historical frameworks influenced the practice of collecting oral traditions as a means of cementing communal identities, thereby contributing to the process of nation-making.

Although the performativity of the tales is inevitably lost in the written medium, traces of gender, language, class, and ethnicity conflict can be found among the lines of the oral traditions that writers and collectors across the centuries have made available for contemporary readers. In line with feminist research in this field, my core objective is to reassess side by side women's forms of engagement with folklore and fairy tales at the turn of the century in

---

9. On the numerous studies devoted to the Great Famine, which raged across Ireland in the years 1845–52 and provoked the death of approximately one million people, see Woodham-Smith (1962), Kinealy (2002), and Crowley et al. (2012).

10. On the process of political myth-making and the various organizations that disseminated nationalistic ideas in nineteenth-century Ireland, see Grote (1994) and White (2004).

Italy and Ireland, by approaching the traditions collected in print "as sites of competing, historically and socially framed, desires, [...] which continue to play a privileged function in the reproduction of various social constructs" (Bacchilega 1993:11). With the all-encompassing term "feminist" applied to folklore studies, I refer to the works of scholars who have delved into the diverse expressions of women's lives by engaging in more or less explicit ways with feminist theories and by uncovering overlooked female figures, genres, and creative acts, thus laying bare omissions and gaps in our understanding of cultural expressions.[11] In Italian and Irish folklore and fairy-tale studies, the work of scholars such as Luisa Rubini, Jack Zipes, Angela Bourke, and Patricia Lysaght have played a crucial role in this respect. By embracing and foregrounding such perspectives, this book readdresses the disequilibrium between critical studies predominantly focused on male canonical figures and scholarly endeavors toward noncanonical contributions by women.

The partial or total neglect of female-authored folkloric writings across the centuries is not an isolated case in the Irish and Italian contexts: undeniably, the same has occurred in other traditions, which also deserve to be investigated with a cross-cultural mindset. However, this book focuses on the Irish and Italian folkloric traditions, and in particular on the insular realities within them, as these contexts are emblematic of how marginal cultures were perceived by dominant nationalistic discourses and how they were located within the complex process of constructing collective identities at the turn of the century. By weaving a thread between the Italian and Irish traditions, I bring to light the sociocultural background of the folkloric writings under scrutiny through an investigation of the personal motivations, methodological criteria, and conceptual frameworks that informed them.

The attention to works by female folklorists provides an alternative perspective to the largely male viewpoint that prevailed in the discipline of folkloristics at the time. The personal experiences of female scholars frequently placed them nearer to the marginal communities that were the object of their studies, with concrete effects on the gathering and selection of the tales and traditions that would be at the heart of their sketches, articles, and anthologies. Nineteenth-century women who were engaged in this essential work of preservation often suffered from a twofold marginalization, rooted in the constrictions related to their gender as well as in the prejudices of intellectual circles, which deemed folk traditions as minor products in the hierarchy of cultural expressions. Conversely, nowadays folklorists and historians turn to these materials

---

11. For an insightful reflection on scholarly engagements with feminist theories in American folkloristics, see Jorgensen (2010).

as invaluable sources that disclose not only the efforts of nineteenth-century scholars but also the subaltern perspectives of their oral informants, thus offering vital data on the cultures that conceived these tales and traditions. In some cases, when women were directly involved in the quest for popular narratives, the connection with female informants was stronger, and as a result the female collectors' attempt to give voice and space to elements that subverted a male-centric worldview was also strengthened. In this light, several folkloric writings analyzed in this volume are reassessed as historical documents that obliquely comment on social and gender injustice. Awareness of the uneven relationship and power dynamics between collectors and informants constitutes a pivotal standpoint to frame the manifold facets of this cultural phenomenon. Gayatri Spivak's poignant question "Can the Subaltern Speak?" (1988) thus resonates retrospectively with the issues revolving around the collection, compilation, and reelaboration of folkloric materials, and functions as a relevant overarching theoretical lens for their contextualization.

This book draws together sources preserved in archives and libraries, including previously unpublished photographs and manuscript materials, such as letters and postcards. Borrowing from Gérard Genette's terminology in *Paratexts: Thresholds of Interpretation* (1997 [1987]), these epitextual elements become essential sources of information to gain a deeper understanding of the intertextuality of the folkloric writings under scrutiny, with attention to female forms of expression and representation. As I will explore in chapter 3, far from being the product of a single author, these texts are the result of a multilayered polyphonic dialogue between collectors, editors, informants, and tradition-bearers across generations, social classes, cultures, and languages. In the liminal spaces of these intersecting textual levels, the quintessentially plurivocal character of folktales, fairy tales, and other genres of oral traditions transposed to the literary realm is reappraised. It is thus important to bear in mind Jennifer Schacker's emphasis on the folklore collection as a cultural artifact "negotiated by a number of players—from storytellers to translators to illustrators to publishers to readers and reviewers—and responsive to its context of reception" (Schacker 2003:11).

The relationship between the oral and literary spheres as well as the transfiguration from a performative act to a printed text represent a significant concern for the analysis of folkloric materials. As Paul Zumthor cogently argued in *Introduction à la poésie orale* (1983), in the performance "se recoupent les deux axes de la communication sociale: celui qui joint le locuteur à l'auteur; et celui sur quoi s'unissent situation et tradition" (Zumthor 1983:32).[12] In the

---

12. "two axes of social communication intersect: one that connects speaker to author, and one that combines situation with tradition."

transcription of oral traditions, these two axes are inexorably compromised. It is not only the voice that is irremediably lost but also the nuances of the gestures and the gazes, the sounds and silences, the interactions with the listeners, the atmosphere and the specificity of the contexts in which narrators share their stories. In this respect, Alan Dundes eloquently commented that a "vast chasm separates an oral tale with its subtle nuances entailing significant body movements, eye expression, pregnant pauses, [...] from the inevitably flat and fixed written record of what was once a live and often compelling storytelling event" (Dundes 1986:259). Additionally, it is difficult to determine the extent to which these narratives of oral origin were accurately recorded or altered due to specific concerns of the collector and other contingent circumstances (Olrik 1992 [1921]:14).

Notwithstanding this radical metamorphosis, which turns written texts into faint echoes of the original performances, folklore and fairy-tale writers, compilers, and collectors frequently attempted to retain signs of orality through stylistic choices aimed at conjuring the performativity of the storytelling event, such as phatic expressions and formulas that directly address the readers, imaginatively involving them in the narration. Their commitment and actions were fundamental: without the transit of these narratives from an oral to a literary system at the hands of both men and women of letters, entire repertoires of ancient traditions would have been erased by the passing of time. Critical debates on the interrelationship between orality and literature, and the theoretical perspectives of subaltern studies and intersectionality, thus provide essential methodological tools to contextualize this corpus. To unravel the complex relationship between collectors and informants in a selection of Italian and Irish folk and fairy-tale collections, I therefore consider the interrelated linguistic, class, and gender dynamics at work in this process. Unfortunately, but perhaps not surprisingly, we only have very feeble historical data on nineteenth-century informants, except in a few instances in which such information can be derived from handwritten letters, other archival materials, or from the collections themselves. When the informants' names and other useful information could be deduced from the primary sources and from the archival materials unearthed, I have highlighted them, although it is not always possible to reconstruct in detail the collecting and editing changes that occurred in the transformation of these narratives from an oral to a written realm.[13]

---

13. For a feminist study that shows how the unfolding of the relationship between an ethnographer and an informant can be documented according to contemporary methodologies and standards, see Patricia Sawin's dialogic reconstruction of the life and stories of Bessie Eldreth (1913–2016), a traditional singer from North Carolina (Sawin 2004).

The tendency to underestimate women who were involved in the preservation and dissemination of folklore and fairy tales in the nineteenth century and to neglect their efforts is fairly common across cultures. In *Women and Tradition: A Neglected Group of Folklorists* (2000), Carmen Blacker and Hilda Ellis Davidson explore the works of several women writers in the anglophone world, namely from Great Britain, Ireland, and North America, in their sociocultural complexity. Despite being frequently undermined and prevented from accessing further education due to the conventional limitations imposed on women throughout the centuries, female folklorists were nonetheless extremely committed to their cause and proved to be "adventurous collectors, bold innovators, gifted linguists and recorders of repute" (Blacker and Davidson 2000:4). Many of them had the opportunity to develop their linguistic knowledge also due to social and educational circumstances that did not hinder their language learning, given that modern languages were not "as respected as the classical ones over which male translators held dominion" (Day 2019:412). Such mastery of multiple languages allowed several women to work as translators, paving the way for the circulation of tales and traditions across different cultural and linguistic spheres. However, as was the case with Leonora Blanche Lang (1851–1933)—the key translator and compiler of the highly acclaimed twenty-five-volume Fairy Book series (1889–1913) for which her husband, Andrew Lang, was praised—the lack of recognition of women's labor is not a rare occurrence.[14]

As highlighted by Jack Zipes in his study of neglected female collectors (Zipes 2012:80–108), several nineteenth-century women were deeply engaged in folkloric practices as scholars and as storytellers, such as Nannette Lévesque (1803–1880) in the area of Fraisses in central France, Rachel Busk (1831–1907) in Rome, and Božena Němcová (1820–1862) in Prague. In this regard, Zipes observes how

> Hardly anyone—and this includes folklorists and other scholars with an interest in fairy tales—has taken the time to study the tales of Gonzenbach, Lévesque, Busk, and Němcová, despite the great advances made in recent feminist studies that led to the rediscovery of important European women fairy-tale writers from the seventeenth century to the present. (Zipes 2012:95)

---

14. Andrea Day reconstructed the strategies of erasure of Nora Lang's role in the creation of the Fairy Book series. The series also benefited from the overlooked work of other female translators, including May Kendall (1861–1943), Margaret Raine Hunt (1831–1912), and Violet Hunt (1862–1942). Day insightfully notes that "[b]y subordinating his wife's intellect to his own, Andrew situates the series in a European fairy-tale tradition that privileges the voice of the white, educated male editor over those of women, peasant, and racialized storytellers" (Day 2019:401). On Andrew Lang's "invisible" translators, see also Lathey (2010:102–9).

Many of these figures challenged the biases and prejudices of the time, which precluded women from public exposure; some of them managed to impose themselves on the folkloric scene, despite orbiting around a world dominated chiefly by male scholars. Although their biographies are often little known, these versatile women produced works that denote a keen interest in oral traditions. The field of late nineteenth-century folklore studies can therefore be rightly included among those "lesser-known or unexplored territories that await further investigation from the specific point of view of women and gender issues" (Mitchell and Sanson 2013:9). In this sense, the gender dimension is a central perspective from which to reassess the endeavors of female folklorists in Italy and Ireland, and particularly the contributions of Gonzenbach, Deledda, Wilde, and Gregory, to the preservation of insular folkloric traditions. The compromises they had to make and the challenges they had to face need to be historically contextualized, so as to provide a pertinent reflection on turn-of-the-century concerns regarding gender expectations and constraints that inevitably had an impact on the genesis and reception of their writings. Furthermore, as Kathleen Ragan reminds us, an awareness of the gender issues involved in the collection and publication of folk and fairy tales "can aid in the recovery of neglected folktale texts by women and can open the possibility of uncovering a corpus of folktales outside of, or at least on the periphery of, the male world" (Ragan 2009:240).

In Italian and Irish cultures, the names and works of pivotal nineteenth-century women writers and folklorists faced a comparable fate, having been either entirely excluded from the canon or framed as exceptional cases. The publishing history of *The Field Day Anthology of Irish Writing* (1991–2002) is emblematic in this respect: nearly a decade after the release of the first three volumes, which were accused of portraying an inaccurate male-centric viewpoint of Irish literature, two further volumes devoted exclusively to Irish women's writings and traditions were published by female scholars in 2002. Irish historian and folklorist Angela Bourke wrote and edited seminal sections devoted to women's oral traditions, in which forgotten "expressive personalities and talented artists" are presented alongside excerpts from their works (Bourke 2002a:1195).

In Italian folkloristics, female scholars were barely mentioned in *Storia del folklore in Italia* (1981) by anthropologist and ethnologist Giuseppe Cocchiara (1904–1965). Nevertheless, in the nineteenth century, there were testimonies of the distinctive efforts made by women in this field. For instance, in a review of a collection of Italian folk songs written by British folklorist Evelyn Martinengo-Cesaresco (1852–1931), philologist Francesco Novati (1859–1915) remarked that "[n]ella schiera, che va ogni giorno diventando più numerosa, dei ricercatori delle tradizioni e delle produzioni popolari, l'elemento femminile ha già acquistata una considerevole importanza"[15] and observed that at the delicate female touch "si schiudono talvolta certe porte che sarebbero rimaste gelosamente custodite, si sprigionano vene di poesia, che sarebbero altrimenti restate chiuse nel loro ricetto" (Novati 1886:602).[16] Although this recognition of women's skills in gathering folklore went hand in hand with a stereotyped view of femininity, it is true that female folklorists, precisely because of their gender and in spite of the limitations they had to endure, were often able to gather tales and traditions that were inaccessible to their male counterparts. These figures, whose works tend to be scarcely remembered even within the niche of folklore studies, let alone in the wider cultural sphere, deserve further study to identify the specificities of their endeavors and of the folk traditions they preserved in print.

The significance of women's involvement in popular traditions was occasionally documented in other cultural contexts in the late nineteenth century: in 1892 Paul Sébillot (1843–1918) dedicated a study to "Les femmes et les traditions populaires," published in *Revue des traditions populaires*, the journal of the Société des traditions populaires (1885). In his excursus aimed at tracing "le tableau du folk-lore féminin" (Sébillot 1892:456),[17] the French folklorist praised women who were active in this field in France and abroad. Furthermore, he highlighted the feminine dimension of storytelling:

> Quel que soit le degré de culture ou la condition sociale de la femme, si elle s'occupe de ses enfants, elle a recours pour les endormir, pour adoucir leurs petites douleurs, ou simplement pour les amuser, à un répertoire de berceuses, de chansonnettes, de formulettes, de petits jeux, ou de contes transmis par sa mère, qui elle-même les tenait de la longue suite des aïeules. Et cette littérature orale a, en passant par leurs lèvres, un charme et une naïveté, parfois un bonheur de formes, que les hommes atteignent plus rarement. (Sébillot 1892:449)[18]

---

15. "In the ranks of researchers of popular traditions and productions, which are increasing every day, the female element has already acquired considerable importance."

16. "certain doors that would have remained jealously guarded sometimes open, veins of poetry are released, which would otherwise have remained closed in their shelter."

17. "the picture of female folklore."

18. "Whatever the degree of culture or the social condition of a woman, if she takes care of her children, puts them to sleep, soothes their little pains, or simply amuses them, she uses a repertoire of lullabies, ditties, short formulas, little games, or tales transmitted by her mother, who herself preserved them from a long series of ancestors. And this oral literature, passing through their lips, has a charm and a naivety, sometimes a happiness of forms, that men attain more rarely."

The association of women with orality is long-standing. Although scholars should not be tempted to consider storytelling a feminine prerogative, it is important to acknowledge that many nineteenth-century collectors relied on female informants. The not-coincidental popular designation of "mere old wives' tales" had significant repercussions on how these narratives were perceived, and trivialized, across the centuries, as Marina Warner illustrates in her seminal study *From the Beast to the Blonde: On Fairy Tales and Their Tellers* (Warner 1994:19).

The analysis of the gender dimension of folk and fairy-tale writings is not devoid of political implications. Tradition is not a static product but rather a mutable process continuously shaped by historical changes (Cirese 1971:95). It is thus worth investigating folklore collections "within history and cultural politics and with an eye to the dynamics of change and rupture" (Bacchilega 2007:3) as well as with attention to women's contributions, which remain an "urgent desideratum" in folklore and fairy-tale studies (Haase 2004:30). As in virtually every other academic discipline, the hegemony of a male-dominated canon rages across these fields of study. Only relatively recently, as a result of the rise of feminist inquiries in folklore and fairy-tale studies from the second half of the twentieth century onward, has the nearly absolute absence of "women-authored and women-centered tales" (Haase 2019:55) been acknowledged and partially mended.[19] In this regard, Cristina Bacchilega recognizes the existence of a "Perrault–Grimm–Andersen–Disney quadrumvirate in popular culture" and underscores the cruciality of translations in forwarding the "anti-colonial project of undermining the authority of the 'classic' European tale" (Bacchilega 2019:35).

The intersection of feminist scholarship and folklore studies led to key publications at the crossroads of these fields in the 1970s and 1980s (Kousaleos 1999). A significant impulse was generated by a special issue of the *Journal of American Folklore* in 1975, titled *Women and Folklore: Images and Genres*, which problematized stereotypical representations of women and explored the "cultural variables influencing the range of expressive and creative activities" they engaged in (Farrer 1975:xii). Approximately a decade later in 1987, another special issue of the *Journal of American Folklore* was devoted to feminist folkloric research, building on the scholarly exchanges that took place at the

---

19. Important anthologies of women-authored and women-centered tales are Rosemary Minard's *Womenfolk and Fairy Tales* (1975), Angela Carter's *The Virago Book of Fairy Tales* (1990) and *The Second Virago Book of Fairy Tales* (1993), and Kathleen Ragan's *Fearless Girls, Wise Women, and Beloved Sisters: Heroines in Folktales from around the World* (1998). For a collection of feminist fairy-tale rewritings and literary criticism, see Zipes (1986). On feminist fairy-tale scholarship, see Haase (2004), Stone (2008), and Joosen (2011).

"Folklore and Feminism Symposium" during the annual meeting of the American Folklore Society in 1986. These studies were pivotal to destabilizing assumptions of folklore theory that historically gave prominence to "male informants and masculine forms of expressive culture" (Saltzman 1987:548). The works of feminist folklorists such as Rosan Jordan and Susan Kalcik's *Women's Folklore, Women's Culture* (1985), and the studies of Joan Radner and Susan Lanser on coding in women's folk culture (1987; 1993), have been equally essential to challenging such biases and to carving spaces for alternative perspectives in folklore studies, with the objective of locating "covert feminist messages, within and across cultures" (Radner and Lanser 1993:3). In their article on "Women and the Study of Folklore," Rosan Jordan and Francis A. de Caro grappled with the complex ways in which women's lives and women's issues had been analyzed in folklore studies up to the 1980s. In the context of this study, they noted a shift in the reevaluation of women as folk performers, thanks to their recognition as "people of creativity, sometimes of genius, as worthy of attention as the artists of literate culture" (Jordan and de Caro 1986:514).

Following the path traced by these foundational scholarly debates, which documented the "gargantuan task" of reappraising obfuscated female forms of cultural expression (Farrer 1975:xiv), I propose to unearth the contributions of nineteenth-century female scholars to folklore and fairy-tale studies starting from an acknowledgment of the political dimension of their endeavors. In the *Encyclopedia of Women's Folklore and Folklife*, the term "politics" is applied to women's folklore to underscore how women, through their manifold traditional practices, were able to blur the boundaries between the private and the public spheres, directly or indirectly intervening in wider cultural and political networks (Senehi and Hawranik 2009:463–69). Framing the "politics" of folklore and fairy-tale collections by female figures thus entails focusing on how women drew on "their folk traditions and the relative inscrutability of the homeplace to articulate an alternative politics," by participating in collective discourses and collaborative practices (Senehi and Hawranik 2009:466). This was the case with several nineteenth-century female folklorists in Italy and Ireland.

While a reappraisal of women's participation in folklore practices took place over the course of the twentieth century, the historic neglect of women, both as collectors and as informants, and the frequent downgrading of their scholarly works echoes the Gramscian concept of subaltern groups, whose cultural expressions have been de facto marginalized or silenced. If there is a pressing need for decolonizing the folk and fairy-tale canon by casting a wider net beyond its Eurocentric perspective (Haase 2010), it is also true that the Western folk and fairy-tale canon itself would benefit greatly from further studies and translations that can lay the foundations for the emergence of noncanonical tales and collectors, with the ultimate objective of "support[ing] a more transnational and multi-directional history of the genre within Europe" (Bacchilega 2019:35). Such a view resonates with Donald Haase's claim for the necessity "to expand the focus of feminist fairy-tale research beyond the Western European and Anglo-American tradition, and even within those traditions to investigate the fairy-tale intertexts in the work of minority writers and performers" (Haase 2004:29).

A growing interest among contemporary scholars in women folklorists, fairy-tale writers, and their works is testified by several post-2020s publications that underscore women's multifaceted ventures into folklore as well as the relationship between feminism and fairy tales. A wide and nuanced reflection on women's roles as heroines in the Western tradition is provided by Maria Tatar in *The Heroine with 1001 Faces* (2021), a book that overturns the gender biases at the core of Joseph Campbell's influential study in comparative mythology, *The Hero with a Thousand Faces* (1949). The work of scholars and translators in disseminating lesser-known fairy tales by women or about women has also witnessed an important turn. In *Women Writing Wonder: An Anthology of Subversive Nineteenth-Century British, French, and German Fairy Tales* (2021), Julie Koehler, Shandi Lynne Wagner, Anne Duggan, and Adrion Dula bring together a fascinating corpus of tales by women writers, thus highlighting female forms of engagement with wonder in the British, French, and German traditions. A similar intent animates the pages of *The Lost Princess*, in which Anne Duggan carries out an "archaeological excavation" into the history of French *conteuses* such as Marie-Catherine d'Aulnoy (1652–1705), Charlotte-Rose Caumont de La Force (1654–1724), and Marie-Jeanne L'Héritier (1664–1734), who left a crucial yet not fully recognized mark on the history of the fairy-tale genre (Duggan 2023:8).[20] This act of excavation aligns with Jack Zipes's relentless quest to rediscover "buried treasures," those tales that disclose the "virtues of the discarded, the marginal, and the dispossessed" (Zipes 2023:7).

In the Italian tradition, several lesser-known narratives by women writers have been included in two anthologies of fairy tales translated into English, Cristina Mazzoni's *The Pomegranates and Other Modern Italian Fairy Tales* (2021) and Nancy Canepa's *The Enchanted Boot: Italian Fairy Tales and Their Tellers* (2023). Equally important is *Fiabe ribelli. Le più belle fiabe italiane delle ragazze in gamba* (2023), one of the many collections of folk and fairy tales translated and edited by Bianca Lazzaro into standard Italian, which greatly contribute to widen access to a wealth of narratives featuring resourceful and

---

20. For a fundamental study on women in the history of the fairy tale from the seventeenth to the twentieth centuries, see Harries (2001). For an anthology of Madame d'Aulnoy's tales translated into English by Jack Zipes and illustrated by Natalie Frank, see d'Aulnoy (2021).

sharp-witted female protagonists, for a long time available only to a limited readership. All these scholars and translators challenge the pervasive assumption that "women in previous ages were voiceless, subservient creatures," as Eddie Lenihan notes in *Defiant Irish Women* (Lenihan 2019:11),[21] yet another empowering book in which the Irish storyteller shows how women's voices reverberate across time under the guise of liberating stories about banshees, hags, witches, and goddesses. It is within the wonder worlds of these narratives that women often reclaim the space for self-expression that their societies have long denied them.[22]

This volume situates itself within this ongoing process of rediscovering women's roles as writers, collectors, transcribers, translators, compilers, tellers, and protagonists of wonder tales. As a whole, this book intends to take a step further in reassessing and recentering the memories of several women in Italian and Irish folklore, building on the foundational works of committed folklorists that have previously investigated some of these figures and traditions. The volume is thus structured into three macrochapters, devoted to (1) the establishment of a parallel study of Italian and Irish cultures from the point of view of nineteenth-century folklore studies and the mapping of the heterogeneous contributions by women from a variety of sociocultural backgrounds; (2) an in-depth reassessment of the positionalities of Laura Gonzenbach, Grazia Deledda, Jane Wilde, and Augusta Gregory, with attention to the genesis and reception of their folkloric works; and (3) a critical analysis of the representation of female figures and insular contexts within their folkloric writings, taking into account the issues revolving around the transposition of oral narratives in written form.[23]

21. The book was first published in 1991 as *Ferocious Irish Women*.

22. A separate discussion would address the wondrous array of contemporary feminist reimaginings that follow in the footsteps of the influential literary fairy tales by Angela Carter (1940–1992), in which compelling rewritings such as the award-winning *Tangleweed and Brine* (2017) and *Savage Her Reply* (2020), by Irish writer Deirdre Sullivan, can be included. Another collection of imaginative tales that falls into this category is Sharon Blackie's *Foxfire, Wolfskin and Other Stories of Shapeshifting Women* (2019), in part inspired by Irish folklore and mythology. It is also worth mentioning contemporary anthologies like *Awake Not Sleeping: Reimagining Fairy Tales for a New Generation* (2021)—part of an initiative promoted by United Nations Women, dedicated to women's empowerment—that reveals an activist commitment to foster gender equity by reimagining old stories (Walsh et al. 2021). On Sullivan's *Tangleweed and Brine*, see Sarti (2023a).

23. Acknowledgment is made to the following articles, in which some of the observations in this book first appeared: Sottilotta, Elena Emma (2021), "From Avalon to Southern Italy: The Afterlife of Fata Morgana in Laura Gonzenbach's *Sicilianische Märchen* (1870)," *Women Language*

More specifically, chapter 1, "The Collection of Folklore in Italy and Ireland: Women's Perspectives," tackles the central questions surrounding the phenomenon of folklore collection. This chapter provides an overview of the transnational dimension of the nineteenth-century European folk revivals and identifies key female figures in Italy and Ireland. In this historical period, marginal contexts became privileged spaces to trace the remotest roots of primitivism. Thus, this first chapter introduces identity issues related to the insular dimension vis-à-vis the broader gendered implications of folklore research by moving gradually from a transnational standpoint to national, regional, and local axes. I therefore zoom in on lesser-known contributions to folkloristics in periodicals and book form, offering new insights into the networks of cultural exchange in the "long nineteenth century."[24] Rather than emphasizing the exceptionality of a few distinguished women, the large and small efforts of various female figures are contextualized and reappraised within and outside the niche of folklore studies, with further consideration of other overlapping fields, such as children's literature, travel writing, dialectology, and ethnomusicology. As will be shown, many women played an important role in preserving folk traditions in Italy and Ireland, often questioning the limits imposed on them through their intellectual pursuits or through the field-based exploration of rural regions. It is outside the scope of this chapter to provide an in-depth study of each of these figures. Rather, chapter 1 aspires to serve as a starting point for further exploration of lesser-known individuals and their works, or to direct interest to scholarly works that explored some of these case studies but did not receive considerable attention.

Chapter 2, "Identity Matters: Framing the Positionalities of Four Women Folklorists," narrows the focus onto the folkloric writings by Gonzenbach, Deledda, Wilde, and Gregory. Each figure is placed alongside other scholars of popular traditions, and their works are reassessed in light of contemporary

---

Literature in Italy / Donne Lingua Letteratura in Italia, 3, 103–21; Sottilotta, Elena Emma (2022), "Maria Savi-Lopez: The Portrait of a Neglected Woman Writer and Folklorist in Post-Unification Italy," *P.R.I.S.M.I. Revue d'études italiennes, Nouvelle série*, 3, 141–63; Sottilotta, Elena Emma (2023), "(Re)Collections of a 'Piccola Streghina' from the Heart of the Mediterranean: Gender and Class Consciousness in Grazia Deledda's Folkloric Writings," *I.S. MED.—Interdisciplinary Studies on the Mediterranean*, 1, 109–29; Sottilotta, Elena Emma (2024), "'Miniere di fiabe': Poetics of Space and Performance within and outside Angela Nardo Cibele's Folk and Fairy-Tale Writings," *Women Language Literature in Italy / Donne Lingua Letteratura in Italia*, 6.

24. British historian Eric Hobsbawm (1917–2012) investigated the historical processes that marked the so-called "long nineteenth century," a term that encompasses the period ranging from the French Revolution to World War I, in his trilogy *The Age of Revolution: 1789–1848* (1962), *The Age of Capital: 1848–1875* (1965), and *The Age of Empire: 1875–1914* (1987).

perspectives on women's and folklore studies. These women were selected as case studies for their emblematic contributions to the discipline of folklore studies at its inception in Italy and Ireland and for their idiosyncratic positionalities. Each subsection details the personal motivations and biographical vicissitudes that paved the way for their involvement in this field. Starting with a section devoted to Laura Gonzenbach in mid-nineteenth-century Sicily and ending with a section devoted to Augusta Gregory in Ireland at the turn of the twentieth century, I adopted a chronological approach so as to retrace not only these women's life trajectories but also the development of Italian and Irish folkloristics more broadly.

Gonzenbach, a fairy-tale collector born into a Swiss-German family in Messina, wrote a collection of Sicilian fairy tales that was, and still is nowadays, groundbreaking for its focus on women both as storytellers and as protagonists of the tales. Her work as a folklorist predates the contributions of illustrious scholars of the time, including Giuseppe Pitrè and Angelo De Gubernatis, who performed the role of mentor to Grazia Deledda in her formative years, the second case study presented. After a contextualization of Deledda's life with a focus on her youth, her gathering of popular traditions from her native island is examined side by side with her correspondence with De Gubernatis. In the third and fourth sections of this chapter, the attention shifts to Jane Wilde and Augusta Gregory in Ireland by reassessing their folklore collections in light of their identities as Anglo-Irish upper-class women who turned their patriotic gaze to the counties and isles in the west of Ireland as sources of inspiration. While Jane Wilde can be considered the first woman who authored a compendium of folklore in nineteenth-century Ireland, she did not interact directly with local informants but rather relied upon materials previously collected by her husband, William Wilde. Conversely, Lady Gregory had a direct contact with Irish peasants, and her folklore anthologies reveal an increasingly systematic study of Irish oral tales and traditions, which not only greatly influenced W. B. Yeats but is also valuable from a cultural and historical viewpoint in its own right. As a whole, the second chapter scrutinizes the ideological beliefs that lie at the core of these case studies in order to outline the situatedness of these women. I then present their folkloric writings, with attention to where they originated and how they were received at the time of their publication. Finally, I juxtapose the linguistic and cultural compromises that these figures had to make when compiling these writings with reference to the dynamics between vernacular and dominant languages in their respective cultural contexts.

To adequately address the gender issues involved, it is necessary to explore the role of women not only as collectors but also as depositories of traditional knowledge. Hence, it is essential to recognize how folkloric writings are the result of a complex interplay between the informants' world and the scholarly world, and thus between the oral and the literary dimensions. Consequently, chapter 3, "Women's Folklore: Reclaiming Voices and Figures in Insular Traditions," explores the politics and poetics of seeking wonder by foregrounding the relationship between collectors, tellers, and tales in these four case studies. In this chapter, I draw connections between real-life and imaginary female figures that appear in these texts as well as between their manifold references to insular contexts. The key themes of subversion and justice set the scene for an exploration of the liminal encounters with supernatural creatures recorded in this heterogeneous corpus, by highlighting their affinities and differences across these distinctive cultural traditions.

While the most renowned fairy-tale anthologies, such as those by Charles Perrault and the Brothers Grimm, have been subjected to numerous critical studies,[25] a parallel analysis of folklore and fairy-tale collections by nineteenth-century women writers and collectors who were active in European insular contexts has not been carried out thus far. The fairy tale is not "a lonely island": with these allusive words from this introduction's epigraph, Hungarian writer, film critic, and author of fascinating fairy-tale narratives Béla Balázs (1884–1949) encapsulates the paradoxes of an elusive genre that escapes straightforward interpretations.[26] This book ultimately wishes to contribute to folklore and fairy-tale studies by "de-isolating" the popular traditions of European islands and women's praiseworthy efforts in these fields.

---

25. Among the many scholarly works on Charles Perrault, see Lewis (1996), Jones (2016), and Haase (2017). On the Brothers Grimm, see Bottigheimer (1987), Haase (1993), Zipes (2002a; 2015), Tatar (2003), and Norberg (2022).

26. For a recent translation into English of his literary fairy tales, inspired by the Chinese aquarelles made by Austrian-Argentine painter Mariette Lydis (1887–1970) and originally published in 1922 in *Der Mantel der Träume: Chinesische Novellen*, see Balázs's *The Cloak of Dreams* (2010, trans. Jack Zipes).

1

The Collection of Folklore in Italy and Ireland

WOMEN'S PERSPECTIVES

> Ritorno sui miei passi, verso la vetrina della collezione di sabbia. Il vero diario segreto da decifrare è qui, tra questi prelievi di spiagge e di deserti sottovetro. Anche qui il collezionista è una donna [...]. Ma per ora non m'interessa darle un volto, una figura; la vedo come una persona astratta, un io che potrei essere io, un meccanismo mentale che cerco d'immaginarmi al lavoro.[1]
> —ITALO CALVINO, *COLLEZIONE DI SABBIA* (1984 [1974]:12)

THE SURGE of folk and fairy-tale collections became a preponderant cultural phenomenon in the shifting panorama of nineteenth-century Europe. In this historical phase, intellectuals, scholars, and popular culture enthusiasts devoted their time and skills to collecting, transcribing, and editing traditional narratives from the "mouth of the people," a frequent metonymic image that makes a claim for the authenticity of these tales.[2] The nineteenth-century folk revivals were part of a European process, to the point that it would be more appropriate to define them as heterogeneous versions of a "European Folk

---

1. "I retrace my steps, towards the case with the collection of sand. The real secret diary to decipher is here, amidst these samples from beaches and deserts now under glass. In this case too the collector is a woman [...]. But just now I am not interested in giving her a face, or features; I see her as an abstract person, an 'I' that could be myself as well, a mental mechanism which I try to imagine at work" (Calvino, trans. Martin McLaughlin, 2013:8).

2. On the recurrence of the "mouth of the people" among nineteenth-century fairy-tale collectors, see Köhler-Zülch and Shojaei Kawan (1990:253) and Rubini (1998:161–63).

Revival," rooted in the belief that an ancient world made of traditions, songs, and stories passed on by word of mouth was doomed to disappear (Campbell and Perraudin 2012:2). The radical sociocultural changes that the first and second industrial revolutions brought about in nineteenth-century Europe spurred a pervasive sense of urgency to preserve the remnants of a peasant world perceived to be under threat.

It is precisely in the mid-nineteenth century that folklore begins to develop as a field of study.[3] Since then, the history of folklore has greatly expanded and intersected with several other disciplines, including ethnography, anthropology, philology, and cultural studies.[4] This first chapter thus aims to establish the basis for the parallel assessment of Italian and Irish folklore studies through a gendered lens and with an eye to the European dimension of this phenomenon. To this end, the first section, "The Nineteenth-Century Transnational Interest in Folklore," introduces the transnational dynamics that distinguished this discipline. The second section, "Between the Margins and the Center: Folklore Studies in Italy and Ireland," investigates the key concerns of this field within these two cultural contexts. Finally, the third and fourth sections, "Women and Folklore in Post-Unification Italy" and "Women and Folklore in Ireland in the Long Nineteenth Century," map the contributions of different women to the preservation of popular traditions in Italy and Ireland, moving from a national to a local dimension.

---

3. The first instance of the usage of this term dates back to William Thoms, who employed this "good Saxon compound, Folk-Lore,—*the Lore of the People*" in an article published in 1846 in *The Athenaeum*, under the pseudonym "Ambrose Merton," to designate "that interesting branch of literary antiquities" (Thoms in Emrich 1946:361–62). Salvatore Battaglia reported the term in the *Grande Dizionario della Lingua Italiana* in its Italianized version, *folclore*, defined as the discipline "che studia le tradizioni popolari, ne ricerca le origini, ne segue lo svolgimento e le compara e confronta fra di loro" [that studies popular traditions, researches their origins, follows their development and compares them with each other] (Battaglia 1961:VI, 107). Battaglia directed readers to the definition provided in Costantino Arlia and Pietro Fanfani's *Lessico dell'infima e corrotta italianità* (1890 [1881]:230). In the latter, Vincenzo Grossi's *Il Folk-lore nella Scienza, nella Letteratura e nell'Arte* (1888) was reported as the first Italian book in which the term appeared. In Modern Irish, *béaloideas* is the term used to designate folklore, a compound word that blends *béal* (mouth) and *oideas* (instruction), literally meaning "oral teaching" (Bourke 2002a:1193). *Béaloideas* is also the title of the journal of the Folklore of Ireland Society (An Cumann Le Béaloideas Éireann), founded by Séamus Ó Duilearga (1899–1980) in 1927.

4. On the history of folklore in Europe, see Cocchiara (1952). On the intersection between folklore and the nation-building process, see Ó Giolláin (2000:63–93) and Baycroft and Hopkin (2012).

The Nineteenth-Century Transnational Interest in Folklore

When Italo Calvino encountered a "collection of sand," which then became the title of his eponymous anthology of essays originally published in 1984, he lingered at length on the visual texture of these diverse universes coming from the most disparate corners of the world, captured in small jars and brought to light for an exposition in Paris. The Italian fabulist curiously scrutinized this collection of sand as a "diario di viaggi, [. . .] di sentimenti, di stati d'animo, di umori"[5] and observed how "[i]l fascino d'una collezione sta in quel tanto che rivela e in quel tanto che nasconde della spinta segreta che ha portato a crearla" (Calvino 1984 [1974]:10–11).[6] If approached as lively and dynamic cultural manifestations, nineteenth-century and early twentieth-century folklore collections, in a similar manner to their sandy counterparts, can reveal the collectors' state of "inbetweenness," the hybrid nature of the oral tales transformed for the written medium, the liminality of this operation of cultural and linguistic mediation, the reasons behind this fascination with popular culture, and the intellectual effort at work in this mediating process.

The phenomenon of folkloric collection in the nineteenth century revolved around a crucial process: the relationship between outsiders and insiders, between "foreign" upper-class collectors and the "folk," who belonged to a lower social class and to a well-defined community. There is an evident ideological paradox at the core of these folkloric practices: on the one hand, from the collectors' point of view, folklorists were moved by the noble ideal to give voice to those who did not have the means to express themselves outside their own community and, consequently, to preserve and transmit that knowledge to posterity; on the other hand, from the informants' point of view, collectors transformed, translated, altered, and edited on multiple levels the original "voice of the folk" to fit the multifaceted purposes of their collections. In the twentieth century, Italian philosopher and political thinker Antonio Gramsci (1891–1937) observed how folklore had been studied chiefly as "elemento 'pittoresco'" and remarked how it ought to be investigated as a "concezione del mondo" of specific social strata (Gramsci 1975, III:2311).[7] The Gramscian conception of folklore acknowledges its complex nature and is prescient of the

---

5. "a diary of travels, [. . .] of feelings, states of mind, moods" (Calvino, trans. Martin McLaughlin, 2013:6).

6. "The fascination of a collection lies just as much in what it reveals as in what it conceals of the secret urge that led to its creation" (Calvino, trans. Martin McLaughlin, 2013:7).

7. "'picturesque' element," "conception of the world" (Gramsci, trans. Joseph A. Buttigieg and Antonio Callari, 2007, I:186).

need to consider the dialectic dialogue between higher and lower forms of cultural expression, in which the popular dimension is deeply interwoven with the creation of a nation.[8] It thus becomes clear that the act of collecting is essentially an act of mediation but also of appropriation, in which several identities encounter and overlap with one another. This was even more true at a time when professional figures in folklore studies were yet to be fully defined: hence, to gain a better understanding of one facet of this cultural phenomenon, it is helpful to view "nineteenth-century collectors as transcribers, translators, mediators, educators, cultivators, and historians rolled into one" (Zipes 2013:xxxvi).

Given the considerable distance between the tales cataloged on the page and the original verbal performance, in the past folklore collections were regarded as obsolete and artificial cultural productions: according to this view, which reclaimed the importance of the living traditions, "[t]he folklore archive is no more than a collection of defunct artifacts, texts selected at random that came into being in rather unusual, in most cases non-authentic conditions" (Honko in Leino 1989:33). However, alternative perspectives on the collection of verbal folklore can bring to the fore the efforts that collectors made to preserve centuries-old narratives, the relationship between collectors and informants, and the gender and class dynamics at stake in this process. In other words, when highlighting the peculiarities of this act of appropriation, the collections of folk and fairy-tale narratives can be approached as multilayered artifacts in which various distant and at times conflicting voices blend and resonate. Their intrinsically polyphonic nature allows for an emergence of diverse viewpoints.

In his reflection on W. B. Yeats's collections, Vito Carrassi, albeit not focusing on the role of gender dynamics in the act of compiling and collecting oral narratives, aptly defines the folklore anthology as "una sorta di area di transizione, di zona franca, di spazio ibrido dove, a prescindere dalle reali o presunte intenzioni dell'*editor*, si verifica una complessa intersezione e interazione di voci, idee, valori, moventi, finalità che, tutti insieme, danno vita a un sistema eterogeneo" (Carrassi 2014:228; original emphasis).[9] In the afterword to his translation of Irish folk and fairy tales into Italian, Antonio Bibbò similarly observes how, since the early nineteenth century, "la storia del folklore

---

8. For a critical investigation of the Gramscian conception of folklore, see Cirese (1976:65–104), Bronzini (2002:195–224), and Gencarella (2010:221–52).

9. "a sort of transition area, free zone, hybrid space where—regardless of the real or presumed intentions of the editor—a complex intersection and interaction of voices, ideas, values, motives, purposes take place, which, all together, give life to a heterogeneous system."

irlandese e della sua scoperta si presenta come un'opera collettiva, nella quale è difficile definire l'apporto delle singole mani" (Bibbò 2022b:175).[10] Hence, when analyzing folktales transmitted in print, it is essential to remember that "editors and tellers do not 'tell' the same story" (Bacchilega 1993:9) and that competing voices are often merged in the written page.

On a geopolitical level, the dichotomy between nationalism and regionalism in relation to nineteenth-century folklore studies is only apparent: it would perhaps be more appropriate to refer to a pervasive nineteenth-century spirit of "romantic regionalism" (Zipes 2013:xxxii) rather than nationalism if one wishes to acknowledge the increasing attention of nineteenth-century folklorists to extremely specific local areas within a wider nationalistic project.[11] In light of the complex relationship between the national and the regional dimensions, it is important to remember that traditional narratives "were not limited by national or indeed any political or administrative boundaries, but transcended them. [...] Folklore was not national, or even regional, it was simultaneously more generalised and more particular" (Hopkin 2012:391).[12] If the nature of folklore surpasses national borders, the multidirectional efforts of folklore collectors unveil the coexistence of diverse agendas behind their works. Marina Warner echoes such reflections when writing that "[n]ineteenth-century collectors set out to capture the national imagination of their country, but time has revealed them to have been unwitting internationalists" (Warner 2018:51). In other words, in the enterprise set by nineteenth-century folklorists, the national and local dimensions are not devoid of a transnational drive, as revealed by their wide-ranging scholarly interests and intricate networks of worldwide exchanges. Such pivotal observations on the geopolitical sphere surrounding the collection of folklore conflate into a statement that constitutes the crucial premise of this book: "collecting folktales was some kind of social and political act" (Zipes 2013:xxxi). In unfolding the complexities of folklorists' social and political acts, the gender perspective can pave the way for untrodden paths in this field of inquiry.

Notably, at the beginning of the nineteenth century, a fundamental impulse for the collection of verbal folklore was triggered in Germany by Jacob Grimm (1785–1863) and Wilhelm Grimm (1786–1859), who represent the polyhedral nineteenth-century philologists, linguists, translators, and revivalists par

---

10. "the history of Irish folklore and its discovery appears as a collective work, in which it is difficult to define the contribution of individual hands."

11. On Romantic nationalism in folkloristics, see Abrahams (1993).

12. On the politics of regionalism in European folklore studies, see also Augusteijn and Storm (2012) and Hopkin (2019). For a study of Italian regionalism and its historical and linguistic ramifications, see Levy (1996).

excellence. As a pebble thrown in a pond creates a motion of concentric and ever-expanding waves, the Grimms' *Kinder- und Hausmärchen* (1812–15) and *Deutsche Sagen* (1816–18) generated a process of emulation and reproduction that Terry Gunnell terms "Grimm Ripples."[13] While acknowledging the central influence of the Brothers Grimm, it is interesting to investigate what happened when the collection of folkloric material was undertaken by women rather than men. Despite being less popular today than their male counterparts, several women writers in nineteenth-century Europe were keenly involved in the practice of collecting folklore. It becomes evident that there is an underexplored area in scholarly studies with regard to nineteenth-century female folklorists and that much more can be disclosed about these women and their works, especially from a transnational perspective. If "[t]hus far, few scholars have [...] studied how gender may play a role in recording, translating, editing, and publishing oral wonder tales" (Zipes 2012:105), it is now time to delve deeper into this field by taking into account the international parameters of the folk revivals in Europe.

In the twentieth century, there was a tendency to examine the folk revivals in the European tradition within the cultural and linguistic limits set by national frontiers. In the words of Matthew Campbell and Michael Perraudin, "[a]fter the early nineteenth century, the paths of the various national revivals increasingly diverged, and that is very much how they tend to be seen now, as isolated national phenomena rather than as aspects of a pan-European process" (Campbell and Perraudin 2012:2). Comparative perspectives have seldom been implemented since "the socio-political implications of folklore studies have all been seen within national boundaries" (Naithani 2010:1). However, there is a visible—and invisible—network of interconnections between the various national folk revivals that deserves to be unraveled. It is therefore essential to place different cultural traditions in relation to other national contexts in order to frame the nineteenth-century phenomenon of folk revival and the roles that women played in it.

As observed by Diarmuid Ó Giolláin, a comparative critical outlook brings into focus the network of relationships between metropolitan and peripheral countries, and between the metropolitan and peripheral dimensions within the same countries, bearing in mind that the same ideas circulated in different European countries but "varied in their ideological potency" (Ó Giolláin

---

13. "Grimm Ripples" is the title of an international project aimed to explore the intersection between nationalism and folk legend collections in Nordic European countries, led by Terry Gunnell at the University of Iceland. See Gunnell (2012:47; 2022a; 2022b) and Hafstein (2015:19–20).

2000:4). The broad distinction between urban and rural areas and between central and peripheral nations is helpful to the extent that it emphasizes the significance that folklore research was charged with in politically marginal and culturally heterogeneous countries that were still aiming to achieve a sense of national belonging, as was the case for Italy and Ireland in the mid-nineteenth century. In this regard, Sadhana Naithani reiterates how the nationalistic impulse that guided folklore collectors in Ireland is "comparable with its European contemporaries" (Naithani 2010:7). A comprehensive investigation of the history of folklore in the Italian and Irish contexts would inevitably fall outside the scope of this study. However, before moving to an exploration of women's roles in the preservation and dissemination of Italian and Irish popular traditions in the long nineteenth century, it is helpful to identify some of the key political, cultural, and linguistic dynamics that animated the emergence of folklore studies in the two countries.

Between the Margins and the Center: Folklore Studies in Italy and Ireland

In the long nineteenth century, the shift toward peripheral regions as depositories of a primitive and purer knowledge was taking place in the context of a highly transnational exchange of knowledge and theories among folklore scholars. Starting from the assumption that the collections of folklore are not neutral in the way they were conceptualized and internally organized, the act of mediation between "the academic world of folklore studies," which was inherently international, and "the authenticity of the local, oral tradition" (Eriksen and Selberg 2015:303) inescapably reflects the worldview, background, and intentions of the collector.

In *Novelle lombarde*, published in 1868, Italian writer and historian Cesare Cantù (1804–1895) ironically observed how "qui da noi né gli scrittori descrivono, né i curiosi osservano le cose nostre; s'ha altro a fare che scendere alle minuzie della vita reale: e vuolsi dover guardare ogni cosa col telescopio— eccellente metodo di raggiungere la verità!" (Cantù 1868:215).[14] With this remark, Cantù underscored the tendency of Italian intellectuals of the time to investigate and to be fascinated by the outside world while disregarding what lay in their immediate surroundings—in this case, the autochthonous

---

14. "here [in Italy] neither the writers describe nor the curious observe our matters; there are more important concerns rather than getting down to the minutiae of real life: and everything has to be observed through a telescope—what an excellent method for reaching the truth!"

traditions of the Italian nation. However, this tendency was destined to be turned upside down by the legions of scholars that drove a process of rediscovery of regional folklore in the last decades of the nineteenth century. Stefano Cavazza describes this process as a "quest for 'domestic' exoticism" (Cavazza 2012:77), a definition that resonates with James Knapp's concept of the "exotic familiar," whereby the "cultural world of folktale and peasant lore which had been virtually invisible to 'civilized' eyes [...] suddenly began to be seen in the reflected light of nineteenth-century Europe's fascination with the more distant exoticism of its world-wide imperial realms" (Knapp 1995:289).[15]

In *The Critical Study of Irish Literature* (1903), which contained a printed version of a lecture he delivered at the National Literary Society in Dublin on November 10, 1902, Celticist Alfred Nutt (1856–1910) remarked that, although at the beginning of the twentieth century several studies sought to reconstruct the history of Gaelic literature, their results were nonetheless "trifling in comparison with what remains to be done. Gaelic literary history is not, as is the Polar region, a *terra incognita*; but it may be likened to the interior of the African continent some forty years ago" (Nutt 1903:12; original emphasis).[16] If on the one hand Nutt negated the equation between Gaelic literature and the polar region as an unexplored branch of knowledge, on the other hand he evoked a comparison with the African hinterland, imbued with imperialist assumptions, casting a vision of Irish literary history as a yet-to-be-mapped field due to the absence of "fixed points of latitude or longitude" (Nutt 1903:12). In this "imaginative geography" of Irish literary history, Nutt's allusion to an uncharted territory places Ireland in the context of postcolonial critical theories long before they were developed (Said 1977:49; 1986); this is not dissimilar to the frequently discriminatory perceptions of Italian southern regions within the newborn state at the turn of the century, although the destiny of these territories was to remain firmly established within the Italian state, whereas Ireland was already set on the turbulent historic path leading to its independence from the British Crown.

The analogies between Italy and Ireland on a political level, particularly between specific areas within the two countries, were rife throughout the late nineteenth and early twentieth centuries. In his study of the perception and reception of Irish literature in Italy, Antonio Bibbò cogently investigates the

---

15. On the interplay between the emergence of folklore studies and the imperialist and colonial dynamics in European nations, with a focus on France, Italy, and Ireland, see Ó Giolláin (2022).

16. On Alfred Nutt, founding member and former president of the Folklore Society, see Wood (1999).

images of Ireland that were refracted in Italian culture in the early twentieth century by focusing on the role of pivotal mediators, including lesser-known figures such as translators, publishers, and editors who acted as agents of transnational exchange between the two countries. As Bibbò points out, "the hetero-images of Ireland that were disseminated in Italy at the start of the century were closely dependent on the British-Irish dynamics that produced them in the first place" (Bibbò 2022a:12). The parallels between the two countries were advanced by the Italian press and often gave voice to opposing ideological stances. For example, in the years following the Irish War of Independence (1919–21), there was a growing sympathy from both Italian republicans and fascists, as well as from Catholics and socialists in Italy, toward the Irish rebellion. To sow support for their own agendas, these disparate parties highlighted "the similarities between the Italian and Irish experiences of nation-building, in order to create a bond of empathy" (Chini 2015:205). The historical echoes between the Irish fight for independence and the Italian Risorgimento were particularly foregrounded, starting from the deeply anchored myths and ideals of martyrdom and national unity that animated both historical processes.[17] In this regard, Italian writer Giuseppe Tomasi di Lampedusa (1896–1957) commented on the paradox of the spiritual union of Irish people, despite the loss of their language as a result of English colonization. In this linguistic and cultural struggle, the literary and political exponents of the Irish Renaissance often had to rely on the language of the enemy to forge a distinctive Irish literature in English. In this respect, Tomasi di Lampedusa allusively invited Italian intellectuals to reflect on the tragedy of this solution: "Per apprezzare l'orrore di queste tragedie noi italiani dobbiamo immaginare il nostro Risorgimento propugnato da un Mazzini che avesse scritto in tedesco e cantato da un Mameli in versi croati" (Tomasi di Lampedusa 1926:39).[18]

The parallel between Italy and Ireland was also motivated by a perceived negative marginal position in Europe. Such a perception led, from the late nineteenth century onward, to controversial associations between Ireland and Southern Italy, allusively called in some instances "l'Irlanda d'Italia,"[19] a label

---

17. On the Italian Risorgimento and Ireland, see also Edwards (1960).

18. "To appreciate the horror of these tragedies, we Italians have to imagine our Risorgimento advocated by a Mazzini who had to write in German and sung by a Mameli in Croatian verses." Political thinker and leader Giuseppe Mazzini (1805–1872) and poet Goffredo Mameli (1827–1849), who wrote a renowned patriotic song destined to become the Italian national anthem, were central figures of the Italian Risorgimento.

19. "the Ireland of Italy." Among the various studies that draw parallels between Irish and Italian cultures, see Rossi (1932), Linati et al. (1940), and Bernardy (1942). On the relationships between the two countries, see also Chini (1996; 2015).

that allows us to draw a link between the semicolonial condition of the Italian "Mezzogiorno"[20] and the colonial status of Ireland at the turn of the twentieth century. Italy and Ireland shared "a common sense of inferiority and marginality with respect to European political power plays; similar economic weaknesses (both economies were predominantly agrarian, dysfunctional and unbalanced); and similarly problematic social dynamics" (Chini 2015:217). In an introductory chapter to the Italian translation of Irish agricultural reformer Horace Plunkett's *Ireland in the New Century* (1904), poignantly entitled "Il problema della rinascenza irlandese e la nostra Questione Meridionale,"[21] Italian economist Gino Borgatta (1888–1949) reinforced the parallel between Southern Italy and Ireland by carrying out a scientific study of the two agricultural systems in place at the time (Borgatta in Plunkett 1914:1–48). In the preface to Plunkett's work, Luigi Einaudi wrote that "[t]utti i paesi hanno in sé stessi un'Irlanda; e sotto certi aspetti l'abbiamo anche noi italiani in una parte del Mezzogiorno" (Einaudi in Plunkett 1914:x).[22] Einaudi agreed with Plunkett's positive view on the valorization of popular traditions encouraged by the Gaelic Revival: "la rinascita della lingua e delle tradizioni nazionali, l'attaccamento ai costumi propri non possono non rafforzare quel sano senso di orgoglio del natìo loco, quell'amore alla casa, quella fiducia in sé stessi che sono fondamento necessario di ogni progresso economico" (Einaudi in Plunkett 1914:ix).[23] Bibbò also draws attention to two works by socialist Dino Fienga (1893–1975), *L'insurrezione irlandese* (1916) and *L'Inghilterra contro l'Irlanda* (1921), in which Ireland is compared to Southern Italy for "its lack of industrialization, depopulation and land-owning policies" (Bibbò 2022a:53), building on the similarities "between the age-old economic distress of Ireland and that of rural Italy" (Bibbò 2022a:57).[24]

---

20. "Southern Italy."

21. "The issue of the Irish renaissance and our Southern Question."

22. "All countries have an Ireland within themselves; and, in some respects, we Italians have it too in a part of Southern Italy."

23. "the revival of the national language and traditions, the attachment to one's customs cannot but strengthen that healthy sense of pride for one's native place, that love for the home, that self-confidence which are the necessary foundation for any economic progress."

24. The perception of such affinities would change over time. In this respect, Bibbò remarks that "[w]hereas until the early 1920s Italian observers were more inclined to compare Ireland's condition to that of some depressed regions of Italy, such as the South or Sicily [...], or to regions which were supposed to strive for independence such as Sardinia, this attitude started to change in the wake of the Great War, with most Italian commentators now more prone to see Ireland as a separate nation, worthy of governing itself, and a potential ally of Fascist Italy" (Bibbò 2022a:179–80).

Beyond the indubitable and objective differences existing between the two political and economic systems, it is evident that Italian and Irish insular spaces share several affinities, which have been explored in various scholarly studies in the last three decades. Máire Nic Mhaoláin, translator into modern Irish of Grazia Deledda's *La madre* (1920), observes how there is a "somiglianza—per molti aspetti—fra la comunità sarda e quella irlandese o, più precisamente, quelle zone dell'Irlanda dove si parla ancora l'irlandese: entrambe le società di impianto eminentemente agricolo-pastorale, tradizionaliste e cattoliche" (Nic Mhaoláin 1992:350–51).[25] The essentially agricultural economy, extreme poverty, high rates of illiteracy, lack of infrastructure, and absence of adequate land reclamation policies as a consequence of a general governmental neglect accentuated the vulnerability of these areas and increased their isolation from the most prosperous centers of their respective nations. In other words, the relationship between southern Italian regions—in particular Sardinia and Sicily—and the Piedmontese state shows affinities with the colonial relationship between Ireland and the British Empire, in that both territories, depressed and impoverished from an economic point of view, were victims of internal colonial politics and subjected to the tyranny and arbitrariness of ruthless centralized governments. In this regard, Iain Chambers identifies a "common nineteenth-century matrix of colonialism" that "establishes the Italian 'Southern Question' in a colonial framework, not too dissimilar to the experiences of Scotland and Ireland and their political, administrative, cultural and military subordination to London and the unification of Great Britain" (Chambers 2015:16).[26]

It is not coincidental that the title of a book that gathers Carlo Cattaneo's and Giuseppe Mazzini's writings on Sardinia, edited by Francesco Cheratzu, is *La terza Irlanda: gli scritti sulla Sardegna di Carlo Cattaneo e Giuseppe Mazzini* (1995).[27] When discussing the debated "Sardinian Question," which locates itself within the broader Italian Southern Question, Birgit Wagner reports that it was Cavour, according to the British press, who allegedly claimed in 1860 that Italy had "tre Irlande" (Wagner 2011:10).[28] Giuseppe Marci returned to this

---

25. "a similarity—in many respects—between the Sardinian and Irish communities or, more precisely, between those areas of Ireland where Irish is still spoken: both are eminently agricultural, pastoral, traditionalist and Catholic societies."

26. On the Southern Question, see also Gramsci (1966) and Moe (2002). On the marginalization of the south, see Cassano (1996).

27. On Cavour's, Cattaneo's, and Mazzini's views on Ireland, see also Pellizzi (2011).

28. The sentence "We have three Irelands, in Sardinia, Genoa and Savoy," which was attributed to Cavour, appeared in the *Morning Post* on February 9, 1860, n. 26, 878, p. 4 (Cheratzu 1995:187–90).

denomination, which alludes to the relationship between the so-called "tre Irlande" that were part of the Kingdom of Piedmont—Savoy, Genoa, and the "third Ireland," Sardinia—and mentioned how, before Italian unification, "gli intellettuali sardi [...] a quell'isola nordica guardavano scorgendovi analogie politiche con la propria terra mediterranea" (Marci 2007:181).[29] As a result of the resonance of Cavour's famed expression, which stressed the subordinate role of Sardinia as a commodity that could be potentially sold to France by the Piedmontese government, there was a tendency in nineteenth-century Italy to associate Sardinia with Ireland. In this regard, on October 9, 1852, Stefano Sampol Gandolfo (ca. 1820–1889), director and editor of the journal *L'Eco della Sardegna*, explicitly blamed the Piedmontese government for the unjust treatment that Sardinia had to endure, commenting rather bitterly that

> È la Sardegna l'Irlanda dell'opulento Piemonte. Colla differenza, soggiungeremo, se avessimo voglia di ridere, che mentre l'opulento Inglese ha oro, e sprezza le patate della povera Irlanda; il Piemonte, della Sardegna, se essa ne avesse, invidierebbe forse infin le patate e la polenta ancora, perché ne è ghiotto. (Sampol Gandolfo in Ortu 1998:149)[30]

Leopoldo Ortu notes how another Italian intellectual of the time, Francesco Ferrara (1810–1900), similarly defined Sicily as "l'Irlanda dell'Italia," with reference to the danger the island would constitute for the Italian state for its autonomist impulses (Ferrara in Ortu 1998:52–53). The "sisterhood" between these different contexts resides in their distinctiveness on a cultural and linguistic level as insular spaces and in the affinities of their economic and political histories, which saw them as victims of colonial enterprises and protagonists of waves of emigration (Marci 2006:9).

In a comparative study of Sardinian and Irish women's writing with a focus on Grazia Deledda and Irish writers such as Katharine Tynan (1859–1931) and George Egerton (1859–1945), Ruth McKee acknowledges that it would be "tempting to embark on a comparison of Deledda and Irish Revival writing, not least because of a shared interest in legend and language" (McKee 2009:5). The Irish revivalists were a lively group of writers, poets, artists, and intellectuals,

---

29. "Sardinian intellectuals [...] used to look at that Northern island and detected political analogies with their own Mediterranean land" (Marci 2007:181). On the nineteenth-century cross-cultural echoes between Sardinia and Ireland, see also Paulis (2006:144).

30. "Sardinia is the Ireland of the opulent Piedmont. With the difference, we would add, if we wanted to laugh, that while the opulent Englishman owns gold and despises the potatoes of poor Ireland, the Piedmontese would perhaps envy Sardinia even for its potatoes and polenta, if it had any, because of his greediness." The original quotation by Sampol Gandolfo comes from *L'Eco della Sardegna*, I, 8, October 9, 1852 (Ortu 1998:142–49).

including Douglas Hyde (1860–1949), J. M. Synge (1871–1909), and W. B. Yeats (1865–1939),[31] who contributed to resuscitating Irish nationalism through their joined efforts, marking a blossoming of Irish cultural manifestations that came to be remembered in history as the Irish Renaissance. In a review of T. F. Thiselton-Dyer's *The Ghost World* (1893) entitled "The Message of the Folk-Lorist,"[32] the high value that Yeats attached to folklore is evident:

> Folk-lore is at once the Bible, the Thirty-nine Articles, and the Book of Common Prayer, and well-nigh all the great poets have lived by its light. Homer, Aeschylus, Sophocles, Shakespeare, and even Dante, Goethe and Keats, were little more than folk-lorists with musical tongues. [...] There is no passion, no vague desire, no tender longing that cannot find fit type or symbol in the legends of the peasantry or in the traditions of the scolds and the gleemen. And these traditions are now being gathered up or translated by a whole army of writers. (Yeats 1999 [1893]:51)

Yeats's reference to a "whole army of writers" is not hyperbolic if one considers the wide range of folklore collections tinged with a rampant nationalist spirit that emerged in that period. Among the central figures devoted to the promotion of cultural nationalism in Ireland, Jane Wilde and Augusta Gregory reinstated the vital importance of Irish popular traditions in their collections, as will be explored in depth in the following chapters. The process of rediscovery of the past that permeated the Irish Revival dates back to the first half of the nineteenth century, with the influential publication of Thomas Moore's *Irish Melodies* in 1808 and Thomas Crofton Croker's *Fairy Legends and Traditions of the South of Ireland* in 1825, which immediately attracted the interest of the Brothers Grimm.[33] Other collections of mythological tales and popular

---

31. For an overview of the protagonists of the Irish Revival, see Ó Giolláin (2000:94–141).

32. T. F. Thiselton-Dyer was an English folklorist who also authored *Folk-Lore of Women as Illustrated by Legendary and Traditionary Tales, Folk-Rhymes, Proverbial Sayings, Superstitions, etc.* in 1906, an early example of a collection of popular narratives about women. The compendium was, however, misogynistic and consisted mostly of "antifemale lore" (Jordan and de Caro 1986:503).

33. Thomas Crofton Croker (1798–1854) was a correspondent of Wilhelm Grimm, who published with his brother *Irische Elfenmärchen* (1826), a translation of Croker's first volume of *Fairy Legends* into German. The third volume of *Fairy Legends*, published in 1828, contained a dedicatory letter by Croker to Grimm. Prior to the publication of *Fairy Legends*, Croker's *Researches in the South of Ireland, Illustrative of the Scenery, Architectural Remains, and the Manners and Superstitions of the Peasantry, with an Appendix Containing a Private Narrative of the Rebellion of 1798* was published in London in 1824. On Croker, see Hennig (1946), Dorson (1955:1–5), Schacker (2003:46–77), Bourke and O'Sullivan (2016).

sketches drawn from the life of the Irish peasantry that influenced this process of revitalization include William Carleton's *Traits and Stories of the Irish Peasantry* (1830); Samuel Lover's *Legends and Stories of Ireland* (1834); Patrick Kennedy's *Legendary Fictions of the Irish Celts* (1866) and *The Fireside Stories of Ireland* (1870); and W. B. Yeats's *Fairy and Folk Tales of the Irish Peasantry* (1888), *Irish Fairy Tales* (1892), and *The Celtic Twilight* (1893).[34] These writers and folklorists were often grappling with a paradox: in the process of rescuing from oblivion Irish traditions and making them available to a larger readership in the English medium, they were radically detaching these tales from Irish culture and language, thus undermining "la possibile diffusione di queste storie nella loro lingua d'origine" (Bibbò 2022b:178).[35]

Following in the footsteps of the heroic tales of the Irish mythological tradition, the late nineteenth-century revivalists frequently devoted their writings to the islands located in the west of Ireland, which became the real counterparts of the otherworldly Tír na nÓg, the Land of the Young. The insular dimension acquired not only specific historical and geographical connotations but also an imaginative aura (Foster 1977:261). The inhabitants of the western isles soon became "mythical islanders" (Zimmermann 2001:318). Emphasis on the remoteness and pristineness of insular contexts in Ireland, such as the Blasket Islands and the Aran Islands, was functional to the creation of a traditional national background, against British political hegemony and the steady advance of modernity. This fascination for insular areas reflected nineteenth-century conceptions of primitivism and linguistic purity, which were influenced by the legacy of Romanticism and the scientific path inaugurated by positivist thought. In this regard, intellectuals such as W. B. Yeats and Augusta Gregory were intentionally transforming the underdeveloped condition of the Irish peasantry into a literary topos, fostering "a fundamentally egoistic use [...] of the poetic spectacle the peasants offered" (Ó Giolláin 2000:145).[36] Both Yeats and Gregory were active members of the Gaelic

---

34. It is worth noting that collections of Irish folklore and mythology were rarely translated into Italian at the time and have been made available to an Italian readership only relatively recently. Bibbò points toward the "low status of popular and particularly fantastic literature in Italy" as a possible reason behind this late circulation and underscores how, "[s]omewhat contradictorily, the romantic view of Ireland that was widespread in Italy [...] made its wealth of stories central to a definition of its character, but did not significantly affect the book market and the production of translations" in Italy (Bibbò 2022a:164–65).

35. "the possible dissemination of these stories in their original language."

36. On the ideological contradictions of W. B. Yeats and Augusta Gregory, see also Goldring (1975).

League (fig. 1.1), which was founded by Douglas Hyde in 1893, who famously advocated for the "necessity for de-anglicising Ireland" in the lecture he delivered on November 25, 1892, before the Irish National Literary Society in Dublin.[37] In this period of fervent intellectual renewal, these figures, alongside many other contributors, were moved by what Declan Kiberd and P. J. Mathews eloquently define as "a marked idealism but also a conviction that ideas could become a basis for practical actions: a deep investment in the future was born out of an intense engagement with the past" (Kiberd and Mathews 2016:25).

Although Hyde initially distanced himself from any political position in order to make the cultural battle for Ireland as inclusive as possible,[38] the cultural nationalism of the late nineteenth century could not be devoid of political implications and greatly stimulated debates that led to the making of the Irish nation. Not coincidentally, Patrick Pearse (1879–1916), political leader and key figure of the Easter Rising, claimed that the foundation of the Gaelic League was the moment when "the Irish revolution began" (Pearse in Mac Aodha 1972:21). Prior to founding the league, Hyde was a member of the Society for the Preservation of the Irish Language, which was founded in 1876 to revive the nearly extinct native language and halt its abrupt decline in the aftermath of the Great Famine and the subsequent waves of emigration.[39]

The exponents of the Irish Renaissance aimed to create "a new sense of cultural and linguistic identity in Ireland by transforming Irish folklore into art and by capturing the rhythms of the Anglo-Irish dialect" (Fleming 1995:1). Hyde wrote several collections of songs in Irish, such as *Leabhar Sgéulaigheachta* (1889); *Abhráin Grádh Chúige Connacht: Love Songs of Connacht* (1893), which contained also his commentary and translations into English; the influential *Beside the Fire: A Collection of Irish Gaelic Folk Stories* (1890); and *Legends of Saints and Sinners* (1915).[40] *Beside the Fire* functioned as a source of inspiration for J. M. Synge, who was persuaded by the importance of collecting tales in the original

---

37. In his lecture, Hyde made reference to Giuseppe Mazzini's thinking on the Irish Question, thus revealing that he was "aware of the international context of ideas of nationality" (Ó Giolláin 2000:117; 2012:410). Mazzini insisted that the Irish Question was not rooted in a nationalist claim but rather "argued that the Irish demand was essentially one for better government only" (Mansergh 1965:96).

38. On Hyde, see also Daly (1974), Hutton (2001), and Morris (2010).

39. On the Society for the Preservation of the Irish Language, see Ó Murchú (1998:365) and Doyle (2015:165).

40. On the *Love Songs of Connacht*, see Hutton (2001). On Hyde's translations into Hiberno-English in *Beside the Fire*, see Cronin (1996:134–38). Cronin interprets his translations as "an agent of aesthetic and political renewal" (Cronin 1996:136).

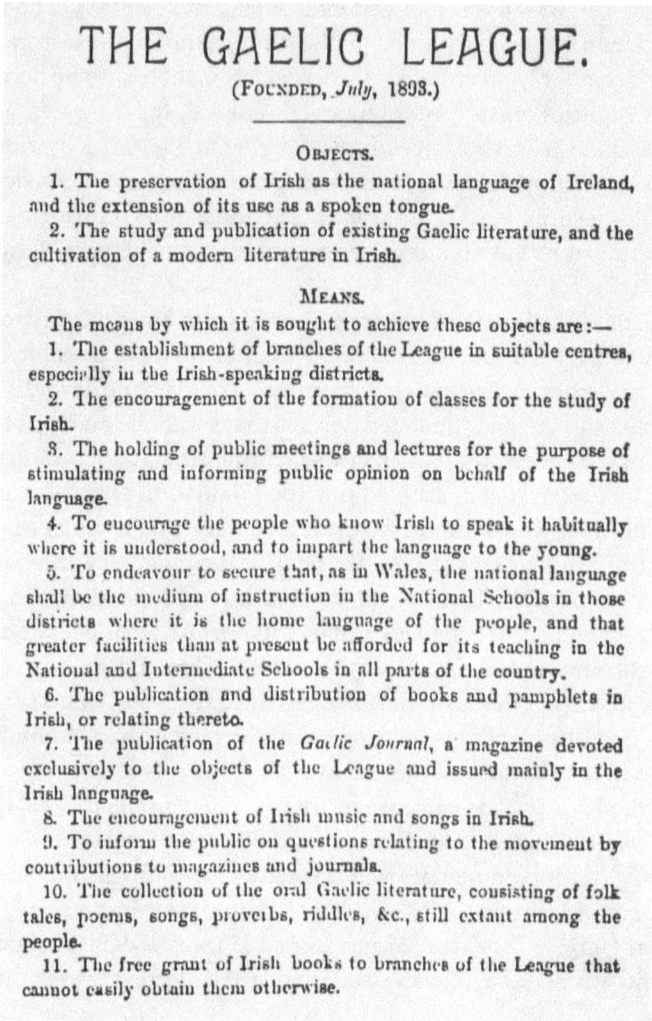

THE GAELIC LEAGUE.
(Founded, *July*, 1893.)

Objects.

1. The preservation of Irish as the national language of Ireland, and the extension of its use as a spoken tongue.
2. The study and publication of existing Gaelic literature, and the cultivation of a modern literature in Irish.

Means.

The means by which it is sought to achieve these objects are:—

1. The establishment of branches of the League in suitable centres, especially in the Irish-speaking districts.
2. The encouragement of the formation of classes for the study of Irish.
3. The holding of public meetings and lectures for the purpose of stimulating and informing public opinion on behalf of the Irish language.
4. To encourage the people who know Irish to speak it habitually where it is understood, and to impart the language to the young.
5. To endeavour to secure that, as in Wales, the national language shall be the medium of instruction in the National Schools in those districts where it is the home language of the people, and that greater facilities than at present be afforded for its teaching in the National and Intermediate Schools in all parts of the country.
6. The publication and distribution of books and pamphlets in Irish, or relating thereto.
7. The publication of the *Gaelic Journal*, a magazine devoted exclusively to the objects of the League and issued mainly in the Irish language.
8. The encouragement of Irish music and songs in Irish.
9. To inform the public on questions relating to the movement by contributions to magazines and journals.
10. The collection of the oral Gaelic literature, consisting of folk tales, poems, songs, proverbs, riddles, &c., still extant among the people.
11. The free grant of Irish books to branches of the League that cannot easily obtain them otherwise.

FIGURE 1.1. A Gaelic League leaflet, National Library of Ireland. Reproduced courtesy of the National Library of Ireland, Dublin.

language and brought the volume during his journeys to the Aran Islands (Kiberd 1979:151–52). His *Aran Islands* (1907) is an exemplary work of literary ethnography, in which Synge's position as a "participant-observer" (Castle 2001:100) becomes enmeshed with the exoticization of the islanders.

The attention to communities and regions located in the west of Ireland, which were initially idealized and then studied with an increasingly detached outlook, is symptomatic of one of the most pressing concerns of folklore studies from its inception as a discipline that aimed to investigate not only the traditional dimensions of culture but also "the *marginal* (in relation to the centres of power and privilege)" as well as "the *ideological* (expressions of belief and systems of knowledge)" (Oring 1986:18; original emphasis). When reflecting on the geography of powers on a cultural level, the emphasis of folklorists on the margins—whether they find a concrete representation in the Irish edge of the Western world or in the Italian islands of the Mediterranean Sea—paradoxically renders these marginal and marginalized spaces central in the dominant discourse of folklore studies on a national scale. By examining the ways the stories and people related to such contexts are repurposed and charged with meaning in folklore collections from Italy and Ireland, it is possible to acknowledge the dynamics that accompanied the nation-building processes in these countries and to recognize the relationships of power that lie beneath the representation of these perceived marginalities, bearing in mind that "in social terms, there are no margins, just ways of seeing or observing places and people as marginal" (Forgacs 2014:5–6).

The power struggle between marginal and central dimensions is evident in the practices surrounding the collection of folklore. Furthermore, this phenomenon was intrinsically related to questions of language and identity. After Italian unification, the centralizing forces linked to the necessity of creating a sense of national belonging went hand in hand with a growing interest in local dialects and traditions. This dynamic is reflected in the *Questione della lingua*,[41] which encapsulates the divergent positions around the linguistic model to be adopted in Italy, a debate that animated Italian literary and linguistic circles from the sixteenth century onward. Italian was for centuries above all a written language—a language of literature—whereas the dialects prevailed in everyday life. Linguistic unity was a challenge given the complex relationship between the widespread usage of dialects and the necessity to promote a shared Italian language (Sanson 2013a:273).[42] Among the proponents of two opposite positions in post-unification Italy, it is worth mentioning prominent man of letters Alessandro Manzoni (1785–1873), who advocated for the use of the educated Florentine vernacular on a national level in *Dell'unità della lingua e dei mezzi di diffonderla* (1868), and linguist Graziadio Isaia Ascoli (1829–1907), founder of Italian dialectology, who believed that linguistic unification

---

41. Language question.

42. The bibliography on the *Questione della lingua* in Italy is vast. See, for instance, Migliorini and Griffith (1984:403–50), Serianni (1989; 1990), Marazzini (2018), and Migliorini (2019:425–51; 750–64). On the role of women within the history of the Italian language and the *Questione della lingua*, see Sanson (2011; 2020).

would be a real and permanent achievement only when cultural exchange in Italian society had become effective and Italy as such more modern and efficient (Ascoli 1975).[43]

The nineteenth-century Irish Renaissance was intertwined with the rise of nationalism and the revitalization of the Irish "native" language.[44] In fact, it is in Ireland that early instances of the usage of the term "native speaker" can be found in the debates surrounding the language revival (O'Reilly 1909; Lepschy and Sanson 1991:83). At the core of this process of linguistic recovery during the initial phase of the revival, there was the opposition between the supporters of nativist positions who advocated for the usage of *caint na ndaoine*, the language spoken by the people, and those who advocated for the use of written Irish drawn from the seventeenth-century literary tradition (O'Leary 1994:45). Central to the revival movement was the reappraisal of the Irish language as a means of protection against external corrupting influences. This process of linguistic revival went hand in hand with an increasing reevaluation of, and fascination with, popular culture.

With regard to the folklorists' predilection for peripheral areas, while the westernmost remote region of the Gaeltacht became a central space of inquiry in late nineteenth-century Irish folklore studies—to the point that this phenomenon can be defined as a "gaelicization of folklore" in Ireland (Ó Giolláin 2000:114)—in the same historical time frame, the impulse toward folkloric research in post-unification Italy was particularly strong in the peripheral southern regions.[45] However, whereas the Gaeltacht became the pivot for the

---

43. On the polemic between Manzoni and Ascoli, see Bruni (1984:116–20) and Castellani (1986). On Ascoli and the *Questione della lingua*, see Dardano (1974) and Belardi (1990). In the second half of the nineteenth century, two fundamental laws, the "Legge Casati" in 1859 and the "Legge Coppino" in 1877, established a compulsory elementary schooling system in Italy that attempted to spread knowledge of the national language, although concrete effects on a large scale would be reached only in the twentieth century with the mass media (De Mauro, 1963: 88–105; Sanson, 2013a:278–79).

44. On the revitalization of the Irish language, see Arnold (1867), Monaghan (1899: xxxi–xxxix), and Hyde (1904:117–61). For contemporary studies on the nineteenth-century Irish language revival, see Crowley (2000:133–221) and Doyle (2015:161–214).

45. On the relationship between regional and national identities in Italy and Ireland, see Cavazza (2012) and Augusteijn (2012), respectively. The process by which Ireland has been traditionally described as marginal and picturesque not only by foreigners but also by Irish people themselves has been conceptualized by Joep Leerssen as "auto-exoticism," that is to say, "a mode of seeing, presenting and representing oneself in one's otherness" (Leerssen 1996:37). In Leerssen's view, this process, typical of nineteenth-century Anglo-Irish fiction, is still present in broader cultural discourses revolving around Irish identity.

revitalization of nationalism and the foundation for cultural manifestations that promoted Irish distinctiveness, the fragmented nature of the newborn Italian state engendered a multiplicity of regional contributions to folklore studies.[46] Such drives, though present throughout the Italian peninsula, were particularly prolific in the south and in the islands.

The thorny Southern Question generated a collective intellectual effort to understand the sociocultural causes of the perceived backwardness of the Mezzogiorno, a double-sided process that anthropologists Luigi Lombardi Satriani and Mariano Meligrana define as the "folklorizzazione del Mezzogiorno" and the "meridionalizzazione della scienza folklorica" (Lombardi Satriani and Meligrana 1975:20).[47] In Sicily, Giuseppe Pitrè played a fundamental role in the development of folkloric research with the publication of the *Biblioteca delle tradizioni popolari siciliane* (1871–1913) in twenty-five volumes and the creation of the first chair in folklore studies at the University of Palermo, which he named "demopsicologia."[48] The institution of this chair in 1911 was the culmination of fifty years of studies in the field of popular traditions. The emergence of this new field of inquiry, in which comparative, philological, and anthropological approaches often converged, celebrated the unity of the Italian nation while simultaneously emphasizing its diverse regional and linguistic composition.[49] Together with Salvatore Salomone-Marino (1847–1916), in 1882 Pitrè founded the *Archivio per lo studio delle tradizioni popolari* (*ASTP*), a journal that was published until 1909. It is not coincidental that the greatest impulse to establish folklore studies would emerge among

---

46. In this regard, it is significant that the first comprehensive collection of Italian folktales would be published only in the mid-twentieth century by Italo Calvino (1956). Prior to Calvino, the publication of folklore collections in Italy, despite being a prolific phenomenon, was largely distinguished by their regional character. Domenico Comparetti's attempt to create a national collection of tales, which resulted in the incomplete *Novelline popolari italiane* (1875), represents an exception to this regionalist trend (Johnson 2010).

47. the "folklorization of the Mezzogiorno" and the "meridionalization of folklore studies."

48. The lectures Pitrè held as a professor of "demopsicologia" in Palermo were published in *La Demopsicologia e la sua storia* (2001). On Pitrè's folkloric writings, see Cocchiara (1951), Zipes (2012:109–34), Bellantonio (2017), and Perricone (2017). Battaglia defined "demopsicologia" as the study of the "psicologia dei popoli attraverso le tradizioni, gli usi, i costumi" [psychology of people through their traditions, mores, customs] (Battaglia 1961:IV, 174). The term is akin to the meaning of the Anglicism "folclore."

49. On the anthropological and folkloric strands in post-Risorgimento Italy, see Ó Giolláin (2022:194–201). On the role of folklore studies in the Risorgimento, see Coppola (2021:41–66).

Sicilian folklorists: as Maurizio Coppola observes, Sicilian folklore studies can be regarded as an "activité 'pédagogique'" of sorts,⁵⁰ aimed at subverting the prevalent view of Sicily as a marginalized, impoverished, and subaltern region, thus reclaiming its fundamental contribution to the emerging national identity (Coppola 2021:111).

Nearly a decade after the foundation of Pitrè and Salomone-Marino's journal, Angelo De Gubernatis (1840–1913) founded the *Rivista delle tradizioni popolari italiane* (*RTPI*) in 1893. Galvanized by common objectives and values, both journals intended to disseminate knowledge of regional customs and popular traditions. De Gubernatis, a renowned orientalist and philologist, professor of Sanskrit and comparative mythology in Florence at the Istituto di Studi Superiori, and of Sanskrit and Italian literature at the Università degli Studi di Roma "La Sapienza," was a prolific man of letters and founder of several journals in Italy.⁵¹ He was particularly sensitive to women's issues, to the extent that he organized the *Esposizione Beatrice* in Florence in 1890, an exhibition devoted to honoring Dante Alighieri's muse, Beatrice Portinari, six hundred years after her alleged death, by celebrating female creativity in its multiple forms.⁵²

With regard to local traditions, De Gubernatis mobilized a cluster of intellectuals and popular culture enthusiasts from various Italian regions to participate in a collective project aiming to "raccogliere gli sparsi tesori della nostra tradizione" (De Gubernatis 1893:3).⁵³ Particularly crucial was the foundation of the Società Nazionale per le Tradizioni Popolari Italiane by De Gubernatis in

---

50. "pedagogical activity."

51. De Gubernatis founded journals such as *L'Italia letteraria* (1862), *Rivista orientale* (1867), *Rivista Europea* (1869), *Natura ed Arte. Rivista illustrata quindicinale italiana e straniera di scienze, lettere ed arti* (1891–1911), among others. On De Gubernatis as a scholar of comparative mythology in Italy, see Cocchiara (2016 [1952]:284–86), Rabault-Feuerhahn (2016:149), and Fabbri (2017). In his role as a founder of the popular magazine *Cordelia* (1881–1942), see Folli (1999: 25–47), Falchi (2000:207–11), and Tasca (2003:278–86). On his work as an orientalist, see Vicente (2012).

52. On this occasion, several women participated in conference presentations centered on the topic of Italian womanhood, such as "La donna italiana nel Medioevo," by Maria Savi-Lopez (1846–1940) and "Le operaie italiane," by Carolina Invernizio (1851–1916). These presentations were then published in Florence in *La donna italiana descritta da scrittrici italiane in una serie di conferenze tenute all'Esposizione Beatrice in Firenze* (1890), edited by Giuseppe Civelli. On the *Esposizione Beatrice*, see Soldi (2015). On De Gubernatis as a supporter of women's participation in cultural initiatives, see Bloom (2015:48–52).

53. "gather the scattered treasures of our tradition" (De Gubernatis 1893:3).

Rome in 1893. The main objective of this organization, which was inspired by the British Folklore Society inaugurated in London in 1878 and supported by Margherita of Savoy (1851–1926), wife of Umberto I and queen of the unified Italian kingdom, was to generate a new impetus for the field of popular traditions in Italy (King 2005:50), expanding the path traced by Pitrè in Sicily. The intentions at the core of the journal of the society were made clear in De Gubernatis's inaugural speech in Rome on November 20, 1893 (De Gubernatis 1893:3–19). Intellectuals were worried that the unrestrained progress brought about by the urbanization, the implementation of railways, and the political unification of the nation could bury the treasures of regional traditions, which needed first and foremost to be known on a national scale. In typical nineteenth-century fashion, the folkloric heritage of the various regions was regarded as a precious source that had to be revived and handed down to subsequent generations.

De Gubernatis was convinced that history recounts only the events concerning the conquering minorities, neglecting the collective life of the masses (De Gubernatis 1893:7). Hence, he intended to give voice to these people by encouraging talented men and women to join his national project of rediscovery. He recognized the merit of illustrious Italian scholars who understood the importance of promoting Italian cultural and linguistic traditions, such as Niccolò Tommaseo, Cesare Cantù and Graziadio Isaia Ascoli. Notably, he also acknowledged the works produced by eminent female scholars, including Evelyn Martinengo-Cesaresco and Rachel Busk, thus confirming his interest in cultural contributions to folklore studies made by women.

Together with the political, linguistic, and cultural dimensions explored so far, it is necessary to consider the gender divide in this field at a time when folklore research had not yet been fully institutionalized. Female folklorists became active in a historical phase characterized by a patriarchal social structure that heavily limited their access to education and participation in scholarly activities. Among the intellectuals who enthusiastically participated in De Gubernatis's project, the self-taught Grazia Deledda stood out for her assiduous effort to gather folkloric narratives from her native region, Sardinia, and to carry out ethnographic studies aimed at describing local uses and customs, as will be shown in chapter 2. Deledda, however, was not an exception within the cosmopolitan circle of women who studied and documented Italian folklore. In post-unification Italy, as detailed in the following section, women from a variety of regional and national backgrounds manifested their fascination with popular culture by participating in the transcription and compilation of local folklore.

Women and Folklore in Post-Unification Italy

Contrary to the recognition of renowned scholars such as Ermolao Rubieri (1818–1879), Costantino Nigra (1828–1907), Alessandro D'Ancona (1835–1914), and Vittorio Imbriani (1840–1886),[54] the endeavors of female collectors in Italian folklore studies have frequently been overlooked, and several of their names have consequently fallen into oblivion. Yet there was evidently a strong bond between women and popular culture in late nineteenth-century and early twentieth-century Italy, as this was perceived as a field of knowledge that attracted women's interest and to which women could also actively contribute.[55] Traces of their involvement remain in their books as well as in the essays and articles that made their appearance in European journals of the time, in line with the transnational parameters of the practice of collecting folklore. The publishing efforts of female folklorists in Italy frequently revolved around the aforementioned central figures of Pitrè and De Gubernatis. The journals *ASTP* and *RTPI* featured numerous contributions by women who collected folktales and traditions in various Italian regions. This section provides an overview of the most prolific female folklorists of the time. Several of them had rich epistolary exchanges with prominent scholars, including Pitrè and De Gubernatis, who more often than not became mentors in the development of their folkloric interests. Although a thorough investigation of these figures would go beyond the scope of this volume, each of them begs further attention and deserves to be studied in depth in a larger-scale exploration of the history and legacy of nineteenth-century female folklorists.

From Calabria to Friuli, from Sicily to Emilia-Romagna, interest in popular traditions was spread across the entire Italian peninsula as well as the islands. Women such as the Friulan Caterina Percoto (1812–1887), who compiled

---

54. On Rubieri, poet, writer, and politician, author of the acclaimed *Storia della poesia popolare italiana* (1877), see Cirese (1969:239–77). On Nigra, philologist, politician, and scholar of Celtic studies, author of *Reliquie celtiche* (1872) and *Canti popolari del Piemonte* (1888), see Ó Giolláin (2022:192) and Coppola (2021:112–16). On D'Ancona, writer, literary critic, and politician, author of *La poesia popolare italiana* (1878) and *Saggi di letteratura popolare* (1913), see Macciocca (1991). On Imbriani, who wrote *La novellaja fiorentina* (1871) and an important study on Giambattista Basile, *Il gran Basile: studio biografico e bibliografico* (1875), see Cocchiara (1981a:96–100).

55. In this regard, it is indicative that, on the occasion of the first "Mostra di Etnografia Italiana" in Rome in 1911, organized by Lamberto Loria (1855–1913), founder of the Società di Etnografia Italiana (1910), one of the target audiences of the exposition was clearly composed of women, as revealed by the numerous articles that appeared in women's magazines at the time (Puccini 2005:158–59). On the 1911 exposition, see also Ó Giolláin (2022:236–40).

various anthologies of legends, traditions, and short stories with a clear pedagogical intent, and Caterina Pigorini Beri (1845–1924) from Emilia-Romagna, who authored *Costumi e superstizioni dell'Appennino marchigiano* (1889) and *In Calabria* (1892), stepped into the field of popular culture and contributed to the preservation of regional customs, legends, and folktales. Percoto was one of the first nineteenth-century folklorists mentioned by Italo Calvino in his introduction to *Fiabe italiane* (2015 [1956]:viii): the "contessa contadina"[56] was praised for her patriotic tales written in local dialect, which made their appearance in short-story collections such as *Racconti* (1858), *Nuovi raccontini* (1870), *Ventisei racconti vecchi e nuovi* (1878), and *Novelle popolari edite ed inedite* (1883).[57] In the preface to *Racconti*, linguist and writer Niccolò Tommaseo (1802–1874) placed emphasis on Percoto's adherence to reality in portraying the customs of the Friulan countryside that she knew so well, a faithfulness that was also reflected in her linguistic choices: "non potendo al dialetto toscano, attinse al proprio dialetto, ch'ella scrive con garbo d'artista; e col linguaggio de' libri lo contemperò come meglio sapeva" (Tommaseo in Percoto 1858:7).[58] Percoto had the ability to embed the traditional values and rituals of her community in her writings, thanks to her in-depth knowledge of local people, turning into an "etnologa vera e profonda" (Gri 2008:65).[59]

Such attention to the rural world lay at the core of Percoto's ethnological inclination, which was in line with the cultural ferment of the time. Indeed, the late nineteenth century saw the establishment of the Società Italiana di Antropologia e di Etnologia in 1871 and the its journal *Archivio per l'Antropologia e la Etnologia*, which was closely linked to the foundation of the Museo di Antropologia ed Etnologia in Florence. In 1890 the recipient of the prize awarded by the Società Italiana di Antropologia e di Etnologia was the aforementioned Caterina Pigorini Beri, for the best work on Italian superstitions (Charuty 2019; Ó Giolláin 2022:195). Pigorini Beri was a self-taught folklorist who worked extensively on the folklore of the Apennines in the Marche region.[60] After a journey on her own in Calabria, she published a report in the journal *Nuova Antologia* and then the book *In Calabria* (1892). Her brother

---

56. "peasant countess."

57. On Percoto, see Chemello (1995; 2009), Scappaticci (1997), Gri (2008), and Sanson (2010; 2020).

58. "since she could not draw from the Tuscan dialect, she drew from her own dialect, which she writes with the grace of an artist; and with the language of books she mitigated it as best she knew."

59. "true and deep ethnologist."

60. On Pigorini Beri, see Lanaro (1979:117–18), De Sanctis Ricciardone (1987; 1990), and Puccini (2011).

Luigi Pigorini was a renowned Italian archaeologist, ethnologist, politician, and founder of the Regio Museo Nazionale Preistorico Etnografico in Rome. Caterina Pigorini Beri devoted a chapter of *Costumi e superstizioni dell'Appennino marchigiano* to the "cantafavole," also called "scantafavole," told to her by peasant women, such as Annuccia, Carminella, and Carolina. She defined these oral performances as a series of words, sometimes nonsensical, told by women "nelle veglie laboriose dell'inverno," "per ingannare il tempo, intanto che riempono il fuso e le spole" (Pigorini Beri 1889:114).[61] She recounted how countryside people were amused by the attention she paid to these performances and often needed to be begged in order to share them with her. One of her informants, Innocenza, knew fairy tales, which were Pigorini Beri's keen interest at that time, and told to the folklorist a version of Cinderella's tale from her region:

> Innocenza però sapeva le fiabe: [...] sapeva nientemeno che la *Cenerentola*, la vecchia *Cenerentola* raccontata in tutte le lingue vive e morte, e nei vecchi dialetti puri delle diverse provincie italiane. [...] Quelle fiabe le avevamo sentite mille volte, ma parevano sempre belle e sempre nuove: le sapevamo a memoria, ma avevano la strana potenza di tenerci inchiodati a sedere per un'ora sul seggiolino, vicini, stretti alla narratrice, che ci sorprendeva e spaventava qualche volta coi racconti popolati di fantasmi e di apparizioni. (Pigorini Beri 1889:123)[62]

Commenting on Pigorini Beri's writings, De Gubernatis wrote that "[g]li scritti della signora Pigorini-Beri hanno tutti un'impronta maschia, e uno stile vigoroso che non manca d'affetto" (De Gubernatis 1879:821), relying on the category of virility to acknowledge her worth.[63] Yet Pigorini considered herself a dilettante, as she wrote in her correspondence with Pitrè: "Lascio dunque ai cultori della scienza i lavori serii [...]; felice soltanto se degli usi e costumi da

---

61. "in the laborious winter vigils," "to pass the time, while they fill the spindle and the spools."

62. "Innocenza, however, knew fairy tales: [...] she knew none other than *Cinderella*, the old *Cinderella* told in all living and dead languages, and in the old pure dialects of the various Italian provinces. [...] We heard those fairy tales a thousand times, but they always seemed beautiful and always new: we knew them by heart, but they had the strange power of keeping us glued to our seats for an hour, close, tied to the female narrator, who surprised us and sometimes scared us with stories filled with ghosts and apparitions." This tale was first published in *ASTP* in the local dialect from Parma with Pigorini Beri's parallel translation into Italian (Pigorini Beri 1883).

63. "Pigorini-Beri's writings have all a masculine imprint, and a vigorous style that does not lack affection." On the use of the category of virility to praise women's writing, see Barbarulli (2003:96–97).

me raccolti con amore, se non con metodo scientifico, potranno giovarsi coloro che cercano la formula per l'esistenza morale dell'umanità."[64] These diminishing remarks, scattered throughout her writings, can be rightly interpreted as a "spazio di libertà creativa e non un'ammissione di debolezza" (Faienza 2023:74).[65] As will be shown, many instances of these rhetorical techniques can be found in female-authored folkloric writings: through this strategic *captatio benevolentiae*, women aimed at protecting their publications from harsh criticism while underlining the courage of their contributions, given their limited or nonexistent access to specific trainings in the field.

A contributor to *ASTP* and *RTPI*, and an interlocutor of both Pitrè and De Gubernatis, was Venetian folklorist Angela Nardo Cibele (1850–1938), an expert in popular traditions from Belluno, which she gathered in *Zoologia popolare veneta, specialmente Bellunese. Credenze, leggende e tradizioni varie* (1887) and *Acque, pregiudizi e leggende bellunesi* (1888).[66] In her epistolary exchange with Pitrè, she explained how challenging it was to convince peasants to share their stories: "Ma che fatica si fa per farsi raccontare! Questa buona gente si mette subito in sospetto di essere canzonata—ma [...] termina poi, col canzonar noi che prendiamo sul serio *quelle fole*."[67] She defined a local young girl from Venice as a "piccola miniera di fiabe,"[68] a metaphor that casts light on the high regard she placed on her informants and their stories. In 1898 she published a collection in which she gathered her father's studies on the dialect of the town of Burano—a small island located in the Venetian lagoon that was renowned for the traditional practice of lacemaking—which she interspersed with references to female informants and workers: "Brutte come le Parche della leggenda, queste tarde

---

64. "Therefore, I leave the serious work to the scientific experts [...]; I am just happy if the habits and customs I collected with love, if not with a scientific method, can benefit those who seek the formula for the moral existence of humanity." Pigorini Beri, *Lettere a Giuseppe Pitrè*, February 17, 1882, P-B-12, letter n. 1:2, BEGP.

65. "space of creative freedom and not an admission of weakness."

66. Calvino quoted *Zoologia popolare veneta* (1887) in his detailed notes to *Fiabe italiane*, in relation to a variant of the rare fairy tale "Il principe granchio" from the Trentino region, which was reported by Nardo Cibele (1887:76–77). I am grateful to the Gladys Krieble Delmas Foundation for supporting my research on Nardo Cibele in libraries and archives in Veneto. For further details on her life and works, see Perco (2010), Duse (2015), and Sottilotta (2024).

67. "But what an effort it takes to be told stories! These good people immediately suspect they are being teased—but [...] they then end up teasing us for taking those stories seriously." Nardo Cibele, *Lettere a Giuseppe Pitrè*, May 18, 1885, P-B-11, letter n. 2:4, BEGP (original emphasis).

68. "A little mine of fairy tales." Nardo Cibele, *Lettere a Giuseppe Pitrè*, June 23, 1885, P-B-11, letter n. 3:3, BEGP.

rappresentanti viventi di un'altra età, sono preziose pei raccoglitori di tradizioni popolari" (Nardo Cibele 1898:21).[69] However, she did not indulge in an unrealistic depiction of womanhood; on the contrary, a class consciousness seeps through her words and comes to the fore when she advocates for a "riforma più radicale"[70] of female lacemakers' working conditions, proposing a reduction of their working hours and the introduction of walks and recreational breaks for these "povere lavoratrici" (Nardo Cibele 1898:39).[71]

Prior to the publication of *Studi sul dialetto di Burano*, she wrote a letter to feminist writer Gualberta Alaide Beccari (1842–1906) on the contribution that women could make to the creation of a comparative dictionary of Italian dialects, advocating for the necessity to rely on women to record terms and customs that pertain to the female sphere.[72] She underlined that it was precisely thanks to women's pivotal roles as depositories of language and traditions that dialects were still alive (Nardo Cibele 1872:2).[73] Such keen interest toward both language and popular culture is one of the numerous examples of the deep interconnection between dialectology and folklore as fields of study.[74] The bond between the two disciplines is not surprising and was motivated both by concrete needs,

---

69. "As ugly as the legendary Fates, these late living representatives of another age are precious for the collectors of popular traditions."

70. "more radical reformation."

71. "poor female workers."

72. The letter, titled "Della parte che come madre e come educatrice potrebbe avere la donna nella formazione del grande Vocabolario comparato dei dialetti italiani" [On the part that the woman could have as a mother and as an educator in the creation of the great comparative vocabulary of Italian dialects], was sent by her father to linguist Niccolò Tommaseo. Nardo Cibele published Tommaseo's answer in *Studi sul dialetto di Burano* (Nardo Cibele 1872:33–35). On the role of mothers as educators in post-unification Italy, see Sanson (2013b:39–63).

73. The conservative connotation of women's language is a motif that emerges throughout history, starting from ancient Greek and Latin classics such as Cicero's *De oratore* and Plato's *Cratylus*; however, contemporary sociolinguistic studies disagree on this claim (Sanson 2007:174). On the other hand, women's role in the preservation of semantic fields that pertain to the domestic sphere has been recognized. For instance, in the issue of the journal *Orbis* titled "Le langage des femmes: Enquête linguistique à l'échelle mondiale," Italian glottologist Giorgio Piccitto (1916–1972) observed that the value of elderly female informants for specific semantic fields could not be underestimated: "[è] naturale che, dal punto di vista lessicale, le donne, specie le più anziane, siano fonte di informazione più sicura e più ricca per quanto riguarda i dominii semantici di loro particolare competenza" (Piccitto 1952:14) [It is natural that, from a lexical point of view, women, especially the older ones, are a more reliable and richer source of information regarding the semantic domains of their particular competence].

74. On folklore and dialectology with a focus on Giuseppe Pitrè's folkloric writings, see Cocchiara (1951:75–83). On the publication of dictionaries, folkloric collections, and popular

given that knowledge of the local dialect was vital to interacting with lower classes and therefore to accessing their folklore, and by a frequent juxtaposition of interests, since many dialectologists were also folklorists and vice versa.

In nineteenth-century Italy, although women collectors were primarily motivated by the compilation of oral traditions that were perceived to be on the verge of oblivion, they concurrently contributed to transcribing and codifying local dialects in their collections (Sanson 2020:81). Carolina Coronedi Berti (1820–1911) was equally committed to folklore and language studies. A contributor to *Rivista Europea* and *ASTP*, she published several works such as *Vocabolario bolognese-italiano* (1869–74), *Novelle popolari bolognesi* (1874), *Appunti di botanica bolognese* (1875), and *Al sgugiol di ragazù. Favole popolari bolognesi* (1883). The latter represents a noteworthy effort not only from a cultural but also from a linguistic point of view as it was transcribed entirely in the dialect of Bologna.[75] Despite a lack of information about the storytellers, in the body of her dedication to her niece Giulietta, she specified that she wrote the majority of the fairy tales "come mi sono state raccontate, senza togliere né aggiungere nulla; e la maggior parte di esse l'ho ascoltata dalla bocca del volgo e de' nostri contadini" (Coronedi Berti 1883:n.p.).[76] This collection is particularly interesting from the perspective of gender representations within the tales (Casali 2012:92; Calvino 2015 [1956]:xxxiv).[77]

---

poetry in post-unification Italy, see Antonelli et al. (2012:261–73). On women as collectors with a focus on language, see Sanson (2020).

75. For a foundational study on Coronedi Berti, see the volume edited by Andrea Battistini (2012) on the centenary of her death. Important background details about her works can be reconstructed from an analysis of her unpublished letters, including the epistolary exchange with Francesco Zambrini (1810–1887), the latter being the first president of the Commissione per i testi di lingua founded in Bologna in 1860. On Coronedi Berti's connection to this association, see Campana (2012).

76. "as they were told to me, without removing or adding anything; and I listened to most of them from the mouth of the people and of our peasants."

77. The first complete translation into Italian of Coronedi Berti's fairy tales by Ombretta Zanetti came to light only in 2021. A complete English translation of these fairy tales has yet to be published. Only two of these tales are available in English: "The Curse of the Seven Children" and "The Crumb in the Beard," which were published by American folklorist Thomas Frederick Crane (1844–1927) in 1885 as tales XI and XXIX, respectively, in *Italian Popular Tales* (Crane 2001 [1885]). Crane's correspondence with Pitrè from 1876 to 1913, which includes thirty-four letters, is preserved in the BEGP (P-B-16). I am grateful to Jack Zipes for pointing me toward this correspondence and for his precious insights into the friendship between Crane and Pitrè, testified not only by their letters but also by Crane's publication of an obituary in Pitrè's honor in *The Nation* in 1916. Their correspondence reveals unknown data on Crane's biography and on the intellectual exchange between him and the Sicilian folklorist.

Coronedi Berti's contribution to folklore and dialectology can be reappraised thanks to her rich unpublished correspondence with Pitrè, who became an important point of reference for her. Their exchanges were permeated by allusions to her methodology as a collector. For instance, in a letter dated June 30, 1874, she explained how her study of herbal properties in popular beliefs required time, since it involved both library research and fieldwork among peasants: "Le notizie intorno all'erbe delle piante, ch'ella mi chiede, potrei guardare di raccorle ma con del tempo; lì per lì non posso fare, bisogna ch'io cerchi nel volgo, nella biblioteca."[78] Pitrè himself praised Coronedi Berti's work, as is evident in his correspondence with De Gubernatis: "Questa egregia donna non è abbastanza conosciuta in Italia; eppure merita di esser presentata a modello di attività unica anziché rara in un genere di studi nuovi per le donne."[79] In the preface to her *Vocabolario bolognese-italiano*, she wrote that it was made with her little wit and "con quel fermo volere, di cui se ne dubita la donna essere capace,"[80] by listening to the living voice of the folk (Coronedi Berti 1869–74:II). Once again, as in the case of Caterina Pigorini Beri, women folklorists' self-effacing modesty comes to the fore: this propensity to minimize their own achievements in the field of popular traditions becomes apparent in several prefaces to female-authored nineteenth-century folkloric collections, in a typical fashion that reflects the topos of *modestia auctoris*.

In a similar vein, Nardo Cibele, after an excursus on the scholars who devoted themselves to the study of folklore and dialect in Venice, bashfully added her own name to the list: "Benché mi sembri temerità nominare qui la mia povera persona, pure lo faccio, dichiarandomi semplicemente come una timida eco di tutte quelle idee che infervoravano allora l'anima del padre mio" (Nardo Cibele 1898:32).[81] Likewise, the Paduan Eugenia Levi (1861–1915), teacher of German, linguist, and author of an anthology of Italian folk songs, *Fiorita di canti tradizionali del popolo italiano* (1895), started her work by claiming: "È una semplice fiorita la mia. Chi dei canti tradizionali del popolo italiano vuol fare

---

78. "I could try to collect the information about the herbs of the plants that you are requesting, but I need some time; I can't do it immediately, I have to search among the folk, in the library." Coronedi Berti, *Lettere a Giuseppe Pitrè*, June 30, 1874, P-A-5, letter n. 15:4, BEGP.

79. "This distinguished woman is not known enough in Italy, yet she deserves to be presented as a model of a unique if not rare engagement with a new genre of studies for women." Pitrè, *Lettere ad Angelo De Gubernatis*, January 24, 1872, cass. 100 n. 19.6, letter 17:1, Fondo "Angelo De Gubernatis," BNCF.

80. "with that firm will of which women are doubted to be capable."

81. "Although it seems to me temerarious to name my poor person here, I will do it, simply declaring myself as a timid echo of all those ideas that filled with fervor my father's soul at that time."

un serio studio ricorre ai lavori magistrali del D'Ancona, del Nigra, del Pitrè" (Levi 1895:v).[82] Immediately after this volume had been printed, Levi sent a letter to Pitrè, in which she asked for his honest opinion: "ella voglia essermi cortese di un giudizio sincero [...]. Ho lavorato molto, moltissimo e con amore, ma il campo era vasto e so che molto avrò errato."[83] Yet the works of these women were far from being amateurish endeavors. While declaring themselves to be inexpert researchers of folklore, they were indeed carving a niche for themselves in this sector, often with less resources and fewer opportunities to access formal education at their disposal in comparison with their male counterparts.

As far as genre is concerned, nineteenth-century collections of folklore tend to be highly hybrid anthologies of popular traditions, ranging from legends, fairy tales, and folk songs to studies of popular customs, proverbs, and beliefs. In some instances, women writers reelaborated previously collected material, and their studies therefore represent scholarly reflections on traditional popular narratives. This was the case of *Leggende del mare* (1894), by Maria Savi-Lopez (1846–1940), a lengthy intertextual study of sea legends across various cultural and national contexts, which she dedicated not coincidentally to Pitrè and De Gubernatis. In this corpus of sea legends, she reported stories "di strani fantasmi, di re fulgenti, di divinità marine, di nordici giganti, di *trolli* innamorati, di fanciulle dalle verdi chiome, che uniscono il canto soave alla voce possente degli epici cantori del mare" (Savi-Lopez 2008 [1894]:25; original emphasis).[84] A forgotten Neapolitan folklorist gifted with a literary talent, Savi-Lopez authored numerous anthologies of legends and popular traditions, such as *Le valli di Lanzo: bozzetti e leggende* (1886), *Leggende delle Alpi* (1889), and *Nani e folletti* (1900). In addition to De Gubernatis and Pitrè, she liaised with various illustrious personalities of the time, such as philosopher and literary critic Benedetto Croce (1866–1952), Nobel Prize winner Giosuè Carducci (1835–1907), novelist Antonio Fogazzaro (1842–1911), postimpressionist painter Mario Puccini (1869–1920), and literary critic Pio Rajna (1847–1930). The letters she sent to these figures constitute invaluable archival sources to retrace the steps of her

---

82. "Mine is a mere anthology of songs. Those who wish to study seriously the traditional songs of the Italian people resort to the masterful works of D'Ancona, Nigra, Pitrè."

83. "Please be so kind to give me a sincere judgment [...]. I worked much, very much and with love, but the field was wide and I am aware that I have made many mistakes." Levi, *Lettere a Giuseppe Pitrè*, February 1, 1895, P-A-8, letter n. 1:2–3, BEGP.

84. "of strange ghosts, of shining kings, of sea divinities, of Nordic giants, of trolls in love, of girls with green hair, who combine the sweet song with the powerful voice of the epic singers of the sea."

life.[85] She often commented that she was leading a peculiar life. She knew that this perceived oddity stemmed from her being a pioneering woman in this field of studies, particularly as a woman from Southern Italy. During the composition of *Le valli di Lanzo: bozzetti e leggende* (1886), which she considered an "immenso tributo d'amore" for Piedmont (Savi-Lopez 1886:7),[86] she highlighted how courageous she had to be to overcome this double discrimination:

> Questi buoni piemontesi hanno giustamente un affetto appassionato tenace pel loro paese, moltissimi amano specialmente le Valli di Lanzo e può immaginare come sia aspettato questo libro scritto da una donna, da una napoletana. Il Direttore della linea Torino Lanzo ne ha già parlato nel consiglio e forse molti uomini serii avranno riso della temerità che ho avuta nel mettermi in questo cimento.[87]

She used to work, in her own words, "pazzamente,"[88] sacrificing sleep in order to write essays, lectures, articles for journals and magazines, while taking care of her son on her own after her husband's death. In a letter to De Gubernatis, tinged with patriotism, she mentioned her wish to explore the role of women in popular traditions, brimming with "fate benevole o crudeli, streghe innumerevoli, perfide ammaliatrici, figlie di re innamorate, perfide matrigne, brutte ragazze invidiose, belle fanciulle oppresse."[89] Her scholarly passion is particularly evident in works concerning the legends of the Alps, which she collected

---

85. Her biography and eclectic work deserve further investigation. I am grateful to the Folklore Society in London for the award of the 2021 Estella Canziani Bursary for Postgraduate Research, which allowed me to carry out archival research on Maria Savi-Lopez. For a preliminary reconstruction of her life and folklore collections based on her unpublished epistolary exchanges, see Sottilotta (2022). On her literary production, see Masoero (1990:63–74), Santoro (1987), Valisa (2018:242), and Perugi (2019). On her letters to Fogazzaro, see Chemello (2010) and Ricaldone (2010).

86. "an immense tribute of love."

87. "These good Piedmontese rightly have a tenacious and passionate affection for their country. Many of them love especially the Lanzo valleys, and you can imagine how they were expecting this book written by a woman, by a Neapolitan woman. The director of the Turin Lanzo line has already talked about it in the council, and perhaps many serious men will have laughed at my recklessness in taking on this challenge." Savi-Lopez, *Lettere ad Antonio Fogazzaro*, November 19, 1885, CFo 30, Pl. 183, letter n. 10:4, Fondo "Antonio Fogazzaro," Biblioteca Civica Bertoliana, Vicenza.

88. "in a frenzy." Savi-Lopez, *Lettere ad Antonio Fogazzaro*, June 24, 1886, CFo 30, Pl. 183, letter n. 16:2, Fondo "Antonio Fogazzaro," Biblioteca Civica Bertoliana, Vicenza.

89. "benevolent or cruel fairies, innumerable witches, wicked enchantresses, enamored kings' daughters, wicked stepmothers, ugly envious girls, beautiful oppressed maidens."

in the field: she regularly traveled through the mountainous paths, facing the night, cold, fog, and high altitudes to gather tales from local people. Although she never had a formal education as a child, as she grew up, she tirelessly spent her time in libraries and archives. The eloquent words she wrote to Fogazzaro on November 4, 1885, constitute a powerful reminder of the importance of recovering forgotten identities:

> Ho preso passione alle carte vecchie, mi pare che se avessi tempo non farei altro che cercare le vecchie memorie, le figure dimenticate, mi piacerebbe illustrare opere che nessuno ha stampato, e che riposano fra i volumi innumerevoli degli archivii, mentre è tanto facile parlare di coloro che tutti conoscono e sarebbe invece opera utile e pietosa ricordare all'Italia i dimenticati.[90]

Alongside these Italian scholars, there were also foreign folklorists who participated in folklore collection and dissemination in Italy. Several of them had Italian origins or traveled to Italy for health reasons and educational purposes, in the footsteps of the early modern Grand Tour that led to the compilation of a copious amount of travel writings by foreign aristocrats.[91] Among them, it is worth remembering Anglo-French writer and photographer Louisa Hamilton Caico (1861–1927), author of the illustrated ethnographic volume *Sicilian Ways and Days* (1910),[92] and British collector Estella Canziani (1887–1964), who wrote extensively on popular traditions from Piedmont and Abruzzo. A London-born painter, travel writer, and folklorist, Canziani wrote *Costumes, Traditions and Songs of Savoy* (1911), *Piedmont* (1913), and *Through the Apennines and the Lands of the Abruzzi* (1928), and was a contributor to the journal of the Folklore Society, of which she became a member in 1910. Her collections lift a curtain on the lives of peasants in marginal areas of the Italian peninsula. Her ethnographic portrayals are paired with illustrations that

---

Savi-Lopez, *Lettere ad Angelo De Gubernatis*, September 13, 1893, cass. 112 n. 29, letter n. 46:3, Fondo "Angelo De Gubernatis," BNCF.

90. "I became passionate for old papers, it seems to me that if I had time I would do nothing but search for old memories and forgotten figures; I would like to illustrate works that no one has ever printed, and which rest among countless volumes in the archives. It is so easy to talk about those that everyone knows, and it would instead be a useful and merciful endeavor to remind Italy of those who were forgotten." Savi-Lopez, *Lettere ad Antonio Fogazzaro*, November 4, 1885, CF0 30, Pl. 183, letter n. 9:3-4, Fondo "Antonio Fogazzaro," Biblioteca Civica Bertoliana, Vicenza.

91. For a recent study of the Grand Tour from a linguistic perspective with a focus on women travelers and gender issues, see Tosi (2020:240–59).

92. For a thorough analysis of *Sicilian Ways and Days*, see Alù (2008).

disclose a wealth of human interactions and local traditions. In her study of *Costumes, Traditions and Songs of Savoy,* Hannah Elizabeth Carroll aptly observes that several of Canziani's illustrations "reveal an underlying respect for the spiritual devotion of the women she encountered" (Carroll 2013:79). This empathic engagement emerges also in *Through the Apennines and the Lands of the Abruzzi.* The meaningful encounters between the British folklorist and local women constitute a substantial part of her travelogue (Guarracino 2023:122).[93] In *Through the Apennines,* Canziani reported that she often encouraged women who posed as models for her illustrations to share with her everything they knew about local traditions. So it happened that the seventeen-year-old girl Maria Mancini, one of her model-informants, told her several wonder tales she once heard from an "old woman of ninety," who "on Sunday afternoons used to have the children of the village sitting round her while she told them stories" (Canziani 1928:243).

Several anthologies that, like Canziani's collections, involved firsthand investigation in local communities place an emphasis on this "authentic" process of collection in their paratexts. An example of this can be seen in Rachel Busk's *The Folk-Lore of Rome* (1874), the subtitle of which makes clear that the folkloric material was "collected by word of mouth from the people." Busk was a member of the Folklore Society in London and was renowned for various works of European folklore.[94] She originally came from a wealthy London family that settled in Rome after several turbulent events.[95] In Italy, she became acquainted with Pitrè, who wrote a chapter for her book *The Folk-Songs of Italy,* published in 1887 (Dorson 1968:385). As she wrote to Pitrè, she gathered folktales "tra le vecchiarelle di Roma."[96] In their study on Busk's work as a collector, Anne Eriksen and Torunn Selberg praise her as "a (highly successful) field-working collector" and "as an upper-middle-class English lady approaching the common people of another nation (and language)" (Eriksen and Selberg 2015:305). In the preface to *The Folk-Lore of Rome,* Busk described how she came to the decision to collect the "legendary lore" of Rome due to

---

93. On Canziani's life and works, see also Coote Lake (1964) and Polezzi (2004).

94. Busk also wrote collections of Spanish and Tirol traditions and legends (Busk 1870; 1871; 1874b).

95. On her biography and family history, see Hopkin (2017; 2018a). She was evidently competent in Italian. It is also important to bear in mind that, in order to access the folklore of Roman people, she needed to have a thorough knowledge of the local dialect: in this regard, it cannot be ruled out that she may have relied on local dialectophone assistants during her folkloric quest.

96. "among the little old women of Rome." Busk, *Lettere a Giuseppe Pitrè,* January 12, 1876, P-B-16, letter n. 1:1, BEGP.

the absence of an "Italian Grimm" (Busk 1874a:vi).[97] She explained to De Gubernatis that in this volume she had "tried to scrape together & put in record a very important item of popular mythology, no collection of which had been made before."[98] Her Roman folktales offered remarkable insights into the practice of collecting folklore from lower-class women.[99] The volume can be categorized as "reflexive ethnography" (Hopkin 2018a): indeed, a sound awareness of the importance of the dynamics in the relationship between collector and informant emerges in these pages. Busk also provided a detailed account of the difficulties she encountered in obtaining fairy tales from her storytellers: for instance, offering "some means of compensation" to the informants for the time granted to the collector was not a straightforward task because "direct payment would be an offence" (Busk 1874a:ix).

Similarly, an elderly peasant named Clementina—the main informant of British folklorist Isabella Anderton (1858–1904),[100] who collected tales from the rural areas surrounding the town of Pistoia in *Tuscan Folk-Lore and Sketches* (1905)—"would take no payment for her time" (Anderton 1905:9–10). The recollection of the encounters between Anderton and her storyteller illuminates how the dissemination and preservation of popular culture was tightly interwoven with the conception of women as conveyors of traditional values and linguistic knowledge. This view is evident in the way female informants

---

97. Pitrè mentioned Busk in his epistolary exchange with De Gubernatis: "Son lieto di dirti che abbiamo in Italia la distintissima mitologa inglese Miss R. H. Busk, che tu tanto conosci. [...] Da più anni ho la fortuna di carteggiare con questa egregia signora; e sempre più mi son dovuto rallegrare di aver conosciuto ed ammirato in lei non solo un'ottima scrittrice, ma anche un'ottima donna. Una Busk in Italia noi non l'abbiamo né tra le ragazze, né tra le signore; ma che dico io tra le signore! Se non l'abbiamo neppure tra gli uomini che coltivano le tradizioni popolari!" [I am happy to tell you that we have in Italy the very distinguished English mythologist Miss R. H. Busk, whom you know so well. (...) For several years I have been lucky enough to exchange letters with this excellent lady, and more and more I have rejoiced knowing and admiring her not only as an excellent writer but also as an excellent woman. We don't have a Busk in Italy either among girls or ladies; but what am I saying, among the ladies! We don't even have someone like her among the men who cultivate popular traditions!]. Pitrè, *Lettere ad Angelo De Gubernatis*, March 11, 1881, cass. 100 n. 19.9, letter n. 9.1, Fondo "Angelo De Gubernatis," BNCF. On Busk's folkloric writings, see Lee (2008), Eriksen and Selberg (2015), and Hopkin (2017; 2018a).

98. Busk, *Lettere ad Angelo De Gubernatis*, March 5, 1881, cass. 18 n. 28, letter n. 1:2, Fondo "Angelo De Gubernatis," BNCF.

99. For subsequent collections of Roman folklore written in the Romanesco dialect, see Zanazzo (1907; 1908).

100. On Isabella Anderton's correspondence with renowned Italian poet Giovanni Pascoli (1855–1912), see Perugi (1989; 1990). On her life and contributions to folklore, see Hopkin (2018b).

were idealized in nineteenth-century collections as uncorrupted sources of ancient wisdom. In this regard, it is worth noting that Anderton's folktale "A Tuscan Snow-White and the Dwarfs" begins precisely with a picturesque portrayal of Clementina:

> It was old Clementina—a white-haired, delicate-featured peasant woman, with a brightly-coloured handkerchief tied cornerwise on her head, a big ball of coarse white wool stuck on a little stick in the right-hand side of the band of her big apron, and the sock she was knitting carried in the other hand. My companion had gone down to Pistoia to do some shopping: I was alone in our rooms in the straggling primitive little village that clings to the hill among the chestnut woods above. Clementina thought I must be very lonely; besides, she was anxious to know what sort of things these extraordinary *"forestieri"*—foreigners—did all by themselves. They wrote, she believed—well, but how did they look when they were writing, and what sort of tools did they use? (Anderton 1905:11)

Clementina's perspective as an uneducated peasant, mediated by Anderton's description, perfectly exemplifies the iconic image of the "musa analfabeta" (Bonomo 2016:14), the illiterate muse that inspired folklorists to put their writing tools to good use. These tools become invested with a quasimagical aura in the eyes of the old woman, thanks to their power to crystallize the wisdom of the folk into written words.

Alongside Anderton's anthology, Tuscan folklore was also the subject of the collections by Francesca Alexander (1837–1917), née Esther Frances, originally from Boston, Massachusetts. She nurtured a passion for painting under the guidance of her father, a renowned portraitist, and moved at an early age to Florence with her family. In Abetone, a village in the province of Pistoia, she became acquainted with Beatrice Bugelli (1802–1885), better known as Beatrice di Pian degli Ontani, an acclaimed illiterate poet of humble origins. Also called "poetessa pastora,"[101] Beatrice Bugelli achieved national prominence among illustrious scholars and intellectuals of the time, including Niccolò Tommaseo, due to her extraordinary ability to improvise poems.[102] As Maurizio

---

101. "shepherd female poet."

102. In his article "Gita nel Pistojese," published in *Antologia. Giornale di Scienze, Lettere e Arti*, Tommaseo related his encounter with Beatrice di Pian degli Ontani. He observed how Beatrice used to spend "ore intere a cantare, sempre ripigliando la rima de' due ultimi versi cantati dal suo compagno" [whole hours singing, always resuming the rhyme of the last two lines sung by her partner] (Tommaseo 1832:26). On Beatrice di Pian degli Ontani, see Bellucci (1986), Rosati (2001), Ciampi (2008), and Borghi (2012). The tradition of poetic improvisation was widespread in eighteenth-century Tuscany as well: on women improvisers such as Maria

Coppola notes in his observations on her role as Tommaseo's primary informant, she is an *"individu-monde"* that symbolizes the intricate bond between the spontaneous voice of the people and the emerging national identity: she concentrates in herself "toute la puissance artistique et historique d'un people, comme dans un coffre idéal capable de conserver tous les trésors de la nation" (Coppola 2021:57; original emphasis).[103] In 1885 Alexander published *Roadside Songs of Tuscany*, with original versions and translations of songs she collected in the region. The text was edited by John Ruskin (1819–1900) and accompanied by her illustrations, including a portrait of Beatrice Bugelli (fig. 1.2).[104] Alexander remembered her with these words:

> These songs and hymns of the poor people have been collected, little by little, in the course of a great many years which I have passed in constant intercourse with the Tuscan contadini. [...] A great many were taught me by the celebrated improvisatrice, Beatrice Bernardi of Pian degli Ontani, whose portrait I have placed in the beginning of the book,—one of the most wonderful women whom I ever knew. [...] *She had no education in the common sense of the word, never learning even the alphabet*, but she had a wonderful memory, and could sing or recite long pieces of poetry. (Alexander 1885:1–2; original emphasis)[105]

A vivid physical description followed by an illustration of Beatrice di Pian degli Ontani in old age can also be found in an article published in *L'Illustrazione Italiana* in 1888 by Clara Schubert (fig. 1.3), who paid homage to the creative power of this talented poet and implicitly mentioned the work of Francesca Alexander, albeit omitting her name at the request of Alexander herself:

> Essa fu di statura piuttosto piccola; era forte ma svelta molto; aveva i capelli neri, tutti arricciolati, che spesso le cadevano sopra la fronte; occhi grandi, nerissimi e di un lustro singolarmente bello; aveva bei denti e belle fattezze,

---

Maddalena Morelli (1727–1800), Fortunata Sulgher Fantastici (1755–1824), and Teresa Bandettini Landucci (1763–1837), linked to the Italian literary academy Arcadia, see Giuli (2003; 2009), Trapani (2010), and Winter (2019). The database on *Donne in Arcadia (1690–1800)*, created by Tatiana Crivelli, gathers bio-bibliographical data on women who participated in the Arcadia (Crivelli 2010). For a recent study of eighteenth-century poetic improvisation, with reference also to female improvisers within this tradition, see Capriotti (2022a:169–82) and his catalog of testimonies of this cultural phenomenon (Capriotti 2022b).

103. "all the artistic and historical power of a people, as in an ideal chest capable of preserving all the treasures of the nation."

104. Giannozzo Pucci partially translated the work into Italian (Alexander 1976; 1980).

105. She was also known as Beatrice Bernardi after her marriage with Matteo Bernardi in 1823.

ma la sua pelle era un po' bruciacchiata.—Così la descrisse a me una signora americana, che l'ha conosciuta e avvicinata per più anni, che le ha voluto un gran bene e che di lei ha fatto un bellissimo ritratto, che si trova riprodotto esattamente nei *Roadside Songs of Tuscany* (Canti popolari Toscani), editi per John Ruskin. E questa signora (che mi ha pregato di non nominarla), non conobbe la Beatrice quand'era giovane, ma quando avrà avuto almeno una quarantina d'anni. (Schubert 1888:52)[106]

Similar to Nardo Cibele's collections, Alexander's writings show a sensitive proximity to the peasants and mountain dwellers she approached during her search for popular songs, often denouncing their difficult living conditions (Bencistà 2011:53–54). Alexander also published other collections such as *Christ's Folk in the Apennine: Reminiscences of Her Friends among the Tuscan Peasantry* (1887), *Tuscan Songs* (1897), and *Hidden Servants and Other Old Stories Told Over* (1900). Being "part artist, part amateur ethnographer" (Feldman, 2002:43), her endeavors situate themselves at the crossroads between art and folklore, offering compelling evidence, both in verbal and visual form, of the intellectuals' rising fascination with peasantry in the nineteenth century.

Women, real and imagined, were often presented as cultural and linguistic informants par excellence. With regard to the transmission of language, it is worth remembering that "Grammar" has frequently been personified as a breastfeeding nurse (Sanson 2011:6). From this mythical characterization to a more markedly historical dimension, women's roles in passing on knowledge and educating children were central in the evolution of nation-states in the nineteenth century. This was also the case in post-unification Italy, when the educational system became more accessible to women both as teachers and pupils of the new emerging nation (Sanson 2013b). This centrality frequently clashed with women's concretely marginalized social condition, although it was precisely because they were at the margins of society that they were highly regarded as bearers of linguistic purity.

A further testimony of the belief that Tuscan rural regions were regarded as repositories of uncontaminated language can be found in Cesare Cantù's

---

106. "She was of rather small stature; she was strong but very quick; she had black hair, all curled, which often fell over her forehead; large, very black eyes with a singularly beautiful shine; she had beautiful teeth and beautiful features, but her skin was a little scorched. She was described to me in such a way by an American lady, who has known and has been close to her for several years, loved her very much and made a beautiful portrait of hers, which is reproduced exactly in the *Roadside Songs of Tuscany* (Canti popolari Toscani), edited by John Ruskin. And this lady (who begged me not to name her), did not know Beatrice when she was young, but when she was at least forty years old."

FIGURE 1.2. Illustration of Beatrice di Pian degli Ontani, *Roadside Songs of Tuscany* (Alexander 1885, I). Photograph by Amélie Deblauwe, Cambridge University Library (Syn.3.88.1). Amélie Deblauwe / Reproduced by kind permission of the Syndics of Cambridge University Library.

La poetessa BEATRICE DI PIAN DEGLI ONTANI.

FIGURE 1.3. Beatrice di Pian degli Ontani in old age, *L'Illustrazione Italiana*, "La pastorella poetessa. Beatrice di Pian degli Ontani," 31 (Schubert 1888:52), Biblioteca Comunale dell'Archiginnasio, Bologna (A.2306). Courtesy of the Biblioteca Comunale dell'Archiginnasio, Bologna.

words to Alessandro Manzoni: the former encouraged Manzoni "di mettersi *per mesi ed anni* nella *montagna di Pistoja o nel Casentino*, e come l'aria respirare a pieno petto quelle squisitezze e *assimilarsele*" (Cantù in Stampa 1885, I:101; original emphasis).[107] The province of Pistoia is precisely the area Anderton and Alexander drew from for their collections, whereas the Casentino features predominantly in Emma Perodi's children's book *Le novelle della nonna: fiabe fantastiche* (1893).[108] The references to gifted spinners of tales became a topos not only in folklore collections but also in literary works for children, increasingly so in the second half of the nineteenth century, when a conspicuous number of folk and fairy tales started to be adapted for a young readership. Emma Perodi (1850–1918), a writer of novels and short stories for children who personally knew Giuseppe Pitrè, worked in Florence, Rome, and Palermo, directing from 1887 the *Giornale dei bambini*, a periodical aimed at a children's readership, published between 1881 and 1889. Although she was not a collector herself, her narratives were steeped in local folklore, which she reinvented for literary ends and imbued with explicit pedagogical messages. In *Le novelle della nonna*, she built a framed narrative set in the Casentino valley. The focal point of the narration is Regina Marcucci, an old grandmother and formidable narrator, who weaves tales that Professor Luigi, an embodiment of the modern ethnologist, writes down feverishly in his notebook. The forty-five tales she narrates are interspersed with asides on the rural life of her relatives, enchanted by her storytelling skills. Her ability to captivate them is well rendered in Carlo Chiostri's illustrations, in which her centrality as a narrator is underscored: all her family members of different ages, and even their poultry, used to gather around her to listen intently to her voice and follow her awe-inspiring gestures, with eyes wide open (fig. 1.4 and fig. 1.5).

It is not far-fetched to suppose that Emma Perodi had Giuseppe Pitrè in mind when she sketched the character of the professor who so eagerly transcribed Regina Marcucci's tales, told with "la voce dolce e il purissimo accento, proprio degli abitanti delle montagne toscane," "senza cambiarvi una parola" (Perodi 1992 [1893]:5, 423).[109] Pitrè also appeared under a fanciful guise in another children's story, the meta-fairy tale "Il racconta-fiabe" (The Fairy-Tale

---

107. "to reside *for months and years* in the *mountains of Pistoja or in the Casentino*, and to breathe fully those delicacies as if they were air and to *assimilate them*."

108. On Perodi's cultural production, see Scapecchi (1993) and Scancarello (2014). On *Le novelle della nonna*, see Faeti (1974), Roversi Monaco (2013), and Agostini-Ouafi (2016).

109. "the sweet voice and the very pure accent that is typical of the inhabitants of the Tuscan mountains," "without changing a word." The first ten stories narrated by Regina Marcucci have been translated by Lori Hetherington (Perodi 2020). The tale "L'Incantatrice" (The Enchantress) has been translated into English by Nancy Canepa (2023:305–17). Three other tales, "The

FIGURE 1.4. Illustration of Regina Marcucci by Carlo Chiostri, *Le novelle della nonna: fiabe fantastiche* (Perodi 1924 [1893], I), Biblioteca Comunale Rilli-Vettori, Poppi (BCRP-17498). Courtesy of the Biblioteca Comunale Rilli-Vettori, Poppi.

Teller) (1893), by Sicilian writer Luigi Capuana (1839–1915). In this ironic reflection on the limits of authorial invention and on the power of imagination, Capuana gave shape to the wizard Tre-Pi—a pun that humorously alludes to Pitrè—who jealously stores in his countless drawers "fiabe imbalsamate,"[110] all

---

She-Mule of Abbess Sofia," "Lavella's Stepmother," and "The Madonna's Veil," have been translated by Cristina Mazzoni (2021:127–62).

110. "embalmed fairy tales."

FIGURE 1.5. Illustration of Regina Marcucci by Carlo Chiostri, *Le novelle della nonna: fiabe fantastiche* (Perodi 1925 [1893], II), Biblioteca Comunale Rilli-Vettori, Poppi (BCRP-17499). Courtesy of the Biblioteca Comunale Rilli-Vettori, Poppi.

perfectly numbered and classified (Capuana 1992 [1893]:111–15). After asking for the wizard Tre-Pi's advice, the protagonist of the story—a storyteller who is unable to innovate his repertoire of fairy tales—starts a quest for the fairy Fantasia, the only one who knows the secret recipe for new stories.[111] Regina

---

111. On Capuana's "Il racconta-fiabe," see Miele (2009:303), Zuccala (2020:89–92), and Canepa (2023:278). For a translation of the tale into English, see Zipes (2009b:369–74).

Marcucci and the wizard Tre-Pi constitute respectively mediated images of fairy-tale storytellers and folklore collectors, suspended between reality and imagination. Such images achieve on a narratological level a mise-en-abîme effect, creating echoes between the oral and the literary dimensions. These literary narratives, reverberating with the practices of transcribing, collecting, and reinventing oral traditions, invite us to rethink the meaning and function of the portrayals of gifted tradition-bearers, who served different purposes depending on the specific context in which their stories were told and on the eyes of the beholders that perpetuated their afterimages in a textual dimension. As I will illustrate in further detail in chapter 3, the works of fin de siècle folk and fairy-tale collectors prompt a reflection on the class dynamics that characterized the uneven relationship between scholars and informants, as well as on the concepts of creativity and cultural transmission in the long nineteenth century.

Tuscan traditions, and in particular folk songs, were also compiled by Scottish translator and editor Grace Warrack (1855–1932), whose *Florilegio di Canti Toscani: Folksongs of the Tuscan Hills with English Renderings* (1914) was dedicated to three women, including Francesca Alexander.[112] In assembling these songs, she drew from previously published collections, which she acknowledged thoroughly in her preface, such as Eugenia Levi's *Fiorita di canti tradizionali* (1895),[113] Alessandro D'Ancona's *Storia della poesia popolare italiana* (1878), Giuseppe Pitrè's *Canti popolari siciliani* (1870), and Ermolao Rubieri's *Storia della poesia popolare italiana* (1877). Being fond of both Italian and Scottish Gaelic folk songs and poetry, Warrack dedicated an appendix to the "Use of Repetition in Tuscan and in Gaelic Traditional Poetry" (Warrack 1914:295), in which she compared the Tuscan "ripresa," the structural reiteration of a word or an idea that was typical of Tuscan folk songs, to the repetition that could be found in old Scottish Gaelic poetry (Warrack 1914:295),[114] commenting that

---

112. The other dedicatees were Mary S. Talbot of Clifton, Bristol, and Phoebe Anna Traquair (1852–1936), a leading figure in the Scottish Arts and Crafts movement at the turn of the century.

113. Warrack was enthusiastic about Eugenia Levi's work. In the preface, she thanked her and commented positively on her collections of folk songs: "For some beautiful songs from other parts of Italy than Tuscany I have to thank Professor Eugenia Levi and the publishers of her *Fiorita di canti tradizionali* [...]. This little treasury of the songs of all the Regions of Italy, with music, gives in its notes invaluable help to readers unfamiliar with the various dialects." See the unpaginated preface to Warrack's *Florilegio di Canti Toscani* (1914).

114. On oral formulaic studies on folk songs, with a focus on Scottish ballads, see Buchan (1972) and Nicolaisen and Moreira (2013).

in the habitual echoing mode of the closing of these Tuscan love-songs there is a "way" that brings to memory things far remote from them—namely, the old religious songs found in the Highlands, and especially about the North-Western shores and the Hebridean Islands of Scotland. (Warrack 1914:295)

Warrack subsequently published another anthology of Italian folk songs entitled *Out of the Heart of Italy: Folk Songs from Venetia to Sardinia* (1925), which included lyrics, lullabies, and children's prayers from various Italian regions.

Prior to the publication of Warrack's anthologies, an academic study of Italian folk songs in the English language was carried out by British folklorist Evelyn Martinengo-Cesaresco (1852–1931), née Carrington, author of *Essays in the Study of Folk-Songs* (1886) and *La Poésie Populaire* (1893). Martinengo-Cesaresco was an intrepid traveler and supporter of the Italian Risorgimento, which she studied in depth (Hopkin 2018c).[115] She approached popular poetry as "un'espressione estetica e psicologica delle classi umili" (Galanti 1956:158) and was esteemed by De Gubernatis, D'Ancona, and Pitrè, for whom she wrote an obituary in 1916.[116] She had a long correspondence with the Sicilian scholar, to whom she used to send her contributions, including the articles she had published in the journal of the Folklore Society in London. For example, on April 15, 1882, she wrote to Pitrè:

I am about to take the liberty of sending to the "Archivio per lo Studio delle Tradizioni popolari" two slight contributions of mine to the study of Folklore, that consists in a few songs to which I have given the name of "singing games" & which have been printed by the English Folk-lore Society. The children & young girls of the village of Bocking have often played & sung these songs in my father's garden when they have met there for a fête.[117]

Martinengo-Cesaresco's education was haphazard, as she confessed in an undated letter rich with autobiographical details preserved in De Gubernatis's archive.[118] Although she did not receive a formal education, she grew up in a

---

115. She knew Italian patriot Giuseppe Garibaldi (1807–1882), whom she met twice, both in England and in Italy. She wrote several works on Italian history, such as *Italian Characters in the Epoch of Unification* (1890), *Cavour* (1898), and *The Liberation of Italy, 1815–1870* (1895). On her Risorgimento writings, see Hopkin (2017; 2018c) and Casalena (2012).

116. "an aesthetic and psychological expression of the humble classes."

117. Martinengo-Cesaresco, *Lettere a Giuseppe Pitrè*, April 15, 1882, P-C-18, letter n. 1:1–2, BEGP.

118. Martinengo-Cesaresco, *Lettere ad Angelo De Gubernatis*, undated letter, cass. 83 n. 20, Fondo "Angelo De Gubernatis," BNCF.

family that encouraged the pursuit of her literary and historical interests: her father, Dean Henry Carrington, was a literary translator, and her mother, Juanita Lyall, was a novelist. Her *Essays in the Study of Folk-Songs* was defined by Paul Sébillot as "une sorte de tour du monde des chansons populaires" (Sébillot, 1892:455).[119] Oscar Wilde reviewed the volume and applauded it greatly, underscoring the worth of popular songs as spontaneous poetic forms (Wilde 1886:5). Martinengo-Cesaresco highlighted the importance of dialects, maintaining that "the local dialects have a charm which standard Italian has not—a charm that consists in clothing their thought after a fashion which, like the national peasant costumes, has an essential suitability to the purpose it is used for" (Martinengo-Cesaresco 1886:124–25). She was well aware of the delicate task of collectors in their attempt to gather valuable remnants of the past: their priority was to gain the trust of illiterate peasants so as to "persuade the natural man to tell us what he still knows of those vanishing beings, and to lend us the key to his general treasure-box before all that is inside be reduced to dust" (Martinengo-Cesaresco 1886:xi–xii).

Such a conception of popular traditions as relics of the past that ought to be preserved in the present and perpetuated in the future is reiterated in *Leggende Napoletane* (1881), a romanticized assemblage of Neapolitan myths and legends retold with artistic license by Matilde Serao (1856–1927), a journalist and writer who was nominated several times for the Nobel Prize in Literature.[120] In the final legend included in her work, "La leggenda dell'avvenire," Serao addressed a "buona e baldanzosa fanciulla" (Serao 1907 [1881]:261),[121] underlining the female audience she was targeting, and suggestively commented that

> Queste storielle sono antiche, alcune antichissime, appartengono al lontanissimo passato che non ritorna più; furono vita e morirono; furono amore e sono un vago ricordo; furono dramma umano e sono parole vane, tradizione oscura e scorretta. Rimane di esse talvolta un quadro, una statua, una chiesa, una tomba, un bosco, talvolta una semplice idea, talvolta un semplice nome; ma è il passato. (Serao 1907 [1881]:262)[122]

---

119. "a sort of world tour of popular songs."

120. For some of the key studies on Matilde Serao, see De Nunzio Schilardi (1986), Frattarolo (1989), Scappaticci (1995), and Fanning (2002). On Serao's reception abroad, see Romani et al. (2022).

121. "a good and bold maiden."

122. "These little stories are ancient, some very ancient, they belong to the distant past that never returns; they were life and they died; they were love and they are a vague memory; they were human tragedy and they are now vain words, an obscure and incorrect tradition. At times

It is perhaps not coincidental that Serao entitled this conclusive legend as "leggenda dell'avvenire," the "legend of the future," as if it were a message left to readers and to posterity. Past and future are inextricably connected, and the historical value of folklore—its very raison d'être as a science—resides in their indissoluble bond. It was undoubtedly this desire to hand down the traditions of the past to future generations that nourished the passion of nineteenth-century folklorists, despite their different approaches and ideological positions, inducing them to devote their time to the research and collection of folkloric materials. Giuseppe Cocchiara, in his reflections on the European "mission" of folklore, observed how "il folklore, lo studio delle sue varie manifestazioni [...] segnava appunto il ponte di passaggio fra il passato e l'avvenire,"[123] promising the possibility of overcoming the limits of each nation (Cocchiara 2016 [1952]:271). It is within this wider perspective that the European dimension of folklore studies can be acknowledged and that women's contributions to the field can be reassessed.

Women and Folklore in Ireland in the Long Nineteenth Century

The preservation and dissemination of a rich array of popular traditions, including folk and fairy tales, melodies and folk songs, ethnographic sketches and customs, saw the participation of various female figures in Ireland and across the British Isles. In addition to Jane Wilde's and Augusta Gregory's collections, which will be examined in the following chapters, several nineteenth-century women, some renowned and others relatively lesser known, published books and essays inspired by Irish folklore. Similar to the female scholars examined thus far in the Italian context, the educational and social circumstances of these figures were not uniform, although they tended to belong to the middle and upper social classes. In a study of women's roles in Celtic linguistics, Bernhard Maier observes that, when drawing some general considerations on the

---

a painting, a statue, a church, a tomb, a forest remain of these stories, at times a simple idea, at times a simple name; but it is the past." In the foreword to the reader, Serao wrote that "[l]a severa arte moderna, dal vasto ideale di verità [...] ci allontana sempre più dalla fantasia" [the severe modern art characterized by the vast ideal of truth [...] takes us further and further away from fantasy] and rhetorically asked readers to be allowed to "dare un addio alle vecchie forme poetiche, scrivendo un libro d'immaginazione e di sogno" [say goodbye to the old poetic forms by writing a book of imagination and dream]. "Un libro d'immaginazione e di sogno" would become the subtitle of her Neapolitan legends in the 1907 edition.

123. "folklore, the study of its various manifestations, [...] marked precisely the bridge between the past and the future."

educational background of women who were active in the broad field of Celtic languages, it is inevitable to take note of the "formidable gaps in our knowledge of the mechanisms at work, because the early education of girls—especially if it took place at home and without formal schooling—can only be reconstructed to the extent that there are relevant sources" (Maier 2020:307).

Despite the difficulties in reconstructing the trajectories of women's private education, several scholars cast light on the "terrain of female education" in nineteenth-century Ireland (Raftery et al. 2010). The numerical discrepancy between male and female scholars in this period can be attributed to the divergence in educational opportunities that were available at the time for men and women. Nevertheless, it was not unusual for young girls from the Anglo-Irish gentry to have access to the libraries of their family members and to gain a solid knowledge in fields such as poetry, modern languages, and music, whereas their male counterparts were used to pursuing a classical education through formal schooling (Raftery et al. 2010:566). A significant increase in female education was achieved in the nineteenth century thanks to the establishment of a free national schooling system for both girls and boys in 1831 and to the foundation of the first Protestant high schools and Catholic convent schools for girls in the 1860s (Raftery et al. 2010:567). Yet there continued to be considerable educational gaps between those who belonged to the Anglo-Irish class, who tended to receive first private education at home and then further official education, and Irish Catholic children who lived in deprived rural areas without the same opportunities. As for university education, the first step for women's access was granted by the Royal University of Ireland in 1879 (Raftery et al. 2010:573).[124] These circumstances had an impact on women's forms of engagement with folklore studies.

For the purposes of this section, I aim to map the roles of different women in Irish folklore. This mapping, which inevitably cannot be exhaustive, offers an overview of individual women who were committed to the perpetuation of oral traditions through retellings, translations, transcriptions, and various forms of rewritings. Women's engagement with Irish folklore frequently interlaced with other disciplines and cultural realms, such as travel writing, children's literature, linguistics, and ethnomusicology. A cursory review of the history of nineteenth-century Irish folklore may suggest that women's involvement in this field was not substantial. However, by paying closer attention to the juxtaposition of folklore with other areas, several contributors can be reappraised and given the recognition they deserve.

---

124. For a history of female education in Ireland, see also Raftery and Parkes (2007) and Harford (2008).

Before delving into the nineteenth century and early twentieth century, it is worth remembering Charlotte Brooke (1740–1793), member of the Protestant Anglo-Irish class from County Cavan and Irish language enthusiast, whom Diarmuid Ó Giolláin and Bernhard Maier acknowledged as a pioneer (Ó Giolláin 2000:95; Maier 2020:308). Her *Reliques of Irish Poetry* (1789), written in Irish with English translations, presented heroic poems, odes, elegies, and songs. This volume was "primarily intra-Irish" (Leerssen 1996:31), that is to say, meant to address Irish readers and not exclusively a British readership (Ó Giolláin 2000:95–96). The interest in Irish oral traditions grew among Anglo-Irish scholars after the publication of James Macpherson's highly influential *Fragments of Ancient Poetry, Collected in the Highlands of Scotland, and Translated from the Gaelic or Erse Language* in 1760. This work, which featured the epic poems of the bard Ossian, sparked controversy not only because of its nonauthenticity but also due to "Macpherson's own contention on the Scottishness of Ossian and on the priority of the Scottish Gaelic tradition over the Irish" (Ó Giolláin 2000:19–20). Charlotte Brooke was aware of this controversy to the point that her book can be regarded as "a subtle assertion of the Irishness of the material that Macpherson used" (Ó Giolláin 2000:95).[125] At the beginning of the volume, in a manner that will immediately evoke the examples of *modestia auctoris* illustrated in the previous section of this chapter, she wrote:

> In a preface to a translation of ancient Irish poetry, the reader will naturally expect to see the subject elucidated and enlarged upon, with the pen of learning and antiquity. I lament that the limited circle of my knowledge does not include the power of answering to just an expectation; but my regret at this circumstance is considerably lessened, when I reflect, that had I been possessed of all the learning requisite for such an undertaking, it would only have qualified me for an unnecessary foil to the names of O'Conor, O'Halloran and Vallancey. My comparatively feeble hand aspires only (like the ladies of ancient Rome) to strew flowers in the paths of these laureled champions of my country. (Brooke 1789:2)[126]

---

125. On the Ossianic controversy and Brooke's role in defending Irish culture, see Gantz (1940).

126. Charles O'Conor (1710–1791) was an Irish antiquarian, author of *Dissertations on the History of Ireland* (1753). Sylvester O'Halloran (1728–1807) wrote *An Introduction to the Study of the Antiquities of Ireland* (1772) and *A General History of Ireland* (1778). Charles Vallancey (ca. 1731–1812), a British general relocated in Ireland, wrote numerous works on Irish antiquarianism and language, including *An Essay on the Antiquity of the Irish Language* (1772) and *A Vindication of the Ancient History of Ireland* (1786).

In spite of these remarks, her translations into English were written in a sophisticated style, and each poem was rife with notes and commentaries that showed the extent of her cultural and linguistic knowledge.

When reassessing women's manifold roles in Irish folklore, it is also worth mentioning the contribution of a female lament-poet in late eighteenth-century Ireland, of whom very little is known: Nóra Ní Shíndile, also called Norrie Singleton, a *bean chaointe*, a keener from Millstreet in County Cork. She sang to the poet Éamonn de Bhál first and then to Domhnall Mac Cáib the lament "Caoineadh Airt Uí Laoghaire," destined to become the most renowned example of Irish traditional keening, a practice that involved women wailing for the dead during funerals. Ní Shíndile's oral recitation was pivotal for the perpetuation of the lament, the composition of which was attributed to Eibhlín Dubh Ní Chonaill (ca. 1743–ca. 1800), widow of Art Ó Laoghaire, to express her sorrow for her husband's tragic death.[127] Angela Bourke defined the practice of *caoineadh* as a "central theatre of women's expression in the Irish language" and commented that it may be seen as a "feminist utterance," given that it is "an art in which women collaborated with other women, both synchronically—taking turns to weep over the same dead body [...]—and diachronically: remembering and quoting each other's laments, often over many generations" (Bourke 2002b:1365–66). In particular, Nóra Ní Shíndile's oral performance was an essential step for ensuring the longevity of this lament's heritage in popular culture across the centuries, and it is therefore a reminder of the importance of preserving oral traditions.

Moving to the first half of the nineteenth century, acclaimed Irish novelist and travel writer Lady Morgan (ca. 1783–1859), née Sydney Owenson, author of the successful epistolary novel *The Wild Irish Girl* (1806), arranged an anthology of Irish airs and poems under the title *Twelve Original Hibernian Melodies* (1805), many of which "were orally collected in what may be deemed the classic wilds of Ireland": as she wrote in the preface, "[w]ith a timid hand I have endeavoured to snatch them from the chilling atmosphere of oblivion" (Owenson 1805:1). Animated by a strong patriotic impetus toward Ireland, she gained a cosmopolitan outlook thanks to her studies and her journeys in Europe. After her stay in Italy in 1819–20 with her husband, Sir Charles Morgan,

---

127. For a translation of the lament into English, see Mary Anne O'Connell's *The Last Colonel of the Irish Brigade* (O'Connell 1892:239–46, I); for the Irish transcription, see O'Connell (1892:327–40, II). For more recent translations from the original into English, see Frank O'Connor's translation in Brendan Kennelly (1970:78) and Thomas Kinsella's translation in Kinsella and Ó Tuama (1981). For versions of the text that "differ significantly from the standard edited text," see Bourke (2002b:1372–84). On "Caoineadh Airt Uí Laoghaire," see Marren (1993) and Ó Giolláin (2022:278).

she wrote *Italy* (1821), a work that can be located "on the borderline between description and interpretation, guidebook and personal diary, pamphlet and history" (Badin 2016:130). In this travelogue she combined acute social observations with political commentaries on the current state of affairs in the Italian peninsula, whose longing for freedom reminded her of the similar yearning of her own country. Her two-volume *Patriotic Sketches of Ireland, written in Connaught* (1807) was centered on "the pensive legend of national woe, or the romantic tale of national heroism" (Owenson 1807, I:1), while *The Lay of an Irish Harp: or, Metrical Fragments* (1807), an anthology of Irish ballads, was permeated by observations on Ireland's glorified historical roots. She made clear that her writing was meant to ignite patriotic feelings: "as a *woman*, a *young woman*, and an *Irish woman*, I felt all the delicacy of undertaking a work which had for the professed theme of its discussion, circumstances of national import, and national interest" (Owenson 1807, I:v; original emphasis). She explained in the first fragment of *The Lay of an Irish Harp* how she came to write this collection after a journey in western Ireland, lamenting the decrease in the use of this typical Irish instrument:

> With an enthusiasm incidental to my natural and national character, I visited the western part of the province of Connaught in the autumn of 1805, full of many an evident expectation that promised to my feelings, and my taste, a *festival* of national enjoyment. The result of this interesting little pilgrimage has already been given to the world in the story of the "Wild Irish Girl," and in a collection of *Irish Melodies*, learned among those who still *"hum'd the Song of other times."* But the hope I had long cherished of hearing the *Irish Harp* played in perfection was not only far from being realized, but infinitely disappointed. That encouragement so nutritive to genius, so indispensably necessary to perseverance, no longer stimulates the Irish bard to excellence, nor rewards him when it is attained; and the decline of that tender and impressive instrument, once so dear to Irish enthusiasm, is as visibly rapid, as it is obviously unimpeded by any effort of national pride or national affection. (Owenson 1808:17–18; original emphasis)

If in this volume can be traced a nostalgic melancholy for the gradual disuse of the harp, in *Patriotic Sketches* she insisted on the "pertinacity with which the Irish adhere to their ancient customs and manners" (Owenson 1807, II:40) and inserted remarks on the bond between vernacular languages and old traditions. In this respect, she reported in a footnote the eloquent words of Irish lawyer and intellectual William Preston (1750–1807):

> The Scotch, Welsh and Irish, though the countries they inhabit have been much subject both to foreign aggression and intestine wars, yet contain

more of their aboriginal inhabitants, and are at this day a less mixed race than the English. They have still in some measure retained in popular use their peculiar dialects, handed down to them from remote ages. They converse in their own language with a conscious delight, and have preserved many of their ancient customs, institutions, traditions, and pastimes, and also many of their metrical compositions. (Preston in Owenson 1807, II:41–42)[128]

Such reflections on the entanglements between language purity and the preservation of cultural roots were widespread at the time, as was the stress on the retention of ancient and uncontaminated traditions in the Celtic world.[129]

Regarding anthologies with a more markedly ethnographic flavor, Irish-born writer Anna Maria Hall (1800–1881), née Fielding, devoted her attention to local customs and published several sketches of Irish life, such as *Sketches of Irish Character* (1829), *Lights and Shadows of Irish Life* (1838), and *Stories of the Irish Peasantry* (1840). In *Lights and Shadows of Irish Life*, she laid claim to her focus on the lower classes by commenting how she had been told "somewhat reproachfully, that I write only of the humbler classes—that my sketches are of peasants and their cabins [...]. I can but urge in excuse, that it is only among such we must look for original character" (Hall 1838, I:vi). Together with her husband, Samuel Carter Hall, editor of *The Art Journal*, she wrote a rich account of their memories and their several journeys to Ireland in three volumes, titled *Ireland: Its Scenery, Character and History* (1841–43), followed by *A Week in Killarney* (1843), the four-volume *Handbooks for Ireland* (1853), and *A Companion to Killarney* (1878). These volumes were interspersed with references to local traditions and were the result of the intellectual collaboration between husband and wife.[130] Hall, who had moved to England from an

---

128. The original quotation can be found in Preston (1806:112).

129. Preston articulated the difference between the Saxon and the Celtic people by highlighting the different natural characterization of their respective countries: "It is easy to account for this difference. The lofty mountains, the woods, defiles and morasses, by which Wales, Scotland and Ireland were defended, afforded natural fortresses, to which the ancient inhabitants retired, from the rage and pursuits of their enemies, and preserved their language and manners pure and unmixed. The progress of invasion was stopped, and some remnant of independence preserved. To this circumstance Ireland superadded a remote insular situation, which originally preserved her from the visitation of the Romans. England, on the contrary, which was better known, lay more open to invasion, and afforded fewer natural means of defence" (Preston 1806:113–14).

130. Jane Wilde and William Wilde represent another renowned example of the collaborative nature of cultural endeavors by married couples, which will be explored in chapter 2. The Irish revivalists Padraic Colum (1881–1972) and Mary Colum (1884–1957), née Mary Gunning

early age, wrote in the introduction to the third edition of *Sketches of Irish Character* that her intention was not just to amuse her readers but, above all, "to picture the Irish character, as to make it more justly appreciated, more rightly estimated, and more respected, in England," with the objective "to do justice to the many estimable qualities of the Irish peasantry, of whom it has been truly said, 'their virtues are their own; but their vices have been forced upon them'" (Hall 1892 [1829]:viii). The volumes by the Halls are exemplary of the intersection of folkloric material with other genres, such as travel writing. The guide published with her husband, *Ireland: Its Scenery, Character and History*, offers insightful remarks on the thorny question of authenticity in the transcription of oral narratives. For instance, when the Halls reported tales related to the Pooka,[131] a shape-shifting creature of Celtic folkloric imagination, they observed with a hint of irony:

> One of these stories, having more than the usual point, we shall repeat, as nearly as we can, in the words in which we received it; only regretting that we have it at second-hand, being unable to record the fact on better authority, in consequence of the decease of the actual adventurer. (Hall and Hall 1841, I:111–12)

Whether truthful or not, these stories often showcased the Halls' "claim to authority" and insistence on objectivity (Murphy 2011:122): although many of them were clearly fictional in nature, they were presented to the readers as reliable sources of information on Irish customs and social life. Yet these writings were far from promoting ideas about Irish independence since the Halls were strong proponents of the peaceful union between Ireland and Britain: indeed, they frequently expressed their disapproval of the Irish battle for freedom in their works, rather advocating for a "friendly relationship" between the two nations (Dochy 2014:2). Their works are exemplary of a colonialist attitude and were primarily aimed at a British middle-class readership. Nonetheless, in the process

---

Maguire, were another collaborative couple worthy of notice for their shared interest in Irish culture and folklore. The couple moved from Ireland to the United States in 1914, where Padraic Colum became a prolific children's writer and collector of Hawaiian folklore, which he published in three volumes: *At the Gateways of the Day: Tales and Legends of Hawaii* (1924), *The Bright Islands: Tales and Legends of Hawaii* (1925), and *Legends of Hawaii* (1937). Mary Colum was a literary critic, editor, co-founder of the magazine *The Irish Review*, and author of *From These Roots: The Ideas That Have Made Modern Literature* (1937), *Life and the Dream* (1947), and *Our Friend James Joyce* (1958), the latter being a recollection of her friendship with James Joyce (1882–1941), written with her husband.

131. As the Halls reported, "Pouke or Pooka means literally the evil one; 'playing the puck,' a common Anglo-Irish phrase, is equivalent to 'playing the devil'" (Hall and Hall 1841, I:109).

of fashioning Ireland as an attractive land of touristic destination, they preserved valuable topographical and folkloric sketches. For example, in a chapter devoted to Waterford, in southeastern Ireland (Hall and Hall 1841–43, I:277–324), they reported in detail the tradition of "pancake tossing" on Shrove Tuesday, the day preceding Ash Wednesday, accompanied by a picturesque illustration of an Irish family gathered around the fireside (fig. 1.6). On this occasion, family members attempted to toss the pancake: whoever managed to toss and turn it upside down in the pan was destined to have good luck, especially so the unwedded girls; indeed, the first to make the attempt was usually "the eldest unmarried daughter of the host" (Hall and Hall 1841–43, I:316).

Moving to County Donegal, a precursor in the collection of folklore in this area was Letitia McClintock (1835–1917),[132] who contributed to several journals, including the *Dublin University Magazine* in the 1870s and *All the Year Round* in the 1880s. Mary Helen Thuente defines her as a "relatively unknown Donegal folklorist" who was greatly appreciated by Yeats for her "idiomatic accuracy and lack of fictional elaboration," which was a rare quality in nineteenth-century collections (Thuente 1981:64–65). In the article "Folk Lore of the County Donegal: Fairy Tales" published in *Dublin University Magazine* in 1877, McClintock reported the tales of local people from the town of Lifford featuring the "wee folk," or "gentry" (McClintock 1877:241), as fairies were called at the time. McClintock's contributions to folklore were openly applauded by Yeats in his introduction to *Fairy and Folk Tales of the Irish Peasantry* (1888), in which he praised her alongside Douglas Hyde. After an excursus on the works of several Irish folklorists, including Thomas Crofton Croker, William Carleton, Patrick Kennedy, and Jane Wilde, he turned to "Miss Letitia Maclintock," who had the merit of writing "accurately and beautifully the half Scotch dialect of Ulster" (Yeats 1888:xv–xvi). He inserted several of the stories she had gathered in his own collection.[133] McClintock's incursions among Donegal's peasants configure themselves as quasidetached accounts of the visions of rural people, without explicitly projecting any ideological view onto them, lacking any "propagandistic biases—moral or political" (Thuente 1981:64–65) and "literary tampering" (Carrassi 2012:50). However, her detached viewpoint as an educated woman sometimes emerges. For instance, in an article appearing in the journal *Belgravia: A London Magazine* in 1878 entitled "Cavan

---

132. In some sources, her surname is also spelled "Maclintock" or "MacClintock."

133. Yeats included in his anthology the following narratives by McClintock: "A Donegal Fairy" (Yeats 1888:46), "Jamie Freel and the Young Lady: A Donegal Tale" (Yeats 1888:52–59), "Far Darrig in Donegal" (Yeats 1888:90–93), "Grace Connor" (Yeats 1888:130–32) and "Bewitched Butter (Donegal)" (Yeats 1888:149–50).

FIGURE 1.6. An Irish family around the fireside in *Ireland: Its Scenery, Character and History* (Hall 1841–43, I:316), HathiTrust Digital Library. Courtesy of HathiTrust Digital Library.

Superstitions," she retold in first person her interactions with local people in County Cavan, noticing that

> Superstition is rampant here as if there were no national schools. I am surrounded by neighbours who have had wives and children stolen by fairies; who have been blighted by the evil eye, or who have had interviews with friends returning from the "undiscovered country" with messages of warning or farewell. The peasants of Cavan are eager to falsify Shakespeare's words, for to them the grave is not "the bourne from whence no traveller returns." (McClintock 1878:90)

Although she gave space to the ironic subtexts of the stories, the dialogue she reported with a "loquacious friend" (McClintock 1878:92) reinforces the distance between the lady who observed the surroundings with the curiosity of an outsider and the perspective of the "very old man, bent and snowy-haired" (McClintock 1878:90), who used to tell anecdotes about encounters with supernatural beings in which he firmly believed.

A few decades after McClintock's folkloric writings, prominent British folklorist Alice Bertha Gomme (1853–1938), née Merck, was among the founding members of the Folklore Society in London.[134] Gomme devoted her studies to children's games, publishing *The Traditional Games of England, Scotland and Ireland* in two volumes in 1894 and 1898. In this popular collection, she gathered in alphabetical order "both indoor and outdoor games, and those played by both girls and boys" (Gomme 1894:viii), reported the tunes of the singing games as well as a list of the collectors and of the counties of origin for each game, detailing each source with great accuracy. Despite being a pioneer in institutionalizing this subgenre of folklore, her work was often belittled and considered as inadequate by her contemporaries, a view that blatantly clashes with the precision and acuity displayed by her collections.[135] Her merit was to recognize that children's games were valuable not only as a source of entertainment but also "as a means of obtaining an insight into many of the customs and beliefs of our ancestors" (Gomme 1894:x).

British ethnologist and president of the Folklore Society Robert Ranulph Marett (1866–1943) placed a similar emphasis on folklore "not as a mere fireside amusement" in the preface he wrote to *Folklore of the British Isles* (1928), by Eleanor Hull (1860–1935). The volume was appreciated as a praiseworthy contribution to the science of folklore that drew "authentic history out of fantastic myth and crazy custom" (Marett in Hull, 1928:v).[136] Hull was president of the Irish Literary Society, founded in 1892 by Yeats together with Thomas William Rolleston and Charles Gavan Duffy, and was one of the founders of the Irish Texts Society in 1898, led by Douglas Hyde and aimed at the promulgation of Irish literary texts. Among her various works that contributed to the promotion of Irish literary heritage, Hull published *The Cuchulain Saga in Irish Literature* (1898) and *The Boys' Cuchulain: Heroic Legends of Ireland* (1904). After her death, she was remembered fondly for being able to "think with the

---

134. The Folklore Society saw the active engagement of several women, including the previously mentioned Estella Canziani and Charlotte Burne (1850–1923), the first female president of the society. On Burne and Gomme, see Ashman (2000) and Boyes (2000).

135. On the prejudices that Gomme had to endure, see Boyes (2001).

136. Among her sources of inspiration, Hull also reported the "books of the late Lady Wilde" (Hull 1928:xi).

folk and about the folk at once and together; she dreamed their dreams and yet was able to interpret them" (Marett 1935:77).

Another noteworthy member of the Irish Texts Society was Norma Borthwick (1862–1934), born in Chester, England. Borthwick first learned Irish in London and then traveled frequently to Ireland, where she became committed to the cause of revitalizing the language. As a co-founder of the Irish Book Company, in 1912 she published an Irish translation of selected fairy tales by Hans Christian Andersen, *Leouirín na Leanav: Royint shgélíní a toug à shgiàltuiv Hans Christian Andersen don äs óg* (Maier 2020:315), together with Celtic scholar Osborn Bergin (1873–1950). She also supported Irish writer and priest Peadar Ó Laoghaire (1839–1920) in the compilation of *Foclóir do Shéadna*, a dictionary for his well-known work *Séadna* (1904). During her journeys in the west of Ireland, she would visit the Gregory family's estate in Coole Park, where she taught Irish to Augusta Gregory herself and to other Anglo-Irish revivalists.[137]

A dedication to the Irish revivalist movement is also evident in the efforts of Pamela Colman Smith (1878–1951), also known as "Pixie," a talented British artist, folklorist, performer, and editor of American origins who was keenly interested in oral tales, especially from Jamaica and Ireland. She left an indelible mark as the illustrator of the Rider-Waite tarot deck, although she was not credited for its design during her lifetime, a glaring omission that has been amended only in recent years (Grossman 2019:173). Smith was acquainted with prominent personalities of the time, including Bram Stoker and W. B. Yeats, whom she met in 1901 (O'Connor 2021:110). Her fascination with Celtic mythology, occultism, and mysticism, intertwined with her feminist activism, grew over time and would lead her to the establishment of her own magazine in London, *The Green Sheaf* (1903–4), consisting of thirteen issues often accompanied by her ornate illustrations and featuring the contributions of several women writers (O'Connor 2021:151). As Lorraine Janzen Kooistra notes, "in the largely male-dominated world of little magazines in fin-de-siècle Great Britain, *The Green Sheaf* is remarkable for its female leadership, eclectic content, and artisanal design" (Kooistra 2023).

Although she cannot be categorized as a folklorist, Irish poet and suffragist Eva Gore-Booth (1870–1926) was nonetheless greatly inspired by Irish folklore.

---

137. Details about Borthwick's Irish lessons can be found in Augusta Gregory's autobiography, *Seventy Years*, published posthumously: "Miss Borthwick, the Irish scholar who had been giving me lessons in London, is staying here and has classes every afternoon at the gate lodge, about eight girls and thirty to forty young men alternately, some walking as far as three miles to attend" (Gregory 1974:319–20). On Borthwick's life and works, see Rouse (2009).

Together with her sister Constance, later known as Countess Markievicz (1868–1927), destined to become an artist, she grew up in a wealthy aristocratic family in County Sligo, where she became acquainted with local heritage, which she then infused in her poetry and plays. After extensive journeys in North America and Europe, in 1896 she moved to Bordighera, in the Liguria region of Northern Italy, where she was hosted on the premises of Scottish writer George MacDonald (1824–1905); there she met the Anglo-Irish suffragist Esther Roper (1868–1938), with whom she started a fierce social campaign against the oppression of female workers. Drawing from the heroic legends of the Ulster Cycle, in 1916 Gore-Booth published a play entitled *The Death of Fionavar from the Triumph of Maeve*, illustrated by her sister. The play represents Gore-Booth's own reimagining of the ancient myth of Maeve, the Queen of Connacht, whose figure prompted her to reflect on Ireland's past and on her personal reaction to the revolutionary events of the Easter Rising against British domination. In the aftermath of the uprising, her sister Constance, who played an active role in the rebellion, was condemned to a death, a sentence later commuted to life imprisonment. Both the historical event and this personal circumstance further inspired Eva's activism and poetical output. She explained her literary engagement with Maeve's vicissitudes in the preface to the play:

> As I have been accused of taking liberties with an ancient myth, I would say in defence that all myths have many meanings, perhaps as many as the minds of those who know them: and it is in the nature of things that where there is a variation of meaning there is also a variation of form. [...] The meaning I got out of the story of Maeve is a symbol of the world-old struggle in the human mind between the forces of dominance and pity, of peace and war. The time has come, in the history of a human soul, when a newly developed and passionate sense of unity undermines the ancient ideals of savage heroism and world-power. Thus the reign of the old warlike gods is rashly broken into and threatened by the fascination of a new idea. (Gore-Booth 1916:11–12)

Such a reinterpretation of an ancient myth provided an opportunity to the Irish poet to reflect on the senseless tragedy of war and on the inner crisis provoked by the replacement of the old world by a new order. A kindred fascination with female figures from the Irish mythological past can be found in *The Golden Legends of the Gael* (1925), by Maud Joynt (1868–1940), from County Roscommon. *The Golden Legends of the Gael* was praised for "making available for the man in the street, what was hitherto only for the enjoyment of the specialist" (Concannon 1925:679). Joynt was educated at the Royal University of Ireland and became an Irish linguist and language activist, while also supporting women's emancipation through education by participating in the Irish Women's

Franchise League. Her volume of legends gathered tales drawn from the Fenian and the Ulster cycles of Irish mythology as well as tales about Christian saints. Her work greatly contributed to popularizing Irish mythological figures.

One area that clearly attracted women's interest entailed folk-song collections, in which many female figures were active not only in Ireland but also in England, Scotland, and Wales, such as Maria Jane Williams (ca. 1795–1873), Frances Tolmie (1840–1926), Marjory Kennedy-Fraser (1857–1930), Rose Maud Young (1865–1947), Eileen Costello (1870–1962), Kate Lee (1860–1904), and Lucy Broadwood (1858–1929).[138] Bernhard Maier makes a distinction between women who were drawn to the collection of folk songs mainly for their interest in musicology, such as Williams, Tolmie, and Kennedy-Fraser, and women who showed a more evident political engagement with the folk material they gathered, such as Young and Costello (Maier 2020:310). Although it would be unrealistic to claim that all writers and intellectuals who showed an interest in folklore had a political agenda, it cannot be denied that many intellectuals who paid attention to the cultural manifestations of the "folk" often strenuously voiced the concerns of the lower classes and frequently "spoke out in defense of their native languages and in the interests of national and regional movements that sought more autonomy for groups with very particular interests" (Zipes 2013:xxx–xxxi). The life trajectory of the

---

138. Williams was the author of the Welsh collection *Ancient National Airs of Gwent and Morganwg* (1844). A central role in the Welsh Revival was played by Charlotte Guest (1812–1895), who translated the medieval prose tales that formed the *Mabinogion*. On Guest and other important figures such as Marie Trevelyan (1853–1922) and Mary Williams (1883–1977) in the Welsh Revival, see Wood (2000). Tolmie, originally from the Isle of Skye in Scotland, substantially contributed to the *Journal of the Folksong Society* by collecting songs mainly from female informants; Kennedy-Fraser was inspired to collect songs from the Scottish archipelago of the Hebrides after a visit to Eriskay, which she then gathered in three volumes under the title *Songs of the Hebrides* between 1909 and 1921. For further details on these folk-song collections, see Maier (2020:309). Another prominent Scottish folklorist was Lady Evelyn Stewart Murray (1868–1940), born in an aristocratic family in Perthshire, Scotland, where she collected a rich repertoire of folk songs and tales. Lee and Broadwood, who were both professional singers and authors of influential collections, were founding members of the Folk-Song Society in London (Bearman 1999; de Val 2011). It is also worth remembering Sophia Morrison (1859–1917), born in a merchant family in Peel, who attended the Trinity College of Music and became a collector of folklore from the Isle of Man and a Manx-language activist, publishing seminal works in the field, such as *Manx Proverbs and Sayings* (1905), with British antiquarian and naturalist Charles Roeder (1848–1911), *Manx Fairy Tales* (1911), and *A Vocabulary of the Anglo-Manx Dialect* (1924), with Manx scholar and linguist Edmund Goodwin (1844–1925). Morrison was one of the founders of the Manx Language Society in 1899 and acted as its secretary for several decades. On Morrison, see Maddrell (2002).

aforementioned Eileen Costello, née Edith Drury, also known as Eibhlín Uí Choisdealbha, testifies to this conjunction of cultural, linguistic, and political entanglements. Born in London, she became a member of the Gaelic League and eventually a senator of the Seanad Éireann, the upper house of the parliament of the Irish Free State, in 1922. Together with her family, she was based in Tuam, County Galway, where she participated in the Anglo-Irish War of Independence in 1919–21. In 1919 she published a collection of songs in Irish entitled *Amhráin Mhuighe Seola: Traditional Folk-Songs from Galway and Mayo.*

The sisters Rose Maud Young (1865–1947) and Ella Young (1867–1956), originally from County Antrim, reinvigorated the dissemination of Celtic mythology in Ireland and beyond. Rose Maud Young, also known as Róis Ní Ó hÓgain, became an Irish-language activist and a collector of songs in Northern Ireland. Her *Duanaire Gaedhilge,* published in three volumes in 1921, 1924, and 1930, included poems and folk songs, some of which she collected personally (Cooper 2009:118). After attending the Cambridge Training College and becoming a member of the Gaelic League in London, she co-founded the traditional festival Feis na nGleann in Antrim (Lunney 2009). Her collection of folk songs was praised for the "interesting series of notes and a glossary of unusual words as an aid to the student"; such annotations were regarded as "an added value to a book which is sure of an enthusiastic welcome from all lovers of Irish poetry" (Anonymous 1922:335). Her sister Ella Young was a poet and scholar who published several volumes of traditional legends, such as *The Coming of Lugh: A Celtic Wonder-Tale* (1909) and *Celtic Wonder-Tales* (1910), both illustrated by nationalist suffragist, artist, and actress Maud Gonne (1866–1953). Ella Young immigrated to the United States and held a chair as a Celtic mythologist at the University of California, Berkeley, where she continued to disseminate her knowledge on Irish myths and folklore. She described her upbringing and passion for mythology in an autobiographical sketch:

> I have always believed that the countryside where one is born leaves its mark on a person. I was born in the house of my grandfather, at Fenagh, County Antrim, Ireland. [. . .] The Celtic Wonderland awaited me in Dublin. [. . .] I lived there through the most splendid period of the Celtic Renaissance, and through the Rising. I had part in these that were the flowering dream of a people, of a civilization, of a country, and then I came to America [. . .]. If I have written about heroes and dragons and fantastic happenings, it is because these things delight me. I hope they may delight a few others, for it seems to me that the human mind is as full of fantastic imaginings as the sky is of stars; and this is good, for even as Hope remained in Pandora's box so Dream remains when things more prized slip through one's fingers. (Young 1951:305–6)

Fantastic happenings from Irish folklore and mythology also made their way into the realm of children's literature. For example, Irish-Canadian writer Moira O'Neill (1864–1955), nom de plume of Agnes Higginson, originally from Cushendun in County Antrim, wrote a children's book titled *The Elf-Errant* (1895) as well as the collections *Songs of the Glens of Antrim* (1900) and *More Songs of the Glens of Antrim* (1921). Other instances of the connection between Irish folklore and children's literature can be found in *Tales of Fairy Folks, Queens and Heroes* (1907), by poet and writer Alice Furlong (1871–1946), who was also an active member of the women's organization Inghinidhe na hÉireann (Daughters of Ireland), founded by Maud Gonne. Marie Bayne, an Irish children's author of whom very little is known, published anthologies of fairy tales that became very popular, such as *Fairy Stories from Erin's Isle* (1908) and *Tales of Ireland for Irish Children* (n.d.). These old heroic tales were meant to inspire younger generations and nurture the hope that "what a nation has been it may be again," because "[s]ome day [...] the Golden Age will dawn once more in Ireland; and all Irish children who live nobly and well are doing their part to bring that day about" (Bayne n.d.:84). In the same period, Scottish writer Elizabeth W. Grierson (1869–1943), renowned for her collections of Scottish folktales, published *The Children's Book of Celtic Stories* (1908). These works show how "the discourses of heroism, story, and patriotism" merged in Irish children's literature at the turn of the century (Hillel 2019:69).[139]

An important visual testimony of the real-life hardship of Irish people at the turn of the century was provided by Rose Shaw, a woman of British origins who lived in County Tyrone in Northern Ireland. Shaw worked as a governess for the Gledstanes, a family originally from Scotland that settled in Northern Ireland and resided in Fardross House, near the village of Clogher (Walker 1977:56). Her direct interaction with local peasantry is documented by the photographs she took in the countryside, which are pervaded by an atmosphere of "arcadian artfulness" (Maguire 2000:60). She published a selection of these

---

139. The influence of Irish, and more broadly Celtic, folklore and mythology on children's literature is significant and lasting. In the mid-twentieth century, books aimed at a children's readership, both in English and in Irish, such as *Áilleacht agus an Beithidheach* (1946), *Fairy Tales of Ireland* (1967), and *The Verdant Valley and Other Stories* (1970), were published by Sinéad de Valera (1878–1975), wife of Éamon de Valera (1882–1975), third president of Ireland. Besides being a prolific children's writer, during her lifetime she was also a teacher of Irish language as well as a member of the Gaelic League and of Inghinidhe na hÉireann. A selection of Sinéad de Valera's tales has been republished in Heiniger (2023). For a study on the reshaping of Celtic mythology in contemporary children's literature, see Fimi (2017).

pictures in *Carleton's Country* (1930),¹⁴⁰ dedicated to Irish writer and folklorist William Carleton (1794–1869), author of *Traits and Stories of the Irish Peasantry* (1830). Writer and diplomat Shane Leslie (1885–1971), in the foreword to the book, lauded the "sketches with pen and camera" Shaw made in Carleton's honor (Leslie in Shaw 1930:17).

Familiar with the works of Yeats and Synge, Shaw ventured into Clogher Valley to immortalize the peasants immersed in their everyday lives: "Full many a glorious morning have I seen flatter the mountain-tops with sovereign eye, when I have gone forth, camera in hand, to seek out Carleton's haunts and Carleton's people in the beautiful Clogher Valley where he was born and reared" (Shaw 1930:83). In these pages, she also narrated her visit to Station Island in Lough Derg, a pilgrimage destination in which "[w]ell-dressed men and refined-looking women, country lads and old dames with shawls over their heads all go bare-foot the whole time of their stay on the island" (Shaw 1930:80). Her words unveil the habits of country-dwellers such as the gamekeeper Ann Holland, who recounted that fairies would often visit her home in the mountains, and the old Cormic O'Holland, who welcomed her around the hearth of his house to listen to his entertaining stories about Irish highwaymen. Shaw's work is another interesting example of the porous nature of folkloristic endeavors, in that it blends anecdotes, tales, and ethnographic considerations with a piercing photographic gaze, devoted to capturing moments of everyday life through the camera's eye, with intimate attention given to female peasants and laborers (fig. 1.7 and fig. 1.8). An intense empathy and dignified realism can be sensed in these photographs of Irish peasants in the area of Clogher. Shaw's romanticizing style never leads to a sensational portrayal of poverty. These poetic visual memories powerfully project the viewers back in time into the life of rural Ireland in the early twentieth century, a historical period of which Shaw was a remarkable witness.

A similarly fascinating use of photography can be found in the 1906 edition of *Irish Idylls* (1892), by Jane Barlow (1856–1917), one of the first Irish women to be awarded a doctor of letters in Ireland and author of popular collections of short stories, such as *Strangers at Lisconnel: A Second Series of Irish Idylls* (1895) and *A Creel of Irish Stories* (1897).¹⁴¹ In the preface to the 1893 edition of *Irish Idylls* she commented that

---

140. Rose Shaw's original photographs are preserved in the Ulster Folk and Transport Museum, Cultra, County Down, Northern Ireland. Drawing inspiration from these striking images, Taidgh Lynch wrote a poetry collection entitled *Home and Abroad: Poems* (Lynch 2019).

141. Reproductions of photographs from the 1906 edition of Barlow's *Irish Idylls* can be found in Kinmonth (2001), accompanied by an extensive commentary on Irish material culture.

FIGURE 1.7. "Field Group Raking Hay," Rose Shaw Collection, © National Museums NI, Ulster Folk Museum Collection (HOYFM.L918.5). Courtesy of National Museums NI, Ulster Folk Museum Collection.

FIGURE 1.8. "Stocking Corn—Harvest," Rose Shaw Collection, © National Museums NI, Ulster Folk Museum Collection (HOYFM.L918.7). Courtesy of National Museums NI, Ulster Folk Museum Collection.

In Lisconnel, and other such places, we have a saying that *there are plenty of things besides turf to be found in a bog*. This little book attempts to record some of these things, including, I hope, a proportion of that "human nature" which a certain humourist has declared to exist in considerable quantities among our species. I hope, too, that the phases of it pictured here may have some special interest for American readers, to whose shores the wild boglands of Connaught send so many a forlorn voyager "over oceans of say." They will perhaps care to glance at his old home, and learn the reasons why he leaves it, which seem to lie very obviously on the surface, and the reasons, less immediately apparent, why his neighbours bide behind. (Barlow 1893; original emphasis)

Despite these stories being the product of her reimagination, Barlow provided significant information regarding the life of peasants in Ireland as well as a wealth of details about the social and working conditions of women at the time. She did not shy away from depicting the "Irish woman as the beast of burden that she often was, saddled with an enormous wicker creel, barefooted and ready to haul turf from the bog or seaweed from the beach" (Kinmonth 2001:171). However, her literary predilection as a novelist sometimes prevailed over a realistic ethnographic portrayal.

With regard to the scientific approaches to folkloristics, until the first three decades of the early twentieth century, individual amateurs and scholars were entrusted with the collection of folklore in Ireland. A more systematic approach was undertaken with the establishment of the Folklore of Ireland Society (An Cumann Le Béaloideas Éireann) in 1927 and its journal *Béaloideas*, followed by the foundation of the Irish Folklore Institute (Institiúid Bhéaloideas Éireann) in 1930 and the Irish Folklore Commission (Coimisiún Béaloideasa Éireann) in 1935.[142] Seán Ó Súilleabháin (1903–1996), author of *A Handbook of Irish Folklore* (1970), was the archivist of the commission, while James H. Delargy (1899–1980), also known as Séamus Ó Duilearga, was the director (Lysaght 1998b). Due to legislative restrictions forced upon women, especially with regard to their employment, the Irish Folklore Commission did not hire any woman on a full-time basis, a gender constraint that had lasting consequences: "Women were not only not employed as full-time collectors, they were significantly under-represented among the Commission's informants" (Briody 2008:58). This male predominance created difficulties in assessing the

---

This study investigates traditional habits in vogue in Ireland at the time and the ways such customs were repurposed through the eyes of outsiders, lingering in depth on the tradition of representing Irish barefooted women.

142. On the objectives, strategies, and structure of these organizations, see Lysaght (2019).

ways in which women participated in the storytelling performances both as collectors and informants: "male priorities, concerns and involvement" have generally been privileged (Harvey 1989:120), with the result that women's roles remained overwhelmingly undocumented.[143]

The commonplace notion of female storytellers being a rarity in the Irish context was echoed in a well-known passage by James Delargy in his seminal work *The Gaelic Story-Teller*, in which he claimed that women, with few exceptions, were mostly passive tradition-bearers and that their privileged genre of storytelling was *seanchas*, "genealogical lore, music, folk-prayers" (Delargy 1945:7). Conversely, the more complex and episodic narratives termed *scéalaíocht*, hero tales, were associated with men (Harvey 1989:111). In spite of the limitations imposed on women on a daily basis, the practice of storytelling in Ireland did not exclude them because of their gender (Ní Dhuibhne 2002:1214). Angela Bourke highlights how women's contribution to Irish folklore, albeit marginalized, has been substantial: "Women turn up as artists of memory and performance in Irish oral traditions, and as the subject of innumerable stories, songs, proverbs, jokes, riddles and sayings" (Bourke 2002a:1195), despite their presence being underrepresented in folklore collections and scholarly works.[144]

Notwithstanding this underrepresentation, before concluding this excursus on women and folklore in Ireland, it is imperative to recall one of the foremost female informants of the Irish Folklore Commission, the legendary *seanchaí* (storyteller) Peig Sayers (1873–1958) from Dún Chaoin, County Kerry, who lived for four decades on the Great Blasket Island (fig. 1.9). Her life, alongside the lives of other female informants, is a testament to "women narrators taking responsibility for maintaining communal as well as individual memory" (Bourke and Lysaght 2002:1198).

Destined to become an Irish icon, Sayers attracted the interest of various folklorists, including Celtic scholar Kenneth Jackson (1909–1991).[145] She dictated to her son Micheál Ó Gaoithín her well-known autobiography, which

---

143. On issues revolving around the relationship between collectors and informants, with a focus on the representations of women in Seán Ó hEochaidh's diaries, a collector of the Irish Folklore Commission, see Ó Laoire (2017).

144. In a study on the folk memories of the Connacht insurrection of 1798, which saw a French expeditionary force landing in County Mayo in an attempt to support the rebellion of the United Irishmen against the British rule, Guy Beiner underlines that women's voices in the reconstruction of this historical event were less documented, although both men and women were interviewed by folklore collectors. This underrepresentation finds its reasons both in the gender dynamics at work and in the "dominant male trends in the Irish folklore-collecting project" (Beiner 2004:213). On the "year of the French," see also Beiner (2007).

145. On Jackson and Sayers, see Almqvist (2010; 2011).

FIGURE 1.9. Peig Sayers (1873–1958). Photograph by Caoimhín Ó Danachair, National Folklore Collection, University College Dublin (M001.18.00299). Courtesy of the National Folklore Collection, University College Dublin, Ireland.

made its first appearance in 1936 under the title *Peig: A Scéal Féin*, followed by *Machtnamh Sheana-Mhná* in 1939.[146] *Peig: A Scéal Féin* offers not only a detailed description of her life's vicissitudes but also a "reflective account of the universal challenges faced by a woman from the rural poor" in the west of Ireland (de Brún 2024:2). Despite having faced a hostile reception due to its institutionalization as a repertoire of "authentic" Irishness and its inclusion in the Irish secondary school curriculum, her autobiographical memoir provides a unique "perspective of an aged woman who draws her authority from her twin experiences of the ways of the world and the tradition to which she belongs" (Lucchitti 2010:79). Her storytelling skills and extraordinary memory were greatly appreciated. Furthermore, it has been noted that she retained a woman-centered perspective in her stories and frequently implemented the

---

146. For a translation of these works into English, see *Peig: The Autobiography of Peig Sayers of the Great Blasket Island* (1974), translated by Bryan MacMahon, and *An Old Woman's Reflections* (1962), translated by Séamus Ennis. For a reassessment of Sayers's autobiographical writings through a feminist lens, see Coughlan (2007).

practice of "coding," through which covert messages are inserted in women's expressions so as to convey their subordination and oppression without open exposure (Radner and Lanser 1987:415–16). Although she inherited her repertoire mainly from her father, Sayers used to retell the narratives with "attention on the hard lot of women" (Radner 2009:96).

The mapping of female figures who took part in different ways in the preservation of Italian and Irish folklore has demonstrated that, when reflecting on women's roles in the collection and dissemination of popular narratives, it is necessary to consider their contributions from multiple perspectives. On the one hand, women upheld an important function as compilers of folklore, who intervened in the texts with editorial, linguistic, and stylistic choices, and as firsthand collectors who tirelessly went from village to village to observe and transcribe the popular traditions they were seeking. Women also acted as informants and tradition-bearers who entrusted literate men and women to transcribe their folklore. Finally, women featured as protagonists of the folkloric texts themselves, and it is therefore worth exploring how they are portrayed as subject matter within the collections. By paying attention to the work of female folklorists, a more nuanced understanding can be gained of these narratives and the way they subtly reflect—and at times even challenge—sociocultural constraints. The following chapters consequently move to an investigation of the folkloric writings by Laura Gonzenbach, Grazia Deledda, Jane Wilde, and Augusta Gregory with these manifold perspectives in mind.

2

Identity Matters

FRAMING THE POSITIONALITIES OF FOUR WOMEN FOLKLORISTS

If [...] the spatial is thought of in the context of space–time and as formed out of social interrelations at all scales, then one view of a place is as a particular articulation of those relations, a particular moment in those networks of social relations and understandings.

—DOREEN MASSEY, *SPACE, PLACE, AND GENDER* (1994:5)

IF NINETEENTH-CENTURY folkloric writings ought to be investigated as complex cultural products deriving from specific places within a wider patriotic project—and thus as intricately tied to conceptions of nationhood, identity, and language—it is imperative to analyze them in light of the sociocultural contexts that inspired and influenced their collectors and compilers. The concept of place is a deeply relational category that cannot be separated from time and is profoundly interlaced with gender constructions (Massey 1994). It is therefore necessary to recall the particular circumstances related to the collectors' upbringing, education, and social relations so as to frame the "relationship between class *habitus* and individual *habitus*" (Bourdieu 1990:60). In light of this premise, this chapter focuses on four case studies by exploring the lives and works of women folklorists who can be considered, in their own distinct ways, forerunners: Laura Gonzenbach in Sicily, Grazia Deledda in Sardinia, and Jane Wilde and Augusta Gregory in Ireland. By investigating these figures, the identity politics at work in their folkloric writings are brought to the fore with attention to issues of gender, class, ethnicity, and language. The emphasis on their biographies and educational backgrounds sheds light on their diverse attitudes toward nineteenth-century folkloristics, on their intentions and motivations as scholars of insular traditions, and on their contributions and legacies in this field.

Laura Gonzenbach, Grazia Deledda, Jane Wilde, and Augusta Gregory acted as intermediaries across linguistic, cultural, and class borders, transcribing, translating, and/or adapting oral traditions that were originally told in different languages. By highlighting their roles as mediators, it is possible to retrace the journey of these traditional narratives in the cultural circuit of the long nineteenth century. With regard to fairy tales, although the same considerations can also be applied to other folkloric genres, Gillian Lathey observes that

> When fairy tales travel across linguistic frontiers an act of translation takes place at some stage on their journey. The transposition of an oral or written text from one language to another [...] adds an inter-lingual and intercultural dimension to an already densely layered narrative. (Lathey 2019:92)

Issues revolving around vernacular and national languages, their knowledge or lack thereof, and the passage from one to the other and vice versa are thus central to a reevaluation of these folklorists' mediating roles. The collection of folklore involved an act of classification intending to explore and chart the narratives and beliefs of lower-class people throughout Europe. Thus, the perspective of the collectors and compilers of these anthologies, their situatedness within or outside the space inhabited by the local communities they encapsulated in their writings, heavily influenced the way such folkloric materials were transcribed, edited, and arranged. It is also worth noting that, while in the case of Deledda and Gregory there is plenty of extratextual data to rely on, a critical assessment of Gonzenbach's and Wilde's ventures in folklore studies needs to rely on scanter data and on the more conspicuous textual traces left by Gonzenbach's sister and by Wilde's husband. Furthermore, a reappraisal of these figures and their folkloric writings must be accompanied by a reflection on the local, regional, national, and transnational dynamics that permeated the discipline of folklore studies since its inception. Defining a national level between the local, the regional, and the transnational dimensions, as well as delineating the relationship between islands and mainlands, is at times problematic because it entails accounting for the often contradictory or elusive ways these scholars located themselves and their works in relation to the nation-building process in their respective countries. Furthermore, these geopolitical categories were not set in stone in the shifting panorama of the long nineteenth century and were conjured up for different purposes in folklore anthologies.

An examination of the positionalities of Gonzenbach, Deledda, Wilde, and Gregory from the point of view of their folkloric writings shows how their roles as collectors and/or compilers of popular traditions can be interpreted as an act of multiple mediations, not only between the communities they represented in their works and the scholarly world of folklore studies, but also between themselves and the imagined target audience they implicitly addressed in their folkloric writings. In other words, an interpretation of these different levels of mediation allows us to move away from what folklorist Richard Bauman defines as the "elementary, dyadic speaker-hearer or sender-receiver models" (Bauman 2004:129) that usually dominate the discourse surrounding ethnographic performances. In this way, recognition of the manifold functional purposes that lie beneath a collector's recasting of oral sources becomes possible. This view underscores the intertextuality of folklore collections and the complex interplay between oral sources and written texts, tailored to specific ends and a well-defined audience. These considerations, however, need to be rooted in the specific geocultural contexts that contributed to the creation of these texts.

Laura Gonzenbach: A Pioneering Collector in Sicily

From the nineteenth century to the early twentieth century, European countries were traversed by diverse cultural movements: Romanticism and positivism, the reevaluation of popular culture and the advent of scientific social studies, the emergence of national identities and the establishment of nationwide educational systems, the birth of class consciousness, and the rise of women's emancipation. In late nineteenth-century Italy, the literary tradition of *verismo*, following the path traced by French naturalism, drew attention to the lives and struggles of marginalized lower classes and became particularly prolific in the Mezzogiorno, with central exponents such as Giovanni Verga (1840–1922), Federico De Roberto (1861–1927), and Luigi Capuana (1839–1915) in Sicily. The impulses that animated these literary trends are also evident in the folklore collections produced in southern Italian regions.[1] At a glance, it may seem surprising that several of the most avant-garde figures in the field of nineteenth-century folkloristics came from some of the areas that had witnessed lower rates of industrial and educational progress in Italy. However, in southern regions such as Sicily, certain enclaves pervaded by a cosmopolitan and cross-cultural spirit allowed these scholars and their studies to germinate. This was undoubtedly the case in mid-nineteenth-century Messina, Laura Gonzenbach's place of birth. From the beginning of the nineteenth century, the Peloritan city, with its strategic port, attracted foreigners from various

---

1. As remarked by Stefano Cavazza, "[o]n the literary plane the enthusiasm for folklore and regional tradition was stoked by realist literature (verismo) and a fashion for composing in dialect" (Cavazza 2012:77).

European countries who became active in the industrial and commercial sectors: their influence went well beyond these spheres, acting as well "sulle mode, i costumi, le attività ricreative, i gusti culturali" of the local inhabitants (Chiara and Principato 2007:11).[2]

Gonzenbach distinguished herself as the first female collector of folkloric narratives in Sicily in the late 1860s, preceding eminent Sicilian men of letters in the transcription of fairy tales from the Ionian coast of the island. Her social habitus and her ethnicity as a woman of Swiss-German origins born and raised in Messina endowed her with valuable skills for the collection of popular tales. These narratives represent unique records of the stories recounted orally by members of local communities in nineteenth-century Sicilian villages, many of whom were women whose imaginative narratives would have otherwise been lost. Yet her anthology *Sicilianische Märchen aus dem Volksmund gesammelt* (1870), the title of which reiterated the leitmotif of the "mouth of the people," was destined to fall into oblivion for nearly a century. Indeed, in the first half of the twentieth century, Gonzenbach's name was almost entirely forgotten outside of the niche of folklore studies. For several linguistic, cultural, and editorial factors that will be outlined in this section, it was only toward the second half of the twentieth century that scholars started devoting attention to Gonzenbach's collection.

The writings that could have provided a clearer picture of her work were lost in the tragic earthquake that struck the Strait of Messina in 1908: "Poco si sapeva di lei: il terremoto di Messina del 1908 ne aveva cancellato la memoria, disperse i testi siciliani delle fiabe da lei raccolte" (Consolo 2019:viii).[3] However, thanks to a foundational scholarly work by Luisa Rubini, the genesis of Gonzenbach's fairy-tale collection has been accurately uncovered. Gonzenbach's life is chiefly shrouded in mystery: in the words of Rudolph Schenda, "questa raccoglitrice di fiabe, silenziosa e modesta com'era stata e come lo sono spesso i grandi folkloristi, lasciò tracce troppo labili della sua esistenza" (Schenda 1986:265).[4] Her fairy-tale anthology is only a "piccola pietra" (pebble) in the vast sea of publications by nineteenth-century Italian folklorists (Schenda 1986:266). Still, it is a pebble worth examining further for its unusual features. Gonzenbach acquired considerable cultural knowledge through the informal education she received at home. She grew up in the Protestant

---

2. "on trends, customs, recreational activities, cultural tastes."

3. "Little was known about her: the earthquake of Messina in 1908 had erased the memory of her, dispersed the Sicilian texts of the fairy tales she had collected."

4. "this fairy-tale collector, silent and modest as she was and as the great folklorists often are, left too faint traces of her existence."

Swiss-German community of Messina under the guidance of her sister Magdalena. An enlightened woman, Magdalena was assiduously involved in her contemporary social context as a supporter of women's education and emancipation. In fact, in 1874 she founded the first female school in Messina, the Istituto Femminile Gonzenbach, later destroyed by the aforementioned earthquake in 1908.

Gonzenbach was born into a large family of eight siblings on December 26, 1842. Peter Viktor Gonzenbach (1808–1885), her father, was a textile merchant originally from St. Gallen and Swiss consul in Messina. Her mother, Julie Aders (1806–1847), came from a bourgeois German family and died when Laura Gonzenbach was only five, leaving her in the care of her sister Magdalena (1831–1906).[5] Both were raised in a highly stimulating environment imbued with progressive values. The open-mindedness that derived from a multicultural background, the knowledge of several languages, and the cultural relations established at an international level by their family members engendered in the Gonzenbach sisters an uncommon curiosity and intellectual vivacity, accompanied by a consciousness of their own value as women. As a result, they were no longer committed exclusively to the domestic roles usually destined to their gender.[6] The political and commercial relationships cultivated by their father undoubtedly contributed to this cultural openness: "Il 'salotto' dei consoli—quello di Peter Viktor era certamente gestito da Magdalena—[...] permetteva alle donne—sottoposte al controllo sociale e con possibilità di movimento assai più limitate—di approfittare, in modo meno mediato, di tali scambi" (Rubini 1998:95).[7] However, their cultural knowledge did not remain confined to their family circles: on the contrary, it spurred them to share their emancipatory ideals.

While direct testimonies of Laura Gonzenbach's involvement in these protofeminist practices are regrettably absent, her sister Magdalena left a more

---

5. For an accurate reconstruction of Gonzenbach's genealogy, see Rubini (1998:295) and Zipes (2006a:xiii).

6. A portrait of Magdalena Gonzenbach and the copy of a photograph likely of Laura Gonzenbach can be found in the appendix to the second edition of the Italian translation of *Fiabe siciliane*, by Luisa Rubini (2019 [1870]:549–52). Magdalena Gonzenbach's portrait was part of the bequest made by the Gonzenbach-Tobler branch of the family to the Staatsarchiv of St. Gallen in Switzerland (StASG, Wy 137), and it was donated to this archive by Gonzenbach's family branch from Thurgau. The latter photograph is a copy owned by the family's heir Hans Gonzenbach (Rubini in Gonzenbach 2019 [1870]:551).

7. "The 'salon' of the consuls—that of Peter Viktor was certainly managed by Magdalena—[...] allowed women—subjected to social control and with much more limited possibilities of movement—to take advantage of such exchanges in a less mediated way."

concrete mark in Italian women's history as an active promoter of female emancipation, which spread across Italy after the Risorgimento. Similar to other female intellectuals of the time, she collaborated not only with the *Rivista Europea*, headed by Angelo De Gubernatis, but also with the periodical *La donna*, translating the works of John Stuart Mill (1806–1873) and the letters on women by Fanny Lewald (1811–1889).[8] As a pedagogue inspired by Fröbelian principles, she participated in international debates concerning new educational methods and the roles of women in bourgeois society (Caminiti 2015). Mill's essay *The Subjection of Women* (1869) was published while Gonzenbach was working on the publication of her fairy tales, and her sister Magdalena wrote an obituary for the British philosopher in *La donna* in 1873. On April 22, 1870, the year of the publication of *Sicilianische Märchen*, Magdalena Gonzenbach wrote a letter to De Gubernatis in which she explicitly addressed the "questione interessante dell'emancipazione della donna":[9]

> È una questione che negli Stati Uniti, in Inghilterra, in Germania ha preso posto tra le questioni più interessanti del nostro tempo, e di giorno in giorno va prendendo un sicuro e rapido sviluppo. Ma se in quei paesi vi sono molti pregiudizi da combattere, mi sembra che in Italia il pregiudizio sia ancora così forte, così radicato, che alla mente dei più non si è nemmeno affacciata la possibilità di una posizione diversa della donna. [. . .] Senza essere Italiana, io amo l'Italia, mia patria adottiva, con tutto il cuore, e mi reputerei felice se potessi concorrere alla sollevazione della donna in Italia all'indipendenza di cui gode altrove.[10]

---

8. Fanny Lewald was a German advocate for women's rights, author of *Für und wider die Frauen. Vierzehn Briefe* (1870), *Lettere sulle donne di Fanny Lewald*, translated into Italian by Magdalena Gonzenbach, *Rivista Europea*, 1870–72 (1870, year I, vol. III, pp. 95–100, 321–30, 551–56; 1870, year I, vol. IV, pp. 124–27, 330–34, 505–7; 1871, year II, vol. II, pp. 118–24; 1871, year II, vol. III, pp. 226–30; 1871 year II, vol. IV, 88–99; 1872, year III, vol. II, pp. 49–54, 299–312, 476–84). These translations were then reprinted in *La donna*, a pivotal journal for the promotion of women's rights in nineteenth-century Italy, established by Gualberta Alaide Beccari (1842–1906) in Padua. On Fanny Lewald in Italy, see Secci (1988).

9. "interesting question of women's emancipation."

10. "In the United States, England, and Germany, [women's emancipation] takes its place among the most interesting questions of our time, and it is developing steadily and rapidly day by day. But if in those countries there are many prejudices to be fought, it seems to me that in Italy the prejudice is still so strong, so deeply rooted, that the possibility of a different position for women has not even occurred to the minds of most people. [. . .] Without being Italian, I love Italy, my adopted homeland, with all my heart, and I would consider myself happy if I could contribute to the elevation of women in Italy to reach the independence they enjoy

It is evident that the two intellectually gifted sisters, despite their foreign origins, had perfectly integrated into the social community of Messina. Their multilingualism facilitated their interaction with different cultural circles. A glimpse into the relationship between Magdalena and Laura Gonzenbach emerges in another letter that the former wrote to De Gubernatis over twenty years later, on July 30, 1893, in response to his request to collect Sicilian folktales for the soon-to-be established Società Nazionale per le Tradizioni Popolari Italiane. By that time, Laura Gonzenbach had already died. Magdalena Gonzenbach earnestly wrote to De Gubernatis that her own contribution to the field of folklore consisted solely in helping her sister:

> Veramente io non ho fatto mai nulla per il folk-lore, se non ché copiare i racconti scritti dalla povera mia sorella. Ciò non di meno accetto con piacere di far parte della Società in questione, almeno sarà ricordato il nome di chi fra le prime raccolse i Mährchen [sic] siciliani. Difficilmente potrò cooperare allo scopo della Società; ma ho presso di me due nipotine culte e intelligenti, appunto le figlie della buona Laura mia sorella, e del colonnello La Racine. Queste in ragione della loro gioventù e dell'educazione ricevuta (in questo momento fanno l'esame di magistero) stanno in relazione più intima coll'anima delle popolane e dei bambini; cercherò di interessarle nella questione, e farò da loro raccogliere quelle notizie di superstizioni e credenze popolari, versi, leggende, ecc. che potranno raccogliere.[11]

In this letter, Magdalena Gonzenbach, while recognizing the limitations of her engagement with folklore, gladly agreed to join the Società Nazionale per le Tradizioni Popolari Italiane, so that her sister's name could be remembered. The reference to Laura Gonzenbach's daughters as possible perpetuators of their mother's work as a collector is worthy of notice, even though there is

---

elsewhere." Magdalena Gonzenbach, *Lettere ad Angelo De Gubernatis*, April 22, 1870, cass. 65 n. 64, letter n. 1:1,3, Fondo "Angelo De Gubernatis," BNCF.

11. "In truth, I have never done anything for folklore, except copying the stories written by my poor sister. Nevertheless, I gladly accept being part of the Society in question; at least the name of the one who was among the first to collect the Sicilian Märchen will be remembered. I will barely be able to contribute to the purpose of the Society, but I have with me two cultured and intelligent nieces, indeed the daughters of my good sister Laura, and of Colonel La Racine. Because of their youth and the education they have received (right now they are taking the magisterium exam), they enjoy a closer relationship with the souls of female commoners and children; I will try to arouse their interest in the matter, and I will have them gather those facts about superstitions and popular beliefs, verses, legends, etc. that they will be able to collect." Magdalena Gonzenbach, *Lettere ad Angelo De Gubernatis*, July 30, 1893, cass. 65 n. 64, letter n. 11:1–2, Fondo "Angelo De Gubernatis," BNCF.

no evidence that the suggestion had concrete consequences since they seem not to have left any traces in this field. Nonetheless, this remark gives a sense of intergenerational continuity to folkloric research.

The Gonzenbach sisters, albeit in distinct fields, were able to situate themselves in a broader historical trajectory that went in the same direction, a trajectory that advocated for greater freedom for women to be accomplished through education, and for their more visible presence in the cultural sphere. Hence, they deserve credit for having been able to grasp the spirit of their times in the form of active engagement in the fields of female education and folklore studies. In other words, Laura Gonzenbach's pioneering work as a folklorist, which anticipated the major late nineteenth-century collections in Italy, paralleled her sister's activism in the pedagogical sector, on the basis of their shared interest in women's issues.

It comes as no surprise, then, that Laura Gonzenbach dedicated her fairy-tale collection to a woman, Johanna Jaeger, daughter-in-law of the Prussian consul Wilhelm Jaeger, who was also the owner of a prominent textile factory in Messina,[12] and devoted her attention to Sicilian women both as storytellers and as protagonists of the tales, letting their courage and resilience speak. The gender dimension of Gonzenbach's work was underscored in a review published by writer and poet Grazia Pierantoni Mancini (1841–1915) in a section of *Rivista Europea* titled "Rivista dell'istruzione femminile":

> Abbiamo sotto gli occhi un libro interessantissimo compilato da una donna e dedicato ad una donna. [...] Una donna ha dato ora, prima, l'esempio ai letterati siciliani della ricchezza di materiali che offre il loro suolo alla leggendologia comparativa; ne piglino essi animo a seguirla con la stessa alacrità e la stessa modestia. (Pierantoni Mancini 1870:572–73)[13]

The label "fairy-tale *verismo*" has been adopted to describe the flavor of these tales (Noyes 2005:341; original emphasis), a definition reminiscent of what Italo Calvino described as the "avvio 'realistico'"[14] of southern Italian fairy tales, which frequently showcase the deeds of peasant protagonists who face and overcome misery, poverty, and hunger (Calvino 2015 [1956]:xlviii).

---

12. On the relationship between the Jaeger and the Gonzenbach families, see Rubini (1998:23). On the contribution of foreign families, including Jaeger's, to the economic, social, and cultural life of the city, see Chiara and Principato (2007).

13. "We have before us a very interesting book compiled by a woman and dedicated to a woman. [...] A woman has been the first to set the example for Sicilian writers of the wealth of materials that their soil offers to the comparative study of legends; they should take it upon themselves to follow her with the same alacrity and the same modesty."

14. "the 'realistic' foundation" (Calvino, trans. Catherine Hill, 1980:xxxii).

Wonder Tales on the Slopes of the Volcano: Sicilianische Märchen

This hybrid corpus of tales of magic, religious tales, tall tales, and animal tales consists of ninety-four narratives in total, of which forty-five can be classified as a single tale type according to the Aarne–Thompson–Uther Index (ATU Index), a well-known tool that allows scholars to categorize, compare, and study folktales,[15] while forty-nine tales present a complex entanglement of different types and motifs (Rubini 1998:232). Gonzenbach was approximately twenty-six when she was commissioned to collect a few fairy tales by German historian Otto Hartwig (1830–1903), intended to be included in *Aus Sizilien: Kultur- und Geschichtsbilder*, a book he was writing on the history of Sicily, published in 1867–69. Hartwig, after studying theology and working as a librarian in Marburg, moved to Sicily for five years in 1860 and became a preacher for the Swiss-German Evangelists' community in Messina (Rubini 1998:57–87).

The spark generated by Hartwig's request triggered in Gonzenbach a desire to document thoroughly local narratives, interacting with storytellers who passed their oral repertoire on to her. Rather than handing him just a couple of tales, as he had requested, Gonzenbach collected ninety-two tales in Sicilian, which she transcribed and translated into German, followed by two tales published in the original local dialect by Don Salvatore Morganti, an "as-yet-unidentified Sicilian collaborator" (Noyes 2005:332).[16] The tales were eventually printed in two volumes edited by Hartwig and accompanied by scholarly notes from Reinhold Köhler (1830–1892), a renowned literary scholar, librarian, and folklorist who corresponded with eminent scholars across Europe (Rubini 1998:270–77). The German edition by Hartwig remained the only one published in the nineteenth century.

In his article on female contributions to folklore studies, Paul Sébillot defined this anthology as an "excellent recueil" (Sébillot 1892:456).[17] Evelyn

---

15. The ATU Index is based on a system of classification first created by Finnish folklorist Antti Aarne (1867–1925) in 1910, updated twice by American folklorist Stith Thompson (1885–1976) in 1928 and 1961, and then revised more recently by German folklorist Hans-Jörg Uther in 2004. See Aarne and Thompson (1961) and Uther (2004). For a critique of the gender biases in Aarne and Thompson's classification system, see Lundell (1986). For a discussion of gender-related issues in the classification of folk and fairy tales, see also Jorgensen (2014).

16. As reported by Licurgo Cappelletti (1842–1921) in his review of Gonzenbach's collection, the last two tales in Sicilian dialect—"Lu cuntu di li du' cumpari" and "Lu cuntu di li tri soru"—were written by "sig. Salvadore [sic] Morganti da Messina" (Cappelletti 1870:150). The reviewer's name in *Rivista Europea* was erroneously spelled as "Capelletti."

17. "excellent collection."

Martinengo-Cesaresco, a folklorist of British origin mentioned in chapter 1, similarly praised *Sicilianische Märchen* in her *Essays in the Study of Folksongs* (1886). When describing Sicilian popular narratives, Martinengo-Cesaresco referred to one of the tales collected by Gonzenbach and reported that

> Laura Gonzenbach was the daughter of the Swiss Consul at Messina, where she was born. At an early age she developed uncommon gifts, and she was hardly twenty when she made her collection of Sicilian stories, almost exclusively gathered from a young servant-girl who did not know how to write or read. [. . .] A relation of hers, from whom I have these particulars, was much surprised to hear that the *Sicilianische Märchen* is widely known as one of the best works of its class. It is somewhat singular that the preservation of Italian folk-tales should have been so substantially aided by two ladies not of Italian origin: Fräulein Gonzenbach and Miss R. H. Busk, author of "The Folk-lore of Rome." (Martinengo-Cesaresco 1886:287)

This praise by Martinengo-Cesaresco is not entirely precise in its historical reconstruction as Gonzenbach was already in her midtwenties when she embarked on the project of collecting oral tales. Despite its inaccuracies, this recognition of Gonzenbach's work as a folklorist is remarkable in that it shows how women who were writing folklore in the second half of the nineteenth century participated in a web of interconnected relationships and were aware of one another's efforts. In this excerpt, Martinengo-Cesaresco referred both to Laura Gonzenbach and Rachel Busk, another British folklorist active in Italy whose work was previously detailed.

The review of Gonzenbach's collection published in *Rivista Sicula di Scienze, Letteratura ed Arti* subtly reveals the mixed feelings surrounding the reception of *Sicilianische Märchen* in Sicily. Although the reviewer paid homage to the "cultissima signora Laura Gonzenbach" (Anonymous 1870:594),[18] emphasis was placed only on the two tales by Salvatore Morganti published in Sicilian dialect at the end of *Sicilianische Märchen*. With regard to Morganti's tales, the reviewer commented that

> la lingua è proprio quella che usa il popolo; i modi e le frasi abbondano di quelle grazie che sono peculiari al siciliano dialetto. Piacevole oltre modo ne riesce quindi la lettura a noi che dalle materne labbra quella lingua apprendemmo. (Anonymous 1870:596)[19]

---

18. "extremely cultured Laura Gonzenbach."

19. "the language is precisely the one used by the people; the modes and phrases abound with the peculiar graces of Sicilian dialect. Therefore the reading is pleasant beyond measure to us who learned that language from motherly lips."

Significantly, the reviewer concluded this remark by asking Morganti, and not Gonzenbach, to collect and narrate even more stories in Sicilian. A similar attitude can be found in another review of Gonzenbach's fairy tales published in 1870 in *Rivista di Scienze e Lettere* by philologist and translator Emilio Teza (1831–1912), who also carried out an Italian translation of two tales, n. 2 "Maria, la cattiva matrigna e i sette ladroni" and n. 56 "Il conte e la sorella," as well as a summary of n. 66 "Il gallo che voleva diventare papa."[20] Teza commented that

> Novelle speranze ci ravviva con le sue promesse la valorosa traduttrice: e forse dopo a' tedeschi si verrà anche a noi: così che o in italiano, o in siciliano, che sarebbe meglio, qualcuno ci narri codeste novelline che sono nel libro del Hartwig e altre ne aggiunga: così che del popolo ci suoni, non l'eco soltanto, la voce. (Teza 1870:212–13)[21]

Teza took care of highlighting the inaccuracies of some of the Sicilian expressions reported in the anthology and specified in a footnote that "[g]ioverebbe che un siciliano rivedesse le parole scritte nel dialetto dell'isola e dove è a correggere correggesse" (Teza 1870:221).[22] In the review by Licurgo Cappelletti published in *Rivista Europea* in 1870, attention is given to Hartwig's own words in his preface to the collection, reported in the Italian translation. Hartwig underscored the solicitude that distinguished Gonzenbach's response to his initiative:

> [M]i rivolsi alla mia egregia amica signora Laura Gonzembach [*sic*] nata in Messina, che conosce i dialetti di quel paese, e da me avuta per eccellente narratrice. E la pregai di trascrivermi alcuni racconti, che io avrei curato di farli stampare come appendice ai due volumi del mio libro. Colla maggiore cortesia e sollecitudine accolse ella la mia preghiera, ed io ricevetti dopo non lungo tempo un manoscritto di dieci racconti. Scrivevami nello stesso tempo la raccoglitrice come scoverte dopo le prime difficoltà alcune buone siciliane contatrici, avesse conosciuto tal numero di racconti da potermene offrire in gran copia. (Hartwig in Cappelletti 1870:150)[23]

---

20. "Maria, the Evil Stepmother, and the Seven Robbers," "The Count and His Sister," "The Rooster Who Wanted to Become Pope" (Gonzenbach, trans. Jack Zipes, 2006).

21. "The valiant translator revives our new hopes with her promises: and perhaps it will be our turn after the Germans, so that someone will narrate to us the *novelline* that can be found in Hartwig's book and add other ones either in Italian or in Sicilian, which would be better, in such a way that we could hear not only the echo but also the voice of the people."

22. "it would be beneficial if a Sicilian could revise the words written in the dialect of the island and amend what needs to be amended."

23. "I turned to my illustrious friend Mrs. Laura Gonzenbach born in Messina, who knows the dialects of that country, and whom I considered to be an excellent storyteller. And I begged

In the preface to the collection, Hartwig also reported a few lines Gonzenbach had once written to him, in which her passion and rigor as a collector materialize. This is the only testimony left of Laura Gonzenbach's words—mediated in this passage by an anonymous translation from German into Italian—which simultaneously highlights the genuineness of her efforts and the hurdles of her task:

> Desidererei ora dirle pure di aver fatto tutto il mio meglio per narrare i racconti così fedelmente come li ebbi udito, ma io non ho potuto ridare ad essi tutto quell'incanto che trovasi nella maniera delle siciliane narratrici. Molte di esse raccontano con infinita vivacità, facendo per tutta la narrazione i gesti più espressivi colle mani, e delle volte alzandosi e girando perfino nella stanza, se occorra. Non usano mai: *egli disse*, dacché cambiando la persona, atteggiano in modo diverso la voce. Ma ciò non toglie che usino con eccesso la parola *dici*, p. e. *o figghiu dici, comu va dici, pri sti parti dici, sulu sulu dici*. (Hartwig 1870:598; original emphasis)[24]

The importance placed on the need to report the tales as faithfully as she heard them recalls the ideal of authenticity that folklorists aimed to achieve in their transcriptions of oral sources.[25] Authenticity in transcription represented more an aspiration than an actual achievement, although the guiding principle of word-for-word transcription as opposed to finding and reinterpreting the traditional folk soul would eventually prevail as folklore studies became a scientific discipline. Gonzenbach was aware of the difficulties in reaching this level of scientific accuracy and acknowledged the "scarto sostanziale tra

---

her to write some stories down, which I would have taken care of printing as an appendix to the two volumes of my book. She accepted my request with the greatest courtesy and solicitude, and after a short time I received a manuscript of ten tales. At the same time, the collector wrote me that, after the initial difficulties, she had encountered some good Sicilian storytellers and had discovered so many stories that she could provide me with a large quantity."

24. Anonymous translation into Italian of Otto Hartwig's preface to *Sicilianische Märchen*, in *Rivista Sicula di Scienze, Letteratura ed Arti* (1870), 2, 3, 594–601 (598): "Now I would also like to tell you that I did my best to tell the stories as faithfully as I had heard them, but I have not been able to give them back all the charm that can be found in the manners of Sicilian storytellers. Many of them tell [the stories] with infinite vivacity, making the most expressive gestures with their hands throughout the narration, sometimes standing up and even going around the room, if necessary. They never use: *egli disse (he said)*, since, when changing the character, they inflect their voice in a different way. But this does not mean that they do not excessively use the word *dici*, for instance, *o figghiu dici, comu va dici, pri sti parti dici, sulu sulu dici*."

25. On the question of authenticity in folkloristics, see Abrahams (1993) and Bendix (1997).

medium orale e scritto" (Rubini 2006:77; original emphasis),[26] the inevitable loss that takes place when the orality of a storytelling performance is transposed into a written text. This gulf inexorably entails the disappearance of all those markers that distinguish oral narration, such as gesticulation, body posture, timbre, intonation, stress, pauses, and silences. From a linguistic point of view, Gonzenbach's care in recording Sicilian dialectal expressions when describing the vivacity of local storytellers is also remarkable. Traces of the original dialect such as the ones reported above survived in her German translation in the form of specific expressions, formulas, and proverbs that Gonzenbach decided to maintain in Sicilian. From these scattered fragments that she took care to report in her annotations, it becomes clear that Gonzenbach was a proficient dialectophone. Bearing in mind that her informants came from Messina and from villages on the southeastern slopes of Mount Etna in the areas of Catania and Acireale, she showed considerable skills in the transcription of the local expressions.[27]

It is worth examining the way Gonzenbach's work was welcomed at the time of its publication by Italian scholars in their private epistolary exchanges. As remarked by Schenda, Italian men of letters showed keen attention, if not apprehension, toward Gonzenbach's work, to the point that it could be claimed that her collection created "un effetto di choc" (Schenda 1986:271).[28] De Gubernatis, in a letter sent to Pitrè on September 13, 1870, recommended that he focus on the geographic area of Palermo since the Ionian side of Sicily had already been covered by Gonzenbach:

> La Gonzenbach ci diede le messinesi e catanesi, e dicesi ne prepari un altro centinaio e più. Avremo così illustrata la provincia di Catania e di Messina. Tu dovresti darci ora le Novelline del contado di Palermo, e credo che non ti sarà difficile metterne insieme un intiero volume.[29]

---

26. "substantial gap between the oral and written *medium*."

27. It is likely that Gonzenbach could understand and transcribe different Sicilian dialects. Besides the usage of terms such as the verb *annari* (to go), which denotes the Messinese origins of some of the tales, instead of the verb *jiri*, which is widespread elsewhere in Sicily, it is possible that she consciously opted for a neutral transcription of the dialects, with a tendency to avoid more locally connotated expressions. However, given the scant presence of complex linguistic expressions in dialect in the text, it is difficult to determine with certainty the Messinese or Catanese provenance of the tales. I am grateful to Silvio Cruschina for his scholarly insights on Sicilian dialects.

28. "a shock effect."

29. "Gonzenbach gave us [the *novelline*] from Messina and Catania, and it is said that another hundred or more are being prepared. Thus, the province of Catania and Messina will be illustrated. You should now give us the *Novelline* of the countryside around Palermo, and I think it

De Gubernatis's comment on the uncorroborated rumor that Gonzenbach was working on another volume of Sicilian tales is worthy of note. Gonzenbach's tales were centred on the areas of Catania and Messina, while Palermo was still an uncharted territory, ready to be documented by Pitrè. In his answer to De Gubernatis, he attempted to deny that Gonzenbach was the first to collect Sicilian folklore:

> Tra le novelle mie però e quelle della Gonzenbach ci sarà molta differenza. Le mie saranno, alcune, lunghissime e piglieranno molto spazio.—Quel che s'è detto del primato della Gonzenbach non è vero: la Sicilia ha de' Cunti pubblicati, fin dal 1842 [...]. Io lavoro nella raccolta de' libri e delle notizie per la prima mia *Lett. siciliana*, la quale vorrà riuscire copiosa di indicazioni e di notizie. Ho aperto relazioni con Girgenti e Trapani e ne aprirò personalmente per Messina e Catania. Dico *personalmente* perché sabato prossimo (1° 8bre) partirò per Messina, donde mi recherò a Catania e all'Etna. [...] Figurati se penserò eccome alle tradizioni, quantunque dopo il Vigo e la Gonzenbach sia difficilissimo raccogliere nulla.[30]

In this passage, Pitrè was referring to Lionardo Vigo (1799–1879), author of *Raccolta di canti popolari siciliani* (1857). Despite claiming that Gonzenbach was not the first collector of Sicilian tales,[31] Pitrè reluctantly admitted that it would be difficult to gather local traditions following Vigo's and Gonzenbach's works. In a subsequent letter to De Gubernatis dated December 14, 1874, Pitrè thanked him for having persuaded him to study German:

> I frutti di questo studio son questi: *se io non avessi studiato il tedesco non avrei potuto capire l'importanza delle tradiz. pop., né istituito i raffronti delle novelle*

---

will not be difficult for you to put together an entire volume." De Gubernatis, *Lettere a Giuseppe Pitrè*, September 13, 1870, P-A-6, letter n. 51:3, BEGP.

30. "But there will be a great difference between my stories and those of Gonzenbach. Some of mine will be very long and will take up a lot of space.—What has been said about Gonzenbach's primacy is not true: tales have been published in Sicily since 1842 [...]. I am working toward the collection of books and data for my first work on Sicilian literature, which is going to be brimming with details. I have established relationships with Girgenti and Trapani, and I will personally establish others for Messina and Catania. I say *personally* because next Saturday (on the first of October) I am going to leave for Messina, from where I am going to Catania and Mount Etna. [...] Of course I will think about traditions, although after Vigo and Gonzenbach it is very difficult to collect anything." Pitrè, *Lettere ad Angelo De Gubernatis*, September 28, 1870, cass. 100 n. 19.6, letter n. 1:3–4, Fondo "Angelo De Gubernatis," BNCF (original emphasis).

31. In *Lettere siciliane*, Pitrè claimed that this record belonged to a professor from Catania, Agatino Longo, author of *Aneddoti siciliani, raccontati dal cav. Agatino Longo* (1845) (Pitrè 1870:123).

sicil. con quelle dello Schneller, della Gonzenbach, del Knust, del Wolf, del Widter ecc. io non avrei conosciuta la roba che ho in casa mia.[32]

It becomes clear that the scholarly encounter with the works of Gonzenbach and other German researchers of popular traditions, combined with the encouragement of his friend De Gubernatis, inspired in Pitrè the need to learn the German language and culture at the dawn of his folkloristic studies in order to compare German and Sicilian folktales. In this way, he could gain a deeper knowledge of the latter by virtue of this comparative assessment.[33] After the publication of Gonzenbach's collection, Roman philologist and folklorist Domenico Comparetti (1835–1927), professor of Greek language and literature at the University of Pisa, voiced his regret about Gonzenbach's record in a letter to Pitrè dated March 30, 1870:

> Spero che le sue ricerche non si limiteranno ai canti ma si estenderanno alle narrazioni per le quali la lacuna è anche maggiore. Disgraziatamente per le narrazioni popolari della Sicilia ci hanno già preceduto, come in tante altre cose, i tedeschi ed il libro testé pubblicato della Gonzenbach toglierà a Lei ed ad ogni altro italiano il merito di essere il primo a rivolgere a quella ricerca la sua attenzione. Ma se il merito di chi comincia è bello anche quello di chi continua ha il suo valore e spero che ne avrà tanto per Lei da tentarla.[34]

---

32. "The fruits of this study are these: *if I had not studied German I would not have been able to understand the importance of popular traditions, nor made the comparisons between the Sicilian stories and those of Schneller, Gonzenbach, Knust, Wolf, Widter, etc. I wouldn't have known the stuff I have in my own house.*" Pitrè, *Lettere ad Angelo De Gubernatis*, December 14, 1874, cass. 100 n. 19.7, letter n. 17:4, Fondo "Angelo De Gubernatis," BNCF (original emphasis and abbreviations). Pitrè was referring to scholars Christian Schneller, author of *Studi sopra i dialetti volgari del Tirolo italiano* (1865) and *Märchen und Sagen aus Wälschtirol* (1867), Hermann Knust, author of *Italienische Märchen* (1866), Georg Widter and Adam Wolf, who published *Volksmärchen aus Venetien. Mit Nachweisen und Vergleichungen verwandter Märchen von R. Köhler* (1866). On the mediators of Italian folklore in Germany, see Rubini (1996).

33. De Gubernatis would praise Pitrè's effort to learn German in *Rivista Europea*, defining it an "atto eroico" [heroic deed] (De Gubernatis 1870:353).

34. "I hope that your research will not be limited to songs but will extend to narratives, of which there is an even greater lack. Unfortunately, the Germans have already preceded us in the popular narratives of Sicily, as in so many other things, and the book just published by Gonzenbach will take away from you and every other Italian the merit of being the first to turn attention to that research. But if the merit of the one who begins is beautiful, that of the one who continues also has its value, and I hope it will have so much value for you that you will be tempted." Comparetti, *Lettere a Giuseppe Pitrè*, March 30, 1870, P-A-7, letter n. 1:1, BEGP.

Though Comparetti confirmed that Gonzenbach's anthology was the first of its kind, he nevertheless urged Pitrè to pursue his research further. Pitrè's commitment to studying Gonzenbach's tales is evident in other exchanges with De Gubernatis. In a letter sent on December 11, 1872, his determination to carry out a systematic comparative study of Sicilian and foreign oral traditions is clear.[35] In 1968 Alberto Mario Cirese stressed the importance of retracing the influences and stimuli that led to Pitrè's inexhaustible scientific knowledge despite coming from an "isola tanto periferica," wondering explicitly to what extent he was influenced by "le note comparative e bibliografiche che Köhler e Hartwig aggiunsero alle fiabe siciliane raccolte e tradotte in tedesco da Laura Gonzenbach" (Cirese 1968:34–35).[36] In line with other Italian scholars, Pitrè felt that his work was competing with her contribution, especially because she was not of Sicilian heritage. This view emerges not only in his private letters but also in the observations he made in his published works on anthologies of Italian folklore published in foreign languages. In the preface to his first volume of Sicilian fairy tales, Pitrè commented somewhat bitterly on the publication of traditional Italian narratives in German and English:

> Così l'Italia [...] deve ora richiamare dalla Germania e dall'Inghilterra i libri che raccontano in tedesco ed in inglese le storielle di *Giufà* e di *Giovannino senza paura*, della *Cenerentola* e della *Bella dalle tre melarance*. Non è la voce delle giovani contadine, delle vecchie nonne, che si ascolta; è bensì l'eco lontana che a stento si riconosce in lingue tanto dai parlari italiani diverse. (Pitrè 1875, I:lxi)[37]

To validate his statement, he mentioned in a footnote the words of British scholar and translator William Ralston Shedden-Ralston (1828–1889) on the "vari parlari di Sicilia" (Pitrè 1875, I:lxii),[38] according to whom the "transfer"

---

35. Pitrè, *Lettere ad Angelo De Gubernatis*, December 11, 1872, cass. 100 n. 19.7, letter n. 9:1, Fondo "Angelo De Gubernatis," BNCF.

36. "such a peripheral island," "the comparative and bibliographic notes that Köhler and Hartwig added to the Sicilian fairy tales collected and translated into German by Laura Gonzenbach."

37. "So Italy [...] must now summon back from Germany and England the books that tell the stories of *Giufà* and *Dauntless Little John*, of Cinderella and the *Beauty with the Three Oranges* in German and English. It is not the voice of the young peasant women, of the old grandmothers, that is heard; it is rather the distant echo that can hardly be recognized in languages so different from the Italian ways of speaking."

38. "various Sicilian ways of speaking." Pitrè, who was also secretary of the Società per gli Studi del Dialetto Siciliano, incorporated at the beginning of the first volume of his fairy-tale collection an essay on Sicilian dialect, "Saggio d'una grammatica del dialetto e delle parlate

from one language to another was perceived as a "storcimento" (distortion), an unnatural twisting of the genuine voice of the people, which becomes even more violent when the change occurs between languages that are entirely disparate (Shedden-Ralston in Pitrè 1875, I:lxii).[39] Despite Pitrè's skepticism toward the controversial linguistic transformation of Sicilian tales into foreign languages, contemporary fairy-tale scholars such as Jack Zipes observe how *Sicilianische Märchen* is "the most important collection of fairy tales, legends, and anecdotes in the nineteenth century, more important perhaps than the Brothers Grimm" (Zipes 2006a:xii), a statement that resonates with Armando Maggi's reevaluation of Gonzenbach's collection as "one of the most fascinating examples of the nineteenth-century obsession with the recovery and preservation of 'authentic' popular storytelling" (Maggi 2015:69). A similar recognition has been made by Nancy Canepa, who comments that these Sicilian tales "gave the island's rich storytelling traditions their first international exposure" (Canepa 2023:192).

Gonzenbach's neglect by the majority of twentieth-century Italian folklorists—quite telling in this regard is her total absence from Giuseppe Cocchiara's seminal *Storia del folklore in Europa* (1952) and her *en passant* mention in *Storia del folklore in Italia* (1981)[40]—can be partially explained by the reluctance to recognize her accomplishment: in Zipes's words, she had "stolen their fire and published 'their' precious native tales in a foreign language before they did in their own" (Zipes 2006a:xi). Gonzenbach's journey as a collector is thus a tale of transcription, translation, and appropriation across different languages: this process of conversion from one language into another is pivotal to retracing the literary and linguistic reception of these narratives and to

---

siciliane," in which he translated, revised, and expanded with his own notes the study of Sicilian dialect by German scholar Christian Friedrich Wentrup, *Beiträge zur Kenntniss der sicilianischen Mundart* (1859). The insertion of this study within a fairy-tale collection is emblematic of the frequent convergence of interests between folklorists and dialectologists in the nineteenth century, as mentioned in chapter 1. On Pitrè's study of Sicilian dialects, see Sottile (2017). For an overview of Sicilian linguistics in the late nineteenth century, see Ruffino (2017).

39. For Pitrè, the accurate transcription of the tales in their original dialect was both a matter of loyalty to the individuality of the performers and an aesthetic issue (Cocchiara 1951:64–65). In a previous essay on Sicilian fairy tales, he explicitly wrote with regard to Gonzenbach's translated tales that "non conservano quella fragranza ed efficacia che si hanno in siciliano" (Pitrè 1873:3) [they do not retain the fragrance and effectiveness that they have in Sicilian].

40. In *Storia del folklore in Italia*, Cocchiara simply reported that "il Pitrè [...] si impadronì delle raccolte che in Italia avevan fatto la Bush [sic], la Gonzenbach, il Wilter [sic] e il Wolf e il Kust [sic]—edite tutte in tedesco" (Cocchiara 1981a:156) [Pitrè took hold of the collections made in Italy by Busk, Gonzenbach, Widter, Wolf, and Knust, all edited in German].

understanding why her collection, despite being recognized today as extraordinary by several eminent scholars, barely entered the so-called "fairy-tale canon" (Haase 2019).

The peculiar publishing history of Gonzenbach's *Sicilianische Märchen* can partially explain the inadequate recognition of her work to the present day. After its original publication in German in Leipzig in 1870, nine of the tales were translated into English by American folklorist Thomas Frederick Crane (1844–1927) and included in his collection of *Italian Popular Tales* in 1885. A first partial translation into Italian was published by Gonzenbach's granddaughter, Renata La Racine, in 1964. La Racine described her grandmother with these words:

> Donna di non comune intelligenza e cultura si interessava vivamente alle tradizioni popolari locali e soprattutto alle favole, di cui era anche un'eccellente narratrice, conoscendo perfettamente il dialetto siciliano. [...] Così nacque questa raccolta, originariamente di 92 fiabe, che mia nonna aveva fedelmente trascritte, senza alterarle in nulla, così come le aveva udite dalla viva voce di semplici popolane illetterate delle province di Messina e di Catania. Da lungo tempo desideravo proporre ai lettori italiani queste deliziose favole, che propriamente favole non sono, almeno nel valore che si suole dare a questa parola. Sono racconti (e per adulti) di leggende, di fatti meravigliosi, e in molte di esse religione, magia e superstizione si mescolano e si intrecciano. (La Racine in Gonzenbach 1964:11–12)[41]

Her selection of thirty-six tales for this first translation paved the way for the wider circulation of Gonzenbach's work in Italy. The collection was then fully translated into Italian by Luisa Rubini, with Vincenzo Consolo's rereading, in 1999, and into English by Jack Zipes in 2006.[42] It is also worth noting that three of Gonzenbach's tales made their first appearance in Italian in Italo Calvino's

---

41. "A woman of uncommon intelligence and culture, she was keenly interested in local folk traditions and above all in fairy tales, of which she was also an excellent narrator, knowing the Sicilian dialect perfectly. [...] Thus this collection was born, originally containing ninety-two fairy tales, which my grandmother had faithfully transcribed, without altering them in any way, as she had heard them from the living voice of simple, illiterate female commoners from the provinces of Messina and Catania. For a long time I have wished to offer Italian readers these delightful fairy tales, which are not really fairy tales, at least in the value that is usually given to this word. They are tales (for adults) of legends, of wonderful happenings, and in many of them religion, magic, and superstition mix and intertwine with each other."

42. In 2019 a new edition of Gonzenbach's *Fiabe siciliane* was published by Donzelli. The complete 2006 English edition was preceded by the publication of *Beautiful Angiola: The Great Treasury of Sicilian Folk and Fairy Tales Collected by Laura Gonzenbach* and *The Robber with a*

Fiabe italiane in 1956.[43] The act of translating a text into another language leads to its insertion and relocation into another cultural system, a process that often led to the appropriation of local narratives through the exoticizing gaze of colonizers, as in the case of the translation and circulation of *The Thousand and One Nights* in Europe (Bacchilega 2012:457). However, Bacchilega comments favorably on Zipes's English-language version of Gonzenbach's tales, observing that, together with translations from other cultures such as the Hawaiian-English bilingual volume by Puakea Nogelmeier, *Ka Moʻolelo O Hiʻiakaikapoliopele: The Epic Tale of Hiʻiakaikapoliopele*, by Hoʻoulumāhiehie (2007), these editions "run counter to this ventriloquizing norm and promote a culture of translation" (Bacchilega 2012:457).

The virtue of this circulation of local stories in other cultural contexts results in a remediation of their critical reception at the time of their first publication, although the transposition of the narratives into a different language inescapably entails a loss of their linguistic peculiarities. This concern, together with the apprehension related to the transformation from oral into written form, was prominent among nineteenth-century folklorists who translated Italian traditional narratives into foreign languages. In this regard, Rachel Busk admitted in the preface to *The Folk-Lore of Rome* that

> It is impossible, in making acquaintance with these stories in their own language, not to regret having to put them into another tongue. Much of what is peculiar in them, and distinguishes them from their counterparts in other lands, is, of course, wrapped up in the form of expression in which they are clothed. Divested of this, they run the risk of losing the national character they have acquired during their residence on Italian soil. (Busk 1874a:xiv–xv)

Busk had originally opted for a bilingual version of her volume on Roman folklore but was then forced to renounce the idea due to space limits, therefore relegating the "vernacular idiosyncrasies" to her footnotes (Busk 1874a:xv).

Beyond these linguistic considerations, Gonzenbach acted as a key cultural mediator between German and Italian folkloristics (Rubini 1996:51). Although belonging to a foreign upper-class community, by engaging in folkloric research she was clearly stepping into a space dominated by male scholars.

Witch's Head: More Stories from the Great Treasury of Sicilian Folk and Fairy Tales Collected by Laura Gonzenbach in 2004, both edited and translated by Jack Zipes.

43. Gonzenbach's fairy tales included in Calvino's collection are: "La volpe Giovannuzza" (n. 185) (Gonzenbach n. 65, "Vom Conte Piro"); "Il bambino che diede da mangiare al Crocifisso" (n. 186) (Gonzenbach n. 86, "Von dem frommen Kinde"); "Massaro Verità" (n. 187) (Gonzenbach n. 8, "Bauer Wahrhaft, Massaru Verità").

However, precisely because of her gender and her knowledge of the local Sicilian dialect, she was able to gain the trust of female peasants, thereby accessing a rare wealth of folk and fairy-tale narratives. Several layers of gender issues are thus at stake when reappraising the sociocultural value of this collection, both on a contextual level as Gonzenbach conducted fieldwork herself chiefly among women informants, and on an intratextual level as atypical strong-willed heroines feature predominantly in her anthology, as will be highlighted in chapter 3. The heroines' firmness in facing and upending a frequently tragic reality, on the one hand, highlights the bravery of these protagonists and, on the other, mirrors the courage of Laura Gonzenbach herself, who rescued these popular stories from oblivion by perpetuating them in the lasting form of the written page.

Sicilianische Märchen, with its attention to the perspective of the lower classes in line with the verist vogue of the time, was published at a time when Sicily was increasingly perceived in the new Italian state as a region brimming with social malaise. In 1876 statesmen Leopoldo Franchetti (1847–1917) and Sidney Sonnino (1847–1922) carried out an inquiry on the political and administrative conditions of the region and its peasants, in an attempt to identify and study the causes of the issues that tormented the island, including corruption, violence, and criminality.[44] Although "una raccolta di fiabe non è il genere letterario più adatto alla denuncia diretta" (Rubini 1998:261),[45] evidence of a quasisociological mindset can be found in Gonzenbach's footnotes to some of the fairy tales, in which her explanations of local habits and idiomatic expressions have deeper implications if read against the backdrop of the *Questione meridionale*. The commentary in a footnote to the tale "Il calzolaio coraggioso" (Gonzenbach 2019 [1870]:238–41)[46] is emblematic of this perspective:

> Chiamandolo compare, il gigante assicura al calzolaio la vita. Il rapporto del comparatico in Sicilia è sacro come i legami di sangue. Il suo patrono particolare è San Giovanni e spesso si sente la definizione: "siamo compari di San Giovanni." A Messina, poco tempo fa, avvenne questo fatto: due famosi camorristi ("coltellatori") si erano pacificati dopo una lunga inimicizia durata anni e, come suggello, uno aveva chiesto all'altro di diventare suo compare. Questi però non aveva accettato. Perciò quello si ritiene

---

44. See Franchetti and Sonnino (1877). On the role of this inquiry in the context of the Southern Question and the emergence of folklore studies in Italy, see Coppola (2021:104–12). On the divergent positions of Hartwig and Pitrè with regard to the inquiry in Sicily, see Rubini (1998:289–90).
45. "a fairy-tale collection is not the most suitable literary genre for a direct denunciation."
46. "The Brave Shoemaker."

convinto che l'altro volesse ucciderlo e, per precederlo, una sera gli sparò. (Gonzenbach 2019 [1870]:239 n.1)[47]

Such an unexpected note introduces readers to the harsh and violent reality of the time with its abrupt explanation of a local episode of crime. Rubini acutely notes that this is a striking example of how "[l]a questione meridionale fa capolino a chiare lettere in una raccolta di fiabe, anche se timidamente [. . .] e forse in modo non del tutto appropriato al contesto narrativo" (Rubini 1998:257).[48] In these instances, Gonzenbach showed that she had a keen eye for the real-life Sicilian traditions embedded in these fictional tales, which turned into a "peasant diagnostic of social conditions" (Noyes 2005:339).

It is possible, given her position and upbringing, that she was aware of the contemporary discussions surrounding the distorted image of Sicily as an "other" within Italy, an "other" that was increasingly being examined and explained from the outside with the aim of being eventually rectified through centralized state interventions. Gonzenbach's diligence and attentiveness as a female folklorist was not an isolated case in post-unification Italy: another remarkable embodiment of such zeal, with similar "otherizing" effects, can be found in the folkloric writings of Grazia Deledda on the island of Sardinia.

Grazia Deledda: A "Novice Folklorist" in Sardinia

Nobel Prize winner in literature in 1926, Grazia Deledda published several folkloric writings at the dawn of her literary career, between 1891 and 1901, including ethnographic sketches, articles on popular traditions, local legends, and fairy tales. However, this aspect of her production has been largely neglected in comparison with the scrutiny devoted to her work as a novelist.[49]

---

47. "The giant guaranteed his life by calling him cousin. Family relations are regarded as blood ties and holy in Sicily. Their special patron saint is Saint Giovanni, and one frequently hears the expression, 'siamo compari di San Giovanni' (we're cousins of Saint Giovanni). There was an event that occurred not long ago in Messina. Two cutlers (coltellatori) reconciled after being enemies for many years, and as a sign to seal their new friendship one of them offered to call the other 'cousin,' but the other cutler did not accept the offer. As a result, the first cutler, who had made the offer, was convinced that his former enemy still wanted to bring about his death, and one evening, in order to beat him to the punch, he shot him dead" (Gonzenbach, trans. Jack Zipes, 2006:120).

48. "the Southern Question peeps out in black and white in a collection of fairy tales, even if timidly [. . .] and perhaps in a way that is not entirely appropriate to the narrative context."

49. Although there is no mention of Deledda in the *Encyclopedia of Women's Folklore and Folklife* (Locke et al. 2009), she rightfully makes her appearance in *The Greenwood Encyclopedia of Folktales and Fairy Tales* (Canepa 2008:262).

Attention to this early stage of Deledda's development as a writer leads to a deeper understanding of both her visceral attachment to her native island and her ambitious endeavor to make herself known on the Italian literary scene.[50] Hence, this section explores her positionality as a folklorist, the reception of her work as a collector, and the challenges she faced in gathering and publishing popular traditions in journals such as *Vita Sarda, Natura ed Arte,* and *RTPI* in the last decade of the nineteenth century. Deledda's liminality as a collector, suspended between her Sardinian peripheral position and her national and international aspirations, will therefore be foregrounded.

Deledda can rightly be regarded as the first woman to perform the role of "raccontatrice dell'epopea popolare, inedita e orale, che fioriva nella sua isola" (Croce 1940:318).[51] Born after Italian unification to a relatively well-off middle-class family in 1871, Deledda grew up in Nuoro, in the heart of Sardinia. Her father, Giovanni Antonio Deledda (1820–1892), a local landowner who had studied law in Cagliari and became mayor of Nuoro in 1863, was often involved in spontaneous poetic performances and frequently welcomed friends to his house, giving space to encounters that became a source of inspiration for the young Deledda. A turning point in her life was her departure from Sardinia in 1900, when she married Palmiro Madesani, for what she frequently referred to as "the continent," that is, the Italian mainland.

Her early life is described in detail in her unfinished autobiographical novel *Cosima* (1937), written in the third person in the final years of her life in Rome when she was dying of cancer.[52] This novel is permeated by a dreamlike atmosphere, a narrative mode that enables Deledda to delve into the memories of her childhood in Sardinia. In these pages, strong emphasis is placed on the imprint that the telling of popular tales around the hearth left on her imagination as a child, suspended between harsh reality and flights of fancy (Dolfi 1992:13–14): as Deledda put it, "le destava una impressione profonda, quasi fisica, il mistero della favola, quel silenzio finale, grave di cose davvero

---

50. Deledda's early life has garnered significant attention beyond the scholarly world, as evidenced by the two biographical films *L'amore e la gloria: la giovane Deledda* (2024), directed by Maria Grazia Perri, and *Grazia*, directed by Paola Columba, in postproduction at the time of this writing.

51. "storyteller of the unknown and oral popular epic that was flourishing in her island."

52. The title of the first publication was *Cosima, quasi Grazia*. Cosima was Deledda's third name at birth. For critical interpretations of this posthumous work, see De Giovanni (1987), Cerina (1992), Pickering-Iazzi (1997:75–88), Fanning (2007), and Bracchi (2010:145–61). For a study of Deledda's *Cosima* alongside the autobiographical writings of other women writers in twentieth-century Italy, see Fanning (2017).

grandiose e terribili" (Deledda 2005 [1937]:53).[53] As Nancy Canepa points out, the Mediterranean island in Deledda's writings frequently turns into a "mythical place cut off from the world of history," in which a "strong sense of place" can be detected (Canepa 2023:319–20). Decades after her folkloric enterprise, in a 1916 article entitled "Ricordi di Sardegna" published in *La rivista del Touring Club Italiano,* Deledda recalled the memories of when peasants, shepherds, and artisans regularly came to her house from nearby villages to do business or to celebrate rural festivities. On these occasions, they used to take part in improvised poetry and folk-song competitions, although Deledda preferred "i canti corali notturni, i canti religiosi, specialmente i *gosos* [...], e soprattutto i canti schiettamente popolari" (Deledda in Turchi 1995:268–69).[54]

Deledda started pursuing her ambition to become a writer from an early age. However, the path to achieve this dream was riddled with obstacles. First, she had limited educational opportunities. She attended a primary school until the fourth grade, which she repeated twice out of her own free will, since there were no other educational opportunities for girls at the time. Ranking first in her class, she was awarded Niccolò Tommaseo's collection of folk songs, *Canti popolari toscani, corsi, illirici, greci* (1841–42) (Deledda 2005 [1937]:57). Afterward, she had private Latin lessons with her uncle Sebastiano and lessons in Italian grammar and composition with a literature teacher who worked at a school for boys in Nuoro (Balducci 1975:61). Deledda learned Italian at school and therefore wrote in a language that was different from her mother tongue,

---

53. "the mystery of the tale awoke in her a profound, almost physical impression—that final silence, heavy with truly magnificent and terrible things" (Deledda, trans. Martha King, 1991:27).

54. "the nocturnal choral songs, religious songs, especially the *gosos* [...], and above all the genuinely popular songs." Deledda commented that the *gosos* "hanno una fisionomia speciale, tra il classico e il popolare, che in qualche modo delinea il sentimento religioso del popolo sardo con le sue enfasi, il suo entusiasmo e la sua calda fantasia. Composti per lo più da popolani imbevuti di una certa tinta di coltura, si accostano meglio alla poesia semi-dotta e arcaica così antipatica, eppure così amata ed usata dai Sardi" [they have a special physiognomy, between the classic and the popular, that somehow outlines the religious sentiment of the Sardinian people with their emphases, enthusiasm, and warm imagination. Composed mostly by people of the folk imbued with a certain tinge of culture, they can be best associated with the semilearned and archaic poetry that is so unpleasant, yet so loved and used by Sardinians] (Deledda 1894f:897). Deledda published a parody of the "Gosos de Sant'Antoni de Lodè" in the first issue of *RTPI* (Deledda 1893d:62–68). In a subsequent issue, she published the "Gosos della V. del Carmine," the "Gosos de N. S. de Gonare" and "Su perdonu" (Deledda 1894g:17–21). On the genre of the *gosos,* with reference to Deledda's "soundscape," see Turtas (2022–23:168).

the Logudorese dialect of the Sardinian language from Nuoro.[55] If this condition of plurilingualism was true for all post-unification writers, it was particularly challenging for women given their restricted access to educational prospects, which often led them to succumb to the prevailing illiteracy.[56] Despite her linguistic and literary self-learning process and admirably strong ambition as a writer, Deledda was dismissed as a regional author and frequently discriminated against her literary style.[57] Sharon Wood highlights how Deledda has been ignored "for being regional, popular, folkloric and female" (Wood 2007:7).[58] The recurrent use of the adjective "folkloric" as a pejorative label for Deledda's writing reveals the negative connotation that the term acquired and implies the dismissal of folklore as a category of study.[59]

By the time Deledda started to contribute to Angelo De Gubernatis's patriotic quest for popular traditions, she had already published her first short story, "Sangue Sardo," in the magazine *L'ultima moda* in 1888, *Nell'Azzurro* (1890), *Amore regale* (1891), *Stella d'oriente* (1891), *Amori fatali*, *La leggenda nera* and *Il ritratto* (1892), *Fior di Sardegna* (1892), *La regina delle tenebre* (1892), and *Sulle montagne sarde. Storie di banditi* (1892).[60] The following section focuses on Deledda's early contributions to folklore studies, which preceded the

---

55. On the Sardinian language, see Wagner (1997 [1951]), Pittalis (1998), Bolognesi and Helsloot (1999).

56. An overview of plurilingualism in Sardinia, with reference to language policies and sociolinguistic research, can be found in Lavinio (2015). For a study of the Sardinian literary landscape at the turn of the century, see Pirodda (1998). For a historical reconstruction of women's writing in Italy from the Renaissance to the modern and contemporary period, see Panizza and Wood (2000).

57. On Deledda's language, see Lavinio (1992), Secci (1966), Cecchi (1987), and Fortini (2010). Her language has been defined as "comune e piuttosto spampanata" [common and quite flattened] (Cecchi 1987:541), replete with "sgrammaticature e improprietà" [grammatical errors and inaccuracies] (Dessì in Lavinio 1992:69) and "imperfezioni linguistiche" [linguistic imperfections] (Secci 1966:125). Going against the traditional judgment of Deledda's style as flawed, Lavinio argues instead for her conscious "sensibilità metalinguistica" [metalinguistic sensitivity] (Lavinio 1992:72).

58. These persistently dismissive attitudes and the fluctuating scholarly interest toward Deledda in twentieth-century literary criticism are brought into focus in a volume aimed at reassessing her literary production, fittingly entitled *Chi ha paura di Grazia Deledda?* (*Who Is Afraid of Grazia Deledda?*), edited by Monica Farnetti (2010).

59. On the decline and negative connotation of the word "folklore" in Italy today, see Alziator (1974:178).

60. In this regard, Anna Dolfi comments that the popular customs in Deledda's early writings are characterized by a "consapevole mistione di storia e alterazione fantastica" [conscious mixture of history and fantastic alteration] (Dolfi 1979:45).

publication of her most renowned novels, such as *Elias Portolu* (1900), *Cenere* (1904), and *Canne al vento* (1913).

The Unjustly Neglected Sardinian Heart: Tradizioni popolari di Nuoro

As previously hinted, Deledda's folkloric writings comprise several articles, legends, and ethnographic sketches on Sardinian customs written for nineteenth-century Italian periodicals, including, in chronological order, "Luoghi della provincia: Nuoro" in *Le cento città d'Italia*, a supplement of the journal *Il Secolo* (1891); "Gonare (Usi e costumi sardi)" in *Vita Sarda* (1892); "Natale (macchiette sarde)" in *Natura ed Arte* (1892); "Per il folk-lore sardo" and "Leggende sarde" in *Vita Sarda* (1893); "La donna in Sardegna" in *Natura ed Arte* (1893); "Tradizioni popolari di Nuoro in Sardegna" in *Rivista delle tradizioni popolari italiane* (1893–95); "Leggende sarde" in *Natura ed Arte* (1894); "Albo di costumi e tipi sardi" in *Rivista per le signorine* (1900); "Tipi e paesaggi sardi" in *Nuova Antologia* (1901). Her work as a folklorist reached its peak with *Tradizioni popolari di Nuoro* (*TPN*),[61] defined as "the most scientific and ethnographic of her writings" (Gunzberg 1983:117), which was initially published in ten monthly installments from August 1894 to May 1895 under De Gubernatis's editorship in *RTPI* and as a volume by the Roman publishing house Forzani.[62]

This series of articles on oral traditions, which Deledda reported in the original dialect of Nuoro with parallel translations in Italian, contains references to proverbs, curses, poems, riddles, children's games, prayers, rituals, and beliefs related to the natural and supernatural worlds, popular remedies, spells, and religious hymns. She also detailed nuptial and funeral customs, traditional dresses, greetings, and festivities. Her approach was clearly influenced by the positivist prejudices that prevailed overseas. Not coincidentally, she dedicated her novel *La via del male* (1896) to Paolo Orano (1875–1945), author of *Psicologia della Sardegna* (1896), and Alfredo Niceforo (1876–1960), author of *La delinquenza in Sardegna* (1897), both inspired by the criminological theories

---

61. The first instalment of *TPN* was preceded by an article published in December 1893 entitled "Preghiere: Lauda di Sant'Antonio" (Deledda 1893d).

62. A translation of this volume into English has yet to be undertaken. The date 1894 is reported in the frontispiece of the volume. However, as remarked by Benvenuta Piredda in her analysis of the influence of Deledda's folkloric research on her literary production, this date "è da considerarsi errata perché in quell'anno erano usciti appena i primi capitoli in *Rivista delle tradizioni popolari italiane*" [it is to be considered incorrect because in that year the first chapters had just been published in *RTPI*] (Piredda 2010:22). On the genesis of *TPN*, see Atzori and Satta (2013:84–88).

of Cesare Lombroso (1835–1909), which became extremely popular after the Italian Risorgimento, a pivotal moment in the history of the Italian nation.[63]

The Risorgimento marked the beginning of radical political, urban, economic, and self-representational changes, summarized by Lucy Riall as "the breakdown of traditional rural society and the birth of modern, urban life, the transition from a feudal to a capitalist economy and the replacement of local or regional identities by a single national culture" (Riall 1994:1). These transformations, far from being homogeneous, led to diverse sociocultural transitions and compromises in the varied regional landscape of the newborn Italian state. Since the eighteenth century, after the Treaty of London in 1718, Sardinia had been part of the Kingdom of Piedmont-Sardinia, governed by the House of Savoy. As established by the treaty, Vittorio Amedeo II obtained Sardinia, which had hitherto been under Spanish dominion.

The second half of the nineteenth century was a critical moment for Sardinian society, which had to endure the consequences of the Piedmontese government's laws that allowed for the privatization of land to the advantage of wealthy landowners (Pirodda 1992:39). The so-called Editto delle Chiudende (Edict of the Enclosures) proclaimed in 1820—by means of which the "government at Turin decided to eliminate free access in favour of landowners" (King 2005:3)—greatly impoverished the lower classes and laid the foundations for an outpouring of banditry. This phenomenon often appears in the guise of the romanticized bandits who populate Deledda's novels, legends, and short stories.[64] The politics of centralization implemented by the unitary government disappointed the intellectual elites of the island, who were nostalgic toward the "tenue autonomia" of the Kingdom of Sardinia (Tanda 1992:7).[65] The roots of

---

63. Niceforo referred explicitly to Deledda in *La delinquenza in Sardegna* (1897), quoting excerpts from *TPN* and defining her as a "geniale scrittrice sarda" [brilliant Sardinian writer] (Niceforo 1897:100). In the second edition of *La via del male*, Deledda's dedication to Niceforo and Orano would disappear, suggesting perhaps Deledda's intention to distance herself from their positions. Heyer-Caput interprets this removal as a "sign of the intellectual independence that defines the revision of *La via del male* in its entirety" (Heyer-Caput 2008:35). In the novel *Cenere* (1904), Deledda inserted an allusion to criminologist Enrico Ferri (1856–1929), former pupil of Cesare Lombroso, whose university lectures on civil and criminal law were attended by the protagonist of the novel, Anania, in Rome. On the influence of criminal anthropology in Deledda's works, see Pirodda (1998:1094–96), Angioni (2010:11–16), and Hiller (2012). On Niceforo's racist anthropological studies, see Coppola (2021:117–26).

64. Fictionalized narratives of outlaws recur in Deledda's literary works and in southern Italian history in general. For an exploration of the "banditismo" and the woman as an outlaw in Deledda's fiction, see Briziarelli (1995).

65. "tenuous autonomy."

the ensuing economic crisis and social malaise were therefore to be found in the "colonialismo in cui l'isola era mantenuta e nella legge delle chiudende che aveva sconvolto l'assetto comunitario stabilito da secoli" (Turchi 1995:30–31).[66]

In post-unification Sardinia, there was a complex network of interrelations between national and regional literatures. Deledda's literary production locates itself in between the national and the insular literary axes, and it was thanks to her collaboration with De Gubernatis that she started to emerge on the national stage, quite literally moving from the margins of her island to the center of the Italian peninsula (Tanda 1992:10–11). What is striking about Deledda's folklore collection is her attempt to record and portray the popular traditions she observed in an apparently detached manner (Piredda 2010:23). To do this, she mastered a different mode of narration from the one she usually adopted as a novelist, a scientific perspective that has subtle implications in terms of class, gender, and identity issues.[67] Nonetheless, her own "self" as a collector is prevalent throughout her folkloric writings, and her voice intentionally, and indeed frequently, emerges in between these descriptive passages.[68] In the final paragraph of the preface to *TPN*, Deledda wrote:

> La raccolta che oggi presentiamo è certamente incompleta. Anzitutto, è il primo lavoro di un novello folk-lorista, a cui manca la coltura e l'erudizione necessaria per rendere più interessante questa specie di lavori. È un volume fatto senza pretese, [...] col solo intento d'invogliare altri a seguirlo ed a completare con lavori e ricerche dotte ciò che ora la sua penna giovane e inesperta non può fare. (Deledda 1894b:653)[69]

Her own label as a "novello folk-lorista" declared that she was simply an inexperienced folklorist while simultaneously creating a space for herself within

---

66. "colonialism in which the island was maintained and in the law of the enclosures that had upset the community structure that had been in force for centuries."

67. In this regard, Enrica Delitala observes how Deledda approached local customs with "un atteggiamento di idealizzazione e distacco" [an idealized and detached attitude] (Delitala 1992:308).

68. This "centrality of self-representation" is common among Sardinian writers, who tend to document insular life as the main focus of their texts, showcasing a fixation, if not obsession, with the island (Sulis 2017:69). On the "attachment" of Sardinian writers to their island, see also Rudas (2004 [1997]:158–64).

69. "The collection that we are presenting today is certainly incomplete. First of all, it is the first work of a novice folklorist, who lacks the culture and erudition necessary to render this kind of work more interesting. It is a volume arranged without pretentions, [...] with the sole intent of encouraging others to follow this work and to complete with scholarly endeavors what this young and inexperienced pen cannot do in the present moment."

this new field of inquiry; this approach characterized her public presence and autobiographical writings, which were suspended between an overt modesty and an inner consciousness of her own talent. Although this attitude aligns with her self-effacing yet resolute personality, this humble definition does not give justice to her work as a folklorist. The downplaying of her own work can be interpreted through the lens of Joan Radner and Susan Lanser's strategies of coding, more specifically as a way to "claim incompetence" (Radner and Lanser 1987:421–23). Such claims represent both "a conventional strategy by which the woman writer says on her own behalf what she knows her audience thinks: that she has little right to be writing, and that her work is bound to be inferior" and a subtle "appropriation of male forms" (Radner and Lanser 1987:423), such as the male-dominated discipline of folklore studies in the late nineteenth century. The frequent disregard for Deledda's contributions as a folklorist may have several motivations: certainly, her work as a novelist received more attention partially because it rendered her famous on an international level, but also because, in terms of the hierarchy of cultural productions, writing novels and short stories was conceived as a higher form of creative engagement with the raw material that she collected when she was a younger and less experienced writer; second, this neglect can be linked to the generally dismissive attitude toward women who participated in the collection of regional folklore in post-unification Italy, whose efforts have traditionally been sidelined, if not entirely forgotten.

In this regard, it is unsurprising that in the canonical *Storia del folklore in Italia* (1981), Giuseppe Cocchiara devoted only a marginal, albeit admiring, footnote to Deledda's role as a folklorist, exemplifying the tendency to relegate women's contributions to the fringes of the discipline.[70] He observed how De Gubernatis's *RTPI* generally welcomed "[a]rticoli brevi e quasi sempre informativi. Soltanto la Deledda vi pubblicò un ampio saggio sulle *Tradizioni popolari di Nuoro*, che è un'acuta indagine di ricerca folkloristica" (Cocchiara 1981a:138, n.36).[71] Even Italo Calvino in his meticulous research on Italian regional folktales did not draw from Deledda's legends and fairy tales, commenting that "[l]a Sardegna non ha grandi raccolte; ma il modo di raccontare triste, magro, senza comunicativa, e pur sempre con una lama d'ironia, mi pare caratteristico dell'isola" (Calvino 2015 [1956]:xxxviii).[72]

---

70. In a previous study, Cocchiara devoted a few pages to Deledda's folkloric research, defining her as a "folklorista militante" [a militant folklorist] (Cocchiara 1959:507).

71. "short and almost always informative articles. Only Deledda published a long essay on the *Tradizioni popolari di Nuoro*, which is an acute investigation of folkloristic research."

72. "Sardinia does not have large collections; but the sad, meager, uncommunicative way of telling stories, and yet with a blade of irony, seems to me to be typical of the island." Calvino

Deledda's folkloric enterprise acquires further value if one keeps in mind that, similar to other women folklorists in the second half of the nineteenth century, she had not received formal training. Furthermore, she promoted herself as a Sardinian collector in a complex social context in which participating in the public sphere was not only unconventional but also scandalous for a woman. Alongside the folkloric contributions made by scholars such as Egidio Bellorini (1865–1946), Giuseppe Calvia (1866–1943), Francesco De Rosa (1854–1938), Luigi Falchi (1873–1940), Giuseppe Ferraro (1845–1907), Francesco Mango (1856–1900), Pietro Nurra (1871–1951), and Andrea Pirodda (1868–1926),[73] Deledda, being the only woman in Sardinia to undertake such a task, was a true pioneer. Almost a century after her Nobel Prize, it is important to acknowledge that she was not only a talented novelist but also a scrupulous divulgator of Sardinian popular life and traditions, in particular from her hometown, Nuoro.

---

inserted seven Sardinian fairy tales in *Fiabe italiane* (2015 [1956]:881–904): "Fra Ignazio" (n. 191), "La potenza della felce maschio" (n. 196), and "Sant'Antonio dà il fuoco agli uomini" (n. 197) from Gino Bottiglioni's *Leggende e tradizioni di Sardegna* (1922); "I consigli di Salomone" (n. 192) from Francesco Mango's *Novelline popolari sarde* (1890); "L'uomo che rubò ai banditi" (n. 193) from Pietro Lutzu's *Due novelline popolari sarde (dialetto campidanese) quale contributo alla Leggenda del Tesoro di Rampsinite Re d'Egitto* (1900); "L'erba dei leoni" (n. 194) and "Il convento di monache e il convento di frati" (n. 195) from Francesco Loriga's *Novelle sarde* (n.d.).

73. Bellorini wrote *Saggio di canti popolari nuoresi* (1892), *Canti popolari amorosi raccolti a Nuoro* (1893), and *Ninne nanne e cantilene infantili raccolte a Nuoro* (1894). Another scholar who worked on Nuorese folk songs was Filippo Valla, who compiled *Alcuni canti popolari nuoresi* (1892). Calvia was a prolific scholar of popular traditions from the Logudoro region, with a focus on his hometown, Mores, publishing studies such as *Usi funebri di Mores (Logudoro)* (1893) and *Giuochi fanciulleschi sardi (Logudoro)* (1894). De Rosa gathered popular traditions from Terranova Pausania (Olbia) and contributed to *RTPI* and *ASTP* between 1894 and 1901. Falchi, director of the journals *Terra dei nuraghes* and *La Sardegna artistica*, collaborated with De Gubernatis and wrote *Storia critica della letteratura e dei costumi sardi dal secolo XVI ad oggi* (1898). Ferraro authored various anthologies of folklore, including *Canti popolari sardi* (1891) and *Folklore dell'agricoltura in Sardegna e nel Monferrato* (1892). Mango (1856–1900) published *Novelline popolari sarde* (1890). Nurra co-edited *Canti popolari sardi* (1893; 1896) with literary critic Vittorio Cian (1862–1951) and wrote various folkloric works, including *Nella Barbagia settentrionale: impressioni di viaggio* (1896). Pirodda focused on traditions from Aggius in Gallura, which he published in *RTPI* and *ASTP* in 1894 and 1895. Deledda mentioned Pirodda, Falchi, Bellorini, and Mango in a letter to De Gubernatis dated May 8, 1893, when she was striving to gain the support of other folklorists in Sardinia (Deledda, *Lettere ad Angelo De Gubernatis*, May 8, 1893, cass. 41 n. 33, letter n. 11:2–3, Fondo "Angelo De Gubernatis," BNCF). For a more detailed overview of these scholars, see Atzori and Satta (2013:79–107).

Nuoro is part of the Barbagia region, which literally means the "land of barbarians." The villages in this area, and Nuoro in particular, used to be represented as "depositaries of traditional Sardinian culture and language," an "identity paradigm" that became popular also thanks to Deledda's literary model (Sulis 2017:72). The town is described by Deledda in the incipit to *TPN* as "il cuore della Sardegna, è la Sardegna stessa con tutte le sue manifestazioni. È il campo aperto dove la civiltà incipiente combatte una lotta silenziosa con la strana barbarie sarda, così esagerata oltre mare" (Deledda 1894b:651)[74]. Deledda set Nuoro aside not only from the Italian peninsula but also from Sardinia itself, in a manner similar to other foreign explorers who ventured to this area such as linguist Max Leopold Wagner (1880–1962), who portrayed it as one of "the innermost regions of the island, less 'contaminated' by foreign cultures, an island within the island" (Serra 2017:284).

Several decades after the publication of *TPN*, another foreign visitor, D. H. Lawrence (1885–1930), came to Deledda's hometown. The impressions of his journey across Sardinia were published in his travel book *Sea and Sardinia* in 1921, accompanied by Jan Juta's illustrations (1895–1990). Lawrence appreciated Deledda's work as a novelist to the point that he wrote the foreword to the 1923 English translation of Deledda's novel *The Mother* and mentioned her explicitly in some passages of his travel memoir (Lawrence 1921:242, 265). If it is true that some sections of this book "reveal his fascination with human psychology, especially with those obscure and powerful forces which shape the unconscious" (Kalnins 2002:xxii), it is also undeniable that Lawrence's perspective is filtered by his viewpoint as an outsider, who projected perhaps too hastily an interpretation of the island as a primitive space. In fact, in the chapter devoted to Nuoro, he described Italy's remotest places as the epitome of primitivism: "Life is so primitive, so pagan, so strangely heathen and half-savage" (Lawrence 2002 [1921]:116). Although elegantly worded, Lawrence's observations disclose a view of Barbagia as a locus of exoticism and otherness. In her own ethnographic sketches, Deledda—rather than denying the perceived primitivism of this region—builds on the picture of the town starting from the perspective that prevailed "beyond the sea," of which a confirmation can be found years later in Lawrence's travel writings.

However, Deledda carves a central position for herself as a representative of Sardinian culture by virtue of her familiarity with it, her rightful belonging to that context. In this respect, it is worth considering how her representation

---

74. "It is the heart of Sardinia, it is Sardinia itself in all its manifestations. It is the open field where the incipient civilization fights a silent struggle with the strange Sardinian barbarism, so exaggerated beyond the sea."

of Sardinia in her ethnographic writings became a means to become a "portavoce o alfiere del mondo isolano" (Cirese 1976:39).[75] Nevertheless, the lack of a distance between the folklorist and the object of her study does not necessarily guarantee that her portrayal of Sardinia is less ideologically laden than the portrayal of an outsider. In other words, it is important to bear in mind that the depiction of Sardinia in Deledda's ethnographic studies remains *her* representation of the island. What she defined as "Sardinian barbarism" corresponds, as a matter of fact, to the harsh conditions of poverty that vexed Sardinia after Italian unification. Although such a representation does not denounce the real condition of Sardinia but rather eternalizes its status of alterity (Cirese 1976:40), it is also true that Deledda embarked on this project with great determination and contributed through her writing to offering a more multifaceted portrayal of her island. In this regard, Martha King observes how Deledda was able to "codify and define the Sardinian customs and mores that she had grown up with, to see them as through the eyes of interested outsiders" (King 2005:54). Furthermore, moments of rebellion against this preconceived vision of Sardinia can be found between the lines of her folkloric writings. Her irony and bitterness toward the state of neglect of her region often seep through her anthropological gaze.

In this respect, the rich correspondence between Deledda and De Gubernatis is central to understanding her sense of commitment and her desire to emerge on the national stage as a representative of Sardinian traditions (fig. 2.1). The first volume with seventy-one letters from Deledda to De Gubernatis was edited by Francesco Di Pilla (1966). De Gubernatis donated the letters to the Biblioteca Nazionale Centrale in Florence, requesting a fifty-year embargo after his death before the letters could be made accessible to readers. For a long time, these were believed to be the only letters that Deledda wrote to De Gubernatis. Only in 2007 did Roberta Masini publish a collection of many more letters that she found in De Gubernatis's archive. Masini discovered that De Gubernatis had intentionally separated the more personal letters from the others, gathering and reconstructing chronologically a total of 170 letters written by Deledda from 1892 to 1909 (Masini 2007).[76] Most recently, Maria Antonietta Piga Martini published *Grazia Deledda: un singolare romanzo (quasi) d'amore* (2013), which focuses on the letters of a more intimate nature

---

75. "spokesperson or standard-bearer of the insular world." For an overview of the contributions of twentieth-century scholars such as Alberto Mario Cirese, Ernesto de Martino, and Giovanni Lilliu to the anthropological study of Sardinia, see Angioni (2015).

76. In 2010 Masini discovered and published five other letters sent by Deledda to De Gubernatis (Masini 2010).

IDENTITY MATTERS 117

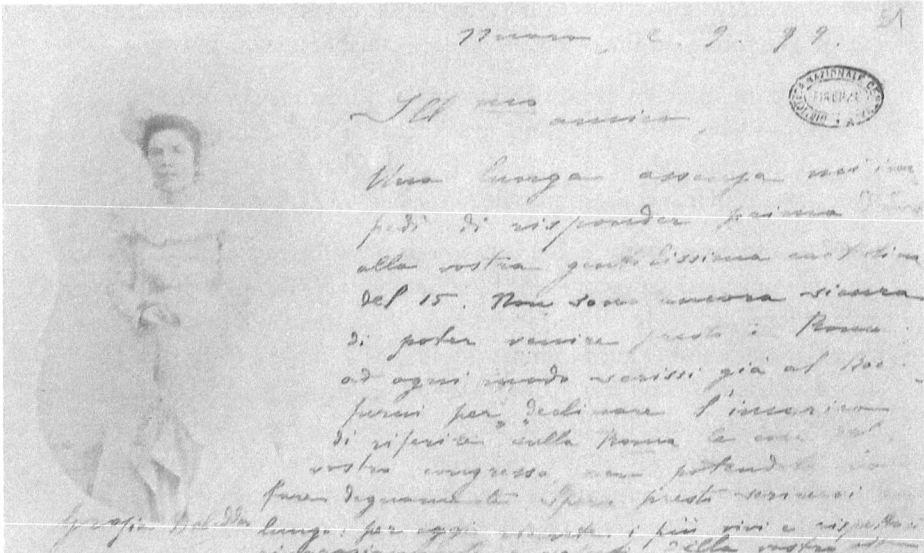

FIGURE 2.1. Grazia Deledda's postcard to Angelo De Gubernatis (September 2, 1899, cass. 41 n. 33, letter n. 51), Fondo "Angelo De Gubernatis," Biblioteca Nazionale Centrale, Florence. Courtesy of the Ministry of Culture / Biblioteca Nazionale Centrale, Florence. No further reproduction or duplication is permitted by any means.

written by Deledda from April 1894 to 1898. Both volumes are essential to exploring the context and motivations behind Deledda's work as a folklorist and her relationship with De Gubernatis. Despite attempts to retrieve them, the letters sent from De Gubernatis to Deledda have never been found (Masini 2010:124). It is therefore possible to read only Deledda's side of the epistolary exchange.

In the first postcard sent on April 14, 1892, Deledda took the initiative to approach De Gubernatis and cleverly asked him to publish some of her writings: "non oso mandarle qualche mio scritto, prima d'esser certa ch'ella vorrà farmi l'onore di pubblicarlo."[77] From Deledda's second missive sent on May 1, 1892, it can be deduced that De Gubernatis answered positively, and she subsequently sent him the short story "Gabina, racconto sardo," which was

---

77. "I do not dare send you some of my writings before being certain that you will grant me the honor of publishing them." Deledda, *Lettere ad Angelo De Gubernatis*, April 14, 1892, cass. 41 n. 33, postcard n. 1, Fondo "Angelo De Gubernatis," BNCF.

published in *Natura ed Arte* in 1892. In this same letter, Deledda introduced herself as a young Sardinian writer, eager to collaborate with him:

> Intanto mi permetto dirle che sono una giovanissima signorina sarda; che sono la sola scrittrice che conti attualmente la Sardegna; che collaboro in molti giornali letterari italiani, e che ... sarei felicissima se anch'Ella volesse annoverarmi fra i collaboratori della sua *Natura ed Arte*.—Spero di sì.[78]

From that moment onward, De Gubernatis turned into a positive figure for the emerging Sardinian writer. He became not only Deledda's point of reference in Italy but also her friend and mentor. In particular, De Gubernatis was a crucial guide in her autonomous training as a "novice folklorist." For instance, in a letter dated July 13, 1893, Deledda explicitly asked De Gubernatis if fairy tales could also be considered as folklore: "Mi dica: c'entrano anche le fiabe nel folk-lore? Ce ne sono di bellissime."[79] Conscious of her own skills and talent but also of the difficulties of her task, Deledda defined herself as a "piccola *streghina* che strega tutti senza volerlo, ma che, come le streghe, non ha mai pace né conforto."[80] As their exchange of letters unfolded, it is possible to discern her growing familiarity with the different genres of oral traditions and the progress she made thanks to her self-learning. After her initial approach, he asked her to participate in the collection of Italian folklore. From the sixth letter that Deledda sent to him on November 8, 1892, onward, it is clear that he had already asked her to contribute to *RTPI*.

Enthused by De Gubernatis's project, on May 2, 1893, Deledda sent a letter to Antonio Scano and Antonio Giuseppe Satta, editors of the journal *Vita Sarda*, which was published first on May 14, 1893, in *Vita Sarda* under the title "Per il folk-lore sardo" and then in *Versi e prose giovanili* (Deledda 1938:241–42).[81] Her letter, to which she attached the program of the Società

---

78. "In the meantime, I would like to tell you that I am a very young Sardinian lady, that I am the only writer who currently recounts Sardinia, that I collaborate with many Italian literary newspapers, and that ... I would be very happy if you could include me among the collaborators of your journal *Natura ed Arte*. I hope so." Deledda, *Lettere ad Angelo De Gubernatis*, May 1, 1892, cass. 41 n. 33, letter n. 2, Fondo "Angelo De Gubernatis," BNCF.

79. "Tell me: do fairy tales also play a part in folklore? There are some very beautiful ones." Deledda, *Lettere ad Angelo De Gubernatis*, July 13, 1893, cass. 41 n. 33, letter n. 19:6, Fondo "Angelo De Gubernatis," BNCF.

80. "A little *witch* who inadvertently bewitches everyone but, similar to witches, never has peace or comfort." Deledda, *Lettere ad Angelo De Gubernatis*, December 27, 1893, cass. 41 n. 33, letter n. 33:8, Fondo "Angelo De Gubernatis," BNCF (original emphasis).

81. When reassessing Deledda's work as a folklorist on a transnational level in connection with other women folklorists, it is also interesting to note that among the pages of *Vita Sarda*

Nazionale per le Tradizioni Popolari Italiane, reveals the importance she placed on this folkloric quest. She underlined how it was De Gubernatis who "ha incaricato me di raccogliere possibilmente il volume riguardante la Sardegna, che l'illustre uomo ritiene per una delle regioni italiane più ricca di tradizioni, leggende, e usanze popolari" (Deledda 1938:241).[82] She accepted this "geloso incarico [...] con entusiasmo e trepidazione,"[83] in the hope that she might receive the support of other Sardinian intellectuals, and defined her collection as an "opera patriottica" and a "crociata intellettuale" (Deledda 1938:241),[84] strong terms that convey the seriousness and rigor with which she embarked on this task. She entrusted the editors of *Vita Nuova* to encourage other Sardinians to take part in the project, since "[i]n ciascun villaggio c'è almeno uno studente che può raccogliere succintamente le credenze, le piccole poesie antiche, gli usi domestici, le superstizioni, le feste popolari" (Deledda 1938:241).[85] They needed only to gather notes and send them to Deledda, who eagerly offered to compile them, order them, and cite their sources. She concluded this ardent letter with a tinge of humility, a recurrent topos for women writers that implicitly reflected the clash between her apparent unpretentiousness and the importance of the task she had taken on. She asked once more to help "questa piccola lavoratrice che ha consacrato la sua vita e i suoi pensieri alla Sardegna, e che sogna ad ogni istante di vederla, se non più conosciuta, liberata almeno

---

there were contributions by renowned women writers such as Fernán Caballero, pseudonym of Cecilia Böhl de Faber (1796–1877), whose Spanish folktales "La buona e la cattiva fortuna" and "La fanciulla dai tre mariti" were included in Italian translation in the issues published on March 13, 1892, and March 27, 1892, respectively, a testimony of the European openness of the Sardinian journal. In *Fiabe novelle e racconti popolari siciliani*, Pitrè commented that "Le donne non sono rimaste estranee a tanto movimento. Una valente signora, che si nasconde sotto il nome maschile di Fernán Caballero, volse le sue cure alle novelle e tradizioni andaluse; la signorina Mijatovies alle serbe; miss Busck [sic] alle tirolesi, alle spagnuole e perfino a quelle della lontana Mongolia e della Calmucchia" (Pitrè 1875, I:lviii–lix). [Women have not been left out from so much movement. A valiant lady, hiding behind the male name of Fernán Caballero, turned her attention to Andalusian tales and traditions, Miss Mijatovies to the Serbian traditions, Miss Busk to the Tyrolean and the Spanish traditions and even to those from the distant Mongolia and Kalmykia].

82. "asked me to collect, if possible, the volume about Sardinia, which the illustrious man regards as one of the richest Italian regions in terms of traditions, legends, and folk customs."

83. "jealous task [...] with enthusiasm and trepidation."

84. "patriotic work" and "intellectual crusade."

85. "in each village there is at least one student who can succinctly collect the beliefs, the small ancient poems, the domestic customs, the superstitions, the popular festivities."

dalle calunnie d'oltre mare" (Deledda 1938:242).[86] This dream emerges preponderantly in one of her ethnographic sketches published in *Natura ed Arte*, "La donna in Sardegna," which will be explored in depth in chapter 3.

The publication of this appeal would give rise to a misunderstanding with De Gubernatis: it can be deduced from Deledda's reply on May 27, 1893, that the task De Gubernatis had entrusted to her consisted only in securing new members for the society rather than taking on such an official position. Deledda was therefore forced to apologize to him for the publication of her unsolicited invitation to Sardinian scholars in *Vita Sarda*. In other words, she was perhaps too hasty and too zealous in her response to De Gubernatis's initiative. In a previous letter dated May 8, 1893 (fig. 2.2), Deledda suggestively commented that

> Se riesco a scuotere i miei amici, a spandere in loro l'entusiasmo che io sento già per questa opera, è certo che la Sardegna porgerà un interessante contingente allo studio del *folk-lore*. Io le prometto di fare tutto il possibile, tutto quello che sta in me. Pur troppo in Sardegna si verifica uno strano e doloroso fenomeno. I sardi gridano ad ogni istante che l'isola loro è la cenerentola italiana, che aspetta tutt'ora una fata benefica, o magari un Cristoforo Colombo che la tragga dall'oscurità e dall'angolo in cui sussiste,— gridano tutti, ma quando si tratta di fare qualcosa, quando si esige da loro un movimento intellettuale, un po' di pratica per le loro teorie, allora nessuno si muove, nessuno si commuove![87]

---

86. "this little worker who has dedicated her life and thoughts to Sardinia, and who constantly dreams to see her region, if not better known, freed at least from the slander coming from overseas."

87. "If I manage to stir my friends, to ignite in them the enthusiasm that I already feel for this work, it is certain that Sardinia will offer an interesting contingent to the study of folklore. I promise you that I will do everything possible, everything that is in me. Unfortunately, a strange and painful phenomenon occurs in Sardinia. Sardinians continuously lament that their island is the Italian Cinderella, still waiting for a good fairy or perhaps a Christopher Columbus who may take her from the darkness and from the corner in which she subsists,—they all shout, but when it is necessary to do something, when an intellectual movement is required of them, a little practice for their theories, then no one moves, no one is moved!" Deledda, *Lettere ad Angelo De Gubernatis*, May 8, 1893, cass. 41 n. 33, letter n. 10:1–2, Fondo "Angelo De Gubernatis," BNCF. The same metaphor appears in Deledda's letter on May 2, 1893, to Scano and Satta: "Tutti gridano che la Sardegna è la Cenerentola d'Italia, che aspetta tutt'ora la fata benefica che la scopra e la tragga dall'oscurità in cui vive" [Everyone cries out that Sardinia is the Cinderella of Italy, still waiting for a good fairy to discover her and take her out of the obscurity in which she lives] (Deledda 1938:241).

Deledda's analogy of Sardinia as the "Cinderella of Italy," the quintessential fairy-tale heroine in distress, was in line with the tendency among local intellectuals to victimize Sardinia, presenting it as a land in dire need of a savior.[88] In this respect, the wish for a Christopher Columbus to intervene and save the island from its obscurity situates Sardinia in a colonialist paradigm, resonating with contemporary reassessments of the island's historical past as "semi-colonial" (Wagner 2011:15–16). This allusion to Columbus recalls the association Alfred Nutt made between Gaelic literature and Africa as quasi-*terrae incognitae* that needed to be discovered and mapped, mentioned in chapter 1 (Nutt 1903:12). Remarkably, the evocative image of Ireland as the "Cinderella of Empire," victim of British hegemony, was circulating in Irish satirical pamphlets and newspapers at the turn of the century, as testified by the range of articles gathered by Abigail Heiniger in the first volume of *Fairy-Tale Revivals: Writing Wonder in Transatlantic Ethnic Literary Revivals, 1850–1950* (2023).[89]

It is worth noting that Deledda identified with great clarity the age-old ills that afflicted her island. On the one hand, by presenting it as a forgotten, exploited, and mistreated region, completely detached from the continent and abandoned to its fate, she described it as if it were a land of colonial conquest, linking its decline and its possible salvation to external political and historical causes. On the other hand, she did not ignore the endogenous roots of this decadence, which she believed to be ingrained in the indolent character of its people, in her view used to posing as victims and reveling in that condition. Deledda saw in De Gubernatis's folkloric initiative an opportunity for her island, and herself, to fit into a continental and international context. She had lucidly interpreted the project to collect popular traditions as a unique chance to enhance not only the Sardinian territory but also its people, connecting

---

88. Letterio Di Francia (1877–1940), in his collection of Calabrian fairy tales, would use the same metaphor to describe another "Italian Cinderella," Calabria: "la Cenerentola d'Italia, bagnata da due mari famosi e ricca di secolari tradizioni, aspettava ancora, senz'alcuna speranza, la venuta provvidenziale del principe, che la togliesse dalla cenere e la collocasse sul trono, come ne aveva ben diritto, per la sua storia millenaria di svariate civiltà e per le ignorate virtù dei suoi abitanti" (Di Francia 2015 [1929]:7). [The Cinderella of Italy, bathed by two famous seas and rich in centuries-old traditions, was still waiting, without any hope, for the providential coming of the prince, who would remove her from the ashes and place her on the throne, and rightfully so, for the millennial history of various civilizations and the ignored virtues of her inhabitants].

89. At the turn of the century, the metaphor of Cinderella as the epitome of oppression was also evoked in other cultural contexts colonized by the British Empire, including the Caribbean islands (Heiniger 2023:1). On the politicized use of Cinderella's tales in the debates surrounding the Irish Question, see also Heiniger (2020).

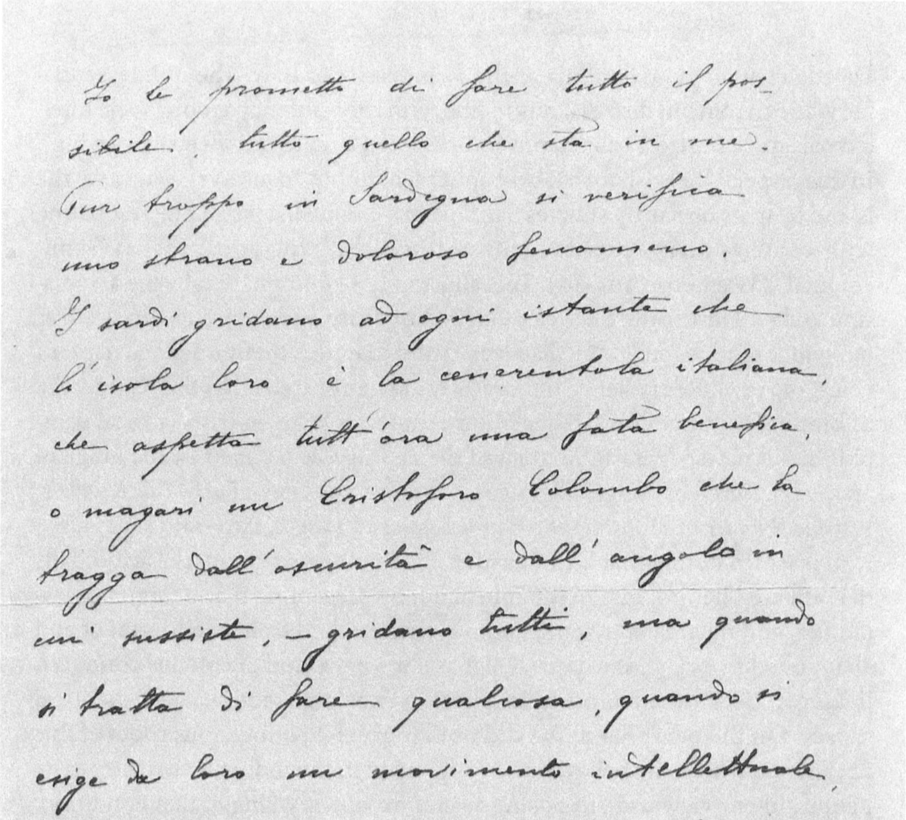

Io le prometto di fare tutto il possibile, tutto quello che sta in me. Pur troppo in Sardegna si verifica uno strano e doloroso fenomeno. I sardi gridano ad ogni istante che l'isola loro è la cenerentola italiana, che aspetta tutt'ora una fata benefica, o magari un Cristoforo Colombo che la tragga dall'oscurità e dall'angolo in cui sussiste, — gridano tutti, ma quando si tratta di fare qualcosa, quando si esige da loro un movimento intellettuale, un po' di pratica per le loro teorie, — allora nessuno si muove, nessuno si commuove! Avverrà così anche questa volta? Speriamo di no. Io dunque suonerò a raccolta e se i sardi non risponderanno all'appello ... tanto peggio per loro!

FIGURE 2.2. Grazia Deledda's letter to Angelo De Gubernatis (May 8, 1893, cass. 41 n. 33, letter n. 10), Fondo "Angelo De Gubernatis," Biblioteca Nazionale Centrale, Florence. Courtesy of the Ministry of Culture / Biblioteca Nazionale Centrale, Florence. No further reproduction or duplication is permitted by any means.

them to an extensive and ever-expanding cultural network. A few weeks later, she wrote:

> Dunque, giacché i grandi sardi sono sconfortati e nessuno di essi vuol mettersi a capo di questa impresa, io stessa mi pongo in testa a questo esercito che comincia a muoversi. E spero. Sono piccina piccina, sa, sono piccola anche in confronto delle donne sarde che sono piccolissime,—ma sono ardita e coraggiosa come un gigante e non temo le battaglie intellettuali. Ora mi son messa in questa e spero di vincerla. In Sardegna sono molto conosciuta ed amata, specialmente dai giovani. Ora io ho fatto l'appello ad essi e son sicura che tutti mi risponderanno, non tanto per amor di patria quanto per amor mio.[90]

This militant fervor emerges in her letter to writer and journalist Luigi Falchi (1873–1940) sent on May 7, 1893, in which she ambitiously wrote: "io mi metto modestamente tra le file; o meglio, sì, mi metto a capo, giacché un capo deve esserci" (Deledda in Falchi 1937:128).[91] Folklore was regarded by Deledda as a flywheel, and if her people were not willing to grasp this opportunity, she was ready to assume this cultural and political mission personally, becoming its chief interpreter. Folklore would thus become her springboard, animating her ethnographic passion and underpinning her novels.

It is evident that Deledda had to face several challenges while working as a collector. In a letter to De Gubernatis dated May 8, 1893, despite stressing her self-determination, she was forced to admit her need to search for and rely on other collaborators, because of the limits imposed by her gender:

> Io, nella mia piccola potenza, le ripeto che farò di tutto. Di Nuoro, che è il centro più caratteristico dell'isola, me ne occuperò io sola [...]. Se fossi abbastanza forte e libera io stessa andrei di villaggio in villaggio alla ricerca di questo *mondo sepolto*, come ella lo chiama; ma pur troppo ciò mi è

---

90. "Therefore, since the great Sardinians are disheartened and none of them want to take charge of this enterprise, I place myself at the head of this army that is beginning to move. And I hope. I am very tiny, you know, I am tiny even in comparison with Sardinian women who are very small, but I am bold and courageous like a giant, and I am not afraid of intellectual battles. Now I have put myself in this one and hope to win it. In Sardinia, I am well known and loved, especially by young people. Now I have appealed to them, and I am sure that everyone will answer me, not so much for the love of country as for love of me." Deledda, *Lettere ad Angelo De Gubernatis*, May 21, 1893, cass. 41 n. 33, letter n. 12:1, Fondo "Angelo De Gubernatis," BNCF.

91. "I modestly place myself in the ranks; or rather, yes, I put myself in charge, since there must be a leader."

impossibile. Ad ogni modo, anche ferma nel mio cantuccio, spero di far assai, col tempo.[92]

A month later, Deledda described an unpleasant episode that occurred while she was reading *Canti popolari amorosi raccolti a Nuoro* (1893), by Egidio Bellorini. Her brother Andrea tore apart some pages of the book that contained traditional love songs called *mutos*, because he deemed them too salacious to be read by a woman (Turchi 1995:26–27; Dedola 2016:128). Regardless of this external censorship, Deledda reclaimed in her letter her right as a scholar "di legger tutto":[93]

> [E]ssendo capitato, prima di leggerlo io, in mano di mio fratello egli ne ha strappato vari fogli di *mutos* e delle loro traduzioni dicendomi che non potevano esser letti neppure da me, benché io, nella mia condizione di studiosa, abbia il diritto di legger tutto. Non posso quindi darle un giudizio su questa parte del volume, che ritengo però per molto riprovevole dal momento che non si permette di leggerla neppure a me.[94]

Although her activity as a folklorist led her to actions that went against the rigid social rules to which women had to comply at the time, Deledda constantly fluctuated between acceptance of these norms and their transgression. For example, when she documented a dense list of Nuorese proverbs, she wrote in a footnote: "Lasciamo da parte alcuni proverbi troppo sudici per essere raccolti da una signorina" (Deledda 1894d:828).[95] This ironic comment acknowledged her awareness that including these scandalous proverbs would reflect poorly on her as a young woman. She described some of the challenges she encountered during her fieldwork in another letter to De Gubernatis, after she had just concluded her collection: she mentioned how her folkloric

---

92. "I can assure you I will do everything I can with my little power. I will take care of Nuoro, which is the most characteristic center of the island, on my own [...]. If I were strong and free enough, I myself would go from village to village in search of this *buried world*, as you call it; but unfortunately this is impossible for me. In any case, even if I am stuck in my little corner, I hope to accomplish a great deal, with time." Deledda, *Lettere ad Angelo De Gubernatis*, May 8, 1893, cass. 41 n. 33, letter n. 10:3–4, Fondo "Angelo De Gubernatis," BNCF (original emphasis).

93. "to read everything."

94. "Since it happened to be in my brother's hands before I could read it, he tore off several sheets of *mutos* and their translations, telling me that they could not be read even by me, although I, in my condition as a scholar, have the right to read everything. I therefore cannot give you an opinion on this part of the volume. I consider this, however, to be very reprehensible since even I am not allowed to read it." Deledda, *Lettere ad Angelo De Gubernatis*, June 12, 1893, cass. 41 n. 33, letter n. 16:3–4, Fondo "Angelo De Gubernatis," BNCF.

95. "Let's leave aside some proverbs that are too dirty to be collected by a young lady."

research led her "negli ovili, nelle case più povere e più oscure, tra il fumo e la miseria,"[96] and emphasized how she adopted stratagems such as telling lies and pretending to be sick to gather popular remedies, which were an integral part of the folk wisdom that she wanted to gather and preserve.

Deledda's contribution to folklore studies was certainly *eccentric*, in that it was unconventional and at odds with the social expectations associated with women in late nineteenth-century Sardinia; but it was also intrinsically *ex-centric* in the original acceptation of the term—that is, peripheral, located outside of the center, here represented by the Italian mainland.[97] Her ethnographic portrayal of the people from Nuoro, albeit permeated by intentional generalizations, both casts light on her knowledge of contemporary discourses surrounding primitivism and indicates her ability to contextualize these assumptions in an attempt to explain the causes behind the alleged criminal impulses intrinsic to Sardinian people. In this regard, she commented that Nuorese people were unjustly feared:

> [I]l Nuorese non è più selvaggio di qualsiasi altro popolo dimenticato e abbandonato a sé stesso. [...] Il Nuorese, che, se non è molestato, è la persona più pacifica del mondo, viene anche accusato di poltroneria perché le sue terre sono incolte [...]; ma come si può coltivare un vastissimo paese allorché mancano le braccia necessarie per dissodarlo e l'agricoltura è ancora allo stato primitivo? Il Nuorese non è ladro per istinto; ruba veramente per fame, parliamo sempre in generale, e ruba nell'aperta campagna, ma non vi toglie l'orologio e la borsa come nei paesi civilissimi. (Deledda 1894b:652)[98]

These words reinforce the perception of extreme otherness that surrounded Nuoro and its people—compared not only to Italy but also to the rest of Sardinia itself. However, in her writings Deledda took care to emphasize with a sympathetic outlook how Nuorese people shared the exact same destiny as other neglected people and that their criminality was not instinctual but rather

---

96. "In the sheepfolds, in the poorest and darkest houses, between smoke and misery." Deledda, *Lettere ad Angelo De Gubernatis*, February 20, 1894, cass. 41 n. 33, letter n. 36:3, Fondo "Angelo De Gubernatis," BNCF.

97. On women writers' eccentricity, see Botta et al. (2003).

98. "The Nuorese is no more savage than any other people who have been forgotten and abandoned to themselves. [...] The Nuorese, who, if he is not harassed, is the most peaceful person in the world, is also accused of laziness because his lands are uncultivated [...]; but how can a huge land be cultivated when there is no manpower to plow it and when agriculture is still in a primitive state? The Nuorese is not a thief by instinct; in truth, he steals out of hunger—we are always speaking in general terms—and he steals in the open countryside, but he does not take away one's watch and purse as happens in very civilized countries."

provoked by external contingencies such as hunger, which rendered their actions perhaps more understandable than the illicit acts of petty thieves in supposedly civilized countries. It becomes clear that Deledda was subtly trying to defend herself and her region from the dominant prejudices of the time, being aware of the theories propounded by criminologists such as Niceforo, who argued that the Barbagia and Nuoro in particular corresponded to a "zona delinquente," "una specie di plaga moralmente ammalata" (Niceforo 1897:31).[99]

The articulation of her defense, suspended between a partial acceptance of these stereotypes and a denial of their truthfulness, shows affinities with the perspective of Jane Wilde in Ireland. Though there were radical differences in their upbringing and respective cultural environments, it is interesting to notice resemblances in the way both writers eloquently attempted to upend the clichéd representations of Sardinian and Irish people through their folklore writings. Although their commentaries remain anchored in an ethnocentric vision of the two cultures that does not exonerate them from blatant stereotyping, such representational strategies invite us to reflect on the similarities between Sardinia and Ireland. The Mediterranean island and the Emerald Isle present "shared historical sufferings (invasion, oppression, marginalisation)" (Adamo 2006:10), since both contexts were shaped by a strong insular identity and marked by a condition of subalternity in relation to the newborn Italian state and to the British Empire. The reflections, asides, and digressions in Deledda's ethnographic sketches expose a political subtext aimed at critiquing hegemonic forces in complex and often contradictory ways, a critical stance that can also be detected in Jane Wilde's collections of Irish folk traditions.

Jane Wilde: A "Gifted Compiler" of Irish Folklore

The creation of an Irish national identity in the nineteenth century was intertwined with the preservation and publication of local folklore: in this respect, the term "local" carries a strong connotation as Irish traditions were regarded first and foremost as "the expression of the *genius loci*," in a context where "localities were not equal in purity or quantity [...] and the best rewarded collectors were those who worked in the Gaeltacht" (Foster 1987:204; original emphasis). Indeed, these areas were marked by a "massive residual orality" (Ong 2002 [1982]:67). The contributions of Jane Wilde to the dissemination of oral traditions from the Gaeltacht are a testimony to the emerging ideals of Irish nationalism, whereby patriotic striving becomes entangled with the rising scholarly interest in popular culture. The notion of tradition conventionally places

---

99. "a delinquent zone," "a sort of morally sick area."

itself at the opposite spectrum of modernity. Yet an investigation of Wilde's views as a woman on the "lore of the people" puts into relief conflicting attitudes toward the representation of the subaltern classes, the perception of the tradition/modernity dichotomy, and the process of national myth-making.

Massey's feminist study on the geopolitics of place reminds us that "[i]ndividuals' identities are not aligned with either place or class; they are probably constructed out of both, as well as a whole complex of other things, most especially 'race' and gender" (Massey 1994:137). The intersection of the categories of ethnicity, class, and gender is especially relevant when outlining how and for what reasons upper-class Anglo-Irish Protestant folklorists published anthologies of verbal lore: their mindset "resembled that of an adult trying to recover the faintly recalled bliss of childhood. [...] [U]pper-class collectors had the outsider's curiosity, condescension, and brashness that resulted in a great quantity of data" (Foster 1987:205). The analogy of the collector as an adult who attempts to regress to a forgotten childlike state suggests the patronizing characterization of peasants as noble savages still rooted in a primordial stage and thus closer to a simpler and purer vision of nature and life. Anglo-Irish folklore collections offer plentiful examples of such a vision. The conceptualization of race in the second half of the nineteenth century left an imprint on Jane Wilde's writings on folklore, in the aftermath of the highly influential publications of Charles Darwin's *On the Origin of Species* (1859) and Edward Burnett Tylor's *Primitive Culture* (1871), the expansion of the British Empire, and the proliferation of positivist theories.

Born Jane Elgee in 1821, Lady Jane Francesca Agnes Wilde was a writer, poet, translator, and folklorist, strongly inspired by national ideals (fig. 2.3).[100] Often remembered as the niece of Charles Maturin (1782–1824), author of the acclaimed gothic novel *Melmoth the Wanderer* (1820), and the mother of Oscar Wilde (1854–1900), she can be regarded as one of the earliest Irish nationalists. She held strong political positions: most notably, under the evocative name of Speranza, she contributed to the weekly journal *The Nation*, founded in 1842 by John Blake Dillon (1814–1866), Thomas Osborn Davis (1814–1845), and Charles Gavan Duffy (1816–1903), strenuous supporters of the Young Ireland (1842–49), a political movement that advocated for the freedom of the island.[101] Despite her political activism and her protofeminist vision that comes

---

100. Although some biographers report 1826 as her date of birth, Eleanor Fitzsimons notes that Jane Wilde wrote December 27, 1821, as her birth date in a grant application submitted to the Royal Literary Fund (Fitzsimons 2015:16). This reliable source has been regarded as evidence of her birth in 1821.

101. On the Young Irelanders, see O'Sullivan (1944), Hutchinson (1987), and Quinn (2015).

FIGURE 2.3. Jane Francesca "Speranza" Wilde (1821–1896), supplement to *The Irish Fireside*, September 2, 1885, National Library of Ireland (EP WILD-JA (1) II). Reproduced courtesy of the National Library of Ireland, Dublin.

to the fore in her contributions to various spheres of knowledge,[102] the reception of Jane Wilde as an intellectual figure has endured persistent "derision and misrepresentation" (Walshe 2023b:136). For a long time, the importance of her scholarly works has been silenced, a neglect that contemporary Wildean

---

102. I embrace the definition of "proto-feminist texts" proposed by Julie Koehler, Shandi Lynne Wagner, Anne Duggan, and Adrion Dula in *Women Writing Wonder*: "texts that represent women as rational subjects endowed with equal rights under the law, in marriage, and in society at large. This includes the right to engage in the public sphere, which can take the form of publicly (even if discreetly) expressing one's opinion in print" (Koehler et al. 2021:20).

scholars such as Eleanor Fitzsimons and Eibhear Walshe have greatly contributed to redressing.

The choice of the Italian pen name "Speranza" (Hope), which Jane Wilde regarded as a "nom de guerre" (Fitzsimons 2015:22), is not a coincidence: she had always been fascinated by Italian culture, to the point of pretending to have Florentine origins. She used to assert that her family name, Elgee, was an Italianized form of Algiati, which in turn derived from Alighieri, thus imaginatively reclaiming a fictitious kinship with Dante Alighieri (Wyndham 1951:13; Fitzsimons 2015:16). In her obituary published in *Freeman's Journal* in 1896, excerpts of an interview with Wilde were reported: the unnamed interviewer commented that Italy was "one of the few themes which moves her to enthusiasm, and with her Italian origin and poetic nature it would be strange indeed if she were not eloquent regarding the land of song" (Anonymous 1896:5).[103] However, her family's genealogy reveals an entirely different history from the one she eccentrically fashioned for herself. In truth, she belonged to the privileged Anglo-Irish Protestant class, and her family was originally from County Durham: her father, Charles Elgee, was a solicitor in Dublin; her grandfather, John Elgee, was rector of Wexford; her mother, Sarah Kingsbury, daughter of the vicar of Kildare, came from a well-off family based in Dublin. In this historical period, there was a deep class divide between the autochthonous Irish population, which was largely Catholic, and the Anglo-Irish Protestant ruling class, which was in charge of all the main political, administrative, and economic positions, embodying the presence of the British Empire in Ireland.[104] Jane Wilde's conservative upbringing did not encourage her revolutionary positions, which were powered instead by her defiant personality, a distinctive trait that made her become an "aristocratic rebel" (O'Connor 1985:100). In this regard, in her obituary it is mentioned that "[h]er connections, her faith, her position in society, all seemed to forbid any sympathy with the popular movement which enveloped Ireland in the forties" (Anonymous 1896:5).

Scant details are available on Wilde's early life: her education is "something of a mystery," as Walshe observes in a study devoted to the chronological reconstruction of her life and reappraisal of her oeuvre (Walshe 2023a:14). She did not have the opportunity to pursue formal education because Trinity College Dublin, attended by her brother, did not admit women at the time

---

103. To the question whether her family was "a purely Irish one," she answered: "No, it migrated in the sixteenth century from Italy, and Elgee is an Irish corruption of the name" (Anonymous 1896:5).

104. On the Anglo-Irish Protestant Ascendancy class, see O'Connor (1985:88).

(Fitzsimons 2015:20). Nevertheless, several scholars report that she read extensively on her own from her father's library and received home tutoring under the guidance of her mother, her uncle, and private governesses (Wyndham 1951:13; Tipper 2002:355). What is certain is that she became highly competent in several languages, and was able to translate from Italian, French, Spanish, Portuguese, German, Swedish, Danish, Turkish, and Russian. As she revealed in her own words,

> I was always very fond of study and of books. My favourite study was languages; I succeeded in mastering ten of the European languages. Till my eighteenth year I never wrote anything. All my time was given to study. Then, one day, a volume of "Ireland's Library," issued from the *Nation* office by Mr Duffy, happened to come in my way. I read it eagerly, and my patriotism was kindled. (Wilde in Anonymous 1896:5)

Notwithstanding her multilingual skills, she did not learn the Irish language, and this lack of knowledge would become apparent in her folkloric writings, as will be shown in detail in the following sections of this chapter.

Jane Wilde's intellectual contributions can be divided into three main fields: poetry, translation, and nonfiction, which included political, social, folkloric, and travel writings. With respect to her poetic output, her admiration for the Young Irelanders—the so-called "men of '48"—is especially evident in the patriotic poems that she published in *The Nation*.[105] One of the often-quoted episodes of Wilde's life in this period concerns her anonymous leading article "Jacta Alea Est," published in *The Nation* on July 29, 1848, in which she fervently invited Irish people to fight against their British oppressors. The publication of the article caused a sensation: Charles Gavan Duffy stated that she provided a piece which "might be issued from the head-quarters of the national army" (Gavan Duffy 1898, I:286–87).[106] She would devote her first book of poetry, *Poems by Speranza* (1864), to Ireland.[107]

---

105. Her poetic production negotiates complex political and gender dynamics, especially given the chiefly male-centered characterization of the Young Ireland movement, the purpose of which was to "articulate the 'otherness' of Ireland around its own centre, both geographically and politically" (Lloyd 1987:3). For a reflection on the tropes of tears and blood, which reveal the affective dimension of nationalism in her poetry in terms of sentimentality, emotional engagement, and violent outbursts, see Howes (1998).

106. At the time, Gavan Duffy had been arrested and imprisoned for the political views he expressed in *The Nation*. Despite Jane Wilde's attempts to reclaim her authorship, this article, which was attributed to him, exacerbated his position.

107. On Jane Wilde's poetic production, see Ní Chuilleanáin (2003) and Walshe (2023a:21–65).

Regarding her work as a translator, her proficiency in different European languages allowed her to publish several acclaimed translations, which were crucial in making her name known in the literary world. Her first book-length translation was the German romance *Sidonia von Bork, die Klosterhexe* (1847),[108] by Pomeranian writer Wilhelm Meinhold (1797–1851), published in 1849 as *Sidonia the Sorceress: The Supposed Destroyer of the Whole Reigning Ducal House of Pomerania*. The book narrates the story of Sidonia von Bork (1548–1620), a noblewoman "accused of having by her sorceries caused sterility in many families" (Meinhold 1849:vii). Following these allegations of witchcraft, she is imprisoned, tortured, sentenced to death, and eventually brutally executed. Her sensational life rendered her a legendary femme fatale who greatly inspired British Pre-Raphaelite artists such as Edward Burne-Jones (1833–1898) and Dante Gabriel Rossetti (1828–1882), who came to know her deeds precisely thanks to Wilde's translation (Wyndham 1951:135). In a review of the book, English critic and poet Edmund Gosse (1849–1928) praised its "fervid authoress" (Gosse 1927:195), commenting on the curious trajectory of this neglected literary work: "How the attention of Speranza, Lady Wilde, was directed to it I am quite unable to report, but it is hardly a paradox to say that this German romance did not begin to exist until an Irishwoman revealed it to a select English circle" (Gosse 1927:197). Karen Tipper reports that Jane Wilde disliked the book, as evidenced in a letter she wrote to an unidentified correspondent (Tipper 2002:362). Despite this statement, and the fact that her main motivation for undertaking this endeavor was likely financial, Wilde's translation of *Sidonia von Bork* might be regarded as an early testament to her burgeoning interest in mysticism and powerful female figures, which would become apparent in her folklore anthologies.

Among her other translations, it is worth mentioning *Pictures of the First French Revolution* (1850) and *The Wanderer and His Home* (1851), by French writer Alphonse Marie Louis de Prat de Lamartine (1790–1869); *The Glacier Land* (1852), by French writer Alexandre Dumas (1802–1870); *The Future Life: Being a Relation of Things Which He Heard and Saw* (1853), by Swedish philosopher and theologian Emanuel Swedenborg (1688–1772); and *The First Temptation; or Eritis sicut Deus, a Philosophical Romance* (1863), by German writer Wilhelmine Friederike Gottliebe Canz (1815–1901).[109]

---

108. Her name is also spelled Sidonia von Borcke.

109. The reviewer of *The First Temptation* commented that in her translation Wilde did not follow "the art-process which photographs an object correctly in its outline, yet rigid and colourless, but that nature-process, which first absorbs everything into itself—then mediates, methodises, and finally reproduces the living representative. It is the rare charm of this book to the English reader that it has all the freedom of original expression of original thought; [...] the

With regard to Jane Wilde's nonfiction writing, prior to the appearance of her folklore collections, the publication of essays and articles in periodicals served as an important step for her emergence on the Irish cultural stage. Several of these writings would later be gathered for publication in her anthologies as well as in *Notes on Men, Women, and Books* (1891) and *Social Studies* (1893). Her collaboration with periodicals thus functioned as a gateway for her affirmation as a public persona.[110] She contributed to numerous journals, as she mentioned in one of her letters to editor, librarian, and biographer David James O'Donoghue (1866–1917) in 1888:

> In answer to the inquiries contained in your note I have to state that I contributed to many periodicals in London, amongst others to *The University Magazine*, *Tinsley's Magazine*, *The Burlington Magazine*, *The Woman's World*, *The Queen*, *The Lady's Pictorial*, *The Pall Mall Gazette*, and others whose names I cannot now recall. The most important writings of recent years are "Driftwood from Scandinavia" (Bentley, 1 vol., 1884), "Ancient Irish Legends" (Ward & Downey, 2 vols., 1887), *The American Irish*, a political pamphlet, Dublin. (Wilde in Tipper 2013:111–12)

In the same letter, she recounted that "[n]ationality was certainly the first awakener of any mental power of genius within me, and the strongest sentiments of my intellectual life" (Wilde in Tipper 2013:112), although at that stage of her life she was more involved in literary endeavors than political ones. Her determination in making herself known on the cultural scene of the time was characteristic of her peculiar protofeminist standpoint: alongside her nationalistic fervor, Wilde was a vigorous campaigner for women's equality, which she firmly believed could be achieved through education. In "The Bondage of Woman," one of the essays in *Social Studies* (1893), the last book she published before her death, she deplored the ignominious conditions women had to endure throughout history. She lamented that "[f]or six thousand years the history of woman has been a mournful record of helpless resignation to social prejudice and legal tyranny" (Wilde 1893:1). She thus used her nonfiction writings to articulate a sharp critique of gender inequality, showing a deep sensitivity toward women's issues. However, as Fitzsimons remarks, Wilde had a "unique brand of proto-feminism" (Fitzsimons 2015:21): if on the one hand she "campaigned vociferously for

---

subtlest skill in management of language and style makes us forget we are reading a German book through an English medium" (Anonymous 1863:69).

110. Especially in late nineteenth-century Ireland, there was a "proliferation of different kinds of newspapers, periodicals, and cultural reviews," which became a source of income for authors and a means for them to establish their names (Hutton 2011:24–25).

women to be granted access to education and the professions," on the other "she also believed that a loyal wife should accommodate any indiscretions perpetrated by her husband" (Fitzsimons 2015:ix).

In *Driftwood from Scandinavia* (1884), which Wilde alluded to in her aforementioned letter to O'Donoghue, she included her travel memoirs and translations of Scandinavian legends and ballads. In this volume, she showcased her interest in the Icelandic, Danish, and Swedish oral patrimonies (Wilde 1884:140, 187–88) and inserted pungent remarks on the political state of affairs in Ireland. For instance, she bitterly commented:

> The South Sea Islanders are better off; they, at least, have a friendly raft or hollow tree to bear them from one island to another; but we in Ireland seem now entirely without the energy to organize a line of passenger ships for ourselves, and with our splendid sea-coast, commanding the portals of both worlds, of Europe and of America, are yet wholly dependent upon England for a latch-key, should we wish to leave our island prison. (Wilde 1884:10)

These travel writings are worthy of notice not only for the observations on the countries that she visited but also for the reflections that this experience of cultural diversity had on her own understanding of the Irish struggle for independence, a topic she would return to in her folkloric collections. Interestingly, in another excerpt from *Driftwood from Scandinavia*, she lingered on the vigor of Italian pride and the resilience of the Celtic national spirit:[111]

> The world gains nothing by the fall and humiliation of any centre of civilization, nor by the annihilation of small states through the dominant force of an alien power. [...] Italy, at the Renaissance, when she gave immortal names and immortal works to the world, was but an aggregate of petty states. Yet all and each were emulous of glory under their own banner and chief; pride in their own people, and reverence for their own traditions [...]. It is cultivation, not vastness, that makes the glory of an empire or of a country. [...] The Celt always resisted dominant empires and bondage to routine, according to the instinct of all passionate, impulsive natures. (Wilde 1884:279–80)

Apart from these intriguing digressions, *Driftwood from Scandinavia* was the account of the journeys that Wilde made in her youth in northern European

---

111. This was not the first time that Wilde celebrated Italian nationalism in her writings: in 1857 she published a book of verse entitled *Ugo Bassi: A Tale of the Italian Revolution*, which narrated in metrical form the story of Ugo Bassi (1801–1849), a patriot and priest from Emilia-Romagna who fought bravely during the First Italian War of Independence and was murdered by Austrian military forces in 1849.

cities, including Copenhagen, Stockholm, and Berlin, in the company of her husband, Sir William Wilde (1815–1876), whom she married in 1851.[112] Although she was not traveling alone, she decided to adopt a first-person voice in her recollections, a remarkable narrative choice that Walshe convincingly interprets as a sign of her agency as a woman writer, at a time when travel writing represented "a radical act of self-assertion" (Walshe 2023a:78).

The Wildes used to live in a house located in 1 Merrion Square in Dublin, where Jane Wilde regularly hosted contemporary cultural figures in her literary salons.[113] In 1865 William Wilde built a country house called Moytura on the shores of Lough Corrib near Cong in County Mayo, where the Wilde family used to spend their holidays (Tipper 2002:567). Their wide-ranging involvement in the cultural life of Victorian Ireland undoubtedly "reach[ed] beyond Ireland and the question of Irish independence to interrogate parallel questions in their contemporary European cultures and societies" (Walshe 2020:2). Their interests merged in at least two fields: the first concerns the Great Famine, which is tackled scientifically in William Wilde's scholarly works and in a lyrical and patriotic manner in Jane Wilde's poetry; the second is Irish folklore, which—far from being emptied of its ideological and sociological implications—became an opportunity for the Wildes to obliquely reflect on the effects of the Great Hunger not only on Irish society but also on Irish traditions.

In the incipit to *Irish Popular Superstitions* (1852), dedicated to his wife, Speranza, William Wilde identified the key factors that provoked radical societal changes in Ireland: "the failure of the potato crop, pestilence, famine, and a most unparalleled extent of emigration, together with bankrupt landlords,

---

112. William Wilde, also known as "An Dochtiúr Mór" [The Great Doctor] (Earls 1992–93:127), authored *Narrative of a Voyage to Madeira, Tenerife and along the Shores of the Mediterranean* (1840), which inserted itself in the "burgeoning genre of medical geography and travel writing" (McGeachie 2016:304), as well as various books on Irish archaeology, topography, and ethnology such as *The Beauties of the Boyne, and Its Tributary, the Blackwater* (1849) and *Lough Corrib, Its Shores and Islands; with Notices of Lough Mask* (1867). He was a keen investigator of Irish culture and traditions and distinguished himself by cataloging Irish antiquities for the Royal Irish Academy in the three-volume *Descriptive Catalogue of the Antiquities in the Museum of the Royal Irish Academy* (1857–62). His contribution as commissioner for the Irish Census in 1851 led him to being knighted in 1864 for his service to "statistical science" (Hanberry 2011:126) and to being awarded the Cunningham Medal by the Royal Irish Academy in 1873. On William Wilde, see Wilson (1942) and Tóibín (2019).

113. For a biographical reconstruction of the key events of their lives, see Lambert (1967) and Tóibín (2019). On Jane Wilde's salons, a tradition she maintained after she moved to London and in which W. B. Yeats also participated, see Tipper (2002:359–60).

pauperizing poor laws, grinding officials, and decimating workhouses" (Wilde 1852:9–10). Through this combination of academic and civic commitment, he gave voice to the sociocultural disaster provoked by the famine and condemned the political and economic incompetence that exacerbated this disastrous event. Jane Wilde similarly blamed the British for the famine, bluntly defining them as "murderers" and exploiters in her renowned poem "The Famine Year," first published on January 23, 1847, in *The Nation*. The British dominion over the Irish is described in strongly derogatory terms, resorting to biblical imagery and metaphors that make the denunciation of their irresponsible ineptitude and criminal inaction reverberate:

> Accursed are we in our own land, yet toil we still and toil;
> But the stranger reaps our harvest—the alien owns our soil.
> [...] A ghastly, spectral army, before the great God we'll stand,
> And arraign ye as our murderers, the spoilers of our land.
> (Wilde 1864:6–7)

Wilde expressed a cry for the freedom of Ireland from the conditions of poverty, starvation, isolation, and distress that characterized it in the mid-nineteenth century. The devastation brought about by the Great Hunger had direct consequences on the country's language and traditions. In an attempt to delay the demise of local lore, William Wilde took all the opportunities he could to record beliefs and traditional artifacts, not only during his frequent explorations of the west of Ireland but also from his own patients as a form of remuneration when they were unable to pay him.[114]

In William Wilde's *Memoir of Gabriel Beranger* (1880), a volume published posthumously in honor of professional Dutch artist Gabriel Beranger (1725–1817), who devoted his art to Irish antiquities, Jane Wilde inserted a "loving tribute to the character, the mind and the heart" of her husband (Walshe 2023a:106). She commented at length on William Wilde's ability to gather knowledge on

---

114. In this regard, Ulick O'Connor reported that "when [Sir William Wilde] was offered presents of butter and fowl by peasants in return for medical assistance he would often ask that a piece of poetry or folklore be recited instead" (O'Connor 1985:100). These unofficial exchanges between doctor and patients were also implemented by Giuseppe Pitrè in Sicily, who used to retrieve oral narratives from the patients who needed his assistance. Pitrè had ingeniously equipped his *calesse* (buggy) with a small desk and filled it with his papers, so that he could read and write while on the way to visit his patients (Cocchiara 1951:171; Manzo 1999:9; Zipes 2009a:3). Contrary to Jane Wilde, who could not speak any Irish, it is likely that William Wilde knew Modern Irish (Wright 2008:18). Tipper is more cautious in this regard and reported that "he may also have been able to converse in Gaelic—though only to write it phonetically" (Tipper 2002:529).

a variety of topics and provided details of his philanthropic relationship with the peasantry, among whom he "was peculiarly loved and trusted, for he had brought back joy and hope to many households"; in return for his generosity as a doctor, "they were ever glad to aid him in his search for antiquities, [...] and in this way many valuable relics were saved from loss" (Wilde 1880:141).

Apprehension regarding the "rapid decay of our Irish vernacular, in which most of our legends, romantic tales, ballads, and bardic annals, the vestiges of Pagan rites, and the relics of fairy charms were preserved" (Wilde 1852:10–11) recasts the widespread idea of the impending threat that oral traditions were facing. This "'last-minute rescue' theme" (Zimmermann 2001:288) was common among nineteenth-century folklorists and antiquarians. However, skepticism toward the alleged immortalization of oral lore by writing it down is evident in William Wilde's assertions in *Irish Popular Superstitions* such as "nothing contributes more to uproot superstitious rites and forms than to print them" (Wilde 1852:vi). In other words, the act of transcription, albeit necessary and valuable, was at times seen as "producing a death certificate in the form of a folklore collection" (Killeen 2013:188). In William Wilde's view, "the spread of education, and the introduction of railroads, colleges, industrial and other educational schools" were contributing to the disappearance of folklore (Wilde 1852:10). It was thus implied that the condition of illiteracy was a hallmark of the so-called *"poetry of the people,* the bond that knit the peasant to the soil" (Wilde 1852:11; original emphasis). Jane Wilde echoed her husband's anxiety when she identified progress and emigration as two of the concomitant causes that could eventually lead to the vanishing of these deep-rooted beliefs:

> In a few years such a collection would be impossible, for the old race is rapidly passing away to other lands, and in the vast working-world of America, with all the new influences of light and progress, the young generation, though still loving the land of their fathers, will scarcely find leisure to dream over the fairy-haunted hills and lakes and raths of ancient Ireland. (Wilde 1887a, I:vii)

The ideological relationship between literate people and the masses in late nineteenth-century Ireland is reflected in Jane Wilde's review of *Irish Minstrelsy: Being a Selection of Irish Songs, Lyrics, and Ballads* (1888), a collection of Irish songs by Henry Halliday Sparling (1860–1924), published in *Pall Mall Gazette* on November 29, 1887:

> The utterance of a people, though always vehement, is often incoherent, and then it is that the *men of education and culture are needed to interpret and formulate the vague longings and ambitions of the passionate hearts around.*

[...] For music and song are part of the life of the people; they give a glow to the stormy twilight of their troubled lives, and strength to bear the tragic terrors of a bitter destiny. [...] Nothing really good in a nation's life is ever lost. [...] [T]he people will never now go back to the servile bondage of the soul and spirit that held them enchained before the fetters were rent and the bonds broken by *the genius and intellectual force, the lofty teaching and the cadenced words of the men of '48*. (Wilde 1887b:3; my emphasis)[115]

Reviews of works such as Sparling's *Irish Minstrelsy* became a vehicle for Wilde to voice her opinions in the public sphere. In her view, it was only through the efforts of intellectuals that the creativity of the masses could be freed and coherently reformulated; educated men and women were therefore conceived as an essential intermediary to elaborate the words of the common people. Her "sguardo aristocratico"[116] (Binelli et al. 2017:287) was omnipresent in her writings: hierarchical structures were not challenged but rather reinforced in the inevitability of their existence. As a result, peasants were quasidehumanized and endowed with a spiritual aura, embodying "the imaginative and mystical bearers of a sort of *docta ignorantia*" (Pulido 1998:219), which Wilde wished to rescue from oblivion in her folklore collections as a way to aid the making of the Irish nation.

The National Heart of the "Uncultured Mind": Ancient Legends *and* Ancient Cures

Jane Wilde's contributions to Irish lore appeared at the end of the 1880s: she edited the folkloric materials previously gathered by her husband and merged them into two assemblages of traditional narratives in 1887 and in 1890 (Melville 1994:199). The two-volume *Ancient Legends, Mystic Charms, and Superstitions of Ireland, with Sketches of the Irish Past* (1887) and *Ancient Cures, Charms, and Usages of Ireland: Contributions to Irish Lore* (1890) were published when she had already moved to London following her husband's death. She was therefore in her mid-sixties when she decided to bequeath these materials to a wider readership. She did not explicitly give credit to her husband for the traditions published in *Ancient Legends* (Walshe 2023a:115). However, W. B. Yeats, who knew her personally, wrote that they were gathered by her husband, possibly with the help of other collectors (Yeats 2004 [1890]:114). A further hint at the provenance of these traditions can be found in the previously mentioned

---

115. This review was then expanded and included in Wilde's collection of folklore *Ancient Cures, Charms, and Usages of Ireland* (1890:169–79).

116. "aristocratic gaze."

volume *Memoir of Gabriel Beranger* (1880), published by Jane Wilde after her husband's death. In the final part of this book, she mentioned that William Wilde had left many "fragments of works" in manuscript form, including a second volume of "Irish Fairy Lore" and "a vast amount of material collected from all parts of the country, many of the strange wild tales being graphically narrated by some eye-witness of evidently intense faith, and forwarded to Sir William by the believing narrator" (Wilde 1880:140). She went on asking rhetorically:

> But who will now finish these half-written works? Who is ever able to take up with the necessary care and precision the threads of another's life-labours, and continue to weave the warp and woof as he would have woven it, fulfilling the idea with all the individuality of thought and form that gave life and colour to his work? (Wilde 1880:140)

It is plausible that the fragments of fairy lore evoked in this passage were the sources that she would eventually include in her collections. Her folklore anthologies are thus emblematic of the husband-wife joint textual collaborations that frequently make it difficult to establish the merits of each individual. If in anthropological and ethnographic writings it is common to find professional couples in which men "who benefited materially from the ethnographic and other labor of their wives mention them in their book acknowledgments or footnotes" (Tedlock 1995:270), in the case of Jane Wilde's folkloric collections there was a role reversal, as she was the one who relied on the fieldwork writings gathered by her husband.

While there is no proof that her son Oscar Wilde helped her in this task, despite suggestions that he may have done so (Wright 2008:19; Markey 2011:43), it is undeniable that he inherited his parents' fascination with Irish folklore. In *De Profundis*, an abridged version of a long letter that Oscar Wilde wrote in 1897 to Lord Alfred Douglas (1870–1945),[117] he mentioned that his parents bestowed on him "a name they had made noble and honoured, not merely in literature, art, archaeology, and science, but in the public history of my own country, in its evolution as a nation" (Wilde 1905:3). However, his own attitude toward folklore greatly differed from his mother's nationalistic and mystical perspective and his father's chiefly antiquarian and sociological interest. In the same years when his mother was working on these folklore collections, Oscar Wilde published two well-known anthologies of fairy tales

---

117. This abridged version was first published by Robert Ross (1869–1918) in 1905. An accurate and complete reproduction of the letter can be found in Holland and Hart-Davis (2000:683–780).

that had a lasting influence on the history of the fairy tale as a literary genre, *The Happy Prince and Other Tales* (1888) and *A House of Pomegranates* (1891). Yet the direct connections with Irish folklore in these tales are mostly "elusive, slippery, ghostly traces" (Killeen 2013:191).[118] It is also worth noting that Constance Wilde (1858–1898), Oscar's wife, née Lloyd, was writing in the same period *There Was Once: Grandma's Stories* (1888), a children's book that contained her retellings of classic fairy tales.[119] Interest in folklore and fairy tales was thus shared among members of the Wilde family.

Jane Wilde's first collection, *Ancient Legends*, predominantly contained so-called *síscéalta*, narratives on fairy folk, and detailed the vast array of supernatural creatures that distinguish Irish folklore as well as beliefs related to Irish festivities. The collection ended with a chapter by the late William Wilde on "The Ancient Races of Ireland" (Wilde 1887a,II:339–70, II:339–70). She was working on the compilation of this collection in 1886, as testified by the letter she wrote on June 26, 1886, to the publishers Kegan Paul:

> I take the liberty of enquiring of you whether you would allow me to forward a manuscript for your opinion as to publication, entitled "Legends & Superstitions of Ireland with Sketches of the Irish Past." It would form one large volume or might be made into two—and a great deal of interesting material is included collected chiefly amongst the Western Irish. (Wilde in Tipper 2013:110–11)

Several of the essays and tales that were then included in her anthology, such as the lengthy introduction and its first two tales, originally appeared in *Dublin University Magazine* under the title "The Fairy Mythology of Ireland" in 1877. The journal editor, Keningale Cook, in a letter written to Oscar Wilde on July 21, 1877, wrote that Jane Wilde's article "receives very pleasant attention" (Cook in Mason 1914:68), an interest that she would capitalize on ten years later with the publication of her first folklore collection.

---

118. On Oscar Wilde's relationship with the Irish folkloric tradition, which he regarded as a lower cultural form that had the potential to generate art and inspire creative genius, see Upchurch (1992), Pine (1995), Toomey (1998), and Markey (2011:51–57). On the cultural legacy bequeathed by his parents, see Ryder (2013). On Oscar Wilde's Irishness, see Ní Fhlathúin (1999).

119. Some of her children's stories were also included in *The Bairn's Annual of Old Fashioned Fairy Tales* (1887), *The Favourite Nursery Stories* (1890), *A Long Time Ago: Favourite Stories Retold by Mrs. Oscar Wilde and Others* (1892), *A Cosy Corner and Other Stories* (1893), and *A Dandy Chair and Other Stories* (1893). For a reconstruction of Constance Lloyd's life and works, see Moyle (2011) and Fitzsimons (2015). For a fictional account of her life, see Guglielmi (2021).

The publishing house that eventually accepted her two volumes under the title of *Ancient Legends* was Ward & Downey, which would also later publish her nonfiction books *Notes on Men, Women, and Books* (1891) and *Social Studies* (1893). Alongside her passion for popular culture, one of Jane Wilde's motivations for rearranging and publishing this folkloric material was her need for income after her husband's death and the urge to cope with the financial difficulties the family endured.[120]

Between the publication of *Ancient Legends* and her subsequent compendium *Ancient Cures*, Wilde published Irish folktales in the magazine *The Woman's World*, previously titled *The Lady's World*, when her son Oscar was already editor in chief.[121] These "Irish peasant tales," including "St. Patrick and the Witch," "A Night with the Fairies," "A Legend of Shark," "The Doctor's Visit," "Fairy Help," and "The Western Isles," were then incorporated in *Ancient Cures* (Wilde 1890:93–96, 135–57). Chiefly focused on how to cure earthly diseases, the anthology *Ancient Cures* (1890) also listed spells, charms, and traditions related to local festivals and peasant games as well as other supernatural legends. At the end of the volume, Wilde included disquisitions on a variety of topics, such as "Ancient Irish Gold," "Primitive Man," "The New Races," and "The American Irish," among others (Wilde 1890:179–244).

Despite the unfeasibility of retracing the editorial changes and authorial interventions that Jane Wilde implemented, it is nevertheless possible to discern her attitude toward the Irish folkloric past as the collections abound with her own thoughts on this subject. Wilde left a tangible mark in the arrangement of these volumes, especially within the paratextual spaces that frame the narratives such as prefaces and introductions, which not only aim

---

120. From a letter Jane Wilde received on August 1, 1888, from Ward & Downey, it can be deduced that she was asking for a percentage of the royalties from *Ancient Legends* that the London publisher had sold to the American publisher Ticknor & Co.; however, the book did not sell well. As the publisher specified, "only 355 copies" were sold (Tipper 2013:197). It is worth mentioning that the Wildes had to face several challenges during their marital life, especially in the aftermath of a scandal related to a trial that took place in 1864. In that year, William Wilde was accused by his former patient Mary Travers to have assaulted her, and Jane Wilde was sued for libel for a letter she wrote to Travers's father, a case that received sensational media coverage at the time (Walshe 2023a:91–97). For a fictional reconstruction of the scandal, see Eibhear Walshe's historical novel *The Diary of Mary Travers* (2014).

121. In 1887 Oscar Wilde became the editor of *The Woman's World*, a journal that, in his own words, aimed "at being the organ of women of intellect, culture, and position" (Wilde's letter to Wemyss Reid, September 5, 1887, reported in Holland and Hart-Davis 2000:317–18). On Oscar Wilde's editorship of *The Woman's World*, see Clayworth (1997) and Fitzsimons (2015:159–73).

at captivating readers but also at "attribut[ing] high value to a subject by demonstrating its importance" (Genette 1997 [1987]:199). With regard to *Ancient Legends*, it has been noted that her "introduction to the book was a book in itself" (Melville 1994:199).

In the preface to her first collection, Wilde clarified that her interest in folklore and ancient Irish beliefs did not represent for her an uncritical and vain refuge in the past nor a means to escape the reality of her times and the political ferment that pervaded Irish society:

> I must disclaim, however, all desire to be considered a melancholy *Laudatrix temporis acti*. These studies of the Irish past are simply the expression of my love for the beautiful island that gave me my first inspiration, my quickest intellectual impulses, and the strongest and best sympathies with genius and country possible to a woman's nature. (Wilde 1887a, I:vii)

In this conscious declaration of intent, Wilde made clear that her love for Ireland, which had previously ignited her lively adherence to the Irish nationalist movement, inspired her research and publications on popular tales and beliefs. With regard to the origins of these narratives, she asserted that they were "obtained chiefly from oral communications made by the peasantry themselves, either in Irish on in the Irish-English which preserves so much of the expressive idiom of the antique tongue" (Wilde 1887a, I:vii). However, she did not indicate the names of the informants, nor did she specify who collected them; in fact, she rather vaguely reported that they came directly "from the national heart" and "were taken down by competent persons skilled in both languages, and as far as possible in the very words of the narrator" (Wilde 1887a, I:vii).

There is a substantial difference between the approaches to folklore implemented by Jane and William Wilde in their respective collections. Lady Wilde "focused less on material conditions than on the spiritual dimension of traditional narratives, beliefs and practices" (Markey 2011:43), as she herself highlighted in the introduction to *Ancient Legends* when describing the qualities of Irish fairies:

> All the solitudes of the island were peopled by these bright, happy, beautiful beings, and to the Irish nature, with its need of the spiritual, its love of the vague, mystic, dreamy, and supernatural, there was something irresistibly fascinating in the belief that gentle spirits were around, filled with sympathy for the mortal who suffered wrong or needed help. (Wilde 1887a, I:10)

Her extensive knowledge of traditional narratives was based on the premise that "the proper appreciation of a country's past is best derived from an appreciation of its language, mythology and ancient monuments" (Wyndham

1951:163–64). However, if Sir Wilde's method was essentially anthropological and scientific, Lady Wilde's venture into folklore was driven by her curiosity toward the "mystic relation between the material and the spiritual world" and the "unseen agencies that influence all human life" (Wilde 1887a, I:vi).

With regard to her methodology as a compiler, what is striking from the outset is the absence of a coherent organizing principle in the assemblage of the narratives both in *Ancient Legends* and *Ancient Cures*, which contain items that are haphazardly gathered into repetitive thematic sections. Such incoherence, which was not unusual in nineteenth-century collections, may be explained by her distinctive approach to folklore. She did not see legends with the eyes of the scientific folklorist but rather gave shape to them with the voice of a poet, attracted above all by "the mytho-poetic faculty" that survived only "in children, poets, and the child-like races, like the Irish—simple, joyous, reverent, and unlettered" (Wilde 1887a, I:11).

Rather than attempting to position herself as an objective scholar speaking from a detached viewpoint, Wilde imbued the collections with her personal voice and subjective commentary, which understandably led to several methodological critiques both at the time of publication and by contemporary scholars. Douglas Hyde's words left no space for doubt in this respect: in his introduction to *Beside the Fire*, he highlighted that, despite providing "a large amount of narrative matter in a folk-lore dress," her collections were devoid of a systematic approach to the subject matter and showed a significant lack of knowledge of the Irish language (Hyde 1890:xiii). He nonetheless praised her as a "gifted compiler" of folklore:

> [L]ike her predecessors, she disdains to quote an authority, and scorns to give us the least inkling as to where such-and-such a legend, or cure, or superstition comes from, from whom it was obtained, who were her informants, whether peasant or other, [...] and all the other collateral information which the modern folk-lorist is sure to expect. [...] Lady Wilde's volumes are, nevertheless, a wonderful and copious record of folk-lore and folk customs, which must lay Irishmen under one more debt of gratitude to the *gifted compiler*. (Hyde 1890:xiii–xiv; my emphasis)

The greatest limitation of Wilde's collections lies in the difficulty of establishing the extent to which she participated in rewriting this wide-ranging assemblage of folk narratives, many of which are set in the Irish western islands. Nevertheless, more recent reassessments of Wilde's collections are less critical than Hyde's perspective. For instance, Irish poet and scholar Eiléan Ní Chuilleanáin highlights the indebtedness of women poets to Wilde's folkloric writings and remarks how they reveal "not naivety but the depth and variety of Irish tradition" (Ní Chuilleanáin 2003:31).

If Hyde expressed a critical stance that emphasized Wilde's inaccuracies, W. B. Yeats's response to her first folklore collection was diametrically opposed. In *Fairy and Folk Tales of the Irish Peasantry* (1888), he commented that the best collection after Thomas Crofton Croker's *Fairy Legends and Traditions of the South of Ireland* was precisely Wilde's *Ancient Legends*: "The humour has all given way to pathos and tenderness. We have here the innermost heart of the Celt [...]. Here is the Celt, only it is the Celt dreaming" (Yeats 1888:xv). Yeats's allusion to the "Celt dreaming" hints at the conceptualization of the Celt proposed by Matthew Arnold (1822–1888), who underscored the spiritual, sentimental, and feminine essence of the Celt in contrast with the "disciplinable and steadily obedient" Anglo-Saxon (Arnold 1867:83), thereby contributing to the exoticizing process of the creation of a Celtic identity that Ernest Renan (1823–1892) had initiated in "La Poésie des races celtiques" (1854).[122]

Yeats's admiration for Wilde's collection is not surprising. His interest in the usage of folklore for literary purposes and as a gateway toward a transcendental world coincides with her inquisitiveness toward those who lived "under the shadow and dread of invisible powers which [...] are awful and mysterious to the uncultured mind" (Wilde 1887a, I:vi–vii). In his review of *Ancient Cures* published in the *Scots Observer* on March 1, 1890, Yeats welcomed with positive words this new volume of Irish proverbs, cures, and folktales, although he also admitted its flaws: "I heartily wish they had been better and more scientifically treated, but I scarce know whom to blame: Lady Wilde, Sir William Wilde, his collectors, or the big box" (Yeats 2004 [1890]:114). With "big box," Yeats was referring to the box that contained the folkloric material previously collected by William Wilde from Irish peasants.[123] Yeats disapproved of the arid treatment of folk traditions that were increasingly being dissected by modern folklorists, as evidenced by his passionate—and apologetic—description of the work of Irish collectors, suspended between art and science:

> The various collectors of Irish folk-lore have, from our point of view, one great merit, and from the point of view of others, one great fault. *They have*

---

122. On Celticism, see Brown (2001:62–64) and Garrigan Mattar (2004). On the mythical construction of the Celt as a "figure of otherness," see Chapman (1992:228).

123. As hinted at earlier, W. B. Yeats reported that "[i]n addition to the peasants [William Wilde] regularly employed to glean the stubble of tradition for him, he got many things from patients at his Dublin hospital; for when grateful patients would offer to send him geese or eggs or butter, he would bargain for a fragment of folk-lore instead. He threw all his gatherings into a big box, and thence it is that Lady Wilde has quarried the materials of her new book: a farrago of spells, cures, fairy-tales, and proverbs—these last beyond price—the districts seldom specified and the dates of discovery never" (Yeats 2004 [1890]:113–14).

made their work literature rather than science, and told us of the Irish peasantry rather than of the primitive religion of mankind, or whatever else these folk-lorists are on the gad after. To be considered scientists they should have tabulated all their tales in forms like grocers' bills—item the fairy king, item the queen. Instead of this *they have caught the very voice of the people, the very pulse of life*, each giving what was most noticed in his day. (Yeats 1888:xiv; my emphasis)

Yeats identified in the legends and beliefs of the Irish peasantry the presence of "half a visionary fatalism" (Yeats 2004 [1890]:116), in which melancholy retains its own aesthetic value and never degrades into bleak pessimism. His fascination for the occult forces that distinguish Irish traditions is in line with the spirit that animates Wilde's folklore collections, despite their inaccuracies. The review of *Ancient Cures* by *The Athenaeum* highlighted the lack of precision in her work as the various cures and charms were "merely jotted down in a disconnected manner" and there was no mention "of the why and wherefore of the absurd cures and charms she has collected" (Anonymous 1890:398). Likewise, Reverend Percy Myles's review of *Ancient Cures* published in *The Academy* brought to the fore the incongruencies of Lady Wilde's volume:

> Everything which real students most desire—mention of authorities, local touches, chronological and topographical details; anything that would render it possible to separate genuine ancient legend from modern invention or artistic embellishment—all these are either carelessly omitted or carefully suppressed. (Myles 1890:266)

Such a critique stresses once again the different position that writers and folklorists were expected to embrace before these oral traditions: it was natural for writers to "alter and adapt" them, since "[f]rom the novelists [...] we cannot expect scientific accuracy"; however, such alterations and adaptations were unacceptable from a scholarly point of view: "with a professed collector of folk-lore such imaginative treatment of the old stories becomes almost a literary crime" (Myles 1890:320).[124]

---

124. In this respect, it is worth remembering the letter written by mythologist and orientalist Max Müller (1823–1900) to Giuseppe Pitrè, dated October 19, 1881, which the Sicilian folklorist reproduced in the incipit of the first volume of *ASTP* in 1882. In this letter, Müller highlighted the importance of collecting old tales as faithfully as possible, "colle *ipsissima verba* del narratore" [with the very same words of the narrator]. With a tinge of irony, he went as far as to suggest that "un collettore, il quale ritocchi e abbellisca una novella, andrebbe frustato; un uomo poi che inventa una novella e la pubblica per genuina, andrebbe fucilato" [a collector who retouches and embellishes a tale should be whipped; a man who invents a tale and publishes it as genuine should be shot] (Müller 1882:7). On Müller, see Cocchiara (2016 [1952]:275–91).

In this "earnest appeal for the reverent handling" of such remnants (Myles 1890:320), the reviewer encapsulated the heated debates that were animating the discipline of folklore studies: folklorists were increasingly concerned with issues of authenticity not merely as a tangential label of sorts to affix to folklore collections, but also as an ethical matter linked to the respect for oral traditions and the ensuing necessity to implement the most accurate standards conceivable in their transcription. W. B. Yeats's skeptical attitude toward the rigorous classification of folklore in an attempt to justify Wilde's unmethodical approach was thus frowned upon since he went "out of his way to gibe at the honest folklorist who tells what he has actually heard, not what he thinks he might have heard, or what he thinks his audience would like to hear" (Myles 1890:266).[125]

Italo Calvino, in his review of the 1981 Italian edition of W. B. Yeats's fairy tales translated by Mariagiovanna Andreolli and Melita Cataldi, rhetorically asked:

> Ma apparterranno proprio al folklore queste leggende, o non piuttosto alle manipolazioni romantiche o preromantiche tra Sette e Ottocento? Credo che per l'Irlanda soprattutto sia difficile dire fin dove arrivano le tradizioni popolari spontanee e fin dove le trasfigurazioni letterarie in chiave nazionalista, destinate a diventare tradizioni popolari a loro volta. (Calvino 1981:14)[126]

In this review, Calvino lingered at length on the tale of the bard Seanchan, drawn by Yeats from Wilde's "Seanchan the Bard and the King of the Cats" (Wilde 1887a, II:24–30), which the Italian fabulist interpreted as "un apologo sui rapporti tra intellettuali e potere" (Calvino 1981:14).[127] While acknowledging the stratification of these tales and the complex refraction of ancient mores and values that they afford to contemporary readers, the doubt remains whether these stories are indeed folklore or "fakelore," which eventually turns into folklore.[128]

---

125. Interestingly, in the issue of *The Academy* published on October 11, 1890, Yeats felt the need to reply to this remark in an eloquent piece titled "Poetry and Science in Folk-lore": "The man of science is too often a person who has exchanged his soul for a formula; and when he captures a folk-tale, nothing remains with him for all his trouble but a wretched lifeless thing with the down rubbed off and a pin thrust through its once all-living body. I object to the 'honest folk-lorist' not because his versions are accurate, but because they are inaccurate, or rather incomplete. What lover of Celtic lore has not been filled with a sacred rage when he came upon some exquisite story, dear to him from childhood, written out in newspaper English and called science?" (Yeats 1890:320).

126. "But do these legends belong to folklore, or rather to the romantic or pre-romantic manipulations between the eighteenth and nineteenth centuries? I believe that especially for Ireland it is difficult to draw a line between the spontaneous popular traditions and the nationalist literary transfigurations, destined to become in turn popular traditions."

127. "an apologue on the relationship between intellectuals and power."

128. The concept of "fakelore" refers to the creation of nongenuine stories that are presented as if derived from an authentic cultural tradition (Dorson 1976).

Jane Wilde's collections were not devoid of allusions to theories that were circulating at the time in the field of folklore studies. In the preface to *Ancient Legends*, she insisted at length on the resemblance of Irish tales to other cultural traditions, supporting diffusionist theories on the origins of all cultures and languages from a "central parent stock" deriving from the East, commenting that "[t]o reconstruct the primal creed and language of humanity from these scattered and broken fragments, is the task which is now exciting so keenly the energies of the ardent and learned ethnographers of Europe" (Wilde 1887a, I:2). In developing her pseudoscientific discourse that aimed at reinforcing the necessity of studying Ireland—the land where "the last wave of the great Iranian migration finally settled," and the language of which was "nearer to Sanskrit than any other of the living and spoken languages of Europe" (Wilde 1887a, I:5–6)—Wilde was implicitly referring to the theories of orientalists such as Theodor Benfey (1809–1881). Benfey was a German scholar specializing in Sanskrit who edited the Indian collection of animal fables *Pantschatantra: Fünf Bücher indischer Fabeln, Märchen und Erzählungen* (1859) and published a history of linguistics and oriental philology, *Geschichte der Sprachwissenschaft und orientalischen Philologie in Deutschland* (1869), giving new impetus to scholars who were researching the migrations of folktales.[129] However, while Benfey argued for the origins of folktales from India, Wilde located Iran at the heart of her discourse on the origins of ancient mythology and polarized such concepts by taking "the idea of a 'diffusion' of folklore to such extremes that it became laughable: she insisted that all Irish culture was originally Persian, that even such stage-Irish expressions as 'arrah' were Middle Eastern" (Garrigan Mattar 2004:46). To strengthen the exceptionalism of Ireland and its traditions, she vehemently highlighted the unchangeability of the Irish compared to other cultures, which was even stronger in the Irish insular contexts: "All other countries have been repeatedly overwhelmed by alien tribes and peoples and races, but the Irish have remained unchanged" (Wilde 1887a, I:7). Furthermore, she interspersed her reflections with comments on the distinctive cultural and physical traits of the Irish, including detailed explanations of how the supposedly oval and slender shape of the Irish head differed from "the globular Teutonic head," offering it as a proof of the Irish instinctual poetic and musical leanings (Wilde 1887a, I:279).

Entangled in a process of "inverted ethnocentrism" aimed at reevaluating the wild and irrational qualities usually attributed to the Celtic people (Zimmermann 2001:591), Wilde was attempting to upend the racist prejudices that the Irish had to endure across the centuries even though she herself was

---

129. On nineteenth-century Indo-European linguistic studies, see Davies (1994:172–79).

relying on stereotypical imagery in order to emphasize their uniqueness from an anti-imperialist perspective, following the path traced by Arnold's disquisition on the different nature of the Celt and the Anglo-Saxon.[130] Such discourses aimed at counterbalancing an extremely negative and deeply racist portrayal of the Irish, who were often depicted as inferior, animal-like creatures in nineteenth-century journals. In this regard, Lewis Perry Curtis remarked that "[t]here is no more vivid example of the equation which some Englishmen made between apes, savages, and Irishmen than some of the cartoons on Irish affairs in *Punch*" (Curtis 1968:59), a British satirical magazine in which the Irish were frequently represented as grotesque beings to stress their otherness and monstrosity.[131]

However, Jane Wilde, though inspired by contemporary racialized anthropological discourses, did not wish to reach these conclusions. Her anti-British position was even more vocal in *Ancient Cures*, in which she openly accused England of having colonized and persecuted Ireland, albeit without succeeding in destroying the Irish spirit, qualities and culture that would allow the Emerald Isle to resurrect with the support of its people.[132] An urge to create a sense of national belonging in Ireland can also be detected in the works of Augusta Gregory, who, as will be elucidated in the following section, shared a similar upper-class background with Jane Wilde but devoted herself to the practice of folklore collection with a decidedly more accurate and methodical gaze.

Augusta Gregory: A Visionary Collector in the West of Ireland

Lady Augusta Gregory, née Isabella Augusta Persse in 1852 to a large family of Anglo-Irish landlords in Roxborough, County Galway, personally collected the raw material that led to her various folkloric collections, which reveal a growing awareness of scientific approaches to folklore. She thus emerges as a key figure not only for her well-known role as a playwright and co-founder of

---

130. On the racial stereotypes that prevailed at the time, see also Brown (1988) and Cheng (1995).

131. The sketch "The Irish Frankenstein," by John Tenniel (1820–1914), is emblematic of the racist humor in vogue: the English illustrator portrayed an Irish man as a monster of gargantuan proportions holding a blood-dripping knife, titling the cartoon after Mary Shelley's eponymous novel. For a reproduction of the sketch, see Curtis (1968:60).

132. The articulation of her racist views would eventually lead her to proclaim the superiority of both the "Teuton, grave, wise and industrious" and the "Celt, brilliant, powerful and proud" in *Social Studies* (1893:170), influenced by white-supremacist prejudices (Mendelssohn 2018:205–8; Ó Giolláin 2022:281).

the Abbey Theatre but also for her lifelong commitment to delving into popular narratives and igniting the Irish Renaissance.[133] The relationship between Irish women writers and nationalist ideals during the Gaelic Revival was complex, since politics intervened in the cultural manifestations of the time in intricate ways (Ingman and Ó Gallchoir 2018:7). In this regard, in spite of traditionally being deemed a mere facilitator of the revival and therefore lacking her own creative genius (Fogarty 2000:101), Gregory's literary, theatrical, and folkloric production became essential for the construction of the Irish nation. Undeniably, Gregory herself partook in this process of concealment: as Judith Hill notes, "she believed that women should put men first, or at least be seen to, and so she concealed some of her successes and made her presence felt indirectly" (Hill 2005:ix). Notwithstanding this self-imposed discretion, her life itself serves as a testament to women's complex and at times contradictory position in Irish society as well as to the roles that soft skills such as leadership and management had in advancing a cultural and political vision of Ireland. Furthermore, as Hill points out, Gregory "needs to be understood as a cutting-edge folklorist, who realised the need to present the voices of her interviewees in as unmediated a way as possible" (Hill 2005:xi).

Gregory's folkloric output was disseminated in the following four volumes, which will be explored in greater detail in the next section of this chapter: *Poets and Dreamers: Studies and Translations from the Irish* (1903), *The Kiltartan History Book* (1909), *The Kiltartan Wonder Book* (1910), and *Visions and Beliefs in the West of Ireland* (1920). Additionally, she published translations from Irish in *The Kiltartan Poetry Book: Prose Translations from the Irish* (1919). She also assembled translations and rewritings of myths in *Gods and Fighting Men: The Story of the Tuatha de Danaan and of the Fianna of Ireland* (1904), *A Book of Saints and Wonders* (1906), and in an acclaimed book focused on the heroic warrior of the Ulster cycle Cú Chulainn, *Cuchulain of Muirthemne: The Story of the Men of the Red Branch of Ulster* (1902).[134] Her exploration of folklore not only became a source of inspiration but also lent depth to her plays: "as the people she spoke to visited springs for water or cures so she went to the epigrammatic, tight, many-layered folk stories for language, insights and themes" (Hill 2005:199).

---

133. The bibliography on Gregory's plays and on her endeavors in establishing and giving prominence to the Abbey Theatre is rich: in this regard, see for instance Kiberd (1995:83–96), Waters (1995), Bowles (1999), Reynolds (2018), and Remport (2018).

134. The volume was based on both oral traditions and previously written sources, including Standish James O'Grady's *History of Ireland: The Heroic Period* (1878) and Standish Hayes O'Grady's *Silva Gadelica* (1892). On Gregory's translations into Hiberno-English, which were often diminished and criticized, see Cronin (1996:139–40).

Together with her sisters, Augusta Gregory received an informal education at home through English governesses during her childhood (Coxhead 1961:10–11). Mary Sheridan, "an Irish-speaking, folktale-telling, staunchly Catholic nationalist with rebel tendencies" (Broderick 2001:32), was her nurse, a traditionally central figure for the transmission of cultural heritage and language.[135] Gregory described her as a "wrinkled and half blind" woman who used to walk around "barefoot through her lifetime" (Gregory 2006 [1920]:50). Sheridan was crucial in acquainting the young Augusta with the ancient stories of the Irish tradition and in arousing her sympathetic interest toward the Irish lower classes (McDiarmid and Waters 1996:xiv). In her dedication of *Cuchulain of Muirthemne* to the people of Kiltartan, the barony in County Galway where she grew up, Gregory paid homage to the woman who first introduced her to Irish lore when commenting on her stylistic decisions as a translator: "I have told the whole story in plain and simple words, in the same way my old nurse Mary Sheridan used to be telling stories from the Irish long ago" (Gregory 1903b:vi). From an early age, she became familiar with the popular Irish tunes by Thomas Moore (1779–1852) in *Irish Melodies* (1808–1834); her favorite was "Let Erin remember the days of old," an early sign of her interest for Irish traditions:

> A little later I came to know other verses, ballads nearer to the tradition of the country than Moore's faint sentiment. For a romantic love of country had awakened in me, perhaps through the wide beauty of my home, from whose hillsides I could see the mountain of Burren and Iar Connacht, and at sunset the silver western sea; or it maybe through the half revealed sympathy of my old nurse for the rebels whose cheering she remembered when the French landed at Killala in '98; or perhaps but through the natural breaking of a younger child of the house from the conservatism of her elders. (Gregory 1919:3–4)[136]

Gregory's visceral connection with the countryside would become a leitmotif in her autobiographical and folkloric writings. She soon expressed a desire to learn Irish, which was hindered by her family; nonetheless, she never desisted from her intent: at first she hoped "to take lessons from an old Scripture-reader who spent a part of his time in the parish of Killinane," whose teachings were based on "the only book then being printed in Irish, the Bible"; however, her proposal, "timid with the fear of mockery, was unheeded" (Gregory 1919:8).

---

135. On Mary Sheridan, see also Hill (2005:13–14).

136. Gregory was alluding to the French expedition in 1798 to Killala, in County Mayo, mentioned in chapter 1. On this historical event, see Beiner (2004; 2007).

Learning the autochthonous language was not only an essential skill to be able to understand and interact with local native speakers; it was also a defiant act: as Elizabeth Coxhead highlights, "she was a rebel against the family thought and traditions; not a flamboyant rebel, but a quiet, dogged, persistent one" (Coxhead 1961:5).

When she visited Italy in 1879 in the company of her mother and brother, she met her future husband, Sir William Gregory (1816–1892), for the first time.[137] He was a middle-aged landlord who owned an estate in Coole Park near Gort in County Galway. He had distinguished himself during his life as governor of Ceylon and as a liberal political figure who encouraged Augusta Gregory's "own liberal attitudes" (Adams 1973:23). After their marriage in 1880, she tried to learn Irish with the help of a gardener and an Irish grammar book, but once again she faced several difficulties, because her teacher "was languid, suspecting it may be some hidden mockery, for those were the days before Irish became the fashion" (Gregory 1919:8–10). Following her husband's death in 1892, she started studying the language more systematically together with the couple's only son, Robert, consulting an Irish Bible and a practical grammar written by Father Eugene O'Growney (1863–1899), titled *Simple Lessons in Irish for Self-Instruction and for Use in Schools* (1894). In 1898 she would start taking lessons with Norma Borthwick, an Irish-language advocate originally from England.[138]

Her Irish-language learning experience, along with the inspiring initiatives of the newly founded Gaelic League in 1893, was the beginning of a radical change, which she famously voiced in epiphanic tones:

> This discovery, this disclosure of the folk learning, the folk poetry, the ancient tradition, was *the small beginning of a weighty change*. It was *an upsetting of the table of values, an astonishing excitement*. The imagination of Ireland had found a new homing place. My own imagination was aroused. I was becoming conscious of a world close to me and that I had been ignorant of. It was not now in the corners of newspapers I looked for poetic emotion, nor even to the singers in the streets. It was among farmers and potato diggers and old men in workhouses and beggars at my own door that I found what was beyond these and yet farther beyond that drawingroom poet of my childhood in the expression of love, and grief, and the pain of parting, that are the disclosure of the individual soul. (Gregory 1919:10–11; my emphasis)

---

137. She documented her visits to Italy in her diaries and sketchbooks, which contain several drawings of Italian scenery. On Gregory's stays in Italy between 1876 and 1909, see Cataldi (2003).

138. On Borthwick, see chapter 1.

While Gregory's liminal situatedness amid English rule and Irish nationalism was an uneasy position to occupy, as it lent and still lends itself to contentious considerations in terms of class, gender, and ethnicity,[139] her work as a folklorist was nonetheless significant and merits exploration from a transnational perspective. The little-known recollections of Italian philosopher Mario Manlio Rossi (1895–1971), an Irish culture enthusiast and eminent expert on philosopher George Berkeley (1685–1753), allow us to approach Gregory's legacy from an alternative perspective. Rossi's scholarly works constitute an interesting point of contact between Irish and Italian culture. He provided fascinating details on Gregory and Yeats in his travelogue *Viaggio in Irlanda* (1932), partially translated into English as *Pilgrimage in the West* by Joseph Maunsell Hone (1882–1959) in 1933. Antonio Bibbò insightfully defines Rossi's travelogue and its English version as "transnational products" (Bibbò 2022a:188), emphasizing the function of Hone's translation as "an example of images *traveling back* and enlarging the scope and international support" for the Irish Revival (Bibbò 2022a:187; original emphasis). *Viaggio in Irlanda* was published shortly after Gregory's death and configures itself as an homage to her, as Rossi made explicit in his dedication (Rossi 1933:3).

These travel memoirs lingered on Coole Park, the estate that Augusta Gregory inherited after her husband's death, destined to become the cultural center of the Irish Revival. In recounting his journey toward the west of Ireland, Rossi addressed her directly:

> You have never pretended to be a guide, to be a chief, to be a mother of Ireland. And therefore you have been more than a guide, more than a national chief: you have created what did not exist, a common soul for the Catholics and for the Protestants, for the poets and artists, for diverse and hostile spirits. [...] But you forget even the forces which you have directed and organized—always without a thought of yourself, always absorbed in the things which you heard or sang, in the men whom you guided—and it appeared to you that your own work was only a secondary work, an almost superfluous collaboration. (Rossi 1933:47–48)

Such remarks express regret for the tendency to consider Augusta Gregory's efforts as less important than those of her contemporaries and the need to rectify this flawed historical interpretation. The extent of Rossi and Gregory's friendship and intellectual exchanges is demonstrated by the invitation to add

---

139. In this regard, Garrigan Mattar underscores Gregory's "duality" as "an increasingly nationalist Irish gentlewoman who socialized in the top circles of British aristocratic society" (Garrigan Mattar 2004:187).

his own initials to the bark of the renowned tree in Coole Park, on which the major exponents of the Irish Revival had carved their names. They remained in contact also after his departure from Ireland, as testified by their exchanges of letters between 1931 and 1932 (Fantaccini 2003:288), preserved in the Archivio "Mario Manlio Rossi" in the Biblioteca "Antonio Panizzi" in Reggio Emilia.[140]

By then, Gregory was approaching the end of her life and showed gratitude for the kind words that Rossi reserved for her: as she wrote to him, "I have come to an age when the appreciation of the young touches me, and gives me a happy feeling that I am not yet a quite withered leaf. And I especially value it from you."[141] She also took care to send him a postcard reproducing her portrait by Antonio Mancini (1852–1930) (fig. 2.4), which the Roman painter had made for her in 1907.[142] The crucial role of the Anglo-Irish cultural exponents in the preservation of Irish folklore, regarded as "the point of support of any possible Irish culture" (Rossi 1933:29), was greatly celebrated in *Pilgrimage in the West*. Rossi's perspective as a "southern European" comes to the fore when he described Galway as "the last Mediterranean shore" (Rossi 1933:37):

> Here in the extreme west, where Europe loses herself in the clouds and in melancholy, has come to die an extreme surge of those Mediterraneans who first wandered over the sea and brought the flash of their eyes and the clean nobility of their lithe bodies to the furthest coasts. Among these Celts the Southern element has remained more evident than elsewhere. What this land, what Galway might have been, if they drew from the South so much blood, and if in it men come from so different a climate were able to find a new fatherland! Only the fundamental gaiety, the passionate fantasy of the Irish can explain this ethnographical wonder. (Rossi 1933:40)

Contrary to the most spirited defenders of the necessity to safeguard folklore in the medium of the Irish language, Rossi claimed that it was precisely thanks to the endeavors of the Anglo-Irish Ascendancy members writing in English that Irish folklore was becoming known across the world: "all this richness, of saga, myth, song and chronicle, would have remained shut away as a curiosity—and it is poetry!—if the 'Ascendancy' living it over again in English and diffusing it through English channels had not given it a spiritual

---

140. The Biblioteca "Antonio Panizzi" also holds the letters Yeats wrote to Rossi. Their correspondence has been reconstructed by Fantaccini (2009:78–81).

141. Gregory, *Lettere a Mario Manlio Rossi*, September 1, 1931, cc. 13, letter n. 1:1–2, Archivio "Mario Manlio Rossi," Biblioteca "Antonio Panizzi," Reggio Emilia.

142. As reported by Kohfeldt (1985:187), she was very fond of this painting. On Mancini's portrait, see De Petris (2004).

FIGURE 2.4. Augusta Gregory's postcard to Mario Manlio Rossi (1931), Biblioteca "Antonio Panizzi," Reggio Emilia. The postcard features Augusta Gregory's portrait by Antonio Mancini. Courtesy of Archivio "Cesare Zavattini"—Biblioteca Panizzi—Comune di Reggio nell'Emilia.

value for the whole world" (Rossi 1933:31). Clearly, his close ties with and great admiration for the Anglo-Irish members of the Gaelic League and their lively contributions to Irish culture in English influenced his views on this matter.

A chapter of Gregory's autobiography, *Seventy Years*, is devoted to "The Changing Ireland" at the turn of the century. Gregory applauded the establishment of the Gaelic League as the central event in the history of the Irish nation (Gregory 1974:306). Her observations encapsulate the key features of the Anglo-Irish revivalist impulses: nostalgia, utopianism, and primitivism (Foster

1987:210). The first two characteristics were linked to temporal dimensions, since the Anglo-Irish intellectuals looked at the past in a romanticized way in order to find the roots to build a new utopian Irish nation; the latter category, primitivism, while evoking the myth of a precivilized society, was spatially linked to the Anglo-Irish fixation on the west of Ireland. In this respect, Michael Collins (1890–1922), leader of the Irish Free State, wrote that the Gaelic League "linked the people with the past and led them to look to a future that would be a noble continuation of it" (Collins in Gregory 1974:306). Gregory tied these reflections on the past and future of Ireland to the spatial dimension of the west, more specifically to Galway and the western Irish islands, where "the bringing together of the people to give the songs and poems, old and new, kept in their memory, led to the discovery, the disclosure, of folk learning" (Gregory 1974:306).

Folklore exerted a strong influence on Gregory's life, as will be outlined in the next section. In her autobiographical writings, she admitted that in her youth she often felt "a hunger, a pain of longing" she could not fully explain while contemplating the Irish landscape (Gregory 1974:309). Only later she came to realize that it was "the artist's desire to capture, to express, the perfect," a powerful urge to seek wonder. Her life would have been desolate "without that poetry of the soil, those words and dreams and cadences of the people" that allowed her to "give some echoed expression to that dragging driving force" (Gregory 1974:309).

Dreams on the Edge of the World:
The Kiltartan Books and Visions and Beliefs

A turning point for Augusta Gregory was her acquaintance with W. B. Yeats. Gregory was so enthralled by the legends he had collected in County Donegal and published in *The Celtic Twilight* (1893) that she decided to devote herself to the enterprise of collecting folklore in the Kiltartan region in Galway:

> The Sligo legends in that little book made me jealous for Galway, and the gathering of legend among my own neighbours became a chief interest and a great part of my work for many years to come. The gathering was for the most part mine, but as it had been begun so it was continued under Yeats' direction so to speak, so far as the lore of vision was concerned. The folk history and folk tales and poems came later and made a foundation for many of my plays; I found suggestion, inspiration, and the means of expression there. (Gregory 1974:308–9)

In Yeats's view, Augusta Gregory embodied the ideal of aristocratic cultural patronage he so strongly admired in Italian Renaissance culture. He became acquainted with this ideal by reading *Il libro del Cortegiano* (1528), the influential book of manners in which Baldassare Castiglione (1478–1529) recounted his experience in the Duchy of Urbino and detailed the features of the ideal courtier.[143] As Fiorenzo Fantaccini observed, Coole and Gregory "rappresentarono per Yeats il correlativo 'soggettivo' di Urbino e della Duchessa Elisabetta Gonzaga" (Fantaccini 2009:38).[144] The encounter with this book under Gregory's suggestion during a 1907 journey to Italy, which they made together with her son, constitutes a fascinating point of convergence between the literary interests of Gregory and Yeats, and the Italian and the Irish cultural traditions more broadly. The recommendations of Castiglione and the account of the lifestyle in the court of Urbino deeply influenced their imaginations and paved the way for the projection of Renaissance ideals onto Coole, which became a literary hub for the Irish Revival.[145]

Yet Gregory's creative genius has been traditionally downplayed, especially when considered in relation to her longtime friend and Nobel Prize winner Yeats: she has repeatedly been labeled as a "minor helper" (Kopper 1976:15) and as a "patron and hostess to Yeats" (Pethica 1987:257), rather than as a literary figure worthy of her own standing. Furthermore, several interviews and recollections from her acquaintances, such as George Moore (1852–1933), credit the evolution of her literary and linguistic inclinations to Yeats instead of Gregory herself: "her gift [...] languished till she met Yeats. He [...] set her going from cabin to cabin taking down stories, and encouraged her to learn the original language of the country" (Moore in Mikhail 1977:5). A biased view of the collaboration between Gregory and Yeats can be perceived in Moore's reminiscence: as noted earlier, the efforts that she made to learn Irish actually harked back to her youth, long before she met Yeats. Yeats's own writings likewise sketch a partial picture of these endeavors: "Lady Gregory, seeing that I was ill, brought me from cottage to cottage to gather folk-belief, tales of the faeries, and the like, and wrote down herself what we had gathered" (Yeats in Mikhail 1977:14). Although this statement may suggest that she engaged with folklore as a mere palliative to Yeats's poor well-being, in truth this was not the case, since "folklore was her new and chief interest before he appeared personally on the scene" (Mikhail 1977:17).

---

143. On Yeats's fascination with *Il libro del Cortegiano*, see Stein (1949) and Salvadori Lonergan (1970).

144. "represented for Yeats the 'subjective' correlative of Urbino and of the Duchess Elisabetta Gonzaga."

145. Gregory would devote a book to the estate and its significance in Irish culture, titled *Coole* (1931). On the mythification of Coole, see Harris (1974). On its transformation into the "literary workshop and cultural center of Ireland," see Winston (2001:205).

Indeed, after an excursion to Inishmore, the largest of the Aran Islands, in 1887, Gregory made another journey to the Aran Islands on her own in 1893, reaching the smallest island, Inisheer, where she lived among Irish native speakers in a cottage. Such a solitary expedition was "a most unusual undertaking for an Ascendancy woman at that time, and particularly for one travelling alone" (Pethica 1996:xx). The reasons for making the trip are not clear, but she was likely inspired by the reading of Jane Barlow's *Irish Idylls* (1892), as evidenced in her diaries (Pethica 1996:xx). In a letter she sent to Scottish politician Sir Mountstuart Elphinstone Grant Duff (1829–1906) dated October 5, 1893, and partially reported in *Notes from a Diary, 1892–1895* (1904), she narrated her first experience in the Aran Islands, providing details on their geological formation and the "endless relics of the past" that could be found there. In the letter, she encouraged Grant Duff to make a visit and even proposed herself as a "qualified guide" (Gregory in Grant Duff 1904, I:276). She also commented on the living conditions of the islanders: "I could hear low ripples of laughter from the evening fireside at Inisheer, but neither are they merry; a potato and fish diet, and the battle with the stones and the sea, settles this" (Gregory in Grant Duff 1904, I:276). These were the earliest documented impressions of her journeys to the Aran Islands, which would become an essential source of inspiration for her folkloric writings.

The first folklore collection by the "matriarch of the Revival" (Guinness 1998:38) was *Poets and Dreamers* (1903), a heterogeneous assemblage of poems, ballads, legends, and plays—including recollections of the blind wandering poet Anthony Raftery (1779–1835)—based on memories collected in 1899 from the inhabitants of County Mayo (Hill 2004:24). In the section entitled "Workhouse dreams," Gregory recounted her three-day stay among "the imaginative class, the holders of the traditions of Ireland, country people in thatched houses, workers in fields and bogs" (Gregory 1903a:129). The words she used to describe these storytelling performances reflect her distanced gaze toward low culture at this stage of her life. After putting aside her initial impatience, she expressed how impressive the creative imagery of these popular tales was:

> But as I listened, I was moved by *the strange contrast between the poverty of the tellers and the splendours of the tales*. These men who had failed in life, and were old and withered, or sickly, or crippled, had not laid up dreams of good houses and fields and sheep and cattle [...]. The stories that they love are of quite visionary things; of swans that turn into kings' daughters, and of castles with crowns over the doors, and lovers' flights on the backs of eagles, and music-loving water-witches, and journeys to the other world, and sleeps that last for seven hundred years. I think *it has always been to such poor people, with little of wealth or comfort to keep their thoughts bound to the*

things about them, that dreams and visions have been given. It is from a deep narrow well the stars can be seen at noonday; it was one left on a bare rocky island who saw the pearl gates and the golden streets that lead to the Tree of Life. (Gregory 1903a:129–30; my emphasis)

In this evocative passage, it is possible to discern how Gregory participated in the well-trodden nineteenth-century tendency of romanticizing the "voice of the people." In line with this view, material poverty and social constraints took on a dignified status, aimed to emphasize the peasants' deeper connection with the intangible world and their spiritual possession of a visionary power that manifested itself in "splendours of the tales."

In the typescript of an undated lecture Gregory prepared for an American audience entitled "The Continuity of Folklore" and preserved in the archives of the Henry W. and Albert A. Berg Collection in the New York Public Library, she remarked that the importance of folklore resided in its continuity of tradition and the possibilities it allowed for the discovery of a connection between the real and the otherworldly dimensions: "The joy of folkloring is in finding here and there a clue, a thread that leads to the watershed that is not itself the end of our search, because it is the plain where things visible and things invisible meet" (Gregory, "The Continuity of Folklore," n.d.:2). In envisioning a future in which all different human ancestries would merge into a single race, she underscored the importance of folklorists in tracing the origins of the various customs and "shreds of beliefs" that melted together:

> It is then we folklorists of today will be held of blessed memory, as are old painters who it may be have left no great name yet have made it possible to tell from which great grandfather [...] the children of today have taken that bar across the forehead, that curl of the lip. (Gregory, "The Continuity of Folklore," n.d.:1)

She went on to explain how she did not initially venture into folklore with scientific seriousness because these beliefs were deemed as mere superstitions and were usually frowned upon: "It was because of this that the people never had spoken to me of them. But now I began to enquire sincerely and with a desire to know, and knowledge came to my hand" (Gregory, "The Continuity of Folklore," n.d.:2). She stressed the importance of memory in her recording practices, stating: "I have cultivated my memory to be as it were phonographic for such things as visions and beliefs and legends" (Gregory, "The Continuity of Folklore," n.d.:3). She was particularly fascinated by the historical retellings of "great personages in the world transformed in the popular mind" (Gregory, "The Continuity of Folklore," n.d.:6), which she defined as "myths in the making"; this is also the title that she considered giving to her collection of folk memories of historical events published in 1909, though she eventually decided on *The Kiltartan History Book* (Gregory 1909:49). The first of her books on Kiltartan traditions, this volume gathered stories that Gregory heard in Galway, Connemara, and Burren from beggars, pipers, and traveling men who used to modify, exaggerate, bowdlerize, and ridicule the deeds of ancient gods and historical figures. This short collection is a testament to her growing awareness of her purpose as a collector who ought not express her own views but merely report the stories as they were told. In this regard, she wrote: "I do not take the credit or the discredit of the opinions given by the various speakers, nor do I go bail for the facts; I do but record what is already in 'the Book of the People'" (Gregory 1909:51).

In *The Kiltartan Wonder Book* (1910), she gathered sixteen traditional folktales, illustrated by Margaret Gregory, her daughter-in-law. In the note placed at the end of the volume, she clarified that she wanted these stories to be as "authentic" as possible, although she admitted to having intervened from time to time to unscramble them:

> I have not changed a word in these stories as they were told to me, but having heard some of them in different versions from different old people, I have sometimes taken a passage or a phrase from one and put it in another where it seemed to fit. (Gregory 1910:104)

Clearly, Gregory's attitude in *The Kiltartan Wonder Book* toward the collection of folktales was not as methodical and scientifically objective as it would become when she compiled her final collection, *Visions and Beliefs in the West of Ireland* (1920). Nonetheless, she testified to her consciousness of what a folklorist was supposed to do by commenting: "I tell this, because folk-lorists in these days are expected to be as exact as workers at any other science" (Gregory 1910:104).

Several contemporary scholars point out the necessity to acknowledge the neglected value of Gregory's enterprise as a folklorist and praise her anthologies, in particular *Visions and Beliefs* (Pethica 1996; Lysaght 1998a; Billington 2000). First released in two volumes in 1920 by the American book publisher G. P. Putnam's Sons, *Visions and Beliefs* is unquestionably the most precise and multilayered of her collections, "one of the best ever compiled because of its fidelity to the storytellers" (Billington 2000:58). This work has been described as a "collection of material that remains almost unique in scope and gender inclusiveness to the present day," the significance of which "has probably yet to be fully recognized" (Lysaght 1998a:276). The anthology was divided into twelve thematic chapters dealing with topics such as sea stories, seers and healers, the evil eye, herbs, charms, warnings, and appearances. These thematic sections were followed by two essays by W. B. Yeats, "Witches and Wizards and Irish Folk-lore" and "Swedenborg, Mediums, and the Desolate Places" (Gregory 2006 [1920]:302–36).

The genesis of this collection dates to the 1890s, when Gregory started her expeditions on the back of her pony Shamrock to rural areas in Galway and the Aran Islands, alone or in the company of Yeats. In the secluded countryside, they found an "untouched peasant culture" (Coxhead in Gregory 2006 [1920]:6). As Yeats specified in the aforementioned essay "Swedenborg, Mediums, and the Desolate Places," they used to go together "from cottage to cottage while she began to collect the stories in this book, and presently when I was at work again she went on with her collection alone till it grew to be, so far as I know, the most considerable book of its kind" (Yeats in Gregory 2006 [1920]:311). Through the lines of this collection, it is possible to catch a glimpse into the sorrows and griefs of those who lived in some of the poorest areas of Ireland in the late nineteenth century. It was, however, only after "a twenty-two-year gestation" (Guinness 1998:40) that the book came to light. In between these visionary "memorates"[146] of Irish islanders and peasants, there are evident markers of the fears and deprivations they endured in one of the harshest periods of modern Irish history.

On a methodological level, Augusta Gregory defined "leisure, patience, reverence, and a good memory" as essential to the act of collecting (Gregory 2006 [1920]:15). Memory was particularly important since she did not write down the stories when the storytelling events took place but rather transcribed them subsequently, thus relying largely on her recollections. As she wrote in her diaries, starting in summer 1897, Gregory and Yeats "searched for folk lore [...]—Then when we came in I wd write them out, & then type them, very good training if I ever want to be private secretary!" (Gregory 1996 [1897]:151).[147] Delayed transcription was encouraged by prominent Irish scholars of the time such as Douglas Hyde, who warned collectors that when writing down "the story *verbatim* with pencil and paper, as an unwary collector might do, you destroy all, or your shanachie[148] becomes irritable" (Hyde 1890:xlvi).

Furthermore, despite her considerable efforts to learn Irish—thanks to which she became a proficient translator—she had some difficulties in understanding the spoken language. For this reason she relied on the help of an interpreter during her excursions (Murphy 1987:147). In *Visions and Beliefs*,

---

146. In folklore studies, the memorate is a "first-hand account of a supernatural experience" (Lee and Preston 2009:354).

147. Augusta Gregory often used shorthand in her writings, as can be noted in this excerpt.

148. Hyde's transcription of the Irish word *seanchaí*, meaning "storyteller."

Gregory decided to report these narratives in first person, a perspective that endowed them with a greater sense of veracity and "evidential weight" (Corrigan Correll 2005:5). She relegated her viewpoint to the preface and to the brief paragraphs that introduce each chapter. Thus, her perspective never intrudes into the narratives of her informants, which are reported one after another, creating a mosaic of polyphonic voices. Her intention was to hold up "a clean mirror to tradition" (Gregory 2006 [1920]:15) in order to objectively present these stories as they were told. However, the informants' image reflected in her mirror was inexorably bent by her standpoint.[149]

In *Lady Gregory's Toothbrush* (2002), Irish novelist Colm Tóibín recounted her life by reporting real-life anecdotes that reveal her double-sided relationship with the Irish peasantry. In a similar manner to Jane Wilde, her upbringing as an Anglo-Irish woman in an upper-class Protestant Ascendancy family complicates simplistic interpretations of her positionality as a folklorist and has frequently worked to her detriment in twentieth-century critical assessments of her contributions. Irish writers and intellectuals such as the aforementioned George Moore and James Joyce (1882–1941) were bitterly critical toward her; in fact, the former once accused her of proselytizing, believing that she used "her influential position as a member of the landed gentry to entice her impoverished Irish peasants to give up their Catholicism" (Mikhail 1977:17).

Contemporary reassessments of the central "triumvirate" of the Irish Revival, namely W. B. Yeats, J. M. Synge, and Augusta Gregory, suggest that Romantic primitivism was an intentional "ideological choice and a cultural-political tool" for her and that "[t]he influence of science was to be felt directly only in the technique Gregory employed to collect and collate the folklore of her tenantry" (Garrigan Mattar 2004:186–87). For her talent in the recording of popular traditions, she was defined by Thomas Wall (1906–1985), librarian of the Irish Folklore Commission, as "the mother of folklore," a sort of "human tape-recorder" who was able to write down the memories of the peasants with a faithfulness comparable to those technological devices that would later be employed by the commission (Coxhead 1961:58).

Her position in relation to the idealized representation of her Irish informants, who more often than not were her own tenants and members of her household, is controversial (Murphy 1991:41). These were the years of the Land War, the rural revolts of impoverished tenants who rose against their landlords and advocated for land reform. Yet Augusta Gregory rarely tackled the issue raised by this conflict of interest (Guinness 1998:42). She rather

---

149. Yeats would also resort to the metaphor of the mirror when he wrote that Gregory "was born to see the glory of the world in a peasant mirror" (Yeats 1999 [1935]:336).

tended to neglect her privileged position as a member of the landed upper class and emphasized the good relationship she and her husband managed to establish with their tenants:

> I am glad to remember that through the twelve years of our married life, 1880–92, my husband and his people were able to keep their liking and respect for each other. For those were the years of the land war, tenant struggling to gain a lasting possession for his children, landlord to keep that which had been given in trust to him for his; each ready in his anger to turn the heritage of the other to desolation; while the vision of some went yet farther, through breaking to the rebuilding of a nation. The passion, the imagination of Ireland were thrown into the fight. (Gregory 1919:7)

If one aims to achieve a truthful reappraisal of Gregory's contribution to folklore, it is therefore important to recognize how specific "attitudes to colonialism, language, religion and gender may have become linked together to cast a shadow over [...] her work" (Lysaght 1998a:267). A reassessment on a transnational level of the works of Augusta Gregory and other folklorists must take into account these culturally and historically constructed factors. Hence, it is essential to critically analyze these narratives and the way they were edited and presented to readers by bearing in mind that folklorists were often motivated by specific ideological views and had to mediate between different cultural and linguistic circuits.

The "Inbetweenness" of the Folklorist: Strategies and Compromises

The lives and works of Laura Gonzenbach, Grazia Deledda, Jane Wilde, and Augusta Gregory are proof of a relentless work of mediation, made possible thanks to the cultural and linguistic strategies they consciously developed and the compromises they inevitably had to make. Their folkloric enterprises were first and foremost the result of their engagement with subaltern cultures, motivated by their determination to make these traditions known to the outside world. In their quests, they confronted questions of nationhood and islandness in their localized declensions: Sicilianness, Sardinianness, and Irishness.[150]

---

150. Sicilianness and Sardinianness refer to the concepts of *sicilianità* and *sardità*, alternatively called *sicilitudine* and *sarditudine*. The term *sicilitudine* was first coined by Crescenzio Cane (1930–2012) and popularized by Leonardo Sciascia (1921–1989), who encapsulated in this concept the idiosyncratic features of Sicilian culture, namely, in his view, "paura, apprensione,

Such identities were refracted in their folklore writings and inextricably tied to issues of language, which contributed to "generating imagined communities" (Anderson 2006 [1983]:133). This was especially so in the nineteenth century, when language became "a badge of cultural and ethnic identity," an essential instrument to shape a sense of unity that could find expression on a regional or national level (Sanson 2013a:272). As scholars of popular traditions, some of these figures had to transform the words of rural peasants from oral to print form and from vernacular to national languages. To this end, they resorted alternatively to domestication and foreignization strategies to either render their texts closer to the target reader or the target reader closer to the original texts. Throughout these processes, they strove to preserve a sense of orality, a style that would appear "simple, accessible, not pretentious or fancy" (Forrester 2020:268), with levels of success that were largely dependent on their knowledge of vernacular languages.

In the lecture "The Continuity of Folklore," Augusta Gregory reported the tale of an "old woman who could not read or write because it would have cost a penny a week to go to school." Her informant told her that she visited from time to time a house of fairies. Gregory asked her: "What language did they speak?" to which the woman responded: "Irish of course; what else would they speak?" (Gregory, "The Continuity of Folklore," n.d.:3–4).[151] Irish was thus regarded as the natural language of otherworldly beings and understandably so, given their rootedness in Irish culture. Gregory sought to preserve the distinctive features of the Irish language in her English writings by coining "her own literary idiom" (Zimmermann 2001:332), called "Kiltartanese." This hybrid usage of English, which aimed to preserve the rhythmic and syntactic peculiarities of Irish, led scholars to criticize its "contrived cadences" and "artificiality" (Garrigan Mattar 2004:195, 267).

This linguistic stratagem gave rise to a style that corresponded to the speech of ordinary Irish people, which diverged from standard English and would be

---

diffidenza, chiuse passioni, incapacità di stabilire rapporti al di fuori degli affetti, violenza, pessimismo, fatalismo" (Sciascia 1970:13) [fear, apprehension, distrust, closed passions, inability to establish relationships outside of affections, violence, pessimism, fatalism]. The terms *sardità* and *sarditudine* were shaped on the basis of their Sicilian counterparts to define the attitudes and characteristics of belonging to Sardinian culture. For a study of these terms with a focus on the nuances between *sicilianità*, more neutral in tone, and *sicilitudine*, more negatively charged, see Orioles (2009).

151. In *Visions and Beliefs*, Augusta Gregory wrote that she had asked this question to Mary Sheridan: "I think of Mrs. Sheridan's answer when I asked in what language the strange unearthly people she had been among had talked: 'Irish of course—what else would they talk'" (Gregory 2006 [1920]:148).

defined as "Hiberno-English" or "Anglo-Irish."[152] The usage of this idiom in the written form expressed "the linguistic conflict between Irish and English" (Gilmartin 2004:2), at a time when Irish was facing a dramatic diminishment and English had become the dominant language. The decline of the Irish language was due not only to the devastating consequences of the Great Famine but also a result of British colonizing policies in the Irish national schooling system, which would radically change after the foundation of the Gaelic League and its fight for an "Irish Ireland" (Laukaitis 2010).[153] Gregory acted as an intermediary between English and Irish on a linguistic level as well, in a manner not dissimilar to Sicilian verist writers such as Giovanni Verga, who attempted to replicate the syntax and color of the Sicilian language in print. In Gregory's case, despite her detached standpoint, this linguistic compromise had significant implications since her use of English with a semblance of Irishness was an attempt to carve a space for Irishness within the dominant English medium. Her standpoint was controversial, since she firmly remained a privileged member of the landed gentry whose class difference pervaded her interactions with the peasants and her efforts to portray them in her writings.

If the Kiltartan style corresponded to a foreignization strategy that made the presence of Irishness more evident in the English language, an entirely different choice was made by Deledda, who opted for a parallel Italian translation of the original Sardinian expressions in Logudorese that she listed in *TPN*. Deledda's contribution to folklore studies is noteworthy from a linguistic

---

152. For a reconstruction of the codification of the Irish language in the period between 1880 and 1920 thanks to the efforts of the Gaelic League, see Doyle (2015). On the decline of the Irish-speaking population in the mid-nineteenth century, see Ó Murchú (1998). On the educational reforms implemented by the Gaelic League, see Laukaitis (2010).

153. In this respect, the implementation of the infamous "tally stick" under the British rule is quite telling. This instrument of linguistic subjugation consisted of a stick on which a mark would be made to keep track of each time a child would speak Irish. At the end of the day, the child would be punished according to the number of marks on the stick (Doyle 2015:132). William Wilde witnessed this practice and reported it in *Irish Popular Superstitions*: "The children gathered round to have a look at the stranger, and one of them, a little boy about eight years of age, addressed a short sentence in Irish to his sister, but meeting the father's eye, he immediately cowered back, having, to all appearance, committed some heinous fault. The man called the child to him, said nothing, but drawing forth from its dress a little stick, commonly called a scoreen or tally, which was suspended by a string round the neck, put an additional notch in it with his penknife. Upon our inquiring into the cause of this proceeding, we were told that it was done to prevent the child speaking Irish; for every time he attempted to do so a new nick was put in his tally, and when these amounted to a certain number, summary punishment was inflicted upon him by the schoolmaster" (Wilde 1852:27).

point of view: her role as a mediator between Sardinian and Italian cultures is foregrounded by her decision to preserve the original oral expressions of her region by recording them side by side with her meticulous Italian translations. She frequently accompanied them by detailed explanations, including ironic remarks on the difficulty to render "il senso perfidissimo" of Sardinian invectives in the national language (Deledda 1894b:651).[154] Deledda's articles are scattered with observations on the semantic loss that occurs in the Italian translations. These notes, besides providing curious remarks on Nuorese dialect, were also a means for Deledda to underscore her multilingual skills.

Deledda's native proficiency in Sardinian was an asset for asserting her authorial voice as a folklorist. The same cannot be said of Jane Wilde: one of the most striking paradoxes of her collections is that they were written entirely in plain English, the language of the oppressor. Not only did she not conduct fieldwork among the Irish peasantry, but she also did not speak any Irish. Her ignorance of the language spoken in her native island, as evinced by the errors in her scant references to Irish words, hindered the appreciation of her volumes by a scrupulous collector and proficient Irish speaker such as Douglas Hyde, who reported in *Beside the Fire* several examples of the mistakes she made:

> Unfortunately, Lady Wilde is always equally extraordinary or unhappy in her informants where Irish is concerned. Thus, she informs us that *bo-banna* (meant for *bo-bainne,* a milch cow) is a "white cow"; that tobar-na-bo (the cow's well) is "the well of the white cow"; that Banshee comes from *van* "the woman"—(*bean* means "*a* woman") [...] etc. Unfortunately, in Ireland it is no disgrace, but really seems rather a recommendation, to be ignorant of Irish, even when writing on Ireland. (Hyde 1890:xiv; original emphasis)

The evident linguistic, ethnic, and class divide that can be traced in Wilde's anthologies involved not only the split between Irish and British identities but also the distinction between the Irish lower-class peasantry and the Anglo-Irish upper-class Ascendancy, of which she was a proud representative. Gino Scatasta cogently remarks that, within such representational strategies, regardless of their positive or negative declinations, "è implicito un messaggio essenzialista, che comporta un annullamento totale della dimensione storica" (Scatasta 1998:18).[155] This historical erasure becomes apparent in Wilde's

---

154. "the most wicked flavor."

155. "an essentialist message is implicit, entailing a total annihilation of the historical dimension."

claims about the immutability of the Irish character, a leitmotif both in *Ancient Legends* and in *Ancient Cures*:

> But the myths, superstitions, and legends (which, are the expression of a people's faith), *remain fixed and fast through successive generations*, and finally become so inwoven with the daily life of the people that they form part of the national character and cannot be dissevered from it. *This is especially true of the Irish, who, having been wholly separated from European thought and culture for countless centuries, by their language and insular position at the extreme limit of the known world, have remained unchanged in temperament and nature.* (Wilde 1890:3; my emphasis)

The topos of the immutability and conservatism of Ireland has been traditionally linked to its insular dimension, which may have "delayed and diluted the effects of some wider European movements" (Zimmermann 2001:13). Wilde's references to the fixity of Irish culture and to the peculiarities of their physical appearance cannot but recall the discriminations that not only the Irish but also the Sardinians had to cope with at this historical juncture. As a reaction to these racist discourses, a very similar emphasis has been historically placed on Sardinia as an island that, despite continuous foreign invasions, remained untouched and faithful to its "authentic" nature. In this regard, archaeologist Giovanni Lilliu (1914–2012) coined the expression "costante resistenziale sarda" (Lilliu 2002:225) to indicate the unchangeability of Sardinia and the intrinsic ability of its inhabitants to resist and survive on an island "sulla quale è calata per i secoli la mano oppressiva del colonizzatore, a cui ha opposto, sistematicamente, il graffio della resistenza" (Lilliu 2002:225).[156]

Wilde and Deledda were attentive to the cultural ferments that raged in the mid-nineteenth century, particularly the positivist pseudoscientific strands that aimed at studying and cataloging human races by making anatomical comparisons between different ethnic groups, in an attempt to create a hierarchy that could support the alleged superiority of the colonizers on the basis of their physical appearance. A considerable number of scientists, naturalists, and anthropologists throughout Europe tried to provide a scientific substrate for these racial theories. The Sardinian case is perhaps less blatant than the Irish one, yet it has palpable affinities with the Irish condition. Both in Italy and in the British Empire, scientists could not appeal to the color of the skin as a scientific basis to justify colonialist enterprises. Hence, the proliferation of theories related to skull shapes and other physical features served to prove

---

156. "Sardinian resistential constant"; "on which the oppressive hand of the colonizer has fallen for centuries, to which it has systematically opposed the scratch of resistance."

the supposed inferiority of people such as the Irish and the Sardinians, compared to the Anglo-Saxons and the continental Italians. The dominant forces looked with suspicion at the cultural diversity and autonomist impulses coming from the areas they failed to subjugate under their hegemonic power. As such, racially based theories offered an alibi for keeping these groups in a condition of subordination. On a cultural and political level, both Ireland and Sardinia became de facto colonies that needed to be linguistically and culturally suppressed, economically exploited, and politically subdued. In order to support the status quo, their inhabitants were accused of being intellectually inferior, primitive, and intrinsically criminal.

Jane Wilde's clumsy attempts to maintain the Irish flavor of the folk traditions translated into English can be regarded as an exemplary form of what folklorist Susan Ritchie defined as "ventriloquist strategies of representation" (Ritchie 1993:366). Furthermore, her authoritative voice is undermined by the absence of a direct interaction with her informants. Contrary to Gonzenbach, Deledda, and Gregory, she was essentially an "armchair folklorist" (Kinahan 1983) who compiled and researched readily available materials. She was thus closer to Yeats in her poetic approach than to fieldwork collectors. While Wilde's zeal for Ireland cannot be denied, at the same time her collections originated from a distinctively condescending view of the Irish masses that denotes an essentialist perspective imbued with a sense of cultural power, which essentially co-opted the indigenous oral traditions of the lower classes in order to make them circulate among a well-educated audience.

In this regard, Jarlath Killeen rightly comments that the endeavors of folklorists in Britain frequently "turned traditional cultures into bodies of information, stratified and classified for consumption by the literate" (Killeen 2013:188). Ventriloquizing practices are predominant in Wilde's collections, especially since the material she rearranged is reported entirely in the language of the colonizers. Her unfamiliarity with Irish was therefore charged with deep political repercussions and made her appear even more distant from the Irish culture that she was attempting to glorify in her writings. In this regard, Hyde further commented:

> [F]olk-lore can only find a fitting garment in the language that comes from the mouths of those whose minds are so primitive that they retain with pleasure those tales which the more sophisticated invariably forget. For this reason folk-lore is presented in an uncertain and unsuitable medium, whenever the contents of the stories are divorced from their original expression in language. (Hyde 1890:xvii)

These remarks are reminiscent of Giuseppe Pitrè's unsympathetic view of the translation of Sicilian folktales into foreign languages. Clearly, language was not a superficial matter but a question endowed with ideological nuances, given the strong identity politics at work in folklore collections. Gonzenbach's translation from the Sicilian dialect spoken in the areas of Messina and Catania was "the product of multiple mediations across languages, class, and genres" (Bacchilega 2012:457) and presupposed a domestication of the tales for an "implied German reader" (Zipes 2012:104). In his preface to Gonzenbach's anthology, Hartwig underlined the double-edged foreign nature of her enterprise: in complimenting her literary German, he commented that "[s]e si pon mente che la nostra raccoglitrice non è stata in Germania che di passaggio, mai nulla ha pubblicato, dovremo tanto più riconoscere, da queste imitazioni della poesia popolare italiana, come essa in alto grado possiede la nostra lingua" (Hartwig 1870:598).[157] Gonzenbach thus occupied a liminal position: as a collector gifted with a unique cultural "hybridity," she was able to navigate more than one cultural and linguistic context thanks to her double identity as a woman of Swiss-German roots born in Sicily who was fluent in several languages, including Italian, Sicilian, German, and French.

Mastery of the local Sicilian dialect was pivotal to allowing Gonzenbach to connect with local female informants of humble origins, who, it can be posited, did not perceive her as a complete outsider. She can be aptly considered "una svizzera molto siciliana," "un'emigrata al contrario, che seppe valorizzare la cultura del paese dal quale fu accolta" (Ottaviano and Ottaviano 2018:72).[158] Her hybridity can therefore be seen as a "duplice appartenenza" or "doppio sradicamento" that determines "un punto d'osservazione particolare che permette distacco oggettivante e partecipazione complice" (Rubini 2006:95).[159] In her reflections on folklore collectors, Lisa Gabbert refers to the great African American anthropologist Zora Neale Hurston (1891–1960), key exponent of the Harlem Renaissance and author of the auto-ethnographical work *Mules and Men* (1935), as an example of a "halfie," building on Kirin Narayan's definition of the term that denotes "a researcher who is both part of the community s/he studies but outside of it as well" (Gabbert 2016:41).[160] To a certain extent, the same may be

---

157. "If one remembers that our collector has been in Germany just for a short period and that she has never published anything, we have to recognize, from these imitations of Italian popular poetry, that she has mastered our language to a high degree."

158. "A very Sicilian Swiss," "an upside-down emigrant, who knew how to enhance the culture of the country that welcomed her."

159. "dual belonging" or "double uprooting," "a particular observation point that allows objectifying detachment and complicit participation."

160. Kirin Narayan's words were originally cited in Abu-Lughod (1991:161, n.1). For a reappraisal of Zora Neale Hurston and other women anthropologists from a feminist standpoint, see Behar and Gordon (1995).

said of Gonzenbach, if one considers her mixed origins and her peculiar situatedness in the Swiss-German community in Sicily. However, if Gonzenbach had to be placed on an insider/outsider continuum, despite her mastery of the local dialect and her ability to create connections with members of the lower classes, she would have remained a foreign upper-class woman in the eyes of the local peasants. It can be further postulated that the members of the Swiss-German community Gonzenbach belonged to had a "colonialist" inclination, in that they acted as "the necessary civilizers of the South, bringing commerce, industry, education, feminism, scholarship, nationalism, and other goods of modernity from abroad" (Noyes 2003:171). Nevertheless, it is likely that Gonzenbach's efforts were well received by the peasants she interacted with. The ending formula of fairy tale n. 70, "Lo scaltro scarparo,"[161] reported in the local dialect, offers an insight into the storytellers' perception of Gonzenbach:

Fàula ntra conca,
E faula ntrô bacili,
ch'è bedda sta Signura
chi mi l'ha fatta diri! (Gonzenbach 2019 [1870]:380; original emphasis)[162]

The positive relationship that Gonzenbach managed to establish with the storytellers can be deduced by their direct address of her with these enthusiastic words, implicitly thanking her for asking them to share their tales. Furthermore, a class distinction can be discerned, since she is called a beautiful *Signura*, a term used to describe someone belonging to the upper class (Rubini 1998:169; 2006:96).[163] It is thus reasonable to posit that the narrators were "compiaciute e forse lusingate che una signora straniera nobile e colta s'interessasse con tanta sincera partecipazione alle loro semplici 'storie'" (Toschi 1964:7).[164]

By alternating back and forth from a regional to a national perspective on the collection of folklore between the second half of the nineteenth century and

---

161. "The Clever Shoemaker."

162. "The sounds of this tale ring from a shell, / The words of this tale flow from a bowl! / How beautiful that lady is / Who told me to tell this tale!" (Gonzenbach, trans. Jack Zipes, 2006:461).

163. Rubini drew attention to the anthropological observations of American ethnologist Charlotte Gower Chapman (1902–1982), conducted in 1928 in Milocca, a village in the southwestern interior of Sicily. In this study, Gower Chapman reported that "[s]trangers in town may be given their proper Italian titles: *Signuri, Signura, Signurina*, and one or two young women of the wealthy class may attempt to insist on being called *Signurina* instead of *Donna*" (Gower Chapman 1971:50; original emphasis).

164. "pleased and perhaps flattered that a noble and cultured foreign lady was interested in their simple 'stories' with such sincere participation."

the early twentieth century, this chapter has investigated the background of four women who were involved in the publication of wonder tales and popular traditions in Italy and Ireland. The reappraisal of the contributions by Laura Gonzenbach, Grazia Deledda, Jane Wilde, and Augusta Gregory carried out thus far suggests that the concepts of alterity, primitivism, and islandness as well as the attention to the rural world and the process of cultural and linguistic mediation are concerns that shaped their approaches to folkloristics. By exploring their lives and works in succession, it is possible to recognize their commonalities as well as the different compromises they had to make while contributing in their specific ways to this field. Despite their different upbringings and cultural contexts, their ventures into folklore represent an important facet of their legacies. Their works give a glimpse into the perceptions of the marginalized rural classes in Italy and Ireland from the viewpoint of upper-class women. The tales and traditions they disseminated, which will be analyzed in depth in the following chapter, reveal their distinctive gazes as women who were actively seeking wonder in their insular cultures.

3

Women's Folklore

RECLAIMING VOICES AND FIGURES IN INSULAR TRADITIONS

> Silences are just as important as voices in a textual economy of folklore and literature that seeks to resist appropriating other, oral or subaltern, cultures [...]. The words of others—groups, individuals, and institutions—inhabit us; we re-inhabit them; and we are responsible for how we exercise these habits because they always require representation, translation, and some exercise of authority over others.
>
> —CRISTINA BACCHILEGA, "FOLKLORE AND LITERATURE" (2012:459)

IN LATE nineteenth-century Ireland, when explaining the criteria for his first anthology on "the fairy literature of the people" (Yeats 1888:xvi), W. B. Yeats claimed that he attempted "to make it representative, as far as so few pages would allow, of every kind of Irish folk-faith" (Yeats 1888:xvi), therefore placing emphasis on representing the various genres of Irish folklore. Similarly, in mid-twentieth-century Italy, Italo Calvino's guiding principle in selecting the tales included in *Fiabe italiane* was the "representativeness" of Italian regional tales both linguistically and geographically, opting for those narratives that were "le più rappresentative, le meno schematiche, e le più impregnate dello spirito dei luoghi" (Calvino 2015 [1956]:xvii).[1] Bearing in mind the importance of representativeness both for the compilation and for the study of verbal folklore, this chapter proposes an analysis of some of the most representative tales, sketches, and traditions that can be found in the heterogeneous works of Laura

---

1. "the most characteristic, the least stereotyped, and the most steeped in local color" (Calvino, trans. Catherine Hill, 1980:xx).

Gonzenbach, Grazia Deledda, Jane Wilde, and Augusta Gregory, adopting as chief criterion for selection the twofold focus on women's textual presence and on insular references.

The first section in this chapter, "The Italian and the Irish Cauldrons of Stories and Their Cooks," introduces the long-standing debates of authorship and creativity in folklore collections, with an eye to the female lineage that lies at the heart of several canonical nineteenth-century anthologies in and beyond Italy and Ireland. The second section, "'Fairy Justice': Women-Oriented Gazes and Narratives of Subversion," explores the corpus under consideration with a focus on women both on extratextual and intratextual levels, as real-life peasants and as fictional characters who subvert the status quo in selected narratives. The third section, "Resisting Evil: Helpers and Healers between Pagan and Christian Beliefs," moves to an analysis of syncretism with an emphasis on beliefs about the evil eye and texts featuring female helpers and healers. Finally, the fourth section, "Creatures 'from the Outside': Magical Femininity in Insular Folklore," delves into the representation of supernatural female entities belonging to Sicilian, Sardinian, and Irish folkloric imaginaries.

The objective of this chapter is not only to analyze a selection of wonder tales and popular customs that illustrate these four folklorists' women-oriented gazes, but also to put them in relation to narratives and traditions gathered and/or rewritten by other renowned contemporary intellectuals in their respective cultural contexts. The folk and fairy tales, legends, and beliefs that constitute this heterogeneous corpus are thus investigated as "transnational genres" (Forrester 2020:277) and as quintessential "transcultural texts" (Haase 2010:29). In this way, these female folklorists' contributions to folklore and fairy-tale studies can be relocated and reappraised within the wider framework of nineteenth-century folkloristics, oral history, and popular culture.

The Italian and the Irish Cauldrons of Stories and Their Cooks

In his essay *On Fairy-Stories* (2014 [1939]), J. R. R. Tolkien resorted to an evocative metaphor to ponder the nature, origins, and effects of fairy tales: the "Cauldron of Story," in which pieces of bones and stew are constantly simmered (Tolkien 2014:44).[2] However, the highly debated topic of where these stories come from and how they came about is not at the center of the present

---

2. This essay was first presented as the Andrew Lang Lecture at the University of St. Andrews on March 8, 1939; it was then revised and completed in 1943.

study. Rather, this chapter explores the relationship between the Cauldron of stories and their "Cooks."[3] Those who oversee the boiling of the "Soup of stories" are, in concrete terms, the storytellers who passed these tales from generation to generation until folklore collectors put them in print. Thus, this chapter offers a critical analysis of the content of what Tolkien defined as "Soup," that is, the fairy tales, legends, anecdotes, and traditions recorded by the four figures under investigation, with attention to the manifold representations of womanhood.

By concentrating on a selection of the Italian and Irish folkloric writings rearranged by Laura Gonzenbach, Grazia Deledda, Jane Wilde, and Augusta Gregory, the different coloring of these tales and traditions will be brought to the fore. Similarities and differences will be highlighted, although it is important to bear in mind that the former do not prove any direct link between Italian and Irish folklore given that analogous figures, motifs, and plots can be found across distinct cultures worldwide. Stith Thompson devoted the first chapter of his foundational study *The Folktale* (1946) to the "universality of the folktale," underlining how the "oral art of taletelling [...] is not bounded by one continent or one civilization. Stories may differ in subject from place to place, [...] and yet everywhere [taletelling] ministers to the same basic social and individual needs" (Thompson 1946:5). If it is undeniable that folk and fairy tales tend to present "common human experiences, hopes, and fears that transcend nation and class," we should nevertheless be skeptical of this universalizing view: in other words, we need to remember that "all fairy tales *have* a history, that they are anything but ageless or timeless," as Elizabeth Wanning Harries firmly stresses (Harries 2001:3; original emphasis).

The substance of folk and fairy-tale narratives is layered and extremely intricate. Their analysis can lead to a myriad of interpretations from different critical approaches. According to Bengt Holbek (1985:25–26), at least eight perspectives can help scholars map the fairy-tale landscape: (1) the viewpoint of the creators of the first versions, which cannot be determined with certainty; (2) the viewpoint of those who conveyed the tales across time; (3) the viewpoint of the storytellers from whom the tales were eventually transcribed; (4) the viewpoint of the audience(s) to whom these tales were addressed; (5) the viewpoint of the collectors; (6) the viewpoint of the publishers; (7) the viewpoint of contemporary readers; and, finally, (8) the viewpoint of the scholars who interpret the tales today. Each perspective corresponds to a level of complexity

---

3. As Tolkien wrote, "if we speak of a Cauldron, we must not wholly forget the Cooks. There are many things in the Cauldron, but the Cooks do not dip in the ladle quite blindly. Their selection is important" (Tolkien 2014 [1939]:47).

that is added to the oral narrative. The function that collectors and publishers performed can be regarded as an "interference," which is nonetheless "a factor of cultural history [...] worthy of study as such" (Holbek 1985:26), especially because without their contribution, many of these narratives and traditions would have been lost.

The politics of cultural identity that lay at the heart of the relationship between collectors and informants lead to reflection on the representation of the "folk" as the "other." This preoccupation emerges clearly in the discipline of folkloristics as the history of the "folk" is inherently a global history "di dominatori e dominati, di accademici e contadini" (Cocchiara 2016 [1952]:17).[4] The struggle between subaltern and dominant classes, and its intersection with gender issues, posits legitimate questions about the validity of folklore collections as representative of the true "voice of the people"—questions that, albeit retro-projected onto the nineteenth century, tangibly resonate with contemporary concerns expressed by postcolonial criticism (Said 1977; Spivak 1988) and theories of intersectionality (Crenshaw et al. 1995; Hancock 2016). Although the presence of informants in nineteenth-century folklore collections is often veiled and negotiated by external interventions, it is inappropriate to define any folklore collection as the property of a solitary creator, since they are embedded with an array of different collective voices. Such complexity prompted Angela Carter to associate the attributes of anonymity and genderlessness to fairy tales due to the difficulty in knowing the original author of any oral story:

> Ours is a highly individualized culture, with a great faith in the work of art as a unique one-off, and the artist as an original, a godlike and inspired creator of unique one-offs. But fairy tales are not like that, nor are their makers. Who first invented meatballs? In what country? Is there a definitive recipe for potato soup? Think in terms of the domestic arts. "This is how *I* make potato soup." (Carter 1990:x; original emphasis)

This polychromy of flavors represents the essence of oral stories. Carter's observations destabilize the concept of authorship itself and push us to rethink creativity not as a spring deriving from a single source but perhaps more fittingly as an ocean with waves that are perennially agitated by concurrent forces. Oral tales are "collective products, emphasizing communities, not individuals" (Köhler-Zülch 1997:207). As a result, there is not an "I" behind folk and fairy-tale narratives but rather several "we's." Thus, when it comes to oral narratives the label of "author" to define the person who has "tamed" the

---

4. "of rulers and ruled, academics and peasants."

orality of the tale is controversial. The manifold mediations, modifications, and domestications by the writers/collectors/compilers/editors who rearrange these narratives into a written text can allow scholars to draw a tentative line between folktales and literary fairy tales, although the oral matrix is always infused, to varying degrees, in both.

As Nicholas Jubber observes in his journey into the lives and works of lesser-known "fairy tellers," this anonymity "conceals the people who did so much to shape the tales," casting "a mist of obscurity" over the historical trajectories of these narratives (Jubber 2022:5). If it is a Sisyphean task to pinpoint the original creator of oral stories given their palimpsest-like nature, the identity of the storytellers at a given moment in time can occasionally be discerned. Nineteenth-century collectors sometimes took care to make explicit reference to their tellers' names within the body of their anthologies, a habit that became increasingly common as the discipline of folklore embraced more scientific approaches. Not coincidentally, these narrators were often women, as the textual and visual portraits of the old peasant Clementina, Beatrice di Pian degli Ontani, and Peig Sayers in chapter 1 have shown. Yet, and perhaps not surprisingly, the art of storytelling was often labeled as a "male art" by a dominant scholarly trend that "washes aside contradictions and absorbs deviations," despite many examples in different cultural traditions pointing to precisely the opposite (Köhler-Zülch 1997:200). Exploring the contradictions and highlighting the deviations frequently overlooked by mainstream research entails acknowledging the feminine dimension of some genres of storytelling, such as the shorter and realistic *seanchas* in Irish culture.[5] This feminine dimension constitutes a widespread historical reality that turned into a prolific literary paradigm, the multiple variations of which can be identified in several folk and fairy-tale collections.

From the myth of Philomela and Procne in Ovid's *Metamorphoses* to the thousand tales narrated by Scheherazade, from the seventeenth-century French *contes de fées* to the Victorian fairy tales written by female authors,[6] numerous real and fictional women turned their vulnerability into an instrument of power through the narration of stories (Rowe 1986). Women's nature has been traditionally associated with the idea of passing on traditions, values, and language. The telling of tales was a privileged vehicle to voice latent

---

5. On the genres of storytelling attributed to women in Ireland, see Harvey (1989:111) and Vejvoda (2004:42).

6. Several Victorian women writers contributed to the genre of the literary fairy tale, such as Anne Thackeray Ritchie (1837–1919), Mary Louisa Molesworth (1839–1921), and Juliana Horatia Ewing (1841–1885). For an anthology of Victorian fairy tales by women writers, see Auerbach and Knoepflmacher (1992).

desires, demonstrate their resilience, and imaginatively transgress the boundaries of an oppressive sociocultural system. In the early nineteenth century, the Brothers Grimm not only greatly inspired other folk revivals across Europe but also reinvigorated the archetype of the old female storyteller and the concept of "a timeless female oral tradition" (de Blécourt 2010:174) by claiming to have relied upon the German storyteller Dorothea Viehmann (1755–1816) as one of their primary informants (fig. 3.1), whose supposedly humble origins were idealized.[7] In doing so, they gave impetus to a scholarly tendency to recast the voices of the female storytellers in folklore collections, accompanied by "the learned commentary of male editors" (Day 2019:400). As Jennifer Schacker remarks, in nineteenth-century folklore anthologies "the figure of the storyteller—imagined as an elderly peasant woman—provided the basis for a new fantasy of cross-cultural encounter" (Schacker 2003:46). This traditional nineteenth-century imagery has significant precedents in the history of the fairy-tale genre.

Numerous instances of the old female storyteller's archetype can be found in various cultural contexts across the centuries.[8] In the seventeenth century, the tales in Charles Perrault's *Histoires ou contes du temps passé, avec des moralités* (1697) were attributed to the French popular character Ma Mère l'Oye.[9]

---

7. As Maria Tatar points out, the informants of the Brothers Grimm "were rarely unlettered peasants who spoke the inimitable language of the 'folk,' but literate men and women from various social classes" (Tatar 2003:24). Jack Zipes observes that "the Brothers Grimm sought to validate the genuine nature of their folk tales with [Dorothea Viehmann's] picture as a 'mythic' peasant woman" and highlights how Edgar Taylor, the first British translator of the Brothers Grimm's *Kinder- und Hausmärchen*, used her image in the frontispiece of the volume *Gammer Grethel; or, German Fairy Tales, and Popular Stories, from the Collection of MM. Grimm, and Other Sources; with Illustrative Notes* (1839) (Zipes 2015:15 and 206, n.22). On the mythologization of Dorothea Viehmann, see Warner (1994:189–93), Tatar (2003:109–10), and Schacker (2003:41).

8. On the archetype of the old wise woman, see Estés (1996). On the motif of the old female crone, see Warner (1994). For an archetypal study of the feminine in fairy tales based on Jungian psychology, see the interpretations proposed by Swiss scholar and psychologist Marie-Louise von Franz (1915–1998) in *The Feminine in Fairy Tales* (2001), originally published as *Das Weibliche im Märchen* (1977).

9. On Perrault's Mother Goose, see Tatar (2003:106). As a tribute to this iconic character, fin de siècle French and foreign folklorists set a monthly meeting fittingly called "Dîner de Ma Mère l'Oye" to facilitate the convivial exchange of ideas on popular traditions. The first of these social occasions took place in 1882 in Paris. Scholars usually gathered at the Cercle historique in the Hôtel des Sociétés. In Italy, folklorist Stanislao Prato (1842–1918) proposed, to no avail, to introduce a similar rendezvous in Rome (Prato 1895:387). On these French dinners, see Privat (2007).

FIGURE 3.1. Portrait of Dorothea Viehmann (1755–1816), by Ludwig Emil Grimm. Public domain, Wikimedia Commons.

Prior to Perrault, the stories written by Giambattista Basile in *Lo cunto de li cunti overo lo trattenemiento de peccerille* (*The Tale of Tales, or Entertainment for Little Ones*), also known as *Il Pentamerone* (1634–36), were told by ten fictional narrators, who were all old crones, parodically mimicking the storytellers in Giovanni Boccaccio's *Decameron* (1349–1351) and "conforming to the type of gossip, old wife, witch and bawd" (Warner 1994:149–50).[10] Following in the footsteps of this enduring tradition revitalized by the Brothers Grimm, the visual and textual portrayals of nineteenth-century storytellers in European

---

10. With regard to the broader category of women as speakers, it is worth remembering that during the Italian Renaissance female speakers featured in the genre of early modern dialogue, which had a "quasi-documentary" quality, since dialogues were often presented as if transcribed directly from oral exchanges (Cox 2013:54).

folklore anthologies show that these narrators were, more often than not, romanticized old female peasants who "nelle lunghe serate d'inverno presso il focolare facevano trascorrere piacevolmente le veglie, o anche, nelle altre stagioni, raccoglievano intorno a sé e intrattenevano i bambini mentre i loro genitori erano impegnati nei lavori campestri" (Toschi 1964:7).[11] References to female peasant storytellers can be found both in the Italian and Irish contexts, as the following examples from canonical anthologies published in the two countries in the nineteenth century demonstrate.

At the opening of "An Irish Story-Teller" introducing *Irish Fairy Tales* (1892), Yeats symbolized this historical time frame as a "century of great engines and spinning-jinnies," acoustically evoked by "the hum of wheels and clatter of printing presses" (Yeats 1892:1). The storyteller Yeats referred to in the tale's title is a woman, "old Biddy Hart." The suggestive portrait drawn by Yeats conjures the image of an old lady who firmly believes in ancient legends and supernatural creatures, a woman who is initially reluctant to share her beliefs but eventually confides in the Irish poet. In the ensuing passage, Yeats retold how he gained Biddy Hart's trust:

> A little talk about my great-grandfather who lived all his life in the valley below, and a few words to remind her how I myself was often under her roof when but seven or eight years old loosened her tongue, however. It would be less dangerous at any rate to talk to me of the fairies than it would be to tell some "Towrow" of them, as she contemptuously called English tourists, for I had lived under the shadow of their own hillsides. (Yeats 1892:2–3)

Although Yeats's writings are permeated less by a scientific folkloric effort than by a spring of poetic imagination, these few lines capture the outsider-versus-insider dynamic that characterized the phenomenon of folkloric collection in the nineteenth century. In this regard, Yeats emphasized how even in western villages strangers found it difficult to obtain traditional tales: it was necessary to "go adroitly to work, and make friends" with local dwellers, among whom the old women were "the most learned, but will not so readily be got to talk, for the fairies are very secretive, and much resent being talked of" (Yeats 1888:xi).

In his subsequent work, *The Celtic Twilight* (1893), Yeats frequently cited some of his informants, including a recurring "old Mayo woman," a further example of the narrative presence of an aged woman who recounts tales from the past. One of his most cherished informants, this old woman was Mary

---

11. "made the wakes pleasant in the long winter evenings around the hearth or, even during other seasons, gathered the children around themselves and entertained them while their parents were busy in rural work."

Battle, a servant in the house of George Pollexfen (1839–1910), Yeats's uncle. She was described by Yeats in a letter to Gregory as "a mine of fairy lore" (Pierce 1995:38, 275 n.19). As reported by Declan Kiberd and P. J. Mathews, she was "reputed in Sligo to have second sight; and this gave her immense prestige in the local community" (Kiberd and Mathews 2016:206). Yeats underscored the connection between women and wisdom in *The Celtic Twilight*: "women come more easily than men to that wisdom which ancient peoples, and all wild peoples even now, think the only wisdom" (Yeats 1893:192). Such an embodied metaphor of elderly womanhood as "authentic" and living depository of traditions has been repurposed by various folk and fairy-tale collectors. For instance, this was also the case of Annunziata Palermo in Palmi, one of the main storytellers who contributed to Letterio Di Francia's *Fiabe e novelle calabresi* (1929),[12] and of Agatuzza Messia in Palermo, the chief female informant consulted by Giuseppe Pitrè for his fairy-tale collections. These are but some examples of the textual appearance of storytellers in folklore anthologies, sometimes accompanied by picturesque illustrations.

In the preface to *Fiabe italiane* (1956), Calvino devoted several pages to Pitrè's work and to his "narratrice-modello" (Calvino 2015 [1956]:xxv).[13] He underlined the uniqueness of the storyteller's performance by drawing attention to the difference between folk songs and folktales. In the former, repetition is key because they are fixed by rhythm, rhyme, and music and are thus less amenable to being used flexibly.[14] Conversely, folktales are more susceptible to change as they are reproduced from person to person:

> [A]l centro del costume di raccontare fiabe è la persona—eccezionale in ogni villaggio o borgo—della novellatrice o del novellatore, con un suo stile, un suo fascino. Ed è attraverso questa persona che si muta il sempre

---

12. Letterio Di Francia, mentioned in chapter 2, was a scholar, teacher, and professor of Italian literature originally from Palmi in Calabria. He lived most of his life in Turin and was committed to literary and folkloric studies, as testified by his anthology of Calabrian fairy tales. He described his main informant as "la più eloquente e sicura delle mie collaboratrici, informatissima dei migliori argomenti, incapace di lasciarsi addietro il menomo particolare, o di avere la più lieve esitazione negli intrecci più complicati" (Di Francia 2015 [1929]:13) [the most eloquent and trustworthy of my female collaborators, well informed on the best topics, incapable of leaving out the tiniest detail or having the slightest hesitation in the most complicated plots].

13. Female "model narrator" (Calvino, trans. Catherine Hill, 1980:xxii).

14. Furthermore, as noted by Enrica Delitala, it should be remembered that "mentre si può cantare da soli, non si può raccontare a se stessi; il raccontare presuppone sempre la presenza di più persone, di una riunione più o meno formale" (Delitala 1985:10) [while one can sing alone, one cannot tell a story to oneself; the act of narrating always presupposes the presence of several people, of a more or less formal meeting].

rinnovato legame della fiaba atemporale col mondo dei suoi ascoltatori, con la Storia. (Calvino 2015 [1956]:xxiv)[15]

Stories do not live in limbo. On the contrary, they are deeply embedded in the social and cultural environment in which they are passed on from generation to generation. The performative element of storytelling transcends the pages of the folkloric collections, and written and oral sources often intermingle over time to the point that it can be difficult to draw a clear-cut line between an oral folktale that has been transcribed in a written text and a literary fairy tale, marked by a more evident authorial intervention. The shift from a performative context to a new literary realm considerably changes the nature of the tales since this relocation fixes "the social arrangements of the instant into a text in ink" (Glassie 1985:10). When it comes to the performativity of storytelling, it is worth taking into consideration the eloquent words that Pitrè wrote with reference to the tales told by Agatuzza:

> Chi legge non trova che la fredda, la nuda parola; ma la narrazione della Messia, più che nella parola, consiste nel muovere irrequieto degli occhi, nell'agitar delle braccia, negli atteggiamenti della persona tutta [. . .]. Della mimica nelle narrazioni, specialmente della Messia, è da tener molto conto, e si può esser certi che, a farne senza, la narrazione perde metà della sua forza ed efficacia. (Pitrè 1875, I:xix–xx)[16]

In a letter sent to philologist Ernesto Monaci (1844–1918) in 1873, Pitrè commented on how astounded he felt before Agatuzza's extraordinary talent: "io mi sento annichilito di fronte a lei. Il suo fraseggio è il fraseggio siciliano modello, e la sua parola così ricca e propria, che non v'è arte o mestiere o condizione di vita cui essa non sappia trattare o ritrarre con voce adatta" (Pitrè in Cocchiara 1959:384).[17] Pitrè drew his tales also from other narrators such as the servant Elisabetta Sanfratello, the blind spinner Rosa Brusca, and the

---

15. "At the core of the narrative is the storyteller, a prominent figure in every village or hamlet, who has his or her own style and appeal. And it is through this individual that the timeless folktale is linked with the world of its listeners and with history" (Calvino, trans. Catherine Hill, 1980:xxii).

16. "Readers find nothing but the cold, bare word, but Messia's narration consists, more than in the word, in the restless motion of the eyes, in the agitation of the arms, in the attitudes of the whole person [. . .]. The narrative mimicry, especially in Messia's case, has to be greatly appreciated, and one can be sure that, without it, the narrative loses half its strength and effectiveness."

17. "I feel annihilated in front of her. Her phrasing is the model Sicilian phrasing, and her words are so rich and unique that there is no art or profession or condition of life that she does not know how to treat or portray with an appropriate voice."

eight-year-old Maria Curatolo.[18] It comes as no surprise then that, in the preface to *Fiabe novelle e racconti popolari siciliani* (1875), before introducing the figure of Agatuzza, Pitrè stated: "Dico narratore e dovrei dire narratrice, perché le persone da cui ho cercate ed avute tante tradizioni, sono state quasi tutte donne" (Pitrè 1875, I:xvi–xvii).[19] The same statement would appear in the preface to *Novelle popolari toscane* (1885), a collection published and rearranged by Pitrè but based on the tales gathered by his friend Giovanni Siciliano in Tuscany: "Dico novellatrici, perché furon donne quelle che fornirono queste novelle, una ventina di donne, varie di età e di mestieri, tutte umili di condizione, e, meno la Dreini di Firenze, la quale leggiucchiava appena, analfabete" (Pitrè 1885a:xxxiv).[20] He stressed their individuality and different skills as storytellers: "non tutte della medesima attitudine a narrare, non sempre franche e spigliate di fronte all'uditore, spiegano le differenze di stile tra una novella e l'altra, sia nella predilezione della forma narrativa, sia in quella del movimento drammatico" (Pitrè 1885a:xxxv).[21] Siciliano took care of reporting the personal details of this intergenerational group of women, many of whom were seamstresses, servants, waiters, and peasants, such as Annina, Beppa and Maria Pierazzoli, Umiltà Minucci, Raffaella Dreini, Teresina Focardi, Maria Gherardi, Paolina

---

18. On Elisabetta Sanfratello's narrative repertoire, see Sanfilippo (2020b). It is worth noting that the very young Maria Curatolo is the narrator of the opening tale of Giuseppe Pitrè's monumental collection of Sicilian fairy tales, entitled "Lu cuntu di 'Si raccunta'" (Pitrè 2013 [1875]:154–57) ["The Tale Told Time and Again," trans. Jack Zipes and Joseph Russo (Pitrè 2009:35)]. In a footnote to this narrative, Pitrè specified that he had gathered all these tales "*ad literam* dalla bocca delle novellatrici" [*ad literam* from the mouth of the female storytellers] and that this first story was told to him by this young child who lived in Erice, in the province of Trapani. During the performance, there were also other professors present alongside Pitrè, as he took care to specify: "il professore V. Di Giovanni, il cav. A. Sieri-Pepoli, il prof. Vito Castronovo e il Dottor Salomone-Marino" (Pitrè 2013 [1875]:156). The presence of these scholars and ethnographers is yet another example of how the collection of folktales became an opportunity for cultural exchange across barriers of age, class, and gender, facilitating the encounter between intellectuals and lower-class members.

19. "I say narrator but I ought to say female narrator, since the people whom I asked for and received many traditions from were almost all women."

20. "I say female narrators, because those who provided these stories were women, about twenty women, of various ages and professions, all of humble condition and illiterate, except for Dreini from Florence, who barely knew how to read."

21. "not all of them have the same aptitude for storytelling, they are not always frank and self-confident in front of the listener, they explain the differences in style between one story and another, both in the predilection for the narrative form and in that of the dramatic movement."

Sarti, Giuseppa Paoli, Zefira Ristori, Teresita and Tancreda Ciabatti, Annina Livacchi, Rosina Casini.

It is significant that across different cultures recurring themes can be identified, such as textual references to women as storytellers.[22] These elements, whether corresponding to an actual reality or reproduced as archetypal models of narration, deserve to be examined further in relation to questions and ideas of womanhood, language, and cultural transmission in the realm of folklore as they also emerge in the works of the female folklorists under scrutiny.

"Fairy Justice": Women-Oriented Gazes and Narratives of Subversion

The folkloric writings compiled by Gonzenbach, Deledda, Wilde, and Gregory constitute an extremely rich and hybrid assemblage not only of folk and fairy-tale narratives but also of other genres derived from oral traditions, including accounts of personal encounters with supernatural creatures, creative rewritings of legends, and ethnographic descriptions of local beliefs.[23] These texts do not focus solely on women as real-life narrators, tradition-bearers, fictional characters, or magical entities. However, a feminine perspective can be teased out of this diverse corpus, disclosing the women-oriented gazes of these four folklorists at different levels of depth. Several of the tales analyzed in this section are exemplary of the utopian potential of folk and fairy tales cogently articulated by Jack Zipes, who built on Ernst Bloch's notion of utopia to explore how such narratives "celebrate humankind's capacity to transform the mundane into the utopian as part of a communal project" (Zipes 2002b:xiii).[24]

In the copious notes to the Italian translation of Gonzenbach's *Sicilianische Märchen*, Luisa Rubini remarks how the first tale of any folklore collection is always endowed with a particular resonance (Rubini in Gonzenbach 2019 [1870]:479). It is not coincidental, then, that the first volume of *Sicilianische Märchen* opened with a tale entitled "La scaltra contadinella" (Gonzenbach

---

22. As mentioned in chapter 1, similar conceptions of women of humble origins as the finest informants can be found in the works of nineteenth-century lexicographers, such as Niccolò Tommaseo (Sanson 2011:286–87).

23. For a classification of folklore genres, see Propp (1984) and Oring (1986).

24. Ernst Bloch (1885–1977), author of philosophical works such as *Geist der Utopie* (1918) and *Das Prinzip Hoffnung* (1954–59), was a German Marxist philosopher. Among his essays that are particularly relevant to the field of fairy-tale studies, it is worth noting "Das Märchen geht selber in der Zeit" (1930), translated by Jack Zipes as "The Fairy Tale Moves on Its Own in Time" (Zipes 2002b:150–53). For a recent scholarly study on Bloch, see Zipes (2019).

2019 [1870]:3–5),[25] which immediately reveals "la cifra peculiare di un volume in cui protagonista è l'elemento femminile" (Rubini in Gonzenbach 2019 [1870]:479).[26] According to the ATU Index, this narrative belongs to the tale type 875A, *Girl's Riddling Answer Betrays a Theft*. The plot revolves around a peasant's daughter who intuitively understood that the gifts the king had sent to her family as a gesture of gratitude had all been deceitfully halved by the servant who carried them. The heroine did not accept this injustice passively but rather shrewdly devised a series of coded messages to be pronounced by the servant to the king, reported rigorously in Sicilian dialect. Through these pseudoriddles, she made sure that the king realized the servant's betrayal while also showcasing her sagacity and intelligence. It was thanks to these qualities that she eventually became queen, thus proving to be a strong-willed and assertive heroine.

The importance of *Sicilianische Märchen* resides in its feminist subtext, which, as the aforementioned opening tale exemplifies, retains "a particular feminine view of Sicilian culture" (Zipes 2012:124). In a review of Gonzenbach's collection published in *Rivista Sicula* in 1870, an anonymous critic commented:

> I due volumi di questa raccolta sono ornati di due bellissimi ritratti. Il primo è di una giovane dalle forme svelte e simpatiche, Caterina Certo di S. Pietro di Monforte; l'altro di una vecchia del borgo presso Catania, che ha vivissimi gli occhi e molta espressione nella figura, Francesca Crialese. In questo modo la nobile Gonzenbach ebbe il gentile pensiero di rimeritare le due contadine siciliane che certo ella stimò le più esperte e valenti narratrici. (Anonymous 1870:595–96)[27]

Several female peasants collaborated as Gonzenbach's informants, including the "young servant-girl" mentioned by Evelyn Martinengo-Cesaresco in her praise of Gonzenbach's work, Caterina Certo from San Pietro di Monforte (fig. 3.2), and the elderly Francesca Crialese from Catania (fig. 3.3).[28] Hartwig reported some of their names in the preface to the collection: among them, it

---

25. "The Clever Farmer's Daughter."

26. "the peculiarity of a volume in which the feminine element is predominant."

27. "The two volumes of this collection are adorned with two beautiful portraits. The first is of a nicely shaped young girl, Caterina Certo from S. Pietro di Monforte; the other of an old woman from a village near Catania, who has very lively eyes and a very expressive figure, Francesca Crialese. In this way, the noble Gonzenbach had the kind thought of paying homage to the two Sicilian female peasants whom she certainly esteemed as the most expert and talented storytellers."

28. Martinengo-Cesaresco's praise is reported in chapter 2. Certo and Crialese's illustrations were based on photographs that reveal the "interesse verista per le nuove apparecchiature" [the

FIGURE 3.2. Caterina Certo, *Sicilianische Märchen* (Gonzenbach 1870, I), Biblioteca Etnografica "Giuseppe Pitrè" (II-B-597). Courtesy of the Biblioteca Etnografica "Giuseppe Pitrè," Palermo.

is worth remembering Bastiana from Via Grande in Acireale, Nunzia Giuffridi, Lucia, Antonia Centorino, Elisabetta and Concetta Martinotti, Francesca Rufullo from Messina, Peppina Guglielmo from the province of Messina, an

---

verist interest for new devices] (Rubini 1998:164). The engravings were made by Adolf Neumann (1825–1884), a German engraver from Leipzig.

FIGURE 3.3. Francesca Crialese, *Sicilianische Märchen* (Gonzenbach 1870, II), Biblioteca Etnografica "Giuseppe Pitrè" (II-B-597). Courtesy of the Biblioteca Etnografica "Giuseppe Pitrè," Palermo.

unnamed female peasant from Randazzo near Catania, and the peasant Alessandro Grasso, who told stories that were handed down to him by his mother (Anonymous 1870:597). These storytellers represent "the last links of a chain that has been broken" (Holbek 1985:26), conveyors of tales and traditions that had been passed down for centuries and that the advent of urbanization and the ensuing radical changes of the mid-nineteenth century were sweeping away.

— 6 —

specialità pel corpetto allacciato dinnanzi, e per la giacchettina di panno o di velluto a bottoni inargentati, pel grembiule a minutissime pieghe e per la veste, di sotto alla quale

vengono fuori due scarpine lucide con fibbie d'argento come quelle dei preti secolari.
Fibbie d'argento in una contadina rozza, anche vestita di festa?
Proprio così! e prego il lettore di crederlo in fede mia.
Ma v'è anche di più.
Le donne di quei comuni, quando indossano le belle vesti, portano spesso collane d' oro.

FIGURE 3.4. "Contadina di Monforte," *Costumi siciliani delle province di Messina e di Palermo* (Pitrè 1895:6), Fondazione Biblioteca "Benedetto Croce" (XX 5 3, 36). Courtesy of the Fondazione Biblioteca "Benedetto Croce," Naples.

Interestingly, the portrait of Caterina Certo was subsequently reproduced at the beginning of a pamphlet by Giuseppe Pitrè on *Costumi siciliani delle province di Messina e di Palermo* (1895), in the form of a sketch realized by Vittorio Turati (1860–1938), a well-known Italian engraver. In this study, Pitrè drew attention to the features of the typical dress worn by this "ragazza di Monforte": "una specialità pel corpetto allacciato dinnanzi, e per la giacchettina di panno o di velluto a bottoni inargentati, pel grembiule a minutissime pieghe e per la veste."[29] This illustration (fig. 3.4) is a stylized replica of Gonzenbach's informant, a further

---

29. "girl from Monforte," "a specialty for the bodice tied at the front, and for the little cloth or velvet jacket with silver buttons, for the apron with minute folds, and for the robe."

lasting afterimage of Caterina Certo as a representative of traditional tales and costumes from the province of Messina.

In the instances in which women were presented as tradition-bearers, they tended to be associated with a conceptualization of folklore as fixed and conservative. This is the case with Pitrè's description of traditional costumes in Sicily. In this sense, tradition and modernity can be simplistically seen as diametrically opposed. However, folklore anthologies at times contain seeds of rupture from conventional models. If it is undeniable that the main model of transmission, in the tradition of nineteenth-century folk and fairy-tale anthologies, consisted of "older women of a lower status handing on the material to younger people, [...] of higher position and expectations, like future ethnographers and writers of tales" (Warner 1994:17), it is also true that there are examples in which this paradigm is both perpetuated and questioned.

The case of Gonzenbach's collection is emblematic: in this regard, the insertion of Caterina Certo's portrait at the very beginning of Gonzenbach's first volume functioned as an unspoken and yet quite blatant acknowledgment that the art of storytelling resided not only in archetypal old crones but could be and indeed was also nourished by younger women. As such, this portrait of a young female storyteller breaks the tradition while simultaneously perpetuating it, a telling emblem of Gonzenbach's work as a whole. Furthermore, the inclusion of this image presumably implies that the typical old female storytellers were once young and that they acquired these tales in different stages of their lives. The emphasis on the female lineage of storytelling is underscored, although the standard static poses of the illustrations, which were in vogue at the time, do not convey a sense of their actual performance.

Unfortunately, beyond Hartwig's comment in his preface to the anthology, any explicit remark on Gonzenbach's personal relationship with her informants has been lost. In Deledda's folkloric writings, there was a tendency to omit specific references to the villagers she interacted with. Sparse comments about the identity of her informants can be found among the pages of the legends she published in *Natura ed Arte* and in her ethnographic articles in *RTPI*. For instance, in "Leggende sarde" (1894), she recounted a tale about the castle of Galtellì—the village where she would set her literary masterpiece *Canne al vento* (1913) decades later—specifying that it was told to her by a woman from Orosei, a nearby hamlet:

> Il suo accento era così sincero e la sua convinzione così radicata che spesso io la fissavo con un indefinibile sussulto, chiedendomi se, per caso, queste bizzarre storie a base di soprannaturale, che corrono pei casolari

del popolo, non hanno un fondamento, e qualcosa di vero. (Deledda 1894a:927)[30]

The informant's ability to convey a sense of authenticity in her storytelling performance is underlined to the point that Deledda herself suspended her disbelief of these supernatural narratives, adding a dramatic effect to her prose. Deledda would then wrap up the tale by directly quoting the words of the informant who had "sketched" this legend for her, thus reminding the readers that this tale was believed to be anchored in truth by local villagers (Deledda 1894a:928). As seen from the picture of a Sardinian woman placed at the beginning of her article (fig. 3.5), the feminine dimension is accentuated by the illustrations inserted as an accompaniment to her "*causerie* sulle dolci leggende sarde,"[31] as she defined these tales in her correspondence with De Gubernatis.[32]

On the one hand, illustrations such as those inserted into Deledda's articles and Gonzenbach's collection partially respond to the implicit mission of folklore scholars to give visibility to the underrepresented, marginalized, and often indistinctly anonymous "women of the folk," in the realistic mode of the verist literary strand. Such women could not otherwise speak for themselves outside their restrictive social context since they were not literate and did not have the means to make their voice heard in a literary form. On the other hand, these reproductions can be critically regarded as "ways of producing marginality" (Forgacs 2014:10), a marginality that was alluring to the eyes of upper-class intellectuals who were voyeuristically fascinated by the romanticized wisdom of the folk.

Despite the inaccuracy in reporting the sources of the tales, Deledda's self-perception as a folklorist, as the examples reported in chapter 2 demonstrated, was widely documented by her own voice. When it comes to delineating Deledda's women-oriented gaze in her folkloric writings, it is worth citing a further reflection drawn from her correspondence with De Gubernatis. In a letter dated November 8, 1892, she confessed how determined she was to accomplish her dream of becoming a writer, against all odds:

[S]ono molto coraggiosa nella via che, per intima vocazione, senza studi, senza esser mai uscita dal mio piccolo nido selvaggio, ho intrapreso. Nessuno mi ha mai ajutato, pochi mi hanno compreso,—neppure nella mia

---

30. "Her accent was so sincere and her conviction so ingrained that I often stared at her with an indefinable gasp, wondering if, by chance, these bizarre supernatural stories, which circulate in the people's farmhouses, do not have a basis [in fact] and something truthful about them."

31. "short article on the sweet Sardinian legends."

32. Deledda, *Lettere ad Angelo De Gubernatis*, February 7, 1893, cass. 41 n. 33, letter n. 7:3, Fondo "Angelo De Gubernatis," BNCF (original emphasis).

LEGGENDE SARDE

— *Contos 'de fuchile* — racconti da focolare, — con questo dolce nome che rievoca tutta la tiepida serenità delle lunghe serate famigliari passate accanto al paterno camino, da noi vengono chiamate le fiabe, le leggende e tutte le narrazioni favolose e meravigliose, smarrite nella nebbia di ère diverse dalla nostra. Il popolo sardo, specialmente nelle montagne selvaggie e negli altipiani desolati, dove il paesaggio ha in sè stesso qualcosa di misterioso e di leggendario con le sue linee silenziose e deserte o con l'ombra intensa dei boschi dirupati, è seriamente immaginoso, pieno di superstizioni bizzarre e infinite. Nella stretta mancanza di denari in cui si trova ha bisogno di figurarsi tesori immensi, senza fine, nascosti sotto i suoi poveri piedi, sicchè, dando retta alle dicerie vaghe, susurrate a mezza voce, con un tremito nell'accento e un lampo negli occhi, si crederebbe che il sotto-suolo di tutta l'isola è sparso di monete d'oro e di perle preziose.

Ogni montagna, ogni chiesa di campagna, ogni rudere di castello, ogni bosco ed ogni grotta nasconde il suo tesoro. Posto da chi?..
Se fate questa domanda vi si dànno delle spiegazioni plausibilissime. Si ha un vago ricordo delle guerre, delle escursioni, dei saccheggi sofferti in ogni tempo dalla Sardegna, e specialmente da Saraceni, da Goti e dai Vandali, e si dice che i nostri antichissimi avi nascondessero in siti impenetrabili i loro tesori, — denaro, gioielli e pietre preziose, — per scamparli dall'espilazione degli invasori, e che la maggior parte di questi tesori, rimasti nei nascondigli per volontà o contro la volontà dei primi possessori, sussista ancora. Sin qui il naturale. Il sovrannaturale è la credenza radicalmente invalsa che a guardia dei tesori vigili il diavolo: il diavolo che, se alla fine di un certo tempo gli uomini non ritrovano il tesoro, se lo appropria lui stesso e se lo porta all'inferno, lasciando nelle anfore o negli scrigni contenenti l'oro e le perle, tanta bella quantità di carbone o di cenere. — La leggenda dei tesori ha così profonde radici da noi che non appena un individuo è riuscito, col suo lavoro e con la sua intelligenza, o magari con l'inganno e la perversità, ad acquistarsi qualche fortuna, subito la voce del popolino afferma che egli ha trovato un *acchisorgiu*, cioè un tesoro.

Mille ricordi mi si affollano su tal proposito al pensiero, e rammento tanti fatti ac-

Donna Sarda.

FIGURE 3.5. First page of Grazia Deledda's "Leggende Sarde," *Natura ed Arte* (1894:921). Courtesy of the Biblioteca Comunale Centrale "Palazzo Sormani," Milan.

famiglia che pure è intelligentissima,—e il poco che ho fatto l'ho fatto tutto da me. Scrivo da quattro anni: il mio sogno, la mia Idea, per non dire il mio ideale, è di fare, un giorno, qualche poco di bene al mio paese: alla mia terra sconosciuta, dimenticata, dilaniata dalla miseria e dall'ignoranza. E spero di riuscire: come, quando, non lo so ancora, ma spero di riuscire perché ho molta buona volontà e un grande coraggio.[33]

In the same letter, Deledda informed De Gubernatis that she would immediately start to "scrivere l'articolo sulle donne sarde, mettendoci, come lei si compiace scrivermi, tutto il mio sapere e tutto l'immenso amore che nutro per il mio paese tanto pittoresco quanto disgraziato."[34] "La donna in Sardegna," the first article to mark her collaboration with De Gubernatis and therefore her venture into the field of folklore studies, was published on March 15, 1893, in *Natura ed Arte*, accompanied by six illustrations of Sardinian female peasants dressed in traditional fashion. Although this article is often listed among her folkloric writings without much relevance attached to it, it shows an awareness of multiple social perspectives and touches upon several issues that characterized Deledda's subsequent literary production, namely her ideological relationship with lower-class women, her self-identification as a middle-class woman, and the increasing consciousness of her mediating role between the prejudiced image of Sardinia in the Italian mainland and the more accurate picture that she wished to convey to the continental readership.

Deledda's spirit of observation and awareness of sociocultural changes emerges in these lines, along with her acute prescience of the gradual enculturing process that was going to radically alter the Sardinian fin de siècle societal landscape. Although she never proclaimed to be a feminist, her sensitivity toward the condition of women is evident not only in her writings but also in her participation in the "Primo Congresso Nazionale delle donne italiane" in

---

33. "I am very brave to have taken this path moved by my intimate vocation, without studies, without having ever left my wild little nest. No one has ever helped me, few have understood me—not even in my family that is very smart—and the little I have done, I have done it all by myself. I have been writing for four years: my dream, my idea, not to say my ideal, is to do, one day, some little good for my country: for my unknown land, forgotten, torn by misery and ignorance. And I hope to succeed: how, when, I do not know yet, but I hope to succeed because I have a lot of goodwill and great courage." Deledda, *Lettere ad Angelo De Gubernatis*, November 8, 1892, cass. 41 n. 33, letter n. 6:3, Fondo "Angelo De Gubernatis," BNCF.

34. "write the article about Sardinian women, putting in it, as you are pleased to write to me, all my knowledge and all the immense love I feel for my picturesque and unfortunate country." Deledda, *Lettere ad Angelo De Gubernatis*, November 8, 1892, cass. 41 n. 33, letter n. 6:1, Fondo "Angelo De Gubernatis," BNCF.

1908.³⁵ Not coincidentally, Deledda dedicated the incipit of the article to Eleonora d'Arborea, Sardinian medieval heroine and promulgator of the *Carta de logu*, a legislative code of great historical value. By placing her at the beginning of her discussion around women in Sardinia, Deledda recognized her importance as an extraordinary historical female figure on the island. The excursus continues with a wide-ranging investigation of Sardinian lower-class women, whose various typologies are skillfully portrayed by connecting their characterization to the towns and villages to which they belong.

Deledda aroused the reader's curiosity by portraying typical Sardinian women in rich detail through vivid images that nearly transform these descriptions into *tableaux vivants*. She explicitly focused on lower-class women rather than the aristocratic "gentlewomen" because the former were the ones she had studied in depth, while she knew the latter only "da lontano o per fama, quindi non posso dir nulla su di esse" (Deledda 1893a:762).³⁶ The first portrait she delineated is that of a Sardinian woman strongly linked to tradition, without ambitions: "Attaccata saldamente alla tradizione segue gli usi, i costumi, le idee di sua madre, come questa aveva conservato quelle della madre sua, e nell'educazione materna le trasmetterà ai suoi figli ed ai suoi nipoti" (Deledda 1893a:751).³⁷ Despite describing lower-class women as uneducated, Deledda showed respect for their beliefs and admiration for their diligence. Though it is possible to discern her self-distancing from them, it can also be assumed that she was attempting to build on the previous knowledge and prejudices of her target continental readers in order to offer a more nuanced depiction of Sardinian womanhood.

In conjunction with an overview of local female costumes, the geography of the Sardinian territory, with its mountains, vegetation, colors, and flavors, is outlined. Deledda would return to these ethnographic descriptions in a subsequent article on "Tipi e paesaggi sardi," published in 1901 in *Nuova Antologia* (fig. 3.6).³⁸ In a positivist fashion, she seemed to acknowledge an intimate

---

35. The "First National Congress of Italian Women." On Deledda and the feminist discourse, see Briziarelli (1995).

36. "from afar or due to reputation, therefore I cannot say anything about them."

37. "Firmly attached to tradition, she follows her mother's habits, customs, ideas, in the same way as her mother had preserved those of her mother, and in her maternal teaching she will pass them on to her children and her grandchildren."

38. Deledda's study was accompanied by twenty-one photographs. At the end of her excursus, Deledda reported that "[p]arecchie di queste fotografie furono eseguite dalla signora Popert, che ora pubblica un albo, all'acqua forte, di costumi sardi" (Deledda 1901:623) [many of these photographs were taken by Mrs. Popert, who has now published a book of etchings of Sardinian costumes]. Carlotta Ida Popert (1848–1923) was a German-Italian painter who had

Donne di Barbagia.

FIGURE 3.6. "Donne di Barbagia," *Nuova Antologia*, "Tipi e paesaggi sardi" (Deledda 1901:615), Biblioteca Comunale dell'Archiginnasio, Bologna (A.2245). Courtesy of the Biblioteca Comunale dell'Archiginnasio, Bologna.

connection between geography and social conditions, which in turn influenced women's characterization. She observed: "Ciascuna [donna] riflette l'ambiente in cui vive, il costume che indossa, il paesaggio che la circonda" (Deledda 1893a:752); "È sempre l'ambiente, sempre la nuova esterna manifestazione della esistenza, che influisce" (Deledda 1893a:754).[39] It is tempting to interpret statements such as "ogni regione ha una specialità, un riflesso della natura nel volto e nello spirito della donna" (Deledda 1893a:755) as a feminization of the geography of the Sardinian landscape.[40] However, in Deledda's view, as elucidated in the subsequent passages of the article, women were far from being a mere background or reflection of Sardinian nature. Their essential function on a societal level is underlined: "dappertutto la donna sarda lavora" (Deledda 1893a:757).[41] Women were the pillars of the familial and

---

also participated in the Exhibition Beatrice in Florence, during which she received a silver medal. De Gubernatis praised her for her "lavori ragguardevoli" [praiseworthy works] (De Gubernatis 1889:386).

39. "Each woman reflects the environment in which she lives, the costume she wears, the landscape that surrounds her"; "It is always the environment, always the new external manifestation of existence, that exerts influence."

40. "Each region has a specialty, a reflection of nature in the face and spirit of the woman."

41. "everywhere the Sardinian woman works."

social structure: "E lavorano, lavorano, povere donne, esposte a tutte le intemperie, mietendo sotto il sol-leone, vendemmiando, raccogliendo ulive in inverno,—nelle miniere, nelle lavorazioni, negli orti e in casa" (Deledda 1893a:756).[42]

Deledda's discussion of local women is interspersed with verses of typical women's songs in Sardinian, followed by translations in Italian in the footnotes. These *mutos*, "bizzarri stornelli,"[43] rhymes and ancient verses, reflect her conception of poetry as "la storia dei popoli" (Deledda 1893a:759).[44] In her first folkloric sketch, Deledda also showcased a knowledge of the economic and social relations existing between city and countryside, namely between the progressive cities of Cagliari and Sassari and the inland with its wild mountains and remote villages, where development and progress were more difficult to attain. The villages were "non ancora solcati dalle microscopiche ferrovie che il governo ci ha regalato" (Deledda 1893a:751),[45] a significant aside in which Deledda's resentment toward the unjust post-unification government comes to the surface.[46] The writer implicitly alluded to the historical issues related to the Southern Question through this sarcastic remark.

Once again, the Barbagia region is described as the most picturesque of Sardinia: the costumes are generally described as "barbari," but for the most important occasions "ci sono vestiti di una delicatezza suprema, che richiamano al pensiero la dolcezza delle foglie dei castagni" (Deledda 1893a:754).[47] Nuoro was called the "Athens of Sardinia" for its cultural liveliness and for being the birthplace of several contemporary intellectuals such as Sebastiano Satta (1867–1914), Antonio Ballero (1864–1932), and Francesco Ciusa (1883–1949). Deledda, after presenting this definition, maintained that Nuoro was one of the few cities touched by modernity. As a consequence, female attitudes

---

42. "And they work and work, poor women, exposed to the bad weather, reaping under the sun, harvesting grapes, gathering olives in winter,—in mines, in the manufacturing field, in the vegetable gardens and at home."

43. "strange folk songs."

44. "the story of the people."

45. "not yet crossed by the microscopic railways that the government has granted us."

46. The implementation of the railway system in Sardinia started in the 1870s: between 1870 and 1874, the railroads Cagliari–Oristano and Ozieri–Porto Torres were created (Casula 1992:497). Deledda did not shy away from expressing her criticism toward the governmental economic policies implemented on the island. For instance, in the short story "Colpi di Scure" (1905), she sharply criticized the exploitation and deforestation provoked by the introduction of the railway system in Sardinia. In this respect, see Caterini (2013).

47. "barbaric," "there are clothes of a supreme delicacy, which recall the sweetness of chestnut leaves."

were more civilized there: it was therefore not unusual to find "qualche popolana col giornale o il romanzo smarrito nel panierino del suo cucito o nel sentirla occupata di elezioni politiche e amministrative" (Deledda 1893a:754).[48] Deledda's irony or perhaps her self-complacency in being a native woman of Nuoro emerges between the lines.

As a whole, in "La donna in Sardegna" Deledda gave further confirmation of her ability as a versatile writer and acute observer. She concluded this ethnographic sketch by claiming that her studies aimed exclusively at giving a picture of the women of the people and not of the bourgeoisie, among whom there were women who were becoming progressively more accustomed to modernity:

> Per ciò noi abbiamo anche donne che frequentano il liceo e si preparono [sic] alle lotte della scienza e dell'arte, abbiamo donne che dipingono, che cantano, che suonano, che studiano, che pensano, che scrivono. Sono in numero ristretto per l'immenso spazio dell'isola,—ma sono abbastanza in confronto al numero della popolazione;—e sono il vago barlume precursore di un'era novella, del sognato Risorgimento sardo, destinate qual sono ad essere madri, maestre, guide ad una nuova, sana, forte e intelligente generazione che solleverà la Sardegna dal tenebrore letterario, artistico, politico, economico e sociale in cui giace. (Deledda 1893a:762)[49]

It was a conclusive message of hope mixed with bitterness, a hope placed in the women of the Sardinian bourgeoisie that, by cultivating arts, letters, and politics, could transfer to the children of the twentieth century "una sana e forte cultura" (Deledda 1893a:762).[50] These final references to "donne della borghesia"[51] are particularly significant: it is not far-fetched to imagine that in this passage Deledda was thinking about herself, her own positioning within Sardinian society as a firsthand listener, observer, and teller of its popular life. Through these optimistic words, she voiced her dream of helping her native

---

48. "a woman of the folk with a newspaper or a novel lost in her sewing basket or to hear her absorbed in political and administrative elections."

49. "We also have women who attend high school and prepare themselves for the struggles of science and art, we have women who paint, sing, play, study, think, write. They are in small number if compared to the immense space of the island, but they are enough if compared to the percentage of the population; and they represent the vague gleam of a new era, the dreamed Sardinian Risorgimento, destined to be mothers, teachers, guides to a new, healthy, strong, and intelligent generation that will raise Sardinia from the literary, artistic, political, economic, and social darkness in which the island lies."

50. "a healthy and strong culture."

51. "bourgeois women."

island resurge from the decadence to which it had been fatally confined up to that point.

If Deledda initiated her ethnographic research with an article on female peasants' costumes, while Gonzenbach chose to start her collection with an illustration of a young storyteller followed by a tale about female linguistic shrewdness, Wilde's *Ancient Legends* (1887) opens with a story in which all the key characters are women, either supernatural or of the earthly world. The protagonist of "The Horned Women" (Wilde 1887a, I:18–21) is a rich lady who was visited during the night by a procession of witches. While she was carding and the rest of her household was asleep, she first let in the Witch of the One Horn, who "sat down by the fire in silence, and began to card the wool with violent haste" (Wilde 1887a, I:18); then, one after another, eleven witches entered the house, each of them with a growing number of horns on their foreheads, all busy turning their spinning wheels while singing in an ancient tongue.[52] The mistress of the house fell under their spell and could neither move nor speak, until one of the witches ordered her in Irish to prepare food. Since the woman needed water to make a cake, the witch told her to take a sieve to a well and come back with water in it, an impossible task to perform. While the woman was away, the horned women made a cake "mixed with the blood drawn from the sleeping family" (Wilde 1887a, I:20).

In the meantime, the lady went to the well but naturally could not fetch water with a sieve. Once she started weeping, the Spirit of the Well came to her aid, suggesting to bind clay and moss and attach them to the sieve so as to be able to carry the water, and recommending to return to the corner of the house facing north, crying three times: "The mountain of the Fenian women and the sky over it is all on fire" (Wilde 1887a, I:19). The pronouncement of this enchanted formula provoked the abrupt flight of the twelve witches. After their departure, the woman of the house began preparing several protections against their return, meticulously following the instructions given to her by the Spirit of the Well. These precautions consisted in sprinkling the water she had previously used to wash the feet of her child outside the door, dividing the witches' cake made of blood and putting pieces of it in the mouth of each sleeping family member, and placing the cloth woven by the witches inside a chest with a padlock. When the witches tried to reenter the house, they were

---

52. The appearance of grotesque female spinners by night recalls the widespread ATU tale type 501, *The Three Old Spinning Women*, although in this case the women are twelve in total and the spinning motif acquires different nuances. Seán Ó Súilleabháin (1903–1996) and Reidar Christiansen (1886–1971) included this story in *The Types of the Irish Folktale* (1963) as type 501*, *The Fairy Hill Is on Fire!* (O'Neill 1991:192).

not able to do so due to these protections. This deeply disturbing legend thus ends on a positive note, with the final remark that one of the witches' mantles, which was accidentally left behind on that eerie night, was preserved and remained in that family for hundreds of years (Wilde 1887a, I:21).

The horns traditionally stand for symbols of nurturing motherhood linked to beliefs associated with the ancient maternal goddess (Guiley 2008:170), an aspect which is turned upside down in this legend, since, rather than being represented as motherly figures, the horned women are depicted as cursing crones. This legend can be found under various guises across Ireland and serves different functions, including "escape, excitement and compensation" (O'Neill 1991:194). However, contrary to other versions of the legend, Wilde's variant escapes ethical categorizations and does not conform to what "moral-hunting readers" would expect (Ní Chuilleanáin 2003:33; Markey 2011:45). Furthermore, as Eiléan Ní Chuilleanáin observes, the prominence given to this distinctively Irish tale placed at the beginning of *Ancient Legends* accentuates the "cultural value of the Irish imagination, and thus, obliquely, it serves Speranza's political ends" (Ní Chuilleanáin 2003:34). The references to the tasks that the woman of the house performed, such as carding, spinning the wheel, making food, and protecting the household, are noteworthy as they act as a reminder of the conventional model of womanhood put to the service of relatives, as opposed to the supernatural power of the witches that threatens to jeopardize the family. The nocturnal scenery renders the tale more unsettling and stands as a warning and implicit condemnation of being involved in such tasks during the night.

The multiple allusions to spinning are interesting from several points of view: first of all, they immediately conjure up one of the key female labors of the time (fig. 3.7); second, they evoke the well-established association between the act of spinning and the act of telling stories, harking back to Philomela and Procne's tale of unspoken violence (Rowe 1986).[53] As Marina Warner eloquently put it:

> Spinning a tale, weaving a plot: the metaphors illuminate the relation; while the structure of fairy stories, with their repetitions, reprises, elaboration and minutiae, replicates the thread and fabric of one of women's principal labours—the making of textiles from the wool or the flax to the finished bolt of cloth. (Warner 1994:23)

---

53. Schacker convincingly argues that the images of spinners conjured the idea of a world on the verge of vanishing due to the emergence of an economic system that was shifting toward a progressive mechanization (Schacker 2003:39–41). On the interconnection between spinning and telling tales, see also Tatar (2003:114).

FIGURE 3.7. An old Irishwoman at her spinning wheel, *The Living Races of Mankind* (Johnston et al. 1901, II:503). Photograph by Amélie Deblauwe, Cambridge University Library (1903.11.31). Amélie Deblauwe / Reproduced by kind permission of the Syndics of Cambridge University Library.

"The Horned Women" thus emerges as a narrative about the power—and threat—of spinning tales, which can be simultaneously instructive, protective, disconcerting, and entertaining. Attesting to the legacy of the opening tale of *Ancient Legends*, these disquieting female figures who drew blood from sleeping prey were believed to be a source of inspiration for another influential writer in fin de siècle Ireland, Bram Stoker (1847–1912), who knew Jane Wilde personally: he may have shaped the blood-sucking "weird sisters" featuring in his masterpiece *Dracula* (1897) after becoming acquainted with this legend rooted in Irish folklore.[54]

Jane Wilde's "The Horned Women" immediately plunges readers into the uncanny atmosphere of Irish legends about encounters with supernatural creatures, the meanings of which are often elusive. Conversely, Augusta Gregory began her collection *Visions and Beliefs* (1920) with a section devoted to narratives collated geographically rather than thematically: "I give the sea-stories first," she wrote at the beginning of her anthology (Gregory 2006 [1920]:16). She explained this choice for the arrangement of her writings by claiming that she had started gathering these narratives precisely "on the coast" (Gregory 2006 [1920]:16), before moving to an exploration of the western isles facing Galway Bay, namely Inishmor, Inishmaan, and Inisheer. Islands and their inhabitants, both real and imagined, are a constant presence in *Visions and Beliefs*. This becomes apparent from the very first pages, as illustrated in this excerpt that gives voice to the words of the islander Colman Kane:

> There's said to be another island out there that's enchanted, and there are some that see it. And it's said that a fisherman landed on it one time, and he saw a little house, and he went in, and a very nice-looking young woman came out and said, "What will you say to me?" and he said, "You are a very nice lady." And a second came and asked him the same thing and a third, and he made the same answer. And after that they said, "You'd best run of [sic] your life," and so he did, and his curragh was floating along and he had but just time to get into it, and the island was gone. But if he had said "God bless you," the island would have been saved. (Gregory 2006 [1920]:21–22)

These memories reveal the vivid imaginary of late nineteenth-century common people living at the edge of Ireland. These secluded geographical areas, together with the rest of the Gaeltacht, were presented as reservoirs of a purer and uncontaminated spirit that was not necessarily representative of Ireland as a whole, being in stark contrast with the skeptical attitude that was starting

---

54. On the connection between Bram Stoker and the Wilde family, see Fitzsimons (2015: 64–70). In particular, on the influence of Jane Wilde's folklore collections on Stoker, see p. 65.

to dominate elsewhere in the country and in the rest of the "civilised world": as W. B. Yeats evocatively put it, "that now old and much respected dogmatist, the Spirit of the Age, has in no manner made his voice heard down there" (Yeats 1888:ix, x). Yet these marginal contexts were chosen to represent precisely the spirit of nationhood that needed to be conjured in order to revitalize the sense of being Irish.

Augusta Gregory's excursions "on the edge of the world" (Gregory 1903a:193), as she defined these areas in *Poets and Dreamers*, allowed her to interact directly with islanders who were still Irish speakers, "proud to show that the language that has been called dead has never died; and glad at the new life that is coming into it" (Gregory 1903a:134). As she recalled in her first folklore collection, several of the people she conversed with during these expeditions, such as a "woman sitting in a donkey-cart" and a "woman with madder-dyed petticoat" (Gregory 1903a:134), were singing melancholic songs about journeys across the Atlantic sea, reminiscing about the old times when they had to leave their land as emigrants.

What emerges from the outset in Gregory's *Visions and Beliefs* is not only the focus on insular narratives against the backdrop of the sea but also their gendered dimension, since she reported verbatim both stories told by men and stories told by women, always specifying the gender of her informants before recounting them. Sometimes the names are reported in full, as in the cases of John Corley, John Nagle, Mrs. Casey, Colman Kane, Pat O'Hagan, Mrs. O'Dea, Mrs. Daly, Peter Donohue, Peter Dolan, and Mary Moran in the section on sea-stories, while in other instances the references to informants were more generic, such as "a little girl," "the man of the house," "a woman from the Connemara side," "a Galway woman." Such vagueness and anonymity is more in tune with the elusiveness that can often be found in folktales, indeterminacy being one of their salient features, whereas personal names provided a greater degree of focus, truthfulness, and reality.

However, Gregory's oscillation between being at times explicit and at times unclear about the villagers' identity is motivated less by stylistic effect than by the ethics of her anthropological approach, as she specified in the preface to the chapter "Appearances" in *Visions and Beliefs*: "I do not give the real names either of those who are living or who have left living relatives" (Gregory 2006 [1920]:202). In other words, such a choice was motivated by her respect toward the informants who were still a breathing part of living communities. It is plausible that several villagers wished to remain unidentified when passing down these tales and anecdotes, both for issues of confidentiality, since many of these stories tackled sensitive topics such as death, illness, or childbirth, and for beliefs dictating that it was preferable not to speak of these matters for fear of the fairies' revenge.

When approaching these folkloric writings from a gender perspective, it is important to keep in mind that the personal beliefs of Gonzenbach, Deledda, Wilde, and Gregory on women's issues may have seeped through them. These issues, albeit veiled by the imagination of the folk, were often connected to women's genuinely harsh living conditions, which were exacerbated by their prescribed roles as daughters, mothers, and wives. However, from the second half of the nineteenth century onward, women's desire for emancipation as independent individuals became increasingly strong and acquired political resonance. Such longings and aspirations of the "women of the folk" take on different nuances when taking into account the extremely varied experiences of these folklorists as women who, in their own terms, challenged the status quo in their respective cultures, leaving an exemplary testimony of how the obstacles that women encountered in their lives could be overcome. These obstacles included not only spatial and educational constraints but also physical and verbal abuse, to which some of these folkloric writings subversively gave voice.

A breakthrough in the Sicilian tradition, as hinted in chapter 2, Gonzenbach's collection presents narratives in which female characters often defy the common stereotypes associated with womanhood as well as vivid descriptions of violence. The attempts to subjugate the female characters frequently leads to an overturning of gender relationships, with the submissive heroines transformed into accomplished women. Brutal episodes such as rape and femicide find space between the lines of these stories, with actions that are frequently "set in motion by material lack" (Noyes 2015:8). For instance, an explicit reference to a rape perpetrated against a young woman can be found in "La serpe che testimoniò in favore di una ragazza," a tale that represents a rarity in Italian folklore (Gonzenbach 2019 [1870]:261–62).[55] In this narrative, which partially belongs to the ATU tale type 672, *The Serpent's Crown*, the female protagonist finds the strength to curse the prince after he takes advantage of her and enlists

---

55. There are evident similarities between this fairy tale and an Albanian variant recorded by Pitrè, "I biri Regghit e Gghialpri (Il figlio del Re e il serpente)" (Pitrè 1875, IV:292–93), although in the latter the representation of the rape is absent and therefore the tone of the tale becomes radically different from the version reported by Gonzenbach (Rubini in Gonzenbach 2019 [1870]:516). Similarities can also be found between this fairy tale and the Jewish legend "Wiesel und Brunnen als Zeugen" (Rubini 2006:89). The tale has been translated into English as "The Snake Who Bore Witness for a Maiden" (Gonzenbach, trans. Jack Zipes, 2006:18–20) and "The Serpent That Testified in Favor of a Girl" (Gonzenbach in Canepa 2023:208–10). As Canepa notes, this tale voices the practice of the "rehabilitating marriage," which was legal in Italy up until 1981, according to which "if a rapist married his victim, he could not be subject to criminal prosecution" (Canepa 2023:208).

a snake as witness: "Se nessuno mi sente nella mia angoscia [...] chiamo a testimone questa serpe: tu, principe non potrai sposare nessun'altra tranne me" (Gonzenbach 2019 [1870]:261).[56] On the day of his announced wedding, this snake impedes the prince from marrying a beautiful princess by wrapping itself around his neck. The young victim of his violence reaches the castle and offers to free him. However, as soon as she starts asking him questions, he pretends not to recognize her. Despite his denial, she firmly asserts her position: "Com'è possibile? [...] Hai dimenticato di essere entrato in casa mia con la violenza e di avermi costretta a sottostare alle tue voglie?" (Gonzenbach 2019 [1870]:262).[57]

The determination and courage of the young female character are exemplified by the image of the snake, which squeezes the prince's neck more tightly after each of his lies until he finally admits that he must keep his commitment. The complicity of the snake, which turns into the girl's avenging weapon, is an emanation of her longing for justice. She is a heroine whose courageous anger leads to her own revenge and self-affirmation, bending the course of events to her will. The climax featuring the snake and the girl towering in front of the prince, worthy of a theatrical performance, is symbolic of an unprecedented desire for self-determination. This narrative is but one example of the rich panoply of resolute fairy-tale heroines who populate Gonzenbach's collection: several of these female characters, rather than requiring the intervention of external saviors, are relentless creators of their own destinies, *deae intra machina* of their own stories. The subversive content of such tales demonstrates the bond of trust between Gonzenbach and the female informants who gave her access to their transgressive imagination, thus exemplifying "the potential for women's cross-cultural communication with one another and their difficult negotiation of class and national differences" (Bacchilega 2009:252).

The representation of women's subversion of spatial and social mores is a recurrent motif in the narratives transcribed by Gonzenbach. Another equally resolute heroine is the protagonist of tale n. 34, "La storia di Sorfarina" (Gonzenbach 2019 [1870]:207–12), a merchant's daughter with unusual intelligence who takes charge of a school during the teacher's absence.[58] This

---

56. "Since nobody hears me in my need [...], I'm calling upon you, oh snake, to bear witness for me: prince, may you never marry anyone but me!" (Gonzenbach, trans. Jack Zipes, 2006:18).

57. "What? [...] Have you forgotten how you charged into my house and forced me to do your will?" (Gonzenbach, trans. Jack Zipes, 2006:19).

58. A renowned nineteenth-century variant of this fairy tale can be found in Pitrè's *Fiabe novelle e racconti popolari siciliani* (1875, I:46–59) under the title "Catarina la Sapienti," told by Agatuzza Messia. For a translation of Pitrè's tale into English, see *Catarina the Wise and Other Wondrous Sicilian Folk and Fairy Tales* (Pitrè 2017:15–23), edited and translated by Jack Zipes.

narrative lends itself to a fascinating interpretation of the theme of subversion in relation to the symbolism of space in fairy tales. The story is initially set in a school. The main characters are Sorfarina and an unnamed king's son, who is sent to her same school to be educated. Yet one day the schoolteacher is forced to leave for a trip and needs to find someone else to manage the school. Sorfarina takes the initiative to replace the "maestro," showing great resourcefulness. The aspiration to emancipate herself finds expression in her desire to take someone else's place, relocating herself in a position of power within a well-defined professional context and, by extension, outside the domestic sphere. This initiative encapsulates a threefold border crossing of age, class, and gender restrictions: first, as a young girl, Sorfarina breaks out of her place in the symbolic world of childhood, landing in the adult world; second, as a merchant's daughter, she changes her social status, improving her condition; finally, as an emerging independent woman, she runs away from her family environment to enter the workplace.

The new position occupied by Sorfarina determines the unfolding of different power dynamics in the tale. One day, while she is giving a lesson, the king's son does not pay attention, and she therefore gives him a slap. He does not react immediately but does not forget her defiant act. Several years later, he decides to marry her. Sorfarina joins the king's son, moving from the school to the kingdom. However, after their marriage, she is literally thrown out of the bedroom. The prince defines the bed as his property and forces her to lie on the floor, a symbolically laden space that suggests the social subalternity of Sorfarina, as a woman, daughter of a merchant, and the prince's new wife. This is the punishment she deserves for the slap that she gave to the prince many years earlier. However, despite his abuses, she holds on to her position and repeats the refrain: *"nun m'aju pintutu, e nun mi pintirò, se n'àutra ci ni voli, ti la darò"* (Gonzenbach 2019 [1870]:208; original emphasis).[59] Her persistence results in a further change in her position: to punish her, the prince subsequently throws her into an empty cistern in the middle of a courtyard, a place inside a

---

However, the variant transcribed by Gonzenbach seems to be more audacious in the representation of the several intercourses between the prince and the female protagonist that occur in various Italian locations, since they do not marry each other repeatedly on each occasion as they do in the variant transcribed by Pitrè (Rubini in Gonzenbach 2019 [1870]:505). The story was clearly circulating, both orally and in print, in the nineteenth century. A mid-nineteenth-century French literary rewriting of the tale by Édouard Laboulaye, "Pif Paf, ou L'art de gouverner les hommes," has been republished and translated into English by Jack Zipes (Laboulaye 2018:31–80).

59. "I didn't regret it, and I don't regret it now. And if you want another slap, you'll get one and how!" (Gonzenbach, trans. Jack Zipes, 2006:2).

place, which suggests isolation and solitude, the deprivation of social and human relations and her subordination to the prince's power.

Afterward, the prince embarks on a journey. Sorfarina asks him if he will travel across the sea or across the land. He answers that he will go to Rome by sea, and so she follows him, secretly, by land. The geographical contrast between the two stands for a relational contrast between husband and wife. In Rome, she settles in a "beautiful house," right in front of the "inn" of the prince, which is actually a brothel, where she uses a disguise to tempt her husband. The cunning Sorfarina does not reveal her identity. The prince is thus unaware that the woman he has slept with is indeed his own wife, whom he thinks he has left at the bottom of the empty cistern in the kingdom. After this first encounter, Sorfarina gives birth to a child named Romano, therefore bearing in his name the geographical connotation of their "illicit" affair. The same scene repeats itself three times: the prince travels to Naples by sea, and Sorfarina reaches him in disguise by land. They see each other again through the window balcony, and Sorfarina conceives another child, this time named Napolitano. Finally, the prince travels to Genoa. Again, Sorfarina follows him and gives birth to Genovesina. Sorfarina eventually returns to the palace of the kingdom with her three sons, and she publicly slaps the prince for his misdeeds in Rome, Naples, and Genoa. In the bedroom, to be sure that the prince would not hurt her, she prepares a doll made of sugar and honey and places it on the bed. The prince cuts off the doll's head and then repents for having murdered the woman he thought was his wife. At this point, Sorfarina appears from underneath the bed, declares her repentance, and the prince forgives her. In the end, the balance between the two protagonists is restored.

This fairy tale masterfully exposes the fluctuating power dynamics between the two main characters. The superiority of the female protagonist emerges preponderantly through her ability to use her husband's betrayal to her own advantage and to follow his steps across Italy, moving effortlessly from the south to the north of the Italian peninsula across different symbolic places. In the process, the interpersonal relations between pupil and teacher, husband and wife, are repeatedly subverted by the female protagonist. Her positionality is atypical in that she chases the man rather than fleeing from him, an important shift in perspective that allows her to assert her own rights. Until the end of the tale, she stubbornly refuses to repent for her action, regardless of his threats. Even after their marriage, she does not submit to his will: when he imprisons her in a well and leaves the kingdom, she cleverly manages to escape and follows him in disguise. Her resolve and perseverance are combined with her shrewdness. It is Sorfarina who pulls the strings of the story, dominates the prince with her strength of character and eventually subdues his arrogance, without ever abdicating her dignity.

Among the pages of *Sicilianische Märchen*, tale n. 64, "La storia della Fata Morgana" (Gonzenbach 2019 [1870]:352–59), provides another instance of a powerful fairy-tale heroine. In this story, Fata Morgana, rather than performing the role of the main character, appears as an external pivotal figure who acts as a catalyst for the unfolding of the main action or, in Rubini's words, as a true *"dea ex machina"* (Rubini 1998:211; original emphasis). According to Renato Aprile, the presence of Morgana in *Sicilianische Märchen* responds to a sublime impulse of the tale, which takes a concrete shape in the fairy, who "regna sull'apparenza illusoria delle cose visibili" (Aprile 1991:219).[60] The figure of Fata Morgana in Southern Italy is deeply interlaced with the optical mirages that can be witnessed in the Strait of Messina.[61] The characterization of Morgana in this tale, whose sweat has a healing power and is capable of restoring the king's lost sight, brings back to mind another figure from Gonzenbach's collection who also performs the function of a *dea ex machina*: Parcemina, who features in tale n. 26, "Il coraggioso figlio del re" (Gonzenbach 2019 [1870]:137–44). Parcemina's name is a further testimony of the intricate relationship between the oral and the written dimensions in the fairy-tale tradition (Sanfilippo 2020a:205). As Rubini points out, Parcemina may derive from the fairy Parchemin, a name that means parchment (Rubini in Gonzenbach 2019 [1870]:498). In a similar vein to the story of Fata Morgana, the quest for the sweat of this sorceress functions as a key plot driver in the fairy tale.[62]

Sorfarina, Fata Morgana, and Parcemina are just a few of the female figures that Gonzenbach gave voice to by transcribing the imaginative words of local female storytellers. The ending of these tales brings us back to the space inhabited by these narrators. Rather than finishing with the well-known phrase "and they all lived happily ever after," the conclusive formula of Sorfarina's tale ironically says: "iddi ristaru filici e cuntenti, / e nui semu ccà senza nenti" (Gonzenbach 2019 [1870]:212).[63] We can only make assumptions about what this fairy tale actually meant for the nineteenth-century female peasants who were recounting it to Gonzenbach. Perhaps none of them had ever left Sicily and could only dream of traveling across Italy; perhaps the informants were subjugated to their husbands' power and through these tales expressed their

---

60. "reigns over the illusory appearance of visible things."

61. For a study of the figure of Morgana and connected folkloric motifs in and beyond *Sicilianische Märchen*, see Sottilotta (2021).

62. It is worth noting that both "Il coraggioso figlio del re" and "La storia della Fata Morgana" partially follow the narrative structure of the ATU tale type 314 *Goldener* (Rubini in Gonzenbach 2019 [1870]:497).

63. "[The king's son and the merchant's daughter] remained happy and content, but we [the storytellers] are still sitting here without a cent" (Gonzenbach, trans. Jack Zipes, 2006:8).

intimate yearning for social change. Such ending formulas expose a scathing attitude toward the abyss between the happy endings of the narratives and the life of deprivation and struggle that the peasant storytellers had to endure. In this regard, Zipes observes how "[t]he tellers remain dispassionate and choose a style that emphasizes distance" (Zipes 2006a:xix), a distance that allows readers to get a glimpse of the narratological presence of nineteenth-century storytellers within the collection.

Similar longings for hope and yearnings for justice, albeit filtered by the imagination of the "folk," can be perceived among the fairy-tale narratives gathered in Wilde's *Ancient Legends*. One of the most eloquent tales in this regard is "Fairy Justice," which retells the story of an ill-tempered man from Shark Island, also known as Inishshark, in County Galway, who used to physically abuse his wife. One day, while crossing the sea, he encounters a company of fairy-spirits who are determined to drown him. Fortunately for him, a red-haired man intervenes to take him back to shore. However, before disappearing, the man says to him:

> [Y]ou are safe, but mind, the spirits are watching you, and if ever again you beat your poor good wife, and knock about the things at home just to torment her out of her life, you will die upon that rock as sure as fate. (Wilde 1887a, I:58–59)

The moral of the tale reiterates this warning: "the threat of retributive justice shows a laudable spirit of indignation on the part of the fairy race against the tyranny of man over the weaker vessel" (Wilde 1887a, I:59). Sometimes only through an imaginative immersion in the otherworld can justice be found for ill-treated women. The beaten wife of this tale is an absent protagonist: she does not speak, she is spoken of. Yet her centrality in the tale is deafening. Wilde's touch in this conclusive comment is palpable: as mentioned in chapter 2, she advocated forcefully for women's emancipation. Her conception of women at the end of the nineteenth century resonates with the hopeful message that Deledda put forward in "La donna in Sardegna": "Now, for the first time in the history of the world, a path is opening to female intellect, energy and talent, and, henceforth, women, perhaps, may lead in the learned professions" (Wilde 1893:93). The plethora of examples that she provided in *Social Studies* (1893) about women's subjugation across different geographical spaces and historical times demonstrates the extent of her cultural references on this subject. These pages vibrate with desire for change in women's status, a wish not so distant from the one that animated the efforts of the Gonzenbach sisters in Sicily.

These women shared a deep sense of social and cultural commitment in favor of female emancipation, publicly and courageously spreading their ideas in an era in which such engagement for women was gaining a foothold, in spite of women's historic difficulties in making their voices heard. They were critical of the oppressive conditions that relegated women to a subordinate position, advocated for women's work as a weapon for social redemption, and supported the need for female education as an essential premise for their emancipation. Magdalena Gonzenbach's pedagogical commitment involved teaching women's work as a means of earning and gaining economic independence. Jane Wilde likewise placed crucial importance on both work and education: "Female professorships might be founded, lecturers appointed, each with a definite income, [...] to give women, not only the means to live, but also a vivid interest in life by the honourable recognition of their gifts and powers" (Wilde 1893:18–19). She also supported the Married Women's Property Rights Act (1882), which decreed women's rights to reclaiming property and retaining a separate legal identity from their husbands, claiming that

> Women have been so long politically non-existent that they almost tremble to assert they have any rights apart from their husbands. They require much training in habits of self-assertion and self-reliance, and full knowledge of their newly acquired legal rights, in order that they may become worthy of the nobler life of freedom. (Wilde in Varty 1998:14)[64]

She was highly critical of women's historic state of enslavement, commenting that across the ages, nothing could be heard but "the clank of their fetters" (Wilde 1893:13), and she demanded higher standards in female education, defining its state of affairs as "mere dilettanteism" since it did not offer "what women really need so much, an assured status, and an honourable independence" (Wilde 1893:21). Such considerations are echoed in the tales featuring subdued female characters in *Ancient Legends*, whose narrative trajectories eventually lead them to a better condition. Alongside the abuse reported in "Fairy Justice," there are other instances of violence perpetrated against women in this volume.

In "The Fairy Child," a tale told by an old female islander, the victim is a young woman who could not bear children: it is narrated that the young protagonist's husband "was a rough, rude fellow, and used to taunt her and beat her often, because she was childless" (Wilde 1887a, I:119). When she eventually became pregnant, her husband realized that their son was actually an elfish imp, and for this reason "he struck her and beat her worse than ever he had done in his life before, so that she screamed aloud for help" (Wilde 1887a,

---

64. Wilde's reflections on women were originally published in the weekly journal *The Gentlewoman* on January 13, 1883. On her views on gender equality, see also Fitzsimons (2015:139–140) and Mendelssohn (2018:14).

I:119). Two strange, red-capped women entered the house and came to her aid: while one of them held the man down, the other one beat him nearly to death. They were the "avengers" who had come for retaliation against the husband who was brutally abusing his wife: "look on us and tremble; for if you ever beat your wife again, we will come and kill you. Kneel down now, and ask her pardon" (Wilde 1887a, I:120).

After this frightening encounter, the man went away and left his wife in peace. As the tale unfolds, it becomes clear that both the child and the husband were actually fairy creatures sent to substitute for the young woman's real child and husband, who returned at the end of the tale and "lived happily from that day forth" (Wilde 1887a, I:124). The passages in which physical violence occur clash against the otherworldly atmosphere of the tale and are described in realistic detail, showing how Jane Wilde could resort both to "a journalistic eye for the graphic, and a poet's ear" (Melville 1994:200). Her idealistic views, then, emerge not only in her nonfiction works but also in her folkloric writings, especially when it comes to restoring the rightful dynamics between men and women, as happens in "Fairy Justice" and "The Fairy Child."

An equally revengeful tone—to the detriment of ill-mannered men—can be detected in *TPN*. For example, by perusing the section "Bestemmie e imprecazioni (Frastimos e irroccos)" listing Nuorese curses in rich detail, it is evident that Deledda was a witness to abusive episodes that were habitually perpetrated against women. She thereby reported instances of what would be defined nowadays as street harassment and enumerated the picturesque curses that local women used as self-defense against the young men in Nuoro:

> I giovinotti, a Nuoro, hanno l'abitudine, proprio di gente incivile e barbara, di toccare le popolane quando le incontrano per le strade. Le più forti reagiscono, scagliando magari delle pietre contro i malcreanzati, altre si contentano di imprecare, mandandoli al diavolo, o augurando loro le mani secche o prese da un cancro. (Deledda 1894b:655–56)[65]

It was therefore possible to hear curses such as "Zustissia ti brusiet" / "Giustizia ti abbruci" and "S'ocru puntu e sa manu frazica" / "L'occhio trapunto e la mano incancrenita" (Deledda 1894b:656).[66] Deledda also reported an imprecation by means of which people wished that divine justice might descend

---

65. "The young men in Nuoro have a habit, which is typical of uncivilized and barbaric people, of touching female peasants when they meet them on the streets. The strongest women react, perhaps throwing stones at these bad-mannered men. Other women are content to curse them, tell them to go to hell, or wish them to have withered or gangrenous hands."

66. "May justice burn you" / "May your eye be pierced and your hand become gangrenous."

upon the earth, leaving the guilty with nothing, not even "chinisa in su fuchile" (Deledda 1894b:660).[67] She specified that this curse had been pronounced in the criminal court by a woman who had been accused of a mysterious felony and had consequently been condemned to thirty years in prison. She also wrote a section on "sos berbos," popular incantations endowed with an aura of mystery and sacrality. They were extremely difficult to find, and yet she managed to retrieve them "[a] stento, a forza di preghiera, di astuzie, di regali e di favori" (Deledda 1895c:241).[68] After having pierced the veil that surrounded them, Deledda listed the spells that could provoke havoc or make miracles. For better or for worse, words were charged with a strong power to effect change, and curses could be deployed not only as a means to defend oneself from aggressors but also as a weapon to attack innocent victims.

In this regard, in a section devoted to courtship practices, Deledda recorded several customs related to unrequited love. When young men were rejected by women, it was common for them to commission obscene songs against their lover, which were then widely sung by people as a form of public shaming: "e la ragazza, in barba al codice penale, resta infamata" (Deledda 1895e:420).[69] In other cases, young men even felt entitled to damage the property of the woman's family, "sempre in modo da sfuggire alla giustizia" (Deledda 1895e:420).[70] The revenge of the lover with wounded pride could assume a strong symbolic value. For instance, when a woman was accused of badmouthing her previous partner, the man would rip off the tongue of an animal from her family's cattle: "Se una donna offende a parole un uomo, questo cerca di strappare la lingua al cavallo od ai buoi della sua famiglia. Vendetta simbolica che dice alla donna: tu sei linguacciuta ed io vorrei strapparti la lingua maledetta" (Deledda 1895e:420).[71] Deledda specified that these vengeful habits were becoming increasingly less common: "Ora gli animi, resi un po' scettici dallo spirito dei tempi che si avanza inconsapevolmente anche tra il popolo, si calmano presto; le canzoni ingiuriose vengono dimenticate, le vendette perdonate" (Deledda 1895e:420).[72]

---

67. "ashes in the hearth."
68. "with difficulty, by dint of prayers, wiles, gifts, and favors."
69. "and the girl, in defiance of the penal code, remains slandered."
70. "always escaping justice."
71. "If a woman verbally offends a man, he tries to tear out the tongue from the horse or from the oxen of her family. A symbolic revenge that says to the woman: you are a jabberer, and I would like to tear out your cursed tongue."
72. "Nowadays the souls soon calm down, as the spirit of the times, which unwittingly advances even among the people, has made them a little skeptical; insulting songs are forgotten, revenges are forgiven."

In this transitional moment shifting from a past depicted as primitive and yet worthy of preservation to a future that held both the promise of progress and the danger of oblivion, intellectuals such as Gonzenbach, Deledda, Wilde, and Gregory managed to capture and offer to future generations a snapshot of folktales and social practices from the past that were on the verge of changing abruptly. Such intertwining of the past world and the future world is also reflected in the singular way in which these folkloric writings are permeated by pagan and Christian references, in an inextricable combination that gives life to stories brimming with miraculous wonder.

Resisting Evil: Helpers and Healers between Pagan and Christian Beliefs

A particular feature of the folkloric writings under scrutiny is their inherent syncretism, that blend of pagan and Christian beliefs which can be found in the Italian and the Irish traditions at large but even more so in the south of Italy and in the west of Ireland. As hinted in chapter 1, "south" and "west," rather than being mere topographical denominators, emerge as categories that reverberate with ideological nuances. As such, these distinctive cardinal points can be juxtaposed when taking into account the long-standing disparity that characterized these areas in the history of the Italian and the Irish nations. The status of sociocultural subalternity in relation to external hegemonic forces animates the core of the concepts of Italian "south" and Irish "west." Southern Italian regions have been historically characterized by a need for psychological shelter from powerful external sources that wield adverse effects on a daily basis. In his influential study on the widespread cultural phenomenon of *jettatura* in Southern Italy,[73] particularly in Naples, Ernesto de Martino unraveled the roots beneath the ideology of "fascinazione" (de Martino 1982:8), rendered in English as "dark binding" (de Martino 2015:xiii), a psychic condition that leaves people helpless before untamable forces:

> [Q]uesta perdurante potenza del negativo si traduce, dal punto di vista esistenziale, nella ricorrente esperienza della *precarietà dei beni vitali elementari*, nella *insicurezza delle prospettive*, nel caos di cozzanti interessi particolaristici e individualistici, e in generale nell'*ininterrotta pressione di forze non dominabili*—naturali o sociali che siano—prementi da tutte le parti e

---

73. As Dorothy Louise Zinn, translator of De Martino's *Sud e magia*, remarks, "jettatura has no exact translation in other languages, but the English-language reader may find it helpful to conceive of it as a form of jinx borne by the glance of the jettatore" (Zinn in de Martino 2015:xiii, n.2).

schiaccianti l'individuo [. . .]. *Ora proprio qui si inserisce il particolare rilievo che assumono, nel sud, il ricorso alle tecniche protettive della bassa magia, la accentuazione magica del cattolicesimo, la molteplicità dei raccordi intermedi magico-religiosi.* (de Martino 1982:165; my emphasis)[74]

In de Martino's view, the historic burden of living in miserable conditions led southern Italian lower classes to find coping mechanisms that transcended the boundaries of rational thinking to face the adversity of everyday life. Popular remedies, spells, curses, and incantations of all sorts can therefore be interpreted not simply as residuals of an archaic past but also as meaningful forms of resistance against a present condition that left individuals powerless before outward forces that could not be subdued otherwise. Such considerations on southern Italian regions prove to be relevant also when considering the hardship and uncertainty faced by the people living in nineteenth-century western Ireland, who were overwhelmed by the devastating effects of the Great Famine and merciless English domination. Such adversities are interlaced with the meanings that popular beliefs were charged with, as well as with how these oral forms of cultural expression were perceived by both insiders and outsiders and eventually reformulated in print in folklore collections.

The insular dimension adds a layer of distinctiveness to these works, since the quintessential feature of islandness implies a sense of difference from the outer world. The cornerstones of this construct hinge on characteristics that can be found in any island beyond the specificities of local contexts, such as an embedded sense of isolation intermingled with a metaphysical condition of being conscious of this separation; a spiritual sense of place, often linked to the awareness of being surrounded by water, which determines a deep bond with nature; and the strong sense of identity within insular communities (Fowles 1978; Conkling 2007). Islandness can thus be approached as a unique way of perceiving the world, which is not an exclusive prerogative of native islanders but which can also be acquired by outsiders who immerse themselves in an island's life and adopt its worldview. Conkling encapsulates the feeling associated with islandness by highlighting its "sacred connectedness to place that blurs the

---

74. "From an existential point of view, this lasting power of the negative translates into the recurring experience of the precariousness of elementary goods for survival, the insecurity of prospects, the chaos of clashing particularistic and individualistic interests. More generally, it translates into an uninterrupted pressure of uncontrollable forces—be they natural or social—pressing in on all sides and crushing the individual [. . .]. It is precisely within this context that we must consider the particular importance in the South of the use of protective techniques of low magic, the magical tone of Catholicism, the multiplicity of intermediate magical-religious connections" (de Martino, trans. Zinn, 2015:178).

sense of time, since the connections to the past feel so omnipresent" (Conkling 2007:199). Linking the category of islandness to folklore studies provides a framework for interpreting the bond between the frequent references to the geographical seclusion of islands and the emphasis on the need to preserve these ancient insular traditions. In island cultures, the relevance of a shared past is merged with a conceptualization of insular space that forges a deep sense of identity, often accompanied by a feeling of defenselessness and an ensuing need to feel safe. It is thus with these insular implications in mind that the intertwining of pagan and Christian beliefs so profoundly ingrained in the nineteenth-century folkloric writings under scrutiny can be analyzed.

In the chapter entitled "The Evil Eye—The Touch—The Penalty" (Gregory 2006 [1920]:80–103), Augusta Gregory documented the reminiscences of several men and women—such as Margaret Bartly, Mrs. Nelly of Knockmogue, Mrs. Clerey, James Fahey, Frank McDaragh, Mrs. Meade, Mrs. Quade, Mrs. Casey, and John Curtis, among others—who heard stories about the "drohuil" (Modern Irish *drochshúil*), the Irish term for "evil eye" (Gregory 2006 [1920]:86), or who had personally experienced its consequences on their family members. Gregory recorded a remarkable number of stories told by islanders who suffered from health issues or who had lost relatives—by and large wives and children—either at childbirth or at a very young age. In popular belief, these tragic events were often linked to the influence of an evil source. The mysterious circumstances surrounding these otherworldly experiences pervade her collection. A puzzling episode is reported in the words of an unnamed "island woman," mother of two young fishermen, who used to work for the head coastguardsman's wife. One day, foreseeing that a misfortune was about to happen, she went to the coast where her boys were fishing in order to give them some bread, as she worried that they "might have got the hunger" (Gregory 2006 [1920]:87). Her younger son had a strange pain in his heel, which caused him to limp. The mother found out that this pain had been provoked by an encounter with a mysterious "woman of the village," who envied him for the fish he had gathered in his basket.

Recollections of the effects of the evil eye on children abound: as mentioned, the heartbreaking loss of infants was frequently interpreted by villagers as a consequence of being "touched" by malicious entities. For instance, the informant Mrs. Casey retold an episode in which the husband of a woman who lived by the sea had to decide to ask a priest to pray for either his wife or their baby's life: only one of them could be spared. Father Rivers prayed for the wife, and both the priest and the baby died shortly after. Other informants reported that the "drohuil" occurred because those stricken by it would forget to utter the words "God bless you," another telling example of how the Irish "kept a foot in both camps—the pagan and the Christian" (Ferguson 2002:1211).

Priests were believed to be able to cure villagers from this evil influence but usually would rather not engage in these matters because they were afraid of the consequences on their own lives. This was the case of Father Gallagher, as reported by Mrs. Clerey. She had asked for his help to cure her sick brother by reading him the mass of the Holy Ghost, but the wealthy priest refused to do so: "He was afraid to go as far as that for fear it might fall on his stock, that he had a great deal of" (Gregory 2006 [1920]:83).

Prior to Gregory's expeditions in the Aran Islands, the widespread beliefs about the evil eye in Ireland were also reported in print by Jane Wilde, who included in her collections several legends in which these beliefs, often imbued with religious connotations, play a central role (Wilde 1887a, I:36–48). For instance, Wilde listed a charm that St. Mary was believed to have given to St. Bridget, according to which if a fairy threw the evil eye at someone, "three greater in heaven" would cast it into the "great and terrible sea" (Wilde 1887a, II:87). In another tale about the power of the evil eye, four female figures are the driving forces for the recovery of a stolen child affected by this malignant influence (Wilde 1887a, I:38–40). Whenever neighbors came to visit a mother in County Galway, they pronounced blessings to wish prosperous health to her son. However, on one occasion, an old woman who came to visit the mother and her child did not utter any benediction. As a result, the child started crying in despair, and none could understand the source of his pain. Another woman, passing by the house, was asked to intervene, for not even the priest could help, as he dreaded the fairies' wrongdoings. The passerby blessed the infant by spitting at him and explained to the mother that her real child had been taken away by the fairies and substituted with a fairy creature. However, no harm could be done to him because he always received many blessings, except on one occasion when a random old woman sat silently next to him. The only way to obtain the real child was therefore to bring this woman back to the house and burn a piece of her cloak to break the spell that was looming over him. The mother managed to lure the old woman into the house by offering her cakes and supper, and her eldest daughter cut off a piece of her cloak. With the help of the father, the piece was burned and the real child eventually came back to his mother.

Remarks about spitting as a remedy and as a form of blessing are pervasive in both Irish and Italian popular traditions. In this regard, Wilde explicitly mentioned that it was necessary to spit on a child in order to reverse the curse provoked by the evil eye:

> To avert the evil eye from child or beast, it is necessary to spit upon it on entering a cabin; and if a stranger looks fixedly and admiringly on a child, he is at once requested to spit upon it; this saving process being perhaps

unknown to him or if he should not understand Irish, and omit the rite that preserves from evil, then the old mother will rise up from her seat by the fire and perform the ceremony herself, that so good luck may not depart from the house. (Wilde 1890:20–21)

The reference to the curse being provoked by a stranger is worthy of notice. Equally interesting is the intervention of the "old mother" if the stranger was not able to perform the rite due to a lack of knowledge of the Irish language. An outsider was evidently considered a greater threat to the community, although the evil eye could be thrown by strangers and islanders alike. Gregory transcribed another anecdote told by an unspecified "old man with a basket" about an islander, Ned Buckley, who was believed to have the power of throwing the evil eye. One day he threw it against a nice young woman who consequently had to lay in bed for several months. To reverse the curse, he was asked "to throw a spit on her" (Gregory 2006 [1920]:88).

In 1885 Giuseppe Pitrè published a study precisely on the act of spitting and the functions of saliva in popular traditions (Pitrè 1885b:233–36), an aspect that he would further explore in his medical work *Medicina popolare siciliana* (Pitrè 1896:225–28), placing emphasis on its apotropaic power. Interestingly, the healing function of saliva plays a central role in Gonzenbach's tale n. 25, "La figlia della Madonna" (Gonzenbach 2019 [1870]:133–36), which belongs to the ATU tale type 706, *The Maiden without Hands*. The Madonna in this narrative is an example of how the sacred and the profane dimensions can intertwine with each other in the fairy-tale tradition (Rubini 1998:223; Delitala 2005:151).[75] Popular wisdom drew and fed on stories that allowed the humblest to come to terms with the abuses they were forced to endure. In this tale, the religious figure of the Madonna assumes the function of tutelary deity of a poor servant who is welcomed into the house of a priest after she is abandoned at birth and left on his doorstep. The statue of the Madonna, near which the child used to rest, comes to life and takes on a maternal role for the child: the Madonna provides advice for her and conveys to her the most appropriate strategies to escape the priest's attempts at rape. There is no censorship of the ignominious behavior of the priest, who is portrayed in a very negative light, constituting an explicit critique of the representatives of the Catholic Church (Rubini 2006:93). With the Madonna's help, the girl takes refuge in a secluded little house where a king who is passing by falls in love with her. He then leads her to his palace where she eventually gives birth to two wonderful boys. The evil priest decides to take revenge on her by killing the children with a knife, which he then hides in her lap. She is consequently accused of killing her own

---

75. For a wide-ranging study on the cult of the Virgin Mary, see Warner (2013 [1976]).

sons, but once again the Madonna comes to her aid, bringing the children back to life with her miraculous saliva. The Madonna and the girl then run away, and the girl spends her life working hard in an inn together with her resuscitated sons. One day the king, passing by the inn in the company of the evil priest, observes the children playing with some golden apples. The Madonna sets up her revenge by hiding the apples in the king's pocket, thus showing him how easy it is to be unjustly blamed, as happened in the past to his wife. Thanks to the intervention of the Madonna, the deceit of the priest is unveiled. After this revelation, the Madonna disappears, having fulfilled her function. In this fairy tale, the Madonna, on the one hand, performs the role of the good fairy and, on the other, can be interpreted as the girl's alter ego, embodying her cunning side and turning her into an assertive woman capable of implementing survival strategies in the face of danger. As a traditional religious entity, the Madonna symbolizes also an external legitimation of the girl's rebellion against the abuse she was enduring and a means to escape violence.

An equally benign function embodied by a fairy-tale Madonna comes to the surface in Grazia Deledda's "Nostra Signora del Buon Consiglio,"[76] which presents all the stylistic markers of "oralità narrativa"[77] identified by Cristina Lavinio: allusions to the listeners/readers within the text; moral and ideological remarks with didactic purposes; inaccuracies and vagueness typical of the fantastic mode; formulas that contribute to the dilation of time and space; and the use of the present as a verbal tense in pivotal moments of the story to convey greater narrative tension (Lavinio 2019:85–88). In this as well as in other narratives by Deledda, folkloric and religious connotations conflate in the representation of the Virgin Mary, who turns into "fairy godmother and mother of God, accomplice and protectress" (Carolan 1999:103), in a mixture of magical spirituality and Christian faith that leads to a "comparable connection between fairies and Madonnas, folktale dreams and Christian visions, magical objects and miraculous rosaries" (Mazzoni 2008:97). As Nancy Canepa observes, it is not uncommon that "religious figures stand in for magic helpers (e.g., fairy godmothers), attesting to Sardinian and Italian popular traditions that syncretically draw on both secular and Christian folklore" (Canepa 2023:321). The positive influence of the Virgin Mary can also be found in Irish

---

76. This tale has been thoroughly analyzed by Cristina Mazzoni (2008), who translated it into English and published it first in 2019. This English translation can also be found in *The Pomegranates and Other Modern Italian Fairy Tales* (Mazzoni 2021:112–22). Another English translation appears in Nancy Canepa's *The Enchanted Boot: Italian Fairy Tales and Their Tellers* (Canepa 2023:321–30), followed by another tale by Deledda, titled "Fairy Tale" (Canepa 2023:331–34).

77. "narrative orality."

traditions. Wilde explicitly commented in the introduction to *Ancient Legends* that the

> pathetic tale of the beautiful young Virgin-Mother and the Child-God [...] touched all the deepest chords of feeling in the tender, loving, and sympathetic Irish heart. The legends of ancient times were not overthrown by it, however, but taken up and incorporated with the new Christian faith. (Wilde 1887a, I:12)

Such stratification of paganism and Christianity can be found in the Irish prayers that mix popular beliefs with religious references to the Virgin Mary, such as the formula reported to cure a wound: "In the name of the Father, Son, and Holy Mary. The wound was red, the cut was deep, and the flesh was sore; but there will be no more blood, and no more pain, till the blessed Virgin Mary bears a child again" (Wilde 1887a, II:87).

The intermingling of pagan and Christian beliefs went hand in hand with the coexistence of supernatural and scientific cures in popular traditions. In *Ancient Cures*, the detailed list of remedies for all sorts of diseases provides a full range of the imaginative combination of popular beliefs and healing methods. In this respect, Wilde included an anecdote about a wise woman, "learned in the mysteries" (Wilde 1890:31), who was capable of curing depression by pronouncing a magic formula in Irish on specific days of the week. The rite was sealed by the baking of a cake and the making of the sign of the cross over it. So great was the peasants' belief in these ancient remedies that "in case of accident or sickness, they would far sooner trust the wise woman of the village than all the dispensary doctors in Ireland" (Wilde 1890:31). Physicians, well aware of these popular practices, would not dissuade their patients from them if these rituals were not harmful, but would rather combine them with scientific treatments; the "medico-religious character" of their cures was believed to be effective (Wilde 1890:5).

References to women as healers abound in folk traditions. Jane Wilde reported the story of a woman of the islands who was considered a "fairy doctress" because the fairies had initiated her into the mysteries and secrets that nature offered those who had the power of controlling them (Wilde 1887a, I:216–17). Augusta Gregory devoted a lengthy section of *Visions and Beliefs* to the most renowned *bean feasa*, "woman of knowledge," of nineteenth-century Ireland, the legendary Biddy Early (Gregory 2006 [1920]:31–50), as well as another shorter chapter to the "wise women" who had the ability to use herbs and charms to support those in need (Gregory 2006 [1920]:148–61).[78] Grazia Deledda, in her article on Sardinian popular remedies, also mentioned a

---

78. On Biddy Early, see Ryan (1978), Lysaght (1998a:273), Jeckins (2007), and Lenihan (2018).

medichessa, a female healer who was able to "measure" diseases with a wool yarn (Deledda 1895e:409–10). These women, learned in the mysteries of life, performed a fundamental social function, becoming a point of reference for people who did not have alternative means to cope with their tribulations and sufferings (Ó Crualaoich 2005). Recorded in this shifting historical period as a result of deep-seated oral traditions, these narratives and customs reveal both the captivating illusions and harsh realities of the local communities from which they originated. These fragments of oral traditions frequently give space to the deeds of magical female figures, whose otherworldly features will be examined in the following section.

Creatures "from the Outside": Magical Femininity in Insular Folklore

Fairies, witches, ogresses, and mermaids, in their countless declensions, left a strong imprint on the collective imaginary of lower classes across the centuries and have persistently been repurposed through different media. Their pervasiveness across various forms of storytelling suggests that they are endowed with a deep cultural significance, in that they were, and still are, able to convey fears and anxieties, hopes and desires related to changing perceptions of womanhood rooted in historical reality. The range of otherworldly creatures that can be found in the Italian and Irish folkloric writings under scrutiny encourages an analysis of magical femininity and its multifaceted meanings across cultures.

In Sicilian folklore, a recurrent supernatural female figure is the *mammadraga*, which Giuseppe Pitrè described as an anthropophagous and bloodthirsty creature standing opposite to the benevolent fairies, akin to the diabolical witches of medieval legacy who are portrayed as constantly fighting against the triumph of good:

> Le draghe o mammadraghe portano il nome dei mariti, e pari ad essi hanno la leggerezza nel segreto e la imprudenza del parlare [...]. Ma tra esse e i mariti v'è una certa differenza di istinti; ché quello de' draghi è di malfare, sebbene le loro minacce facciano temere di peggio, e quello delle draghe è di mangiar carne umana e di cercarla ad ogni costo. La draga è sanguinaria, e si pasce rubando, come il mostro della novella-mito di Polifemo, pecore, capre e buoi [...]. In altre versioni di queste novelle le draghe son sostituite dalle streghe, che come quelle si presentano sotto vesti di vecchie tapine e brutte quanto sia dato immaginare. (Pitrè 1875, I:cxxii–cxxiii)[79]

---

[79]. "The *draghe* or *mammadraghe* bear the name of their husbands, and like them they have the lightness of secrecy and the imprudence of speaking [...]. But between them and their husbands there is a certain difference in instincts; for the male *draghi*'s instinct is ill repute,

In fairy tale n. 15 transcribed by Gonzenbach in *Sicilianische Märchen*, entitled "Re Cardiddu" (Gonzenbach 2019 [1870]:82–89), the *mammadraga* features as the antagonist who creates obstacles aimed at preventing the marriage between the king and a shoemaker's daughter, the birth of their son, and the ensuing happy ending.[80] She is presented as a wicked old ogress who tries to pull the strings of the story by pushing the king to marry her own offspring rather than the shoemaker's daughter.

The tale presents echoes evidently derived from the tale of Cupid and Psyche in Apuleius's *Metamorphoses*, which Armando Maggi (2015:68–86) examined by focusing on the narrative trajectory of the unnamed lower-class maiden who turns into a motherly queen by the end of the story.[81] The *mammadraga* is an equally interesting character to analyze since her subterfuges allow for the transformation of the girl into a subservient wife. The *mammadraga* in this tale represents a residual image of Venus, the vengeful mother who attempts to disrupt the union of Cupid with a mortal woman. The maiden's only chance to escape death is to conform to the model of submissive womanhood that the husband and the surrogate mother-in-law demand her to perform. On a subtler level, it can be argued that the *mammadraga* herself triggers the metamorphosis that will lead to the girl being crowned as a wife and mother through her series of trials, in a sort of implicit bequeathing process by which she reiterates the pivotal roles associated with conventional womanhood. As such, through the figures of the evil *mammadraga* and of the king masked as a helper, this tale reveals the heavy constrictions that limited women's lives.

Even though the *mammadraga* in this tale is the personification of wickedness, traditionally *mammadragas* are not always evil: in some variants, they are

---

although their threats make one fear for the worse, and that of the female *draghe* is to eat human flesh and seek it at any cost. The *draga* is bloodthirsty, and she grazes herself by stealing sheep, goats, and oxen, like the monster in the myth of Polyphemus [...]. In other versions of these novellas, the *draghe* are replaced by witches, who similarly appear under the guise of old wretches, as ugly as can be imagined." For a study of the figure of the *mammadraga* in Pitrè's *Fiabe novelle e racconti popolari siciliani*, see Castiglione (2018:37–45).

80. The fairy tale is a variant of the ATU tale type 425A, *The Animal as Bridegroom*, intermingled with ATU 313, *The Magic Flight* (Rubini in Gonzenbach 2019 [1870]:488). An example of a literary fairy tale featuring this magical creature can be found in Luigi Capuana's "La mammadraga" (1893): in this tale, the figure is vividly described as an anthropophagous witch. Such details can be considered the fruits of Capuana's literary reelaboration, whereas in the oral tradition descriptions are scant (Capuana 1992:148–56).

81. A literary antecedent of this tale type is Giambattista Basile's "Il ceppo d'oro" (The Golden Trunk) in *Lo cunto de li cunti* (Basile 1994 [1634–36]:545–55).

presented as "fate premiatrici di buone, e punitrici di cattive opere" (Pitrè, 1875, I:cxxiii).[82] Despite having a negative function in the tale transcribed by Gonzenbach in which she is diametrically opposed to the positive role of the fairies, the *mammadraga*'s portrayal as a supernatural creature is more ambiguous than it may seem at first. This apparent good-versus-evil dichotomy links the *mammadragas* to other female figures who are well known in the Sicilian folkloric tradition, the *doñas de fuera*. This term harks back to the sixteenth-century witch trials that took place during the Spanish domination of the Mediterranean island. In Sicilian and in Italian, *doñas de fuera* can be translated "donni di fuora" and "donne di fuori," respectively, literally meaning "ladies from the outside" (Henningsen 1990:193; Zipes 2012:74). Giuseppe Pitrè provided a detailed account of the different names with which these entities were addressed, with emphasis on their duality:

> Le *Donni di fuora*, dette pure *Donni di locu, Dunnuzzi di locu* (Sambuca), *Donni di notti* (Caltanissetta, Francofonte), *Donni di casa* (Nicosia), *Donni, Dunzelli, Signuri, Belli Signuri, Patruni di casa* (Contea di Modica), *Patruni d' 'u locu, Diu l'accrisci,* sono esseri soprannaturali, un po' streghe, un po' fate, senza potersi discernere in che veramente differiscano dalle une e dalle altre. Genî benefici o malefici, disposti e fermamente decisi a giovare o a nuocere, ad arricchire o ad impoverire, a far belli o a render brutti, esse non hanno altro movente se non il capriccio, la bizzarria e una certa lor maniera di vedere e di giudicare le cose. [...] [A]mano la pulitezza e la compostezza fino allo scrupolo; e nelle case dove vanno vogliono trovare tutto in bell'ordine, ben rifatto il letto, bianche e odorose le lenzuola, sprimacciati i guanciali, splendido il rame della cucina, benissimo spazzate le stanze. (Pitrè 1889, IV:153–54)[83]

This description highlights their intrinsically contradictory nature, being characterized both as good and evil, gracious yet whimsical, embodying elements

---

82. "fairy rewarders of good deeds, and punishers of wrongdoings."

83. "The *Donni di fuora*, also called *Donni di locu, Dunnuzzi di locu* (Sambuca), *Donni di notti* (Caltanissetta, Francofonte), *Donni di casa* (Nicosia), *Donni, Dunzelli, Signuri, Belli Signuri, Patruni di casa* (Contea di Modica), *Patruni d' 'u locu, Diu l'accrisci,* are supernatural beings, part witches, part fairies, it is not possible to discern how they really differ from one another. Beneficial or evil geniuses, willing and firmly determined to benefit or harm people, to enrich or impoverish them, to render them beautiful or ugly, they have no other motivation than whim, strangeness, and a certain way of seeing and judging matters. [...] They scrupulously love cleanliness and composure; and in the houses they go to, they want to find everything in good order, the bed well made, the sheets white and fragrant, the pillows fluffed, the copper in the kitchen resplendent, the rooms thoroughly swept."

of the fairy and the witch (Zipes 2012:74).[84] Their oddity and otherness is stressed, since, despite being powerful and thus dangerous, they also paradoxically personify the essential features of perfect femininity, such as cleanliness and composure, performing household chores like impeccably making the bed and sweeping the floor with diligence. Pitrè noted how these "women from the outside" blended witch and fairy traits, as exemplified in a legend linked to a very specific place in Palermo: the Curtigghiu di li setti Fati (Pitrè 1889, IV:176),[85] located in front of the church of Santa Chiara, not far from the Ballarò street market in the heart of the city, which still exists today under the name Piazzetta Sette Fate.[86] The dancing *doñas de fuera* were believed to bring women or men of their choice into this patio by night, showing them wonderful visions and then disappearing at the crack of dawn. In an empowering children's book loosely inspired by this legend, contemporary Sicilian writer Nadia Terranova observes that *curtigghiu*—the dialect term for courtyard—retains a double meaning: beyond its topographical connotation, it stands for "gossip," precisely because it was in the courtyards that women would often gather to talk (Terranova 2022). Once again, we are reminded of the place-bound dimension of these oral narratives, with their "chatty asides, apparently spontaneous exclamations, direct appeals to the imaginary circle round the hearth, rambling descriptions, gossipy parentheses," all different facets that are intermingled in the old wives' tales (Warner 1994:25).

In addition to these women's conflicting fairy-witch portrayals, an aspect worthy of notice is their liminality, which is a persistent characteristic of otherworldly femininity in Irish folklore as well. The *doñas de fuera* are both human and animal, shapeshifting into toads according to numerous local tales (Pitrè 1889, IV:154) and on rare occasions into snakes, ducks, turkeys, or even into a fierce wind capable of taking the roof off (Pitrè 1889, IV:160). Half tutelary geniuses, half witches, they can be vengeful and are therefore feared, so much so that "si nomina Dio con voce intelligibile, e si parla con le Donne di

---

84. Zipes refers to another significant scholarly study in which the link between fairies and witches is underscored, namely Carlo Ginzburg's *Storia notturna: una decifrazione del Sabba* (1989). In this book, building on his previous study *I benandanti: stregoneria e culti agrari tra Cinquecento e Seicento* (1966), Ginzburg further explores the rituals of the *benandanti*, members of communities that practiced fertility cults in sixteenth- and seventeenth-century Friuli (Zipes 2012:74).

85. "courtyard of the seven fairies."

86. "square of the seven fairies." Interestingly, Ester Rizzo noted that this is one of the 256 locations entitled to women in Italy, in contrast with the 2,288 places dedicated to men, as reported by the association Toponomastica femminile (Rizzo 2022).

fuora a bassa voce" (Pitrè 1889, IV:173).⁸⁷ They are both visible and invisible, belonging to *this* world and to the *other* world, a transcendental space in between sea and land, where they most frequently live, preferring the poorest and most isolated houses to woods and gardens (Pitrè 1889, IV:154).⁸⁸

The belief that these creatures had a predilection for secluded and impoverished houses shows their proximity on an imaginative level to women from the lower social classes, the informants who most frequently voiced these fairy beliefs. In this regard, Gustav Henningsen comments that "the Sicilian fairy-cult was a daydream religion that allowed poor people to experience in dreams and visions all the splendours denied them in real life" (Henningsen 1990:200). Such a reflection evokes the words that Augusta Gregory expressed in *Poets and Dreamers* about "the strange contrast between the poverty of the tellers and the splendours of the tales" (Gregory 1903a:129). Through these flights of fancy, members of the lower classes projected their own beliefs, hopes, and dreams into a parallel world made of words and imagination, in which poverty could be replaced by wealth, deadly diseases could be miraculously healed, and female subjugation—despite leaving traces even in this imaginary dimension—could blend into models of powerful femininity.

A striking similarity between Sicilian and Celtic folklore can be found in the popular tales and beliefs concerning child abduction, which in the Sicilian tradition are closely related to the *doñas de fuera*. It was said that the latter were naturally attracted to children, taking care of them but also frightening them when they misbehaved. In Sicilian popular beliefs, it was suggested that they could even substitute children, provoking their physical and emotional decay:

> Ma esse gli fanno le più strane cose: lo cambiano e lo sostituiscono con un altro più bello o più brutto, con un altro poverissimo se quello è di agiata famiglia, e viceversa; il che si dice *canciari*. Il bambino *canciatu* o *canciateddu* è il bambino affatturato e lo si giudica tale perché perde il colore del

---

87. "God is named with an intelligible voice, and one talks with the Ladies from the outside in a low voice."

88. In this regard, Pitrè wrote: "È superfluo l'avvertire che esse non son visibili a chicchessia né sempre; anzi può reputarsi fortunato chi riesce a vederle e, vedutele, a cattivarsene l'animo indocilmente bizzarro. [...] Abitano più in terra che in mare, ed ai giardini, ai boschi, alle macchie, dove pur sogliono fermarsi, preferiscono le case anche poverissime e fuori mano. Ecco perché si dicono anche *Donni di casa*" (Pitrè 1889, IV:154) [It is superfluous to warn that they are not visible to anyone nor always; on the contrary, those who are able to see them and, after seeing them, to capture their unruly, bizarre soul can consider themselves lucky. [...] They live mostly on land rather than in the sea, and they prefer houses, even very poor and out of the way, to gardens, woods, and scrublands, where they nonetheless usually stop. That's why they are also called *Women of the house*].

viso, emacia a vista d'occhio, intristisce miseramente, senza che se ne comprenda il come ed il perché. Ogni virtù di farmaco, ogni umano argomento che la medicina e l'amore consigli, riesce frustraneo. (Pitrè 1889, IV:170)[89]

They could misplace children from their cradle for their own amusement, but they could also watch over them and make them laugh while they slept. Ignazio Arturo Trombatore, a contributor to *RTPI* from Catania, devoted an article to the "Donne di casa" in which he recounted a story told to him by "una donnicciuola moglie di un marinaio."[90] The particulars supplied by this female informant confirmed these entities' malicious tendency of stealing children from the cradle (Trombatore 1894a:764). Their supernatural strength was greatly underscored: "Camminano con una velocità mirabile, da per tutto e senza paura: valicano il mare immenso e tempestoso, superano le montagne scarpate e altissime, entrano nei labirinti intricati delle foreste buie" (Trombatore 1894b:930).[91]

In *Storie di figli cambiati* (2014), Riccardo Castellana carried out a thorough investigation into the affinities and differences that can be traced in a wide range of Sicilian and northern European folkloric sources and literary reelaborations of the motif of children's abduction and substitution by supernatural entities. In particular, Castellana draws attention to the Sicilian novella "Il figlio cambiato," by Luigi Pirandello (1867–1936), which first appeared in a slightly different form in *La riviera ligure* in 1902 under the title "Le nonne" and

---

89. "But they do the strangest things to the child: they change him and replace him with another more beautiful or uglier, with a very poor one if he comes from a well-to-do family, and vice versa; this is called *canciari* [to change]. The *canciatu* or *canciateddu* [changed] child is the haunted child and is deemed as such because he turns pale, emaciates visibly, saddens miserably, without understanding how and why. Every virtue of drugs, every human advice that medicine and love recommends, is vain." It was also reported that in Corleone "[c]erte femminucce ritengono che le *Donne di fuora* cangino i bambini in quelle case che trovano non ispazzate, né pulite. Esse vogliono, esigono pulitezza e fragranza" (Pitrè 1889, IV:170) [some little girls are of the opinion that the *Donne di fuora* change children in the houses that they found unswept and unclean. They want, they require cleanliness and fragrance].

90. "a giddy woman, the wife of a sailor."

91. "They walk with admirable speed, everywhere and without fear: they cross the immense and stormy sea, overcome extremely steep and high mountains, enter the intricate labyrinths of dark forests." Trombatore also compiled *Folk-lore catanese* (1896), in which his observations on the "donne di casa" were republished (Trombatore 1896:11–16). Riccardo Castellana notes that in Trombatore's study only the motif of abduction is present, whereas the child's substitution is not mentioned; he also reports that Luigi Pirandello harshly criticized this book in a review published on November 29, 1896, in *Rassegna settimanale universale* (Castellana 2014:26).

then in *Corriere della sera* in 1923 (Pirandello 1987, II:496–501).⁹² Pirandello's tale and his subsequent theater play *La favola del figlio cambiato* (1933) are built around this folkloric motif. At the heart of the narrative lies the substitution of a child at the hands of the *doñas de fuera*. In this bitterly ironic short story about the tragic consequences of popular beliefs, the *doñas de fuera* are depicted as mysterious flying witches prone to mischief, and the changed son is destined to become a social outcast.

The belief in children's substitution is also deeply ingrained in Irish popular beliefs: the children taken away by fairies were identified with the term "changeling."⁹³ In both the Sicilian and Celtic traditions, these supernatural figures have a predilection for kidnapping children, a motif that clearly voiced the contradictory and precarious nature of the societies that conceived such creatures, turning them into "emblemi *magici* dell'oppressione provocata da continue invasioni" (Bombara 2015:3; original emphasis).⁹⁴ Jane Wilde and Augusta Gregory reported in their anthologies a copious amount of tales and anecdotes concerning fairy changelings.⁹⁵ They belonged to the "*Sidhe*, or spirit race" (Wilde 1887a, I:68),⁹⁶ the Irish term that became widespread in the literary works that came to light during the Celtic Revival in order to address the "fairy race" that was banned from heaven, partially plummeting to earth and partially descending into the sea. Thomas Crofton Croker provided an etymology of this term and of several other words connected to it:

> *Sia, sigh, sighe, sigheann, siabhra, siachaire, siogidh*, are Irish words, evidently springing from a common root, used to express a fairy or goblin, and even a hag or witch. [...] The close of day is called *Sia*, because twilight, "That sweet hour, when day is almost closing," is the time when the fairies are most frequently seen. Again, *Sigh* is a hill or hillock, because the fairies

---

92. Curiously, in some instances these supernatural *donne* [women] were called *nonne* [grandmothers] (Castellana 2014:27). Besides the first version of Pirandello's tale, another example in which this denomination appears is Luigi Capuana's *Scurpiddu* (1898): the protagonist of this narrative, Mommo, once heard his mother telling that these *nonne* had stolen her child, who was then found dead (Capuana 1987 [1898]:22).

93. The changeling motif is catalogued as F321.1 in Stith Thompson's *Motif-Index of Folk-Literature* (Thompson 1956:61).

94. "magical emblems of the oppression provoked by continuous invasions."

95. On traditions and stories revolving around fairy changelings, see also Katharine Briggs's *The Vanishing People: Fairy Lore and Legends* (1978:93–103).

96. With regard to the spelling of *sí* and *síthe*, I use the modern Irish form *sí* in the singular nominative case and the form *síthe* in the plural nominative case. Occasionally, these terms appear without accent in the original texts or in the alternative form *sidhe*: in these cases, I spell the words as they are written in the primary sources that I am quoting.

are believed to dwell within. *Sidhe, sidheadh,* and *sigh* are names for a blast or blight, because it is supposed to proceed from the fairies. (Croker 1828:xx–xxi)

Gregory recounted that the *síthe* were once called "gods or children of gods," being the angels "cast out of heaven" (Gregory 2006 [1920]:11). The fairy people lived both in "the clefts of the hills" and in "beautiful fairy palaces of crystal and pearl underneath the waves," where they used to dance "on the greensward under the ancient trees" (Wilde 1887a, I:68). Their dyadic nature was stressed: they could be categorized into two distinct races, one "tall and handsome, gay, and given to jesting and to playing pranks, leading us astray in the fields, giving gold that turns to withered leaves or to dust"; the other "small, malicious, wide-bellied" (Gregory 2006 [1920]:10).

Comparable to the *mammadragas* and the *doñas de fuera*, the *síthe* could be simultaneously peaceful and diabolical, "given to evil and malicious deeds" (Wilde 1887a, I:68), depending on how they were treated by human beings. Wilde reported that peasants did not consider them as deities worth of worshipping but nonetheless respected them out of fear of their powers.[97] One of the greatest popular anxieties in Irish traditions resides precisely in the abduction of children in the cradle:

> The *Sidhe* often strive to carry off the handsome children, who are then reared in the beautiful fairy palaces under the earth, and wedded to fairy mates when they grow up. The people dread the idea of a fairy changeling being left in the cradle in place of their own lovely child; and if a wizened little thing is found there, it is sometimes taken out at night and laid in an open grave till morning, when they hope to find their own child restored, although more often nothing is found save the cold corpse of the poor outcast. (Wilde 1887a, I:70)

Beauty and youth were the features that appealed most to the *síthe*, according to local legends, and therefore children and young women were particularly in danger of falling victim to their powers. As a result, if a stolen child eventually turned out to be ugly, he was given back to the mortals because fairies "love beauty above all things; and the fairy chiefs greatly desire a handsome

---

97. In this regard, it was said that "[t]he witch women who have been taught by them, and have thus becomes tools of the Evil One, are the terror of the neighbourhood; for they have all the power of the fairies and all the malice of the devil, who reveals to them secrets of times and days, and secrets of herbs, and secrets of evil spells; and by the power of magic they can effect all their purposes, whether for good or ill" (Wilde 1887a, I:69).

mortal wife, so that a handsome girl must be well guarded, or they will carry her off" (Wilde 1887a, II:99).

Tales of changelings are scattered throughout Jane Wilde's *Ancient Legends*. Fire was believed to protect children's cradles from the threat of being abducted by the fairies. In the section "The Trial by Fire," for instance, in order to demonstrate that a child was actually a fairy changeling, it was reported that a man invited a woman to place her dead child on the fire, pronouncing the words, "Burn, burn, burn—if of the devil, burn; but if of God and the Saints, be safe from harm" (Wilde 1887a, I:73). Following these words and touching the hot turf, the fairy changeling vanished. A similar legend was reported in "The Fairy Changeling": in this tale, a man overhearing two women who were plotting the abduction of a child, leaving a changeling in the cradle in his place, eventually succeeds in unveiling the deception and saving the true child, after throwing the surrogate creature on the fire (Wilde 1887a, I:170–72). In *Ancient Cures*, Wilde underlined how these beliefs were particularly rooted in the primitive mind of the islanders inhabiting the western isles, who attempted to find an explanation for the calamities that frequently occurred in their lives:

> The islanders seem to live for ever in the presence of the spiritual; and every event of their lives, whether for good or ill luck, is attributed to the influence of unseen beings, who are sometimes good, but more often malign to mortals. Every sickness or accident or misfortune is believed to be the work of the invisible *Sidhe*, or fairy race; and all the primitive science of the people, their knowledge of herbs, and of powerful charms and incantation, is used to break the spells and counteract the sinister designs of the active sprites who haunt the house, and are especially anxious to get possession of the children and carry them off to the fairy homes. (Wilde 1890:155)

Tales of infants and children falling under the spell of the fairies were often connected to the idea that there would be consequences if the *síthe* were disrespected. For instance, "The Fairies' Revenge" recounts the story of Johnstone, a rich farmer who dared to build a house on a fairy rath,[98] uprooting a sacred hawthorn bush. The protagonist of this legend skeptically regarded these beliefs as "mere old-wives' tales" (Wilde 1887a, I:83) and blatantly ignored the neighbors' warnings not to profane the rath. After this ignominious act, a blue-cloaked little old woman visited Johnstone's wife twice: the first time, she kindly asked for some milk but was rejected and reproached as a "tramp" (Wilde 1887a, I:83); the second time, after pleading for food, she was

---

98. Fairy raths, also known as ringforts, were prehistoric circular mounds that were believed to be the dwellings of fairies.

chased away and addressed as a "wicked old wretch" (Wilde 1887a, I:84). On the first occasion, Mrs. Johnstone's cow died; on the second occasion, the same terrible fate befell the farmers' only child, who "began to grow queer and strange, and was disturbed in his sleep; for he said the fairies came round him at night and pinched and beat him, and some sat on his chest and he could neither breathe or move" (Wilde 1887a, I:84). As his health worsened, the child claimed that every night he was carried away to the hills by the fairies. Nothing could help the young boy, not even the intervention of a priest.

The boy's tragic destiny was seen as retribution for the father's unholy exploitation of the fairies' revered ground, which caused his family's ruin. As a consequence of his shameful insolence, the father ceased to look after his farm and cattle, lost everything he cared for, and died shortly after his son's demise. His wife, now a "childless mother" (Wilde 1887a, I:86), was estranged by the rest of the village as if plague-ridden, "a warning to all who would arouse the vengeance of the fairies by interfering with their ancient rights and possessions and privileges" (Wilde 1887a, I:86). This folktale, imbued with a sense of foreboding that calls to mind the dark overtones of the gothic literary genre, narrates the unfolding of this family decay, implicitly conveys an urge to respect old traditions and beliefs, and bequeaths to future generations a reverence for local nature that ought to be kept in high regard, ultimately dissuading against the arrogance derived from wealth and cynicism.[99]

As folklorist Katharine Briggs (1898–1980) noted, several of the narratives collected by Jane Wilde gesture toward "a strong connection between the fairies and the dead" (Briggs 1978:31). Many of these tales express the deep anxieties surrounding children's health in mid-nineteenth-century Ireland. In some instances, Wilde acknowledged the great dangers of believing in such supernatural entities, since, according to some of the anecdotes that she reported, these beliefs could lead to the death of the sickly children, allegedly substituted by fairies, at the hands of their own family members:[100]

---

[99]. Such environmental awareness persists in contemporary Irish culture, as evidenced by the ecological activism of Eddie Lenihan. The Irish storyteller received extensive media coverage when he raised his voice against the uprooting of a hawthorn bush in Latoon, in County Clare, in 1999. The bond between fairy beliefs and reverence for nature in the tales collected by the Irish *seanchaí* has been cogently illustrated by Luca Sarti, who also explores Lenihan's personal commitment to preserve local nature (Sarti 2023b).

[100]. A notorious case of murder linked to the belief in fairy substitution was the burning of Bridget Cleary, née Boland (ca. 1867–1895), a young dressmaker from County Tipperary. Cleary was brutally killed by her husband, who was convinced that she had been replaced by a changeling. Angela Bourke reconstructs the vicissitudes that led to this atrocious crime and the ensuing trial in *The Burning of Bridget Cleary* (Bourke 1999).

If an infant is very small and weakly, it is supposed to be a fairy changeling, and under a curse. To test its nature, the child is placed upon a shovel before the fire. If it is a fairy imp, it will assuredly, after a little while, fly up the chimney, and disappear; but, while waiting for the solution of the question, the poor baby is often so dreadfully burned that it dies in great torture, though its cries are heard with callous indifference by the family around. (Wilde 1890:49)

If on the one hand the manifold references to fairy changelings disseminated throughout Wilde's collections demonstrate how widespread fears were at the time about children's often tragic fate, on the other hand, it can be posited that the selection and insertion into her anthologies of tales about child mortality may have resonated with her personal life. Her daughter Isola Francesca Emily Wilde (1857–1867) died prematurely at the age of nine on February 23, 1867, a heartbreaking event that deeply marked the Wilde family. As Wilde confessed in a letter written on April 16, 1867, to her friend Lotten von Kræmer (1828–1912), Swedish philanthropist and supporter of women's enfranchisement, she was devastated by this event: "Isola was the radiant angel of our home [. . .]. We never dreamed the word *death* was meant for her. Yet I had an uncontrollable sadness over me all last winter—a foreboding of evil" (Wilde in Tipper 2008:46; original emphasis).

These few lines encapsulate the extent of the calamity that befell the Wilde family and Speranza's predisposition for popular belief, an inclination that her son Oscar shared with her (Fitzsimons 2015:53). In February 1896, when he was already imprisoned in Reading Gaol, a well-known episode that exemplifies the degree of such faith in Irish popular beliefs occurred: he had a vision of his mother who came to visit him; afterward, he heard the lament of a banshee, which he interpreted as a clear omen of death. In that moment he knew that his mother had died, before his wife, Constance, would come to visit him to announce his mother's death (Ellmann 1988:467; Scatasta 1998:4).[101] Jane Wilde dedicated several pages to the banshee—a term deriving from the Irish *bean sí*, literally meaning "woman of the fairy mound"—in her folklore collections.[102] She defined this creature as "the spirit of doom" (Wilde 1887a,

---

101. A subsequent dream in which Jane Wilde appeared to him in prison is mentioned in Oscar's correspondence with Robert Ross on May 28, 1897: "My dream was that my mother was speaking to me with some sternness, and that she was in trouble. I quite see that whenever I am in danger she will in some way warn me" (Wilde in Holland and Hart-Davis 2000:858). On these biographical episodes, see also Fitzsimons (2015:274–75).

102. Pitrè noted the similarity between the *doñas de fuera* and the banshees: "Cercando poi nella mitologia comparata antica e moderna potrebbero riscontrarsi isolatamente alcuni

I:259; 1890:75), who used to appear exclusively to families of aristocratic birth.[103] The banshee, according to the sources reported by Wilde, sometimes took the form of a beautiful young maiden, who could be seen "at night as a shrouded woman, crouched beneath the trees, lamenting with veiled face" (Wilde 1887a, I:260) or "with long, red-gold hair, and wearing a green kirtle and scarlet mantle, brooched with gold, after the Irish fashion" (Wilde 1890:84). Her appearance was not necessarily foreboding in itself, unless she started crying: her sorrowful wail prophesied the death of a family member so that her spirit could finally reach heaven and be substituted on earth by another soul. She was capable of traveling long distances, so great was her power. Her shriek was described in hyperbolic terms as "weird," "unearthly," "bitter," and "as of one in deepest agony and sorrow" (Wilde 1887a, I:260). Wilde provided several anecdotes of her fateful appearance, including a story of a banshee who came to visit the O'Gradys, a family of Irish origin who had immigrated to Canada, whose cry announced the death of the father and his son, who would eventually drown in the sea.[104]

The accounts of banshees in nineteenth-century folklore collections were often introduced or interspersed with remarks about the truthfulness of these stories. Augusta Gregory herself commented she had "reason to believe" in the existence of the banshee (Gregory 2006 [1920]:15). In the chapter "Banshees and Warnings" (Gregory 2006 [1920]:170–79), she reported dreams and visions of peasants, doctors, and army men who believed to have encountered

---

caratteri di queste Donne nelle *Dames Blanches* e nelle *Dames vertes* di qualche luogo della Francia, nelle *Benshies* [sic] della Scozia, ne' *Lari* degli Etruschi e de' Latini e forse nelle *Deae Matres* latine, delle quali così poco sappiamo" (Pitrè 1889, IV:177) [If then one looks into ancient and modern comparative mythology, some features of these Women could be found in isolation in the *Dames Blanches* and in the *Dames vertes* of some places in France, in the *Benshies* [sic] of Scotland, in the *Lares* of the Etruscans and Latins and perhaps in the Latin *Deae Matres*, of which we know so little].

103. The aristocratic lineage of the banshees is believed to be linked to the sixteenth- and seventeenth-century English requisition of Irish lands. At the origins of this class connotation, therefore, lies the characterization of the banshee "not merely as a defender of Irish nobility, but as a protector of Irish land" (Stapleton-Corcoran 2009:31).

104. Prior to Jane Wilde's accounts, legends of the banshee were inserted in *Fairy Legends and Traditions of the South of Ireland*, by Thomas Crofton Croker (1828:10; 1834:98–126). Other testimonies of families who firmly believed in banshees can be found in *Ireland: Its Scenery, Character and History*, by Anna Maria Hall and Samuel Carter Hall (1841–43, III:104–13), who also provided the notation of a banshee's mournful wail. They commented that this death-warning spirit could appear as "a young and beautiful woman arrayed in white; but more frequently as a frightful hag" (Hall and Hall 1841–43, III:104).

the "keening woman of the sidhe" (Gregory 2006 [1920]:170). Sometimes the warnings were perceived as indistinct sounds: a local doctor recounted how desperate a boy's parents were, after his mother heard a sinister sound that she interpreted as a harbinger of death; in truth, her son merely had a cold, but since his brother had died of phthisis, his family feared the worst (Gregory 2006 [1920]:178). In other cases, the warnings took on the distinct visual and aural traits of the banshee. According to one of her informants, "Old King," the banshee's cry "was as mournful as the oldest of the old women could make it, that was best at crying the dead" (Gregory 2006 [1920]:178). In this respect, Patricia Lysaght, in her thorough study on the figure of the banshee in Irish folklore, noted that "the stress on the mournful and sad aspects of the death-messenger's cry" was particularly common in western regions, where "the practice of keening survived until the turn of the century" (Lysaght 1997 [1986]:72). In one instance, Gregory wrote that a spinning woman claimed to have seen a banshee with a red petticoat in her youth, while she was picking potatoes; on another occasion, a seaside woman heard the banshee's shriek, "the grandest cry ever you heard," which was often audible "out there where the turf-boat is lying with its sail down, outside Aughanish, there the Banshee does always be crying, crying, for some that went down there some time" (Gregory 2006 [1920]:173).

When considering the geo-poetical sphere of such fragments of oral narratives, the sea rises to an "othered" space bestowed with a mystical power before the eyes of islanders and nonislanders alike. The sea can defend but can also isolate. It is both a protective border and a limit to overcome, a nurturing source that provides sustenance and a threatening basin that provokes death. All these nuances can be found in folktales and oral traditions set against the backdrop of the sea and its wonders. The shore is a particularly alluring liminal space, in which encounters with supernatural entities are rife. Such powerful connotations ring true both for the "narrow shoreline in the almost tideless Mediterranean and the much wider intertidal littoral of the Atlantic" (Cunliffe 2017:7).

In the initial pages of *Visions and Beliefs*, after the retelling of visions of seahorses riding the waves and eating oats, the first reference to a *maighdean mara*, a mermaid, can be found: she was "partly like a fish and the rest like a woman" and fled once the fisherman who saw her pronounced the name of God (Gregory 2006 [1920]:16). Another retelling of an encounter with a sea woman features shortly after, once again told in first person: the informant's father once witnessed a woman with "eyes shining like candles" emerging from the waves and landing on the boat (Gregory 2006 [1920]:16). He thus rushed to obtain some holy water from the priest and a pinch of salt as means to protect himself from these creatures. "Whatever's on the land, there's the same in the sea," the informant solemnly claimed (Gregory 2006 [1920]:18), including magical entities.

In *The Kiltartan Wonder Book* (1910), published prior to *Visions and Beliefs*, Gregory inserted a story about female submission and regaining of power, entitled "The Man That Served the Sea" (Gregory 1910:52–55). Building on the motif of the abduction of a "mer-wife" (Bacchilega and Alohalani Brown 2019:xviii), in this narrative a man finds a mermaid combing her hair in the water, grabs her, and takes her home. Once he captures his wife-to-be, he hides her "cover," the garment that reveals her identity as a sea-creature. The theft of a protective element follows the plot trajectory of the widespread tales in Celtic and Norse mythology about seal women, also known as *selkies*, who in several narratives are coerced into marriage after their skin or hood is stolen.[105] Capturing the mermaid against her will and hiding her cover symbolizes a double act of violence and subjugation since this impedes her from returning to her world and forces her to stay somewhere where she does not belong, unable to fully be herself. In the tale transcribed by Gregory, while being together for seven years and giving birth to three sons, the mermaid "never spoke a word" (Gregory 1910:52) and only laughed three times. The unwillingness to speak is a further resonating reminder of her coercion into an unwanted relationship, whereas her liberating and inexplicable laugh symbolically represents an act of defiance.

Each occasion when the mermaid laughs corresponds to a key space and moment of domestic life. The first time she bursts into laughter around the hearth while dinner is on the fire after a stranger enters the house, refuses to eat, and pronounces a curse. The second time, it happens while dinner is boiling in the pot, and she observes her husband's mother forgetting to remove the top, a gesture that would have prevented the food from being spoiled. The third time, the laugh occurs as she sees her husband's mother accidentally

---

105. Folkloric narratives about *selkies* abound in and beyond the Irish tradition. Reidar Christiansen classified these tales as "migratory legend type 4080," titled "The Seal Woman" (Christiansen 1958:75). Two tales featuring a mermaid and a *selkie*, respectively, can be found in *Fairy Legends and Traditions of the South of Ireland*, by Thomas Crofton Croker (1834:177–85), and in *Tales of the Fairies and of the Ghost World*, by Jeremiah Curtin (1895:151–54). In Croker's "The Lady of Gollerus," the future husband takes possession of the mermaid's *cohuleen driuth*, a "little enchanted cap" (Croker 1834:178). The lady in the tale is defined as *merrow*, the anglicized Irish term often used in place of the English term *mermaid* (Croker 1834:206). Similarly, in Curtin's "Tom Moore and the Seal Woman," the male protagonist steals a hood from the head of a seal woman, takes the maiden home with him, and marries her, legitimizing his actions by repeating that it was God's will to do so. For scholarly reflections on tales about mermaids and seal women, see Darwin (2015) and Ní Fhrighil (2017). For an overview of mermaids, merrows, and *selkies*, see Daimler (2020). A selection of cross-cultural tales featuring mermaids and *selkies* can be found in Bacchilega and Alohalani Brown (2019). For a wide-ranging overview of sea creatures in various cultural traditions, see also Chainey and Winsham (2021).

falling while she is about to enter the parlor. After seven years, the mermaid manages by chance to get hold of her cover again. She puts it on and flees into the sea together with her sons. One day the man, who kept looking for her, sees her sitting on a rock and tries to capture her again, but she decisively says he will never see her again. She will only allow him to take with him their eldest son as long as the father agrees to give him all his possessions.

The final dialogue between husband and merwife reveals why she had laughed three times. On the first occasion, she laughed because the man's curse reduced the food to nothing. On the second occasion, she knew that the negligence of the husband's mother turned the food to poison. Finally, when the husband's mother fell, she laughed because the mother had stumbled upon a pot of gold standing at the parlor's threshold without even realizing it. Following the mermaid's recommendation, husband and son find the treasure and become rich, while the mermaid never returns to their world. Gregory did not specify who told her this tale, which ended with the voice of the storyteller saying: "That is all, my lady, I know about it; and that is one of the old stories of Ireland" (Gregory 1910:55). As a whole, "The Man That Served the Sea" can be interpreted as a tale in which justice is eventually restored: the mermaid frees herself and rejoins her world with two of her sons, while her husband can carry on with his life comfortably, provided he bequeaths all his fortunes to his eldest son.

However, tales about mermaids often present them in a darker and sinister tone as figures seeking revenge rather than justice, as monsters rather than victims. For instance, in the Sicilian tales n. 33, "La sorella di Muntifiuri" (Gonzenbach 2019 [1870]:188–93), and n. 34, "Quaddaruni e sua sorella" (Gonzenbach 2019 [1870]:194–200)—variants of the ATU tale type 403, *The Black and the White Bride*—a wicked sister plots against her beautiful sibling, who is then captured by a "*sirena du mari*," a mermaid that imprisons her in the sea abyss with a golden chain until a valiant king frees her. The motif of imprisonment at the hands of a mermaid features also in Jane Wilde's "The Dead Soldier" (Wilde 1887a, I:164–65), set in a small island located in the River Shannon. It was believed that if a mermaid was found sitting on the rocks there, it meant that some criminal action had been perpetrated. The legend provided inspiration for Oscar Wilde's literary fairy tale "The Fisherman and His Soul," which upended "The Little Mermaid" by Hans Christian Andersen, blending elements from the well-known novella *Undine* (1811), by German writer Friedrich de la Motte Fouqué (1777–1843), as well as motifs from Irish folklore (Fitzsimons 2015:184).[106]

---

106. Pine (1995) and Markey (2011) report that another source of inspiration for Wilde's fairy tale was Thomas Crofton Croker's "The Soul Cages," a prime example of "fakelore," which, by

"The Dead Soldier" narrates that a young fisherman, caught up by a storm, is led by the current toward the small island, following a "streak of red blood" (Wilde 1887a, I:164). There he finds a mermaid, who, as if in a dream, offers him a drink of wine. After he refuses, the dreamlike atmosphere suddenly turns into a nightmare, in which a vision of a soldier who had cut his throat appears to him. The fisherman then comes to his senses and finds himself still in the boat agitated by waves, where he is eventually rescued by his friends. Once back home, he hears that a soldier from the Athlone Barracks, a strategic military spot in the middle of Ireland, has killed himself while being chased. The fisherman realizes that this was the same man who had appeared in his vision in the mermaid's den. Only the exorcism of a priest helps him find peace after this disquieting adventure. The characterization of the mermaid brings to mind the captivating nymph dwelling in the caverns underneath the sea in the poem "The Fisherman" that Jane Wilde wrote in her youth, in which the sea creature entices a fisherman to follow her with her enchanting voice, leading him to sink beneath the seawater (Wilde 1864:186–87). Similarly, in "The Dead Soldier," the mermaid, rather than being a victim, is depicted as a powerful, haunting figure who "tries to lure victims to their death" (Wilde 1887a, I:164).

What is interesting to note in this very short yet dense legend is the topographical hint at Athlone Barracks, since it alludes to a significant place and moment in Irish history: during the Williamite War in Ireland (1689–91), this area was besieged by the army led by William of Orange fighting against the Irish Catholic Jacobite army, and eventually turned into an encampment for the British Army. Furthermore, the detailed descriptions of the perils faced by fishermen in the sea due to unstable weather conditions mirrored a dangerous reality that sailors had to face on a daily basis. In these supernatural legends, there are deep crevices that incorporate both historical events and real-life dangers.

Despite being at times obscure and difficult to untangle, the dissident and "subversive potential" of these stories still breathes through the written page (Zipes 2006b:108). Folktales can thus be fittingly considered "a reflection of social and cultural values" (Ben-Amos 2010:374), although their subversive subtext was at times tamed by the collectors and compilers who assembled the tales, censoring and tweaking them to suit their own values. Particularly when it comes to Jane Wilde's folklore collections, it should not be forgotten that these stories were changed less to reflect the tellers' mindset than to

---

admission of Croker's collaborator Thomas Keightley (1789–1872), was not rooted in Irish folklore but rather adapted from one of the legends included in the Brothers Grimm's *Deutsche Sagen* (1816–18), "The Peasant and the Waterman" (Earls 1992–93:101; Markey 2011:55–56). On the notion of "fakelore," see Dorson (1976).

express the compiler's views. It comes as no surprise, then, that the "nonsensical and eccentric nature" of some of the tales put together by Wilde has been explained as proof of her authorial interventions (Almqvist 1991:12).

The narratives by Deledda, albeit inspired by folk traditions, similarly leaned toward the realm of literature. The duality of fairy creatures that distinguishes the *síthe* can also be found in Sardinian traditions. In her articles, and later in her novels and short stories, Deledda made reference to imprecations and legends related to the *janas*, Sardinian fairies described as "per lo più malefiche" (Deledda 1895e:416),[107] who, according to popular belief, lived in the *domus de janas*, a term that literally means "fairy houses," tombs with origins in the prehistoric period that preceded the advent of the Nuragic civilization on the island.[108] Dialectologist and folklorist Gino Bottiglioni (1887–1963), in his well-known work *Leggende e tradizioni di Sardegna* (1922), listed the various names used to define these little fairy creatures in various parts of the island: *nanos, gianas, giannèddas, mergianas, margianas, bírghines, li faddi* (Bottiglioni 1922:5). Dolores Turchi reported that the *janas* were believed to approach the cradle of newborn children and decree their fate (Turchi 1984:51).[109] Like the Sicilian *doñas de fuera*, the *janas* were believed to be ambiguous creatures: although they were considered quintessentially good-natured, they used to become vengeful toward those who disrespected them, hence the popular imprecation that Deledda reported: "Mala jana ti jucat" (Deledda 1894b:658), "may you be carried away by an evil *jana*."[110] Despite featuring in popular curses, the *janas* could also perform benevolent

---

107. "mostly evil."

108. Legends of the *janas* were also transcribed by Deledda's friend Maria Manca, founder of the first female periodical in Sardinia, *La donna sarda*. It was thanks to Deledda that Manca started a correspondence with Angelo De Gubernatis, as Manca specified in her first letter to him (Manca, *Lettere ad Angelo De Gubernatis*, December 6, 1893, cass. 80 n. 48, letter n. 1:1, Fondo "Angelo De Gubernatis," BNCF). Manca became a contributor to *RTPI*. Her "Leggenda sarda di compare Peddiù" (Manca 1895:466–71) was included in the same issue of *RTPI* that featured some of Deledda's articles on Sardinian popular traditions. Furthermore, Manca's untitled legend about three brothers and three *janas* was published in *Vita Sarda* by Deledda on December 10, 1893. For a translation into English of this tale, see Mazzoni (2021:123–26).

109. Bottiglioni and Turchi suggest that the word "jana" may derive from the Latin goddess of the moon Diana, an etymology that may explain why in many tales the *janas* go out by night, emanating a strong light (Bottiglioni 1922:5, n.6; Turchi 1984:51, n.1). The *janas* also feature in a twentieth-century anthology of Sardinian fairy tales rewritten by Sergio Atzeni and Rossana Copez, largely based on Bottiglioni's collection (Atzeni and Copez 2018 [1978]:65–67). On Atzeni and Copez's fairy tales, see Sulis (2001:9–10).

110. Deledda would report this curse in the incipit of her short story "L'anellino d'argento," a fascinating tale told in first person by a female narrator who is eager to explore the Sardinian fairy houses (Deledda 2013 [1930]:83–87).

deeds. A telling example is the positive characterization of the "fairies on the island of Sardinia," who came to the aid of the protagonist Zezolla in the first European literary version of Cinderella's tale by Giambattista Basile in *Lo cunto de li cunti* (Basile 2007 [1634–36]:84, trans. Nancy Canepa).

The connection of the *janas* with the Sardinian territory is deep. In the research she carried out for De Gubernatis's journal, Deledda reported how these "dommos de sas janas" were believed to be inhabited by monsters and could be gateways to hell (Deledda 1895e:416). Years later, in the article "Tipi e paesaggi sardi" (1901), she described her visit to one of these caves near Nuoro in which she found some ashes and a little ripped piece of paper featuring a poem in Sardinian about Eleonora d'Arborea, which she interpreted as the sign of the presence of a fugitive in the cavern (Deledda 1901:601). The imagery of the *janas* had enchanted Deledda's imagination since she was a child. A testament to her fascination with these fairies can be found in *Cosima* (1937), where she described her grandmother as a *jana*:

> Cosima provava uno strano senso di sogno quando la vedeva comparire d'improvviso. Ma più che di sogno era un senso fisico di ricordo inafferrabile, una lieve vertigine, come un baleno sanguigno, che più tardi ella si spiegò col crederlo un affiorare e subito di nuovo sommergersi di vita anteriore rimasta o rinata nel suo subcosciente. La nonna, poi, le ricordava,—ma questo un po' volontariamente,—certe donne favolose, o piccole fate, buone o cattive secondo l'occasione, che la leggenda popolare affermava abitassero un tempo in piccole case di pietra, scavate nella roccia, specialmente negli altipiani granitici del luogo. E queste minuscole abitazioni preistoriche esistevano ed esistono ancora, monumenti megalitici che risalgono a epoche remote, chiamati appunto le case delle piccole fate (janas). (Deledda 2005 [1937]:40)[111]

It was through the figure of her grandmother that Deledda's alter ego Cosima inherited the art of storytelling in a "consegna genealogica della tradizione" from the oral to the literary realm (Piano 1998:17).[112] In Deledda's posthumous

---

111. "Cosima got a strange dreamlike feeling when she would see her suddenly. But more than a dream, it was a physical sense of indelible memories, a slight dizziness like a sudden shock that she later explained to herself as a surfacing and sudden resubmersion of her earlier life that remained or was reborn in her subconscious. Her grandmother reminded her at that time—but this a little deliberately—of certain legendary little women, or little fairies, good or bad according to the occasion, affirmed by popular legend as having lived one time in small stone houses carved out of rock, especially in the granite plateaus of the area. And these minuscule prehistoric dwellings existed and exist today, megalithic monuments dating from remote times, called the Houses of the Little Fairies" (Deledda, trans. Martha King, 1991:10).

112. "genealogical delivery of tradition."

autobiographical novel, the narrator reports how Cosima, after her first vision of the sea during an excursion with her brother, felt like an outsider, surrounded by her brothers' friends who made fun of her while she remained silent. In this passage, Deledda's alter ego compared herself to a *jana*, one of those "piccole fate ambigue, non sai se buone o cattive, che popolano le grotte del monte e da millenni vi tessono, dentro, nei loro telai d'oro, reti per imprigionare i falchi, i venti, le nuvole, i sogni degli uomini" (Deledda 2005 [1937]:80).[113] The *janas* were hardworking weavers that could determine human destiny, to the point that the term "jana" itself came to be associated with the concept of fate (Bottiglioni 1922:7). These Sardinian fairies so deeply ingrained in Deledda's imagination can be interpreted both as a symbol of collective female creativity and as a metaphor of women's often-obfuscated labor (Sulis 2022–23:15). Not coincidentally, they are evoked in the works of various prominent female figures in Sardinian culture, including textile artist Maria Lai (1919–2013), whose sculptures, canvases, and "sewn fairy tales" speak of and to women's creative expressions beyond the borders of the island.

Sardinian writer, feminist advocate, and political activist Michela Murgia (1972–2023), who played the role of Grazia Deledda in the theater play *Quasi Grazia* (2016), written by Marcello Fois and directed by Veronica Cruciani, dedicated several reflections to the *janas* in her travelogue *Viaggio in Sardegna. Undici percorsi nell'isola che non si vede* (2008). Not only does the very first line of the book conjure the image of the Sardinian "holes" that housed these fairies, but the unearthly power of these entities also reemerges from their secretive crannies in other passages of her journey. Murgia underlines how Sardinian female deities from ancient religions underwent a mechanism of demonization. Through this process, the figures of the *janas* acquired negative connotations:

> Così andare a cercare le *janas*, bellissime piccole fate tessitrici d'oro che abitano gli anfratti delle rocce, può farti trovare tesori incommensurabili, ma anche sottrarti per sempre al tuo mondo, facendoti perdere il senso del tempo come nella mitica Avalon dei celti: al tuo ritorno nessuno dei tuoi cari sarà più vivo da decenni. (Murgia 2008:178)[114]

---

113. "ambiguous fairies, good or bad, who populate the mountain caves and who for thousands of years have been weaving nets on their golden looms to imprison hawks, winds, clouds, man's dreams" (Deledda, trans. Martha King, 1991:62).

114. "So when searching for the *janas*, these extremely beautiful little fairies who weave gold and live in the crevices of the rocks, you can find immeasurable treasures but you can also be stolen away from your world, making you lose your sense of time as in the mythical Avalon of the Celts: upon your return, none of your loved ones will have been alive for decades."

The dualism of otherworldly femininity finds expression in many shapes and realms: Murgia's allusion to Avalon is entangled with the Sardinian writer's deep-seated fascination with the figure of Morgan le Fay, the powerful enchantress from the Arthurian cycle that has been alternatively represented as a witch or as a fairy. In her view, Morgan le Fay's shifting nature stands for a telling reminder of women's condition, which is often vulnerable to whims of the male gaze:

> [L]a sua percezione e rappresentazione cambia a seconda delle circostanze e dello sguardo che si ha su di lei. [...] Questo ovviamente paga lo sguardo maschile: se Morgana serve il trono è una fata, e sul trono c'è il re; se Morgana serve le sue convinzioni diventa una strega. Questa è la parabola che capita a tutte le donne che cercano di definirsi in rapporto al patriarcato in maniera non servile, non ancillare. (Murgia in Delmedico and Sottilotta 2022–23:284)[115]

As an epitome of this fairy-witch paradigm, Morgan le Fay shares this ambiguous portrayal with the fairies of the Sardinian folk tradition. What characterizes the fantastic representation of the *janas* in Sardinian legends is their extreme ambivalence: they are never univocal, they can be bearers of good or bad luck, fairies or witches, ugly or beautiful. The *janas* would also appear in the renowned incipit of Deledda's *Canne al vento* (1913) when the protagonist Efix crosses the Sardinian landscape at twilight, the ideal liminal time during which the boundaries between the visible and the invisible worlds fade away, and it is thus possible to encounter the magical creatures that populate Sardinian folkloric imagery, including *janas*, giants, and *panas*.[116] Deledda's cultural formation was nourished by the folkloric substratum that connected her to Sardinia. In her novels, Deledda would reinterpret and repurpose this corpus of traditions and legends beyond her island as a vital lymph for her creative imagination and for the readership of the new Italian nation.[117] As she maintained in "Leggende sarde," "[l]a leggenda richiama l'attenzione del poeta e dello storico che la sfronda per

---

115. "Her perception and representation change depending on the circumstances and the gaze one has on her. [...] This is obviously a consequence of the male gaze: if Morgana serves the throne she is a fairy, and the king is on the throne; if Morgana serves her beliefs she becomes a witch. This is the parable that occurs to all women who try to define themselves in relation to patriarchy in a nonslavish, nonancillary way."

116. The *panas* were women who had died in childbirth and returned to the earthly world to wash the clothes of their children on the riverbanks (Bottiglioni 1922:31). They show affinities with the Scottish *bean nighe*, who was believed to have died in childbirth and to wash clothes stained with the blood of those who were about to perish (Stapleton-Corcoran 2009:31).

117. For a study of the impact that Deledda's folkloric quest had on her literary production, see Piredda (2010).

trovare nel suo fusto le tracce delle generazioni sepolte, l'indole delle generazioni viventi e il germe di quella delle generazioni future" (Deledda 1893c:7).[118]

Mammadragas, mermaids, *doñas de fuera*, banshees, and *janas* have in common a status of ambivalent otherness that could carry both positive and negative connotations. This dichotomy is entrenched in the marvelous female entities investigated so far, which were both feared and revered. In this regard, it can be maintained that these representations of magical femininity contributed to the "elaborazione di un modo femminile di prefigurare il futuro, servendosi del supporto favolistico tradizionale" (Schram-Pighi 2003:65).[119] Tradition and modernity were thus inextricably embedded in these tales as well as in the practice of folklore collection as a whole. In many ways, several of the folkloric writings analyzed in this chapter represent not merely patrimonies of a nostalgic past but also forward-looking narratives, capable of conveying what Cristina Bacchilega ingeniously defines as "otherwise stories" that evoke "a counterworld, a dreamworld of justice, and feed the hope of making it possible" (Bacchilega 2023:62).

The kaleidoscope of insular folk and fairy-tale creatures, tales, anecdotes, spells, cures, and curses examined in this chapter exemplifies the power that words have been endowed with in oral cultures at a key historical juncture when literacy, nationalism, industrialization, and urbanization were about to drastically change the social habitus of Sicilian, Sardinian, and Irish rural communities, paving the way for a new world in which the spoken word would gradually lose its portentous energy. Speaking, making one's voice heard, was a formidable source of healing that bonded communities together. Oral communication could be both entertaining and threatening, with the power to instill fear and conjure a terrifying fate for one's enemies. This rings particularly true when it comes to marginalized cultures: as Jane Wilde maintained in the essay "The American Irish," first published as a pamphlet in 1877 and then placed at the end of *Ancient Cures* (Wilde 1890:198–244), "[a]ll oppressed nations are eloquent. When laws forbid a people to arm, they can only speak or sing. Words become their weapons" (Wilde 1890:199). Either as shields or arms, words undoubtedly expressed the hidden fears and hopes of those who voiced them, whose stories and beliefs, distant in time and place from us, still deserve to be remembered because they speak of hardship, of resistance, of desire for a better future.

---

118. "The legend draws the attention of the poet and the historian who trim it to find in its stem the traces of buried generations, the disposition of living generations, and the germ of the temperament of future generations."

119. "elaboration of a feminine way of foreshadowing the future, using the fairy-tale tradition as a basis."

EPILOGUE

On Memory and Oblivion beyond Islandness

[Nella trascrittura della parola parlata] [a]ncora trapelano la vitalità, l'energia, le fatiche, gli sforzi, il continuo esperire, e il patire, sul mare delle donne delle Isole. [. . .] Dimenticarle significherebbe infatti perdere per sempre anche un patrimonio di conoscenze e valori, unico e irripetibile, che oggi appartiene a tutti gli isolani. Significherebbe altresì perdere il senso vero e profondo dei luoghi.[1]

—MACRINA MARILENA MAFFEI, *DONNE DI MARE* (2013:14–16)

AFTER MORE than thirty years of fieldwork in the Aeolian Islands, off the northeastern coast of Sicily, contemporary anthropologist Macrina Marilena Maffei compiled a captivating collection of testimonies of the islanders whom she personally interviewed, who shared with her their memories of the lives and struggles of local fisherwomen, animated by the objective of "strapparle dal mondo della trasparenza" (Maffei 2013:13).[2] Albeit ingrained in Aeolian culture, her reflections in *Donne di mare* resonate deeply with the issues raised in this book. Spivak observes that "[i]f, in the context of colonial production, the subaltern has no history and cannot speak, the subaltern as female is ever more deeply in shadow" (Spivak 1988:287). If this double marginalization can be a relevant perspective to frame the legacy of several nineteenth-century

---

1. "The vitality, the energy, the fatigue, the efforts, the continuous trials, and the sufferings on the sea of the women of the Islands still transpire in the transcription of the spoken word. [. . .] As a matter of fact, forgetting them would also mean losing forever a unique and unrepeatable heritage of knowledge and values, which today belongs to all the islanders. In other words, it would mean losing the true and profound meaning of places."

2. "tearing them away from the world of transparency."

female folklorists who continue to occupy a marginal position within the Italian and the Irish canons, this condition of subalternity is even stronger when taking into account the positionality of their female informants, who could not make their voices heard beyond their enclosed social circles without the collectors' intervention.

Transparency, shadow, invisibility, oblivion: these often are the destinies that nineteenth-century female collectors, informants, and their traditions have long endured, not only for being sidelined in the history of their nations but also for being frequently dismissed by the critical gaze of contemporary scholars. The investigation I have carried out is thus a threefold act of recovery and recentering of the lives and works of female collectors and compilers who undertook these efforts, of their informants, and of the tales and traditions they bequeathed to them, so that the echoes of their voices can emerge from the partial or total invisibility to which they were relegated. The commitment to folklore research that characterized the female folklorists presented in this study reminds us that places, borders, villages, and islands can represent not only limits but also opportunities, not only prisons but also open doors that can be crossed by those who actively participate in human exchanges beyond preestablished spatial and social enclosures. By mediating marginalized voices from the past and immortalizing them in their works, women such as Laura Gonzenbach, Grazia Deledda, Jane Wilde, and Augusta Gregory, among many others, rather than being chained to subordinate female roles, became, in their own distinctive ways, cultural forerunners.

The places that saw their birth were an inspiration to them, an arc that threw them beyond the geographical and cultural barriers of their time, beyond the walls usually ascribed to their gender. If places do not have single but rather multiple identities, if they are not frozen in time but are rather fluid and mutable, then these women's lives are a perfect embodiment of this multifaceted conception of place (Massey 1994). The premises related to the geographical context in which they were born could have easily led to a different development. This aspect rings true for Gonzenbach and Deledda as both of them were born in southern Mediterranean islands in a historical period when women's subjugation and widespread illiteracy were still the norm. However, it is also relevant for Wilde and Gregory given the social and educational constraints that still limited women's contributions to intellectual life in mid-nineteenth-century Ireland. Yet these seekers of wonder became the protagonists of a different story. They found their own place in their native islands by diving into their cultural roots and by turning an attentive gaze toward the feminine world. By being consciously rooted in their milieus, they were able to inhabit the world of nineteenth-century Italian and Irish societies while at the same time projecting themselves beyond their national boundaries.

Gonzenbach's tomb lies abandoned in the English cemetery of Messina, her gravestone erased and rendered nearly anonymous by the passing of time. This cemetery has become "un luogo della memoria dimenticato, che testimonia il doppio legame reciso: con la patria d'origine e con quella acquisita" (Rubini 1998:5).[3] The figure of Jane Wilde, who died in disgrace after Oscar Wilde's imprisonment, has been overshadowed by the much greater fame of her son and her husband. For a long time her writings, despite the increasing scholarly attention, have regrettably represented "a body of work lost in the fissures of the Irish literary canon" (Walshe 2023a:152). On the façade of their house in Merrion Square, a commemorating inscription lists Sir Wilde's multifarious contributions as "aural and ophthalmic surgeon, archaeologist, ethnologist, antiquarian, biographer, statistician, naturalist, topographer, historian, folklorist" (Ryder 2013:15). Only as recently as 2021, another plaque in both Irish and English was added in Jane Wilde's memory to celebrate her commitment as "file, scríbhneoir, gníomhaí / poet, writer, activist." Augusta Gregory's estate at Coole Park, the center of the Irish Renaissance, fell into ruin after her death and was demolished in 1941, an act that hindered "the memory of someone who had done so much for Ireland" (Billington 2000:57). These forms of cultural obliteration recall the paradoxical destiny of Deledda's oeuvre, which has repeatedly been diminished by critics who considered her "nothing more than a late imitator of old literary models" (Sulis 2011:1174) in spite of her recognition as a Nobel Prize laureate. Notwithstanding this contradictory neglect, the place of Gonzenbach, Deledda, Wilde, and Gregory in folklore studies and in women's history has not been forgotten.

The endeavors of these figures in folkloristics took place at different stages of their lives; the driving force behind them was their eagerness to learn more about popular culture, so that local traditions could be remembered. With the exception of Gonzenbach, who died prematurely and left only her fairy-tale collection, for Deledda, Wilde, and Gregory folklore was just one facet of their manifold cultural contributions: they were not only folklorists but also translators, writers, playwrights, and contributors to various periodicals, and it is perhaps because of their greater accomplishments in other fields that their work as folklorists has been partially obfuscated. This carelessness finds its roots not only in gender prejudices but also in "scholarly biases that fail to regard editing, translation and journalism, among other endeavours, as the serious work of creative genius" (Reynolds 2018:145–46). Such disregard was, and still is, part and parcel of a deep-seated misconception toward works that

---

3. "a forgotten place of memory, which testifies to the severed double bond: from the homeland of origin and from the adopted one."

tend to be considered less valuable in the hierarchy of cultural manifestations. Furthermore, working as translators and folklore collectors involved stepping back as "authors" in order to emphasize neutrality and professional detachment from the tales and traditions that they disseminated in print, an objective standpoint that worked to the detriment of their recognition. As a whole, their folkloric quest epitomized not only an important apprenticeship but also a performative means to make themselves known on a national level and beyond. As such, it can be seen as a political choice that allowed them to deepen their knowledge of Sicilian, Sardinian, and Irish cultures by delving into their traditions. Venturing into folklore studies thus gave them the opportunity to place themselves at the center of the investigation into the habits and customs of insular communities by poetically reinforcing their own bonds with their native islands.

In the cases of Deledda and Gregory, these endeavors led them to assemble a folkloric repertoire that would eventually permeate the narrative fabric of their literary and theatrical productions at later stages of their lives. Their folkloric writings thus ultimately constituted a fertile ground from which they drew heavily for their subsequent works, transfiguring and transfusing for literary ends the rich material drawn directly from the "voice of the people." These efforts allowed them to set the scene for their own performances as scholars of popular traditions and reveal their dedication in approaching the study of folklore either as a source of spiritual and nationalistic inspiration, as was the case with Wilde, or as a scientific discipline, as with Gonzenbach, Deledda, and Gregory, that ought to be addressed and treated with respect, despite the negative judgments that detractors frequently leveled at their works. However, the clash between art and science in folkloric writings is only illusory, since even the most scientific folkloric works can retain a distinctive poetic quality. The gazes of these folklorists were never cold nor aseptic. Rather, they immersed themselves in these endeavors with all their strength and fervor.

Through this parallel study of Italian and Irish folklore and their collectors, it has been possible to recognize the similar challenges that female figures had to face at the turn of the century and their shared efforts toward the making of their nations and the preservation of cultural heritage. Folklore was for them a "lingua franca" (Markey 2006:33), a vehicle to communicate across different social classes, creating opportunities for encounter between the literate and the illiterate worlds. However, this negotiation of class differences did not lead to their erasure. In this process of mediation, they did not always succeed in portraying local culture, despite their commitment to leaving an imprint in their respective social circles. The stories and traditions they assembled are distant from the original performances: their transcriptions and compilations cannot reproduce them, but they can nonetheless allow us to remember these performances and to pay homage to the storytellers and tradition-bearers whose legacy would have otherwise been lost.

The mapping of women's contributions to nineteenth-century folkloristics begs further investigation in the fields of women's studies and folklore, both inwardly and outwardly: on the one hand, each of the figures presented in chapter 1 deserves in-depth studies that can reveal unknown details of their lives and works; on the other hand, another promising line of research would entail exploring further the network of transnational exchanges that was taking place at the turn of the century in this field, by digging in greater depth into the rich, unpublished archival materials that these intellectuals left behind. This process of recovery of female figures and folkloric writings has significant implications for a new understanding of macrohistorical events through the "microstories" of the "folk" and their collectors. Furthermore, this research has the potential to explore new local and global directions by investigating through gendered lenses other peripheral and insular areas, both within lesser-explored European traditions and outside European frontiers.

By casting a critical gaze beyond the fences of the folk and fairy-tale canon, a more diverse range of stories can be brought to light, unveiling unknown affinities between distinct traditions. The parallel focus on Italian and Irish cultures has demonstrated that, in exploring the legacy of women folklorists whose contributions did not meet the same fortune as other nineteenth-century canonical works, we can gain a more multilayered understanding of these centuries-old narratives, which are still breathing and relevant in today's cultural landscape. Furthermore, by approaching women's engagement with popular traditions in these two contexts, it has been possible to acknowledge the transnational circuit of knowledge that these different figures followed. The Italian and Irish insular writings examined in this volume were suspended between a reclamation of identity and a sense of alterity, an urgency for preservation and an anxiety for communication with the outside world. The themes of women's fears and hopes for social redemption that can be traced in some of these writings transcend islandness, in the same way that the women who collected and compiled these traditions overcame the boundaries of their insular condition in order to draw attention to these historically marginalized cultures.

This journey into the contributions of different women to nineteenth-century and early twentieth-century folklore can now end with a wondrous metaphor conjured by fairy-tale writer Beatrice Solinas Donghi (1923–2015), who well encapsulates the power of these narratives to cross national, regional, and insular borders:

[L]'intreccio fiabesco potrebbe paragonarsi a una zattera messa insieme in epoche remote con pezzi di relitti ancora più antichi, residui di mondi e modi d'esistere ormai inghiottiti dall'oceano del tempo e giunti fino a noi soltanto perché essa—la zattera, la fiaba—era così solidamente congegnata da galleggiare per millenni. (Solinas Donghi 2022:232–33)[4]

We may add that this enchanting fairy-tale raft reached us not only for its endless durability but also thanks to the imaginative voices of the storytellers and the written words of the collectors who tied these pieces of wood together, sailing them across time. These figures, their lives and tales, invite us to seek uncharted waters, immersing ourselves fully in these wonder worlds as an act of remembrance and as a way of envisioning alternative futures.

4. "The fairy-tale plot could be compared to a raft put together in distant times with pieces of even more ancient wrecks, remnants of worlds and ways of existing now swallowed up by the ocean of time and which have come down to us only because the raft, the fairy tale, was so solidly crafted that it has floated for millennia."

BIBLIOGRAPHY

Archival and Manuscript Sources

Busk, Rachel Harriette. *Lettere a Giuseppe Pitrè* (1876–95), P-B-16, 49 letters, Biblioteca Etnografica "Giuseppe Pitrè," Palermo.

Busk, Rachel Harriette. *Lettere ad Angelo De Gubernatis* (1881–90), cass. 18 n. 28, 21 letters, Fondo "Angelo De Gubernatis," Biblioteca Nazionale Centrale, Florence.

Comparetti, Domenico. *Lettere a Giuseppe Pitrè* (1870–97), P-A-7, 12 letters, Biblioteca Etnografica "Giuseppe Pitrè," Palermo.

Coronedi Berti, Carolina. *Lettere a Giuseppe Pitrè* (1871–1904), P-A-5, 100 letters, Biblioteca Etnografica "Giuseppe Pitrè," Palermo.

Coronedi Berti, Carolina. *Lettere a Francesco Zambrini* (1868–80), Lettere personali, Caravelli Vittorio—Curti D., 130, nn. 1610-1637, 38 letters, Fondo "Francesco Zambrini," Archivio della Commissione per i Testi di Lingua, Biblioteca Casa Carducci, Bologna.

Coronedi Berti, Carolina. *Lettere ad Angelo De Gubernatis* (1872–94), cass. 31 n. 39, 23 letters (1876–94), cass. 11 n. 76, 5 letters, Fondo "Angelo De Gubernatis," Biblioteca Nazionale Centrale, Florence.

Crane, Thomas Frederick. *Lettere a Giuseppe Pitrè* (1876–1913), P-B-16, 34 letters, Biblioteca Etnografica "Giuseppe Pitrè," Palermo.

De Gubernatis, Angelo. *Lettere a Giuseppe Pitrè* (1864–1911), P-A-6, 120 letters, Biblioteca Etnografica "Giuseppe Pitrè," Palermo.

Deledda, Grazia. *Lettere ad Angelo De Gubernatis* (1892–1909), cass. 41 n. 33, 71 letters, Fondo "Angelo De Gubernatis," Biblioteca Nazionale Centrale, Florence.

Gonzenbach, Magdalena. *Lettere ad Angelo De Gubernatis* (1870–93), cass. 65 n. 64, 11 letters, Fondo "Angelo De Gubernatis," Biblioteca Nazionale Centrale, Florence.

Gregory, Augusta. "The Continuity of Folklore" (undated). Incomplete typescript of a lecture with the author's manuscript corrections and with holograph notes. Henry W. and Albert A. Berg Collection of English and American Literature, New York Public Library, Astor, Lenox and Tilden Foundations.

Gregory, Augusta. *Lettere a Mario Manlio Rossi* (1931–32), cc. 13, 10 letters, Archivio "Mario Manlio Rossi," Biblioteca "Antonio Panizzi," Reggio Emilia.

Levi, Eugenia. *Lettere a Giuseppe Pitrè* (1895–1907), P-A-8, 3 letters, Biblioteca Etnografica "Giuseppe Pitrè," Palermo.

Manca, Maria. *Lettere ad Angelo De Gubernatis* (1893–95), cass. 80 n. 48, 12 letters, Fondo "Angelo De Gubernatis," Biblioteca Nazionale Centrale, Florence.

Martinengo-Cesaresco, Evelyn. *Lettere a Giuseppe Pitrè* (1882–1915), P-C-18, 57 letters, Biblioteca Etnografica "Giuseppe Pitrè," Palermo.

Martinengo-Cesaresco, Evelyn. *Lettere ad Angelo De Gubernatis* (1882–1915), cass. 83 n. 20, 60 letters, Fondo "Angelo De Gubernatis," Biblioteca Nazionale Centrale, Florence.

Nardo Cibele, Angela. *Lettere a Giuseppe Pitrè* (1885–1914), P-B-11, 93 letters, Biblioteca Etnografica "Giuseppe Pitrè," Palermo.
Nardo Cibele, Angela. *Lettere ad Angelo De Gubernatis* (1888–1901), cass. 91 n. 25, 8 letters, Fondo "Angelo De Gubernatis," Biblioteca Nazionale Centrale, Florence.
Pigorini Beri, Caterina. *Lettere a Giuseppe Pitrè* (1882–99), P-B-12, 14 letters, Biblioteca Etnografica "Giuseppe Pitrè," Palermo.
Pitrè, Giuseppe. *Lettere ad Angelo De Gubernatis* (1864–1912), cass. 100 n. 19, 206 letters, Fondo "Angelo De Gubernatis," Biblioteca Nazionale Centrale, Florence.
Savi-Lopez, Maria. *Lettere a Benedetto Croce* (1893–1920), cor. 254, 482, 483, 484, 5 letters, Archivio "Benedetto Croce," Fondazione Biblioteca "Benedetto Croce," Naples.
Savi-Lopez, Maria. *Lettere a Enrico Bemporad* (1891–1930), 115.6, 39 letters, Archivio Storico Giunti Editore, Florence.
Savi-Lopez, Maria. *Lettere a Giosuè Carducci* (1887–97), Corrispondenti Cart. CII, 49, 3 letters, Biblioteca Casa Carducci Bologna.
Savi-Lopez, Maria. *Lettere a Giuseppe Pitrè* (1887–98), P-B-13, 21 letters, Biblioteca Etnografica "Giuseppe Pitrè," Palermo.
Savi-Lopez, Maria. *Lettere a Mario Puccini* (1927), IT ACGV MP, 5 letters, Fondo "Mario Puccini," Archivio Contemporaneo "Alessandro Bonsanti," Florence.
Savi-Lopez, Maria. *Lettere a Pio Rajna* (1919–29), c.Ra.1477.1–13, 13 letters, Fondo "Pio Rajna," Biblioteca Marucelliana, Florence.
Savi-Lopez, Maria. *Lettere ad Angelo De Gubernatis* (1888–94), cass. 112 n. 29, 64 letters, Fondo "Angelo De Gubernatis," Biblioteca Nazionale Centrale, Florence.
Savi-Lopez, Maria. *Lettere ad Antonio Fogazzaro* (1885–97), CFo 30, Pl. 183, 37 letters, Fondo "Antonio Fogazzaro," Biblioteca Civica Bertoliana, Vicenza.
Shaw, Rose. *Photographs* (undated), Rose Shaw Collection, 27 photographs, National Museums NI, Ulster Folk Museum, Cultra, County Down, Northern Ireland.
Yeats, W. B. *Lettere a Mario Manlio Rossi* (1931–39), cc. 34, 8 letters, Archivio "Mario Manlio Rossi," Biblioteca "Antonio Panizzi," Reggio Emilia.

Primary Sources

Alexander, Francesca (1885). *Roadside Songs of Tuscany*. Sunnyside, Orpington: George Allen.
Alexander, Francesca (1887). *Christ's Folk in the Apennines: Reminiscences of Her Friends among the Tuscan Peasantry*. Sunnyside, Orpington: George Allen.
Alexander, Francesca (1897). *Tuscan Songs*. Boston: Houghton, Mifflin.
Alexander, Francesca (1900). *The Hidden Servants and Other Very Old Stories Told Over Again*. Boston: Little, Brown.
Alexander, Francesca (1976). *Storia del popolo. Beatrice di Pian degli Ontani*, trans. Giannozzo Pucci. Florence: Quaderni di Ontignano, Libreria Editrice Fiorentina, I.
Alexander, Francesca (1980). *Canti lungo i sentieri di Toscana. Storie di popolo*, trans. Giannozzo Pucci. Florence: Quaderni di Ontignano, Libreria Editrice Fiorentina, II.
Anderton, Isabella M. (1905). *Tuscan Folk-Lore and Sketches, Together with Some Other Papers*, ed. with a biographical note by her brothers, H. Orsmond Anderton and Basil Anderton. London: Arnold Fairbairns.
Arnold, Matthew (1867). *On the Study of Celtic Literature*. London: Smith, Elder.
Ascoli, Graziadio Isaia (1975). *Scritti sulla questione della lingua*, ed. Corrado Grassi. Turin: Einaudi.
Atzeni, Sergio, and Rossana Copez (2018 [1978]). *Fiabe sarde*, illustrated by Jenny Atzeni. Cagliari: Condaghes.
Auerbach, Nina, and Ulrich Camillus Knoepflmacher (eds.) (1992). *Forbidden Journeys: Fairy Tales and Fantasies by Victorian Women Writers*. Chicago: University of Chicago Press.

Bacchilega, Cristina, and Marie Alohalani Brown (eds.) (2019). *The Penguin Book of Mermaids*. New York: Penguin.
Balázs, Béla (2010). *The Cloak of Dreams: Chinese Fairy Tales*, ed. and trans. Jack Zipes, illustrated by Mariette Lydis. Princeton: Princeton University Press.
Barlow, Jane (1893). *Irish Idylls*. New York: Dodd, Mead & Company.
Basile, Giambattista (1994 [1634–36]). *Il racconto dei racconti, ovvero il trattenimento dei piccoli*, trans. Ruggero Guarini, ed. Alessandra Burani and Ruggero Guarini. Milan: Adelphi.
Basile, Giambattista (2007 [1634–36]). *The Tale of Tales, or Entertainment for Little Ones*, trans. Nancy Canepa. Detroit: Wayne State University Press.
Bayne, Marie (n.d.). *Tales of Ireland for Irish Children*. Dublin: Fallon Brothers.
Blackie, Sharon (2019). *Foxfire, Wolfskin and Other Stories of Shapeshifting Women*. London: September.
Bottiglioni, Gino (1922). *Leggende e tradizioni di Sardegna (Testi dialettali in grafia fonetica)*. Genève: Leo S. Olschki.
Brooke, Charlotte (1789). *Reliques of Irish Poetry, Consisting of Heroic Poems, Odes, Elegies, and Songs, Translated into English Verse with Notes Explanatory and Historical and the Originals in the Irish Character, to Which Is Subjoined an Irish Tale*. Dublin: George Bonham.
Busk, Rachel Harriette (1870). *Patrañas or Spanish Stories, Legendary and Traditional*. London: Gilbert and Rivington.
Busk, Rachel Harriette (1871). *Household Stories from the Land of Hofer; or, Popular Myths of Tirol*. London: Griffith and Farran.
Busk, Rachel Harriette (1874a). *The Folk-Lore of Rome, Collected by Word of the Mouth from the People*. London: Longmans, Green.
Busk, Rachel Harriette (1874b). *Valleys of Tirol: Their Traditions and Customs and How to Visit Them*. London: Longmans, Green.
Busk, Rachel Harriette (1887). *The Folk-Songs of Italy: Specimens with Translations and Notes, from Each Province, and Prefatory Treatise*. London: Swan Sonnenschein.
Calvino, Italo (1980). *Italian Folktales Selected and Retold by Italo Calvino*, trans. George Martin, with an introduction translated by Catherine Hill. New York: Pantheon Books.
Calvino, Italo (2015 [1956]). *Fiabe italiane*, 3 vols. Milan: Mondadori.
Campo, Cristina (1991 [1977]). "Diario bizantino," in *La tigre assenza*, ed. Margherita Pieracci Harwell. Milan: Adelphi, pp. 45–50.
Cantù, Cesare (1868). *Novelle lombarde*. Milan: Paolo Carrara.
Canziani, Estella (1911). *Costumes, Traditions and Songs of Savoy, Illustrated with Fifty Reproductions of Pictures by the Author, and with Many Line Drawings*. London: Chatto & Windus.
Canziani, Estella (1928). *Through the Apennines and the Lands of the Abruzzi: Landscape and Peasant Life, Described and Drawn by Estella Canziani*. Cambridge: W. Heffer & Sons.
Capuana, Luigi (1987 [1898]). *Scurpiddu*. Turin: Edizioni Paoline.
Capuana, Luigi (1992). *Tutte le fiabe*. Rome: Newton Compton.
Carter, Angela (ed.) (1990). *The Virago Book of Fairy Tales*, illustrated by Corinna Sargood. London: Virago.
Carter, Angela (ed.) (1993). *The Second Virago Book of Fairy Tales*, illustrated by Corinna Sargood. London: Virago.
Coronedi Berti, Carolina (1869–74). *Vocabolario bolognese-italiano*, 2 vols. Bologna: G. Monti.
Coronedi Berti, Carolina (1874). *Novelle popolari bolognesi raccolte da Carolina Coronedi Berti*. Bologna: Fava and Garagnani.
Coronedi Berti, Carolina (1883). *Al sgugiol di ragazù. Favole popolari bolognesi raccolte e pubblicate da Carolina Coronedi Berti*. Bologna: Premiato Stab. Tip. a Vapore Succ. Monti.
Coronedi Berti, Carolina (2021). *Favole bolognesi*, trans. Ombretta Zanetti. Bologna: Persiani.
Crane, Thomas Frederick (2001 [1885]). *Italian Popular Tales*, ed. Jack Zipes. Santa Barbara: ABC-Clio.

Croker, Thomas Crofton (1825). *Fairy Legends and Traditions of the South of Ireland*. London: John Murray.
Croker, Thomas Crofton (1828). *Fairy Legends and Traditions of the South of Ireland. Part III.* London: John Murray.
Croker, Thomas Crofton (1829). *Legends of the Lakes; or, Sayings and Doings at Killarney, Collected Chiefly from the Manuscripts of R. Adolphus Lynch*. London: John Ebers.
Croker, Thomas Crofton (1834). *Fairy Legends and Traditions of the South of Ireland*. London: John Murray.
Croker, Thomas Crofton (1969 [1824]). *Researches in the South of Ireland, Illustrative of the Scenery, Architectural Remains, and the Manners and Superstitions of the Peasantry, with an Appendix Containing a Private Narrative of the Rebellion of 1798*. New York: Barnes and Noble.
Croker, Thomas Crofton (1998). *Fairy Legends and Traditions of the South of Ireland*, ed. Francesca Diano. Cork: Collins Press.
Curtin, Jeremiah (1894). *Hero-Tales of Ireland*. London: Macmillan.
Curtin, Jeremiah (1895). *Tales of the Fairies and of the Ghost World Collected from Oral Tradition in South-West Munster*. London: David Nutt.
Curtin, Jeremiah (1975 [1890]). *Myths and Folk-Lore of Ireland*. New York: Dover.
d'Aulnoy, Marie-Catherine (2021). *The Island of Happiness: Tales of Madame d'Aulnoy*, illustrated by Natalie Frank, trans. by Jack Zipes. Princeton: Princeton University Press.
De Gubernatis, Angelo (1869). *Le novelline di Santo Stefano, raccolte da Angelo de Gubernatis e precedute da una introduzione sulla parentela del mito con la novellina*. Turin: Augusto Negro.
Deledda, Grazia (1891). "Luoghi della provincia: Nuoro," *Le cento città d'Italia*, Supplement of *Il Secolo*, XXVI, 70–71.
Deledda, Grazia (1892a). "Gonare (Usi e costumi sardi)," *Vita Sarda*, II, 19:2–4; 20:3–4; 22:8; 23:5–6; 24:5–6.
Deledda, Grazia (1892b). "Natale (macchiette sarde)," *Natura ed Arte*, I, 2, 144–54.
Deledda, Grazia (1893a). "La donna in Sardegna," *Natura ed Arte*, I, 8, 750–62.
Deledda, Grazia (1893b). "Per il folk-lore sardo," *Vita Sarda*, III, 8, 3.
Deledda, Grazia (1893c). "Leggende sarde," *Vita Sarda*, III, 23, 6–8.
Deledda, Grazia (1893d). "Preghiere: lauda di Sant'Antonio," *Rivista delle tradizioni popolari italiane*, I, 1, 62–68.
Deledda, Grazia (1894a). "Leggende sarde," *Natura ed Arte*, I, 10, 921–31.
Deledda, Grazia (1894b). "Tradizioni popolari di Nuoro in Sardegna: Nuoro," "Bestemmie e imprecazioni (Frastimos e irroccos)," *Rivista delle tradizioni popolari italiane*, I, 9, 651–62.
Deledda, Grazia (1894c). "Giuramenti (Iuramentos)," *Rivista delle tradizioni popolari italiane*, I, 10, 742–44.
Deledda, Grazia (1894d). "Proverbi e detti popolari nuoresi (Proverbios e testos nugoresos)," *Rivista delle tradizioni popolari italiane*, I, 11, 821–30.
Deledda, Grazia (1894e). "Nomi e nomignoli (Numenes e zistros)," *Rivista delle tradizioni popolari italiane*, I, 12, 1894, 893–98.
Deledda, Grazia (1894f). "Preghiere e voti," *Rivista delle tradizioni popolari italiane*, I, 12, 896–98.
Deledda, Grazia (1894g). "Lauda della V. del Carmelo (Gosos della V. del Carmine)," "Lauda di N. S. di Gonare (Gosos de N. S. de Gonare)," "Il perdono (Su perdonu)," *Rivista delle tradizioni popolari italiane*, II, 1, 17–21.
Deledda, Grazia (1894h). *Tradizioni popolari di Nuoro in Sardegna*. Rome: Forzani.
Deledda, Grazia (1895a). "Poesie," *Rivista delle tradizioni popolari italiane*, II, 2, 93–96.
Deledda, Grazia (1895b). "Filastrocche—Ninne-Nanne—Attitedos, ecc.," *Rivista delle tradizioni popolari italiane*, II, 3, 213–23.
Deledda, Grazia (1895c). "Sos berbos o verbos," *Rivista delle tradizioni popolari italiane*, II, 4, 241–46.

Deledda, Grazia (1895d). "Superstizioni, credenze e medicine popolari," *Rivista delle tradizioni popolari italiane*, II, 5, 332–40.
Deledda, Grazia (1895e). "Indovinelli," "Superstizioni, credenze e medicine popolari," "Usi e costumi: amoreggiamenti," "Nozze," "Battesimi," "Spauracchi dei bimbi," "Su candelarju," "Usi funebri," "Saluti ed auguri," "Elemosine," "Feste," "Usi vari," "Passatempi," "I barraccelli (Sos barraccellos)," "Vivande," "Vestimenta," *Rivista delle tradizioni popolari italiane*, II, 6, 401–50.
Deledda, Grazia (1900). "Albo di costumi e tipi sardi," *Rivista per le signorine*, X, 1.
Deledda, Grazia (1901). "Tipi e paesaggi sardi (*con 21 illustrazioni*)," *Nuova Antologia*, 720, 593–623.
Deledda, Grazia (1938). *Versi e prose giovanili*, ed. Antonio Scano. Milan: Treves.
Deledda, Grazia (1991). *Cosima*, trans. Martha King. London: Quartet.
Deledda, Grazia (1994). *Fiabe e leggende*, ed. Bruno Rombi. Milan: Rusconi.
Deledda, Grazia (1996). *Novelle: Nell'azzurro, Racconti sardi, L'ospite, Le tentazioni*, 6 vols., ed. Giovanna Cerina. Nuoro: Ilisso.
Deledda, Grazia (1999). *Leggende sarde*, ed. Dolores Turchi. Rome: Newton Compton.
Deledda, Grazia (2005 [1937]). *Cosima*. Nuoro: Ilisso.
Deledda, Grazia (2013). *Fiabe e leggende sarde*, ed. Carlo Mulas. Indibooks: eReading Life.
Deledda, Grazia, and Dolores Turchi (1995). *Tradizioni popolari di Sardegna: credenze magiche, antiche feste, superstizioni e riti di una volta nei più significativi scritti etnografici dell'autrice sarda.* Rome: Newton Compton.
Delitala, Enrica (1985). *Fiabe e leggende nelle tradizioni popolari della Sardegna*. Sassari: Editrice Mediterranea.
Di Francia, Letterio (2015 [1929]). *Fiabe e novelle calabresi*. Rome: Donzelli.
Glassie, Henry (ed.) (1985). *Irish Folktales*. New York: Pantheon.
Gomme, Alice Bertha (1894–1898). *The Traditional Games of England, Scotland and Ireland: With Tunes, Singing Rhymes and Methods of Playing According to the Variants Extant and Recorded in Different Parts of the Kingdom*, 2 vols. London: David Nutt.
Gonzenbach, Laura (1870). *Sicilianische Märchen. Aus dem Volksmund gesammelt von Laura Gonzenbach*, 2 vols., ed. Otto Hartwig and notes by Reinhold Köhler. Leipzig: W. Engelmann.
Gonzenbach, Laura (1964). *Tradizione popolare nelle fiabe siciliane di Laura von Gonzenbach*, ed. and trans. Renata La Racine. Messina: D'Anna.
Gonzenbach, Laura (2006). *Beautiful Angiola: The Lost Sicilian Folk and Fairy Tales of Laura Gonzenbach*, ed. and trans. Jack Zipes. New York: Routledge.
Gonzenbach, Laura (2019 [1870]). *Fiabe Siciliane. Nuova edizione interamente riveduta e aggiornata condotta sull'originale tedesco del 1870*, ed. and trans. Luisa Rubini, reread by Vincenzo Consolo. Rome: Donzelli.
Gonzenbach, Magdalena (1880). *Istituto femminile Gonzenbach, giardino d'infanzia-scuola elementare e corsi superiori: ordinamento e programmi*. Messina: Stamperia e Stereotipia Capra.
Gower Chapman, Charlotte (1971). *Milocca. A Sicilian Village*. Cambridge, MA, and London: Schenkman.
Gregory, Augusta (1903a). *Poets and Dreamers: Studies and Translations from the Irish*. Dublin: Hodges, Figgis.
Gregory, Augusta (1903b). *Cuchulain of Muirthemne: The Story of the Men of the Red Branch of Ulster*, with a preface by W. B. Yeats. New York: Charles Scribner's Sons.
Gregory, Augusta (1906). *A Book of Saints and Wonders, Put Down Here by Lady Gregory According to the Old Writings and the Memory of the People of Ireland*. Dundrum: Dun Emer Press.
Gregory, Augusta (1909). *The Kiltartan History Book*, illustrated by Robert Gregory. Dublin: Maunsel.
Gregory, Augusta (1910). *The Kiltartan Wonder Book*. Dublin: Maunsel.
Gregory, Augusta (1919). *The Kiltartan Poetry Book: Prose Translations from the Irish*. New York and London: G. P. Putnam's Sons, Knickerbocker Press.

Gregory, Augusta (1971 [1931]). *Coole*, ed. Colin Smythe, with a foreword by Edward Malins. Dublin: Dolmen Press.
Gregory, Augusta (1974). *Seventy Years: Being the Autobiography of Lady Gregory*, ed. Colin Smythe. Gerrards Cross: Colin Smythe.
Gregory, Augusta (1996). *Lady Gregory's Diaries 1892–1902*, ed. James Pethica. Gerrards Cross: Colin Smythe.
Gregory, Augusta (2006 [1920]). *Visions and Beliefs in the West of Ireland*, with a foreword by Elizabeth Coxhead. Gerrards Cross: Colin Smythe.
Grimm, Jacob, and Wilhelm Grimm (1816–18). *Deutsche Sagen. Herausgegeben von den Brüdern Grimm*. Berlin: Nicolaische Buchhandlung.
Grimm, Jacob, and Wilhelm Grimm (1826). *Kinder- und Haus-Märchen. Gesammelt durch die Brüder Grimm*. Stuttgart: Bei A.F. Macklot.
Grimm, Jacob, and Wilhelm Grimm (1839). *Gammer Grethel; or, German Fairy Tales, and Popular Stories, from the Collection of MM. Grimm, and Other Sources; with Illustrative Notes*, ed. and trans. Edgar Taylor. London: John Green.
Grimm, Jacob, and Wilhelm Grimm (1981). *The German Legends of the Brothers Grimm*, ed. and trans. Donald Ward, 2 vols. Philadelphia: Institute for the Study of Human Issues.
Grimm, Jacob, and Wilhelm Grimm (2014). *The Original Folk and Fairy Tales of the Brothers Grimm: The Complete First Edition*, ed. and trans. Jack Zipes, illustrated by Andrea Dezsö. Princeton: Princeton University Press.
Guglielmi, Laura (2021). *Lady Constance Lloyd. L'importanza di chiamarsi Wilde*. Milan: Morellini.
Hall, Anna Maria (1892 [1829]). *Sketches of Irish Character*. London: Chatto & Windus.
Hall, Anna Maria, and Samuel Carter Hall (1841–43). *Ireland: Its Scenery, Character and History, Illustrated from Paintings by F. S. Walker and Photographs*, 3 vols. New York: R. Worthington.
Holland, Merlin, and Rupert Hart-Davis (eds.) (2000). *The Complete Letters of Oscar Wilde*. London: Fourth Estate.
Hull, Eleanor (1928). *Folklore of the British Isles*, with a preface by R. R. Marett. London: Methuen.
Hyde, Douglas (1889). *Leabhar Sgéulaigheachta*. Baile Átha Cliath: Gill.
Hyde, Douglas (1890). *Beside the Fire: A Collection of Irish Gaelic Folk Stories*. London: David Nutt.
Hyde, Douglas (1893). *Abhráin grádh chúige Connacht. Love Songs of Connacht: Being the Fourth Chapter of The Songs of Connacht*. Dublin: M. H. Gill & Son.
Hyde, Douglas (1904 [1892]). "The Necessity for De-Anglicising Ireland," in *The Revival of Irish Literature: Addresses by Sir Charles Gavan Duffy, K.C.M.G, Dr. George Sigerson, and Dr. Douglas Hyde*. London: T. Fisher Unwin, pp. 117–61.
Joynt, Maud (1925). *The Golden Legends of the Gael*. Dublin: Talbot Press.
Kennelly, Brendan (1970). *The Penguin Book of Irish Verse*. Harmondsworth: Penguin.
Kinsella, Thomas, and Seán Ó Tuama (1981). *An Duanaire, 1600–1900: Poems of the Dispossessed*. Portlaoise: Dolmen Press.
Laboulaye, Édouard (2018). *Smack-Bam, or The Art of Governing Men: Political Fairy Tales of Édouard Laboulaye*, ed. and trans. Jack Zipes. Princeton: Princeton University Press.
Lawrence, David Herbert (2002 [1921]). *Sea and Sardinia*, ed. Mara Kalnins. Cambridge: Cambridge University Press.
Lazzaro, Bianca (2023). *Fiabe ribelli. Le più belle fiabe italiane delle ragazze in gamba*, ed. and trans. by Bianca Lazzaro, illustrated by Cinzia Ghigliano. Rome: Donzelli.
Levi, Eugenia (1895). *Fiorita di canti tradizionali del popolo italiano scelti nei vari dialetti e annotati da Eugenia Levi, con cinquanta melodie popolari tradizionali*. Florence: Bemporad.

Manca, Maria (1895). "Leggenda sarda di compare Peddiù," *Rivista delle tradizioni popolari italiane*, II, 6, 466–71.
Martinengo-Cesaresco, Evelyn (1886). *Essays in the Study of Folk-Songs*. London: G. Redway.
Martinengo-Cesaresco, Evelyn (1890). *Italian Characters in the Epoch of Unification*. London: T. Fisher Unwin.
Martinengo-Cesaresco, Evelyn (1893). *La Poésie populaire*. Paris: Émile Lechevalier.
Martinengo-Cesaresco, Evelyn (1895). *The Liberation of Italy, 1815–1870*. London: Seeley.
Martinengo-Cesaresco, Evelyn (1898). *Cavour*. London: Macmillan.
Martinengo-Cesaresco, Evelyn (1909). *The Place of Animals in Human Thought*. New York: Charles Scribner's Sons.
Martinengo-Cesaresco, Evelyn (1916). "Obituary: Giuseppe Pitrè," *Folklore*, 27, 314–16.
Mazzoni, Cristina (ed.) (2021). *The Pomegranates and Other Italian Fairy Tales*, ed. and trans. Cristina Mazzoni. Princeton: Princeton University Press.
McClintock, Letitia (1876). "Folk-Lore of the County Donegal," *Dublin University Magazine*, 88, 607–14.
McClintock, Letitia (1877). "Folk Lore of the County Donegal: Fairy Tales," *Dublin University Magazine*, 89, 241–49.
McClintock, Letitia (1878). "Cavan Superstitions," *Belgravia: A London Magazine*, 37, 145, 90–97.
McClintock, Letitia (1880). "Folk-Lore of the County Donegal," *All The Year Round*, 24, 464–68.
McClintock, Letitia (1881). "Ulster Folklore," *All The Year Round*, 25, 16–20.
McClintock, Letitia (1882). "Fairy Legends of the County Donegal," *All The Year Round*, 28, 461–69.
Meinhold, Wilhelm (1849). *Sidonia the Sorceress: The Supposed Destroyer of the Whole Reigning Ducal House of Pomerania*, trans. Jane Wilde. Belfast: Simms and M'Intyre.
Minard, Rosemary (ed.) (1975). *Womenfolk and Fairy Tales*, illustrated by Suzanna Klein. Boston: Houghton Mifflin.
Nardo Cibele, Angela (1872). "Sulla parte che può avere la donna nella formazione del vocabolario comparativo de' dialetti italiani: lettera a Gualberta Alaide Beccari," Excerpt from the journal *La Donna*, 191, September 7, 1872. Venice: Tip. Del Commercio.
Nardo Cibele, Angela (1887). *Zoologia popolare veneta, specialmente Bellunese. Credenze, leggende e tradizioni varie*. Palermo: Luigi Pedone Lauriel.
Nardo Cibele, Angela (1888). "Fiabe bellunesi," *Archivio per lo studio delle tradizioni popolari Palermo*, VII, 475–81.
Nardo Cibele, Angela (1898). *Studi sul dialetto di Burano*. Venice: Premiata Tipografia Fratelli Visentini.
Niceforo, Alfredo (1897). *La delinquenza in Sardegna*. Palermo: Remo Sandron.
O'Connell, Mrs. Morgan John (Mary Anne) (1892). *The Last Colonel of the Irish Brigade: Count O'Connell and Old Irish Life at Home and Abroad (1745–1833)*, 2 vols. London: Kegan, Trench, Trübner.
Orano, Paolo (1896). *Psicologia della Sardegna. Impressioni ed appunti*. Rome: Tipografia della casa editrice italiana.
Owenson, Sydney (1805). *Twelve Original Hibernian Melodies, with English Words, Imitated and Translated from the Works of the Ancient Irish Bards*. London: Preston.
Owenson, Sydney (1807). *Patriotic Sketches of Ireland, Written in Connaught*, 2 vols. London: Richard Phillips.
Owenson, Sydney (1808). *The Lay of an Irish Harp; or, Metrical Fragments*. New York: Sargeant, Longworth, Jansen.
Percoto, Caterina (1858). *Racconti*. Florence: Le Monnier.
Perodi, Emma (1924 [1893]). *Le novelle della nonna: fiabe fantastiche*, illustrated by Carlo Chiostri. Florence: Salani, I.

Perodi, Emma (1925 [1893]). *Le novelle della nonna: fiabe fantastiche*, illustrated by Carlo Chiostri. Florence: Salani, II.
Perodi, Emma (1992 [1893]). *Le novelle della nonna: fiabe fantastiche*. Rome: Newton Compton.
Perodi, Emma (2020). *Tuscan Tales: The Fantastic Fables of Emma Perodi*, ed. and trans. Lori Hetherington. n.p.: Amazon Books.
Pigorini Beri, Caterina (1883). "La Cenerentola a Parma e Camerino," *Archivio per lo studio delle tradizioni popolari*, II, 45–58.
Pigorini Beri, Caterina (1889). *Costumi e superstizioni dell'Appennino marchigiano*. Città di Castello: S. Lapi Tipografo.
Pigorini Beri, Caterina (2000 [1892]). *In Calabria*, ed. Francesco Giuseppe Graceffa. Soveria Mannelli: Rubbettino.
Pirandello, Luigi (1987). "Il figlio cambiato," in *Novelle per un anno*, ed. Mario Costanzo. Milan: Mondadori, II, 496–01.
Pitrè, Giuseppe (1864). *Profili biografici di contemporanei italiani*. Palermo: Francesco Lao.
Pitrè, Giuseppe (1870). "Lettere Siciliane," *Rivista Europea*, 2, I, 122–29.
Pitrè, Giuseppe (1873). *Nuovo saggio di fiabe e novella popolari siciliane raccolte ed illustrate da Giuseppe Pitrè*. Imola: Ignazio Galeati e Figlio.
Pitrè, Giuseppe (1875). *Fiabe novelle e racconti popolari siciliani*, 4 vols. Palermo: Luigi Pedone Lauriel.
Pitrè, Giuseppe (1885a). *Novelle popolari toscane*. Florence: Barbera.
Pitrè, Giuseppe (1885b). "Lo sputo e la saliva nelle tradizioni popolari di Sicilia," *Archivio per lo studio delle tradizioni popolari*, IV, 233–36.
Pitrè, Giuseppe (1889). *Usi e costumi, credenze e pregiudizi del popolo siciliano, raccolti e descritti da Giuseppe Pitrè*, 4 vols. Palermo: Il Vespro.
Pitrè, Giuseppe (1895). *Costumi siciliani delle province di Messina e di Palermo*. Palermo: Giornale di Sicilia.
Pitrè, Giuseppe (1896). *Medicina popolare siciliana raccolta ed ordinata da Giuseppe Pitrè*. Turin: Carlo Clausen.
Pitrè, Giuseppe (1904). *Studi di leggende popolari in Sicilia e nuova raccolta di leggende siciliane*. Turin: Carlo Clausen.
Pitrè, Giuseppe (2001). *La Demopsicologia e la sua storia*, ed. Loredana Bellantonio. Comiso: Documenta, Ila Palma.
Pitrè, Giuseppe (2009). *The Collected Sicilian Folk and Fairy Tales of Giuseppe Pitrè*, ed. and trans. by Jack Zipes and Joseph Russo, illustrated by Carmelo Bene. New York: Routledge.
Pitrè, Giuseppe (2013 [1875]). *Fiabe novelle e racconti popolari siciliani*, 4 vols., trans. Bianca Lazzaro, with an introduction by Jack Zipes and a preface by Giovanni Puglisi. Rome: Donzelli.
Pitrè, Giuseppe (2017). *Catarina the Wise and Other Wondrous Sicilian Folk and Fairy Tales*, ed. and trans. Jack Zipes, illustrated by Adeetje Bouma. Chicago: University of Chicago Press.
Ragan, Kathleen (ed.) (1998). *Fearless Girls, Wise Women, and Beloved Sisters: Heroines in Folktales from around the World*. New York: W. W. Norton.
Rossi, Mario Manlio (1932). *Viaggio in Irlanda*. Milan: Doxa.
Rossi, Mario Manlio (1933). *Pilgrimage in the West*, trans. Joseph Maunsell Hone. Dublin: Cuala Press.
Savi-Lopez, Maria (1886). *Le valli di Lanzo: bozzetti e leggende*. Turin: Brero.
Savi-Lopez, Maria (1889). *Leggende delle Alpi*, with sixty illustrations by Carlo Chessa. Turin: Ermanno Loescher.
Savi-Lopez, Maria (2008 [1894]). *Leggende del mare*. Palermo: Sellerio.

Sayers, Peig (1936). *Peig: A Scéal Féin*, ed. Máire Ní Chinnéide. Dublin: Talbot Press.
Sayers, Peig (1939). *Machtnamh Sheana-Mhná*, ed. Máire Ní Chinnéide. Baile Átha Cliath: Oifig an tSoláthair.
Sayers, Peig (1962). *An Old Woman's Reflections*, trans. Séamus Ennis. Oxford: Oxford University Press.
Sayers, Peig (1974). *Peig: The Autobiography of Peig Sayers of the Great Blasket Island*. trans. Bryan MacMahon. Dublin: Talbot Press.
Serao, Matilde (1907 [1881]). *Leggende Napoletane. Libro d'immaginazione e di sogno*. Naples: Libreria Economica.
Shaw, Rose (1930). *Carleton's Country*. Dublin: The Talbot Press.
Sullivan, Deirdre (2017). *Tangleweed and Brine*. Dublin: Little Island Books.
Sullivan, Deirdre (2020). *Savage Her Reply*. Dublin: Little Island Books.
Terranova, Nadia (2022). *Il cortile delle sette fate*, illustrated by Simona Mulazzani. Milan: Ugo Guanda.
Thiselton-Dyer, T. F. (1906). *Folk-Lore of Women as Illustrated by Legendary and Traditionary Tales, Folk-Rhymes, Proverbial Sayings, Superstitions, etc.* Chicago: A. C. McClurg.
Turchi, Dolores (ed.) (1984). *Leggende e racconti popolari della Sardegna*. Rome: Newton Compton.
Walsh, Angela, Kalina Maleska, Donna Jo Napoli, and Nadia Albert (eds.) (2021). *Awake Not Sleeping: Reimagining Fairy Tales for a New Generation*, illustrated by Natasa Konjevic. UN Women Regional Office for Europe and Central Asia: United Nations Entity for Gender Equality and the Empowerment of Women. https://eca.unwomen.org/en/digital-library/publications/2021/11/awake-not-sleeping-reimagining-fairy-tales-for-a-new-generation (last accessed June 30, 2024).
Walshe, Eibhear (2014). *The Diary of Mary Travers*. Dromore: Somerville Press.
Warrack, Grace Harriet (1914). *Florilegio di Canti Toscani: Folksongs of the Tuscan Hills with English Renderings*. London: Alexander Moring.
Wilde, Constance (1888). *There Was Once: Grandma's Stories*, with colour pictures by John Lawson. London: Nister.
Wilde, Jane (1864). *Poems by Speranza*. Dublin: James Duffy.
Wilde, Jane (1877). "The Fairy Mythology of Ireland," *Dublin University Magazine*, 90, 70–83.
Wilde, Jane (1880). "Concluding Portion of *The Memoir of Gabriel Beranger*," in William Wilde's *Memoir of Gabriel Beranger and His Labours in the Cause of Irish Art and Antiquities, from 1760 to 1780*. Dublin: M. H. Gill and Son, pp. 131–76.
Wilde, Jane (1884). *Driftwood from Scandinavia*. London: Richard Bentley and Son.
Wilde, Jane (1887a). *Ancient Legends, Mystic Charms, and Superstitions of Ireland, with Sketches of the Irish Past*, 2 vols. Boston: Ticknor.
Wilde, Jane (1887b). "Irish Minstrelsy," *Pall Mall Gazette*, November 29, 3.
Wilde, Jane (1890). *Ancient Cures, Charms, and Usages of Ireland: Contributions to Irish Lore*. London: Ward & Downey.
Wilde, Jane (1893). *Social Studies*. London: Ward & Downey.
Wilde, Oscar (1905). *De Profundis*. New York and London: G. P. Putnam's Sons, Knickerbocker Press.
Wilde, William (1852). *Irish Popular Superstitions*. Dublin: James McGlashan.
Yeats, William Butler (1888). *Fairy and Folk Tales of the Irish Peasantry*. London: Walter Scott.
Yeats, William Butler (1892). *Irish Fairy Tales*. London: Unwin.
Yeats, William Butler (1893). *The Celtic Twilight: Men and Women, Dhouls and Faeries*. London: A. H. Bullen.
Yeats, William Butler (1981). *Fiabe irlandesi*, trans. Melita Cataldi and Mariagiovanna Andreolli. Turin: Einaudi.

Yeats, William Butler (1999 [1935]). "Dramatis Personae: 1896–1902 (w. 1934, publ. 1935)," in *Autobiographies: The Collected Works of W. B. Yeats*, 14 vols., ed. William H. O'Donnell and Douglas N. Archibald. New York: Scribner, III, pp. 287–37.

Zanazzo, Giggi (1907). *Novelle, Favole e Leggende Romanesche*. Turin: Società Tipografico-editrice Nazionale.

Zanazzo, Giggi (1908). *Usi costumi e pregiudizi del popolo di Roma*. Turin: Società Tipografico-editrice Nazionale.

Secondary Sources

Aarne, Antti, and Stith Thompson (1961). *The Types of the Folktale: A Classification and Bibliography*. Helsinki: Academia Scientiarum Fennica.

Abrahams, Roger (1993). "Phantoms of Romantic Nationalism in Folkloristics," *Journal of American Folklore*, 106, 419, 3–37.

Abu-Lughod, Lila (1991). "Writing against Culture," in *Recapturing Anthropology: Working in the Present*, ed. Richard G. Fox. Santa Fe: School of American Research Press, pp. 137–62.

Adamo, Giuliana (2006). "Beneath Two Skies: Diversely Azure," in Adamo and Marci 2006:10–12.

Adamo, Giuliana, and Giuseppe Marci (eds.) (2006). *Nae: Rivista trimestrale di cultura*. Speciale Irlanda. Cagliari: CUEC.

Adams, Hazard (1973). *Lady Gregory*. Lewisburg: Bucknell University Press.

Agostini-Ouafi, Viviana (2016). "Le novelle della nonna di Emma Perodi. Un congegno narrativo 'popolare-nazionale' ante litteram," *Chroniques italiennes*, 31, 1, 87–110.

Almqvist, Bo (1991). "Irish Migratory Legends on the Supernatural: Sources, Studies and Problems," *Béaloideas*, 59, *The Fairy Hill Is on Fire! Proceedings of the Symposium on the Supernatural in Irish and Scottish Migratory Legends*, ed. Bo Almqvist and Pádraig Ó Héalaí, 1–43.

Almqvist, Bo (2010). "Kenneth Jackson and Peig Sayers: The Creation of *Scéalta ón mBlascaod*," *Béaloideas*, 78, 99–125.

Almqvist, Bo (2011). "Kenneth Jackson and Peig Sayers: The Perfect Memory," *Béaloideas*, 79, 22–43.

Alù, Giorgia (2008). *Beyond the Traveller's Gaze: Expatriate Ladies Writing in Sicily (1848–1910)*. Oxford: Peter Lang.

Alziator, Francesco (1974). "Grazia Deledda e le tradizioni popolari," in *Convegno nazionale di studi deleddiani, Nuoro, 30 settembre 1972. Atti*. Cagliari: Editrice sarda Fossataro, pp. 175–89.

Anderson, Benedict (2006 [1983]). *Imagined Communities: Reflections on the Origin and Spread of Nationalism*. London: Verso.

Angioni, Giulio (2010). "Prefazione," in Grazia Deledda's *Tradizioni popolari di Nuoro*. Nuoro: Ilisso, pp. 7–29.

Angioni, Giulio (2015). "Una scuola antropologica sarda?" in *La Sardegna contemporanea*, ed. Luciano Marrocu, Francesco Bachis, and Valeria Deplano. Rome: Donzelli, pp. 647–72.

Anonymous (1863). "Review of *The First Temptation; or Eritis sicut Deus, a Philosophical Romance* (1863) by Wilhelmine Friederike Gottliebe Canz, trans. Lady Wilde," *Duffy's Hibernian Magazine: A Monthly Journal of Literature, Science, and Art*, IV, 63–69.

Anonymous (1870). "Recensione di *Sicilianische Märchen* di Laura Gonzenbach," *Rivista Sicula di Scienze, Letteratura ed Arti*, 2, 3, 594–601.

Anonymous (1890). "Review of *Ancient Cures, Charms, and Usages of Ireland: Contributions to Irish Lore*. By Lady Wilde. (Ward & Downey)," *The Athenaeum*, 398.

Anonymous (1896). "Death of Lady Wilde," *Freeman's Journal*, February 6, 5.

Anonymous (1922). "Review of Rose Maud Young's *Duanaire Gaedhilge*," *Studies: An Irish Quarterly Review*, 11, 42, 335.
Antonelli, Giuseppe, Emiliano Picchiorri, and Marcello Ravesi (2012). "La riscoperta dei dialetti: dizionari, raccolte folkloriche e poesia," in *Atlante della letteratura italiana. Dal Romanticismo a oggi*, 3 vols., ed. Sergio Luzzatto and Gabriele Pedullà. Turin: Einaudi, III, pp. 261–73.
Aprile, Renato (1991). *Fiabe di magia in Sicilia*. Palermo: Sellerio.
Arlia, Costantino, and Pietro Fanfani (1890 [1881]). "Folk-lore," in *Lessico dell'infima e corrotta italianità*. Milan: Carrara, p. 230.
Ashman, Gordon (2000). "Charlotte Burne (1850–1923)," in Blacker and Davidson 2000:33–44.
Atzori, Mario, and Maria Margherita Satta (2013). "Antologia delle tradizioni popolari in Sardegna," in *Prima etnografia d'Italia: gli studi di folklore tra '800 e '900 nel quadro europeo*, ed. Gian Luigi Bravo. Milan: Franco Angeli, pp. 79–107.
Augusteijn, Joost, and Eric Storm (eds.) (2012). *Region and State in Nineteenth-Century Europe: Nation-Building, Regional Identities and Separatism*. Basingstoke: Palgrave Macmillan.
Augusteijn, Joost (2012). "Irish Nationalism and Unionism between State, Region and Nation," in Augusteijn and Storm 2012:192–208.
Ayres-Bennett, Wendy, and Helena Sanson (eds.) (2020). *Women in the History of Linguistics*. Oxford: Oxford University Press.
Bacchilega, Cristina (1993). "An Introduction to the 'Innocent Persecuted Heroine' Fairy Tale," *Western Folklore*, Special issue: *Perspectives on the Innocent Persecuted Heroine in Fairy Tales*, ed. Cristina Bacchilega and Steven Swann Jones, 52, 1, 1–12.
Bacchilega, Cristina (2007). *Legendary Hawai'i and the Politics of Place: Tradition, Translation, and Tourism*. Philadelphia: University of Pennsylvania Press.
Bacchilega, Cristina (2009). "Folktale," in Locke et al. 2009, I:247–56.
Bacchilega, Cristina (2012). "Folklore and Literature," in Bendix and Hasan-Rokem 2012:447–63.
Bacchilega, Cristina (2013). *Fairy Tales Transformed? Twenty-First Century Adaptations and the Politics of Wonder*. Detroit: Wayne State University Press.
Bacchilega, Cristina (2019). "'Decolonizing' the Canon: Critical Challenges to Eurocentrism," in *The Fairy Tale World*, ed. Andrew Teverson. New York: Routledge, pp. 33–44.
Bacchilega, Cristina (2023). "Fairy Stories and the World's Wonder Tales," in *Realms of Imagination. Essays from the Wide Worlds of Fantasy*, ed. Tanya Kirk and Matthew Sangster, with a preface by Neil Gaiman. London: British Library, pp. 47–62.
Bacchilega, Cristina, and Marie Alohalani Brown (2019). "Introduction: The Stories We Tell about Mermaids and Other Spirits," in *The Penguin Book of Mermaids*. New York: Penguin, pp. ix–xxiv.
Badin, Donatella Abbate (2016). "Lady Morgan in Italy: A Traveller with an Agenda," *Studi irlandesi. A Journal of Irish Studies*, 6, 127–48.
Baldacchino, Godfrey (2004). "The Coming of Age of Island Studies," *Tijdschrift voor Economische en Sociale Geografie*, 95, 3, 272–83.
Balducci, Carolyn (1975). *A Self-Made Woman: Biography of Nobel-Prize-Winner Grazia Deledda*. Boston: Houghton Mifflin.
Bani, Luca (ed.) (2010). *Carte Private: taccuini, carteggi e documenti autografi tra Otto e Novecento, Atti del convegno nazionale di studi, Bergamo, 26–28 febbraio 2009*. Bergamo: Moretti & Vitali.
Barbarulli, Clotilde (2003). "La parola senza genere per domestici conforti," in Botta et al. 2003:95–106.
Battaglia, Salvatore (1961–2001). *Grande dizionario della lingua italiana*, 21 vols. Turin: UTET.
Battistini, Andrea (ed.) (2012). *At vòi cuntèr na fòla. Carolina Coronedi Berti e la cultura del suo tempo*. Bologna: CLUEB.

Bauman, Richard (2004). *A World of Others' Words: Cross-Cultural Perspectives on Intertextuality.* Oxford: Blackwell.

Baycroft, Timothy, and David Hopkin (eds.) (2012). *Folklore and Nationalism in Europe During the Long Nineteenth Century.* Leiden: National Cultivation of Culture, Brill.

Bearman, C. J. (1999). "Kate Lee and the Foundation of the Folk-Song Society," *Folk Music Journal*, 7, 5, 627–43.

Behar, Ruth, and Deborah A. Gordon (1995). *Women Writing Culture.* Berkeley: University of California Press.

Beiner, Guy (2004). "Who Were 'the Men of the West'? Folk Historiographies and the Reconstruction of Democratic Histories," *Folklore*, 115, 2, 201–21.

Beiner, Guy (2007). *Remembering the Year of the French: Irish Folk History and Social Memory.* Madison: University of Wisconsin Press.

Belardi, Walter B. (1990). "'Parlare utilmente con la penna,' ovvero il ruolo della lingua scritta nella 'questione della lingua' secondo G. I. Ascoli," in *Linguistica generale, filologia e critica dell'espressione*, 2 vols. Rome: Bonacci, II, pp. 317–39.

Bellantonio, Loredana (2017). "Riflessioni sull'opera di Giuseppe Pitrè nel primo centenario della scomparsa. Gli scritti inediti," *Palaver*, 6, 1, 136–46.

Bellucci, Paolo (1986). *Poetessa pastora. La storia e i canti di Beatrice di Pian degli Ontani, scoperta dal Tommaseo e amata dal Ruskin; con una raccolta inedita di versi da lei cantati e una nota su Francesca Alexander e John Ruskin.* Florence: Medicea.

Ben-Amos, Dan (2010). "Introduction: The European Fairy-Tale Tradition between Orality and Literacy," *Journal of American Folklore*, 123, 490, 373–76.

Bencistà, Alessandro (2011). "Beatrice di Pian degli Ontani. Una pastora diventata mito," in Francesco Chierroni, *Vita della gran poetessa Beatrice e sue poesie cantate insieme col poeta Francesco Chierroni e viaggio di lui che mitologicamente figura di andarla a trovare in paradiso, con aggiunta ancora della di lui vita, tutto in ottava rima*, ed. Jean Pierre Cavaillé and Alessandro Bencistà. Florence: Semper, pp. 53–54.

Bendix, Regina (1997). *In Search of Authenticity: The Formation of Folklore Studies.* Madison: University of Wisconsin Press.

Bendix, Regina, and Galit Hasan-Rokem (eds.) (2012). *A Companion to Folklore.* Malden: Wiley-Blackwell.

Bernardy, Amy Allemand (1942). *Irlanda e Roma.* Rome: Istituto Nazionale per le Relazioni Culturali con l'Estero I.R.C.E.

Bibbò, Antonio (2022a). *Irish Literature in Italy in the Era of the World Wars.* Cham: Palgrave Macmillan.

Bibbò, Antonio (2022b). "Postfazione," in *Spiriti, santi ed eroi. Storie popolari irlandesi.* Milan: Feltrinelli, pp. 173–91.

Billington, Sandra (2000). "Augusta Gregory. 1852–1932," in Blacker and Davidson 2000: 47–61.

Binelli, Andrea, Giorgia Falceri, and Chiara Polli (2017). "Bardi, streghe e altre creature magiche. Tradurre l'Irlanda di Lady Wilde," *Ticontre. Teoria Testo Traduzione*, 7, 285–300.

Bitel, Lisa M. (1998). *Land of Women: Tales of Sex and Gender from Early Ireland.* Ithaca: Cornell University Press.

Blacker, Carmen, and Hilda Ellis Davidson (2000). *Women and Tradition: A Neglected Group of Folklorists.* Durham, NC: Carolina Academic Press.

Bloom, Karin (2015). "*Cordelia*, 1881–1942. Profilo storico di una rivista per ragazze." PhD diss., Stockholms Universitet.

Bolognesi, Roberto, and Catharine Josephine Helsloot (eds.) (1999). *La lingua sarda: l'identità socioculturale della Sardegna nel prossimo millennio. Atti del convegno, Quartu Sant'Elena, 9–10 Maggio 1997.* Cagliari: Condaghes.

Bombara, Daniela (2015). "Il fantastico siciliano dell'Ottocento crocevia di culture e occasione di denuncia sociale nelle opere di Pitrè, Bisazza e Navarro," *AATI Online Working Papers, Proceeding of the AATI Conference in Siena, Italy, 17–21 June 2015*, ed. Andrea Dini, Daria Mizza, and Ilaria Serra, 1–11.

Bonomo, Giuseppe (2016). "Prefazione alla nuova edizione (1971)," in Giuseppe Cocchiara, *Storia del folklore in Europa*. Turin: Bollati Boringhieri, pp. 13–17.

Borghi, Gian Paolo (2012). "'Poesia popolare' e folkloriste tra Emilia e Toscana," in Battistini 2012:93–122.

Botta, Anna, Monica Farnetti, and Giorgio Rimondi (eds.) (2003). *Le eccentriche: scrittrici del Novecento*. Mantova: Tre Lune.

Bottigheimer, Ruth B. (ed.) (1986). *Fairy Tales and Society: Illusion, Allusion and Paradigm*. Philadelphia: University of Pennsylvania Press.

Bottigheimer, Ruth B. (1987). *Grimms' Bad Girls and Bold Boys: The Moral and Social Vision of the Tales*. New Haven: Yale University Press.

Bourdieu, Pierre (1990). *The Logic of Practice*, trans. Richard Nice. Stanford: Stanford University Press.

Bourke, Angela (1999). *The Burning of Bridget Cleary: A True Story*. London: Pimlico.

Bourke, Angela (2002a). "Oral Traditions," in *The Field Day Anthology of Irish Writing: Irish Women's Writing and Traditions*, ed. Angela Bourke. New York: New York University Press, IV, pp. 1191–97.

Bourke, Angela (2002b). "Lamenting the Dead," in *The Field Day Anthology of Irish Writing: Irish Women's Writing and Traditions*, ed. Angela Bourke. New York: New York University Press, IV, pp. 1365–98.

Bourke, Angela, and Patricia Lysaght (2002). "Peig Sayers (1873–1958)," in *The Field Day Anthology of Irish Writing: Irish Women's Writing and Traditions*, ed. Angela Bourke. New York: New York University Press, IV, pp. 1198–1205.

Bourke, Angela, and Niamh O'Sullivan (2016). "A Fairy Legend, a Friendship, a Painting: Thomas Crofton Croker, James McDaniel, and Daniel Macdonald's *Sídhe Gaoithe / The Fairy Blast*," *Éire-Ireland*, 51, 3–4, 7–22.

Bowles, Noelle (1999). "Nationalism and Feminism in Lady Gregory's 'Kincora,' 'Dervorgilla,' and 'Grania,'" *New Hibernia Review*, 3, 3, 116–30.

Boyes, Georgina (2000). "Alice Gomme (1852–1932)," in Blacker and Davidson 2000:65–83.

Boyes, Georgina (2001). "A Proper Limitation: Stereotypes of Alice Gomme," *Musical Traditions*. www.mustrad.org.uk/articles/gomme.htm (last accessed June 30, 2024).

Bracchi, Cristina (2010). "Cosima o l'Altra necessaria del paradigma autobiografico," in Farnetti 2010:145–61.

Briggs, Katharine (1978). *The Vanishing People: Fairy Lore and Legends*, illustrated by Mary French. New York: Pantheon Books.

Briody, Mícheál (2008). *The Irish Folklore Commission, 1935–1970: History, Ideology, Methodology*. Helsinki: Studia Fennica Folkloristika.

Briziarelli, Susan (1995). "Woman as Outlaw: Grazia Deledda and the Politics of Gender," *Modern Language Notes*, 110, 1, 20–31.

Broderick, Marian (2001). *Wild Irish Women: Extraordinary Lives from History*. Dublin: O'Brien Press.

Bronzini, Giovanni Battista (2002). "Come nacquero le *Osservazioni sul folclore* di Gramsci," *Lares*, 68, 2, 195–224.

Brown, Terence (1988). *Ireland's Literature: Selected Essays*. Mullingar: Lilliput Press.

Brown, Terence (2001). *The Life of W. B. Yeats: A Critical Biography*. Dublin: Gill and Macmillan.

Bruni, Francesco (1984). *L'italiano: elementi di storia della lingua e della cultura*. Turin: UTET.

Buchan, David (1972). *The Ballad and the Folk*. London: Routledge.
Calvino, Italo (1981). "Il poeta mangiato da un gatto," *La Repubblica*, December 11, 14.
Calvino, Italo (1984 [1974]). *Collezione di sabbia. Emblemi bizzarri e inquietanti del nostro passato e del nostro futuro. Gli oggetti raccontano il mondo*. Milan: Garzanti.
Calvino, Italo (2013). *Collection of Sand: Essays*, trans. Martin McLaughlin. New York: Houghton Mifflin Harcourt.
Caminiti, Luciana (2015). "Magdalena Gonzenbach. Una pedagogista risorgimentale tra ideali, teoria e pratica," in *Echi dalla Sicilia. Scritti per Amelia Ioli Gigante*, ed. Corradina Polto. Bologna: Pàtron, pp. 101–13.
Campana, Andrea (2012). "Carolina Coronedi Berti socia della Commissione per i Testi di Lingua di Bologna," in Battistini 2012:29–40.
Campbell, Matthew, and Michael Perraudin (eds.) (2012). *The Voice of the People: Writing the European Folk Revival, 1760–1914*. London: Anthem Press.
Canepa, Nancy (2008). "Deledda, Grazia (1871–1936)," in *The Greenwood Encyclopedia of Folktales and Fairy Tales*, 3 vols., ed. Donald Haase. Westport: Greenwood, I, pp. 262–63.
Canepa, Nancy (ed.) (2023). *The Enchanted Boot: Italian Fairy Tales and Their Tellers*. Detroit: Wayne State University Press.
Cappelletti, Licurgo (1870). "I racconti popolari siciliani raccolti dalla signora Laura Gonzembach [sic]," *Rivista Europea*, 1, IV, I, 149–51.
Capriotti, Marco (2022a). *L'improvvisazione poetica nell'Italia del Settecento: la storia e le forme*. Rome: Accademia dell'Arcadia.
Capriotti, Marco (2022b). *L'improvvisazione poetica nell'Italia del Settecento: un catalogo*. Rome: Accademia dell'Arcadia.
Carolan, Mary Ann McDonald (1999). "Icon, Intercession and Insight: The Madonna as Interpretative Key to Grazia Deledda," *Quaderni d'italianistica*, 20, 1–2, 103–17.
Carrassi, Vito (2012). *The Irish Fairy Tale: A Narrative Tradition from the Middle Ages to Yeats and Stephens*, trans. Kevin Wren. Lanham, MD: John Cabot University Press.
Carrassi, Vito (2014). "Polifonia nelle anthologie di W. B. Yeats: il dialogo complesso tra folklore e letteratura," *Studi irlandesi. A Journal of Irish Studies*, 4, 225–43.
Carroll, Hannah Elizabeth (2013). "Travels through Text and Image: Estella Canziani's 'Costumes, Traditions and Songs of Savoy' (1911)." MPhil thesis, University of Birmingham.
Casalena, Maria Pia (2012). *Biografie: la scrittura delle vite in Italia tra politica, società e cultura (1796–1915)*. Milan: Bruno Mondadori.
Casali, Elide (2012). "I 'mille volti' dell'eroina ne *Al sgugiol di ragazù* di Carolina Coronedi Berti," in Battistini 2012:81–92.
Cassano, Franco (1996). *Il pensiero meridiano*. Rome, Bari: Laterza.
Castellana, Riccardo (2014). *Storie di figli cambiati. Fate, demoni e sostituzioni magiche tra folklore e letteratura*. Siena: Pacini.
Castellani, Arrigo (1986). "Consuntivo della polemica Ascoli–Manzoni," *Studi linguistici italiani*, 12, 105–29.
Castiglione, Marina (2018). *Fiabe e racconti della tradizione orale siciliana. Testi e analisi*, with the collaboration of Alessia De Caro and Miryam Lo Dato. Palermo: Centro di Studi Filologici e Linguistici Siciliani.
Castle, Gregory (2001). "'Synge-On-Aran': The Aran Islands and the Subject of Revivalist Ethnography," in *Modernism and the Celtic Revival*, ed. Gregory Castle. Cambridge: Cambridge University Press, pp. 98–133.
Casula, Francesco Cesare (1992). *La storia di Sardegna*. Sassari: Delfino.
Cataldi, Melita (2003). "Lady Gregory's Italian Sketchbooks," in Deandrea and Tchernichova 2003:303–16.

Caterini, Fiorenzo (2013). *Colpi di scure e sensi di colpa. Storia del disboscamento della Sardegna dalle origini a oggi*. Sassari: Carlo Delfino Editore.
Cavallo, Federica Letizia (2013). "Oggetti geografici, soggetti simbolici. Isole e insularità in geografia culturale," in *Luoghi ritrovati. Itinerari di geografia umana tra natura e paesaggio*, ed. Antonio Paolillo. Vidor: Ishtar, pp. 177–205.
Cavazza, Stefano (2012). "Regionalism in Italy: A Critique," in Augusteijn and Storm 2012: 69–89.
Cecchi, Emilio (1987). "Prosatori e narratori," in *Storia della letteratura italiana. Il Novecento*, 9 vols., ed. Emilio Cecchi and Natalino Sapegno. Milan: Garzanti, IX, pp. 533–727.
Cerina, Giovanna (1992). *Deledda e altri narratori. Mito dell'isola e coscienza dell'insularità*. Cagliari: CUEC.
Chambers, Iain (2015). "The 'Southern Question' . . . Again," in *The Routledge Handbook of Contemporary Italy: History, Politics, Society*, ed. Andrea Mammone, Ercole Giap Parini, and Giuseppe A. Veltri. New York: Routledge, pp. 13–22.
Chainey, Dee Dee and Willow Winsham (eds.) (2021). *Treasury of Folklore. Seas and Rivers: Sirens, Selkies and Ghost Ships*. London: Batsford Books.
Chapman, Malcolm (1992). *The Celts: The Construction of a Myth*. Basingstoke: Macmillan.
Charuty, Giordana (2019). "Histoires croisées de l'anthropologie italienne (XIXe–XXIe siècle)," *Bérose—Encyclopédie internationale des histoires de l'anthropologie*, Paris. www.berose.fr/article1781.html?lang=fr (last accessed June 30, 2024).
Chemello, Adriana (1995). "Le Penelopi campagnole di Caterina Percoto," in *"Libri di lettura per le donne." L'etica del lavoro nella letteratura di fine Ottocento*. Alessandria: Edizioni dell'Orso, pp. 1–37.
Chemello, Adriana (2009). "Caterina Percoto e l'educazione della donna," in *Donna al lavoro: ieri, oggi, domani*, ed. Saveria Chemotti. Padua: Il Poligrafo, pp. 305–33.
Chemello, Adriana (2010). "Le lettere di Maria Savi-Lopez ad Antonio Fogazzaro," in Bani 2010: 50–65.
Cheng, Vincent John (1995). *Joyce, Race, and Empire*. Cambridge: Cambridge University Press.
Cheratzu, Francesco (1995). *La terza Irlanda: gli scritti sulla Sardegna di Carlo Cattaneo e Giuseppe Mazzini*. Sassari: Condaghes.
Chiara, Luigi, and Nino Principato (2007). *Famiglie straniere a Messina nell'Ottocento: i segni della presenza*. Messina: Armando Siciliano Editore.
Chini, Chiara (1996). *Ai confini d'Europa. Italia ed Irlanda tra le due guerre*. Florence: Florence University Press.
Chini, Chiara (2015). "Italy and the 'Irish Risorgimento': Italian Perspectives on the Irish War of Independence, 1919–1921," in *Britain, Ireland and the Italian Risorgimento*, ed. Nick Carter. New York: Palgrave Macmillan, pp. 204–23.
Christiansen, Reidar (1958). *The Migratory Legends*. Helsinki: Academia Scientiarum Fennica.
Ciampi, Paolo (2008). *Beatrice. Il canto dell'Appennino che conquistò la capitale*. Florence: Sarnus.
Cirese, Alberto Mario (1968). "Giuseppe Pitrè tra storia locale e antropologia," in *Pitrè e Salomone Marino. Atti del convegno di studi per il 50° anniversario della morte di Giuseppe Pitrè e Salvatore Salomone Marino, Palermo, 25–27 novembre 1966*. Palermo: Flaccovio, pp. 19–49.
Cirese, Alberto Mario (1969). "Gli studi di poesia popolare nell'Ottocento: Ermolao Rubieri e Costantino Nigra," in *Letteratura italiana*, 5 vols., ed. Gianni Grana. Milan: Marzorati, I, pp. 239–77.
Cirese, Alberto Mario (1971). *Cultura egemonica e culture subalterne*. Palermo: Palumbo.
Cirese, Alberto Mario (1976). *Intellettuali, folklore e istinto di classe. Note su Verga, Deledda, Scotellaro, Gramsci*. Turin: Einaudi.

Clayworth, Anya (1997). "*The Woman's World:* Oscar Wilde as Editor," *Victorian Periodicals Review*, 30, 2, 84–101.
Cocchiara, Giuseppe (1951). *Pitrè, la Sicilia e il folklore*. Messina: D'Alma.
Cocchiara, Giuseppe (1959). *Popolo e letteratura in Italia*. Turin: Boringhieri.
Cocchiara, Giuseppe (1981a). *Storia del folklore in Italia*. Palermo: Sellerio.
Cocchiara, Giuseppe (1981b). *The History of Folklore in Europe*, trans. John N. McDaniel. Philadelphia: Institute for the Study of Human Issues.
Cocchiara, Giuseppe (2016 [1952]). *Storia del folklore in Europa*. Turin: Bollati Boringhieri.
Collu, Ugo (ed.) (1992). *Grazia Deledda nella cultura contemporanea. Atti del seminario di studi "Grazia Deledda e la cultura sarda fra '800 e '900,"* 2 vols. Nuoro: Consorzio per la Pubblica Lettura "Sebastiano Satta."
Concannon, Helena (1925). Review of Maud Joynt's *The Golden Legends of the Gael*, *Studies: An Irish Quarterly Review*, 14, 56, 679.
Conkling, Philip (2007). "On Islanders and Islandness," *Geographical Review*, 97, 2, 191–201.
Consolo, Vincenzo (2019). "Presentazione a *Fiabe siciliane* di Laura Gonzenbach," trans. Luisa Rubini, reread by Vincenzo Consolo. Rome: Donzelli, pp. vii–ix.
Conrad, JoAnn (2008). "Wonder Tale," in *The Greenwood Encyclopedia of Folktales and Fairy Tales*, ed. Donald Haase. Westport: Greenwood, III, pp. 1041–42.
Cooper, David (2009). *The Musical Traditions of Northern Ireland and Its Diaspora: Community and Conflict*. Farnham, Surrey: Ashgate.
Coote Lake, E. F. (1964). "Obituary: Estella Canziani," *Folklore*, 75, 3, 206–8.
Coppola, Maurizio (2021). *Construire l'italianité: Traditions populaires et identité nationale (1800–1932)*. Paris: L'Harmattan.
Corrigan Correll, Timothy (2005). "Believers, Sceptics, and Charlatans: Evidential Rhetoric, the Fairies, and Fairy Healers in Irish Oral Narrative and Belief," *Folklore*, 11, 6, 1, 1–18.
Coughlan, Patricia (2007). "Rereading Peig Sayers: Women's Autobiography, Social History and Narrative Art," in *Opening the Field: Irish Women, Texts and Contexts*, ed. Patricia Boyle Haberstroh and Christine St. Peter. Cork: Cork University Press, pp. 58–73.
Cox, Virginia (2013). "The Female Voice in Italian Renaissance Dialogue," *MLN*, 128, 1, 53–78.
Coxhead, Elizabeth (1961). *Lady Gregory: A Literary Portrait*. New York: Harcourt Brace.
Crane, Thomas Frederick (1916). "Giuseppe Pitrè and Sicilian Folklore," *The Nation*, 103, 234–36.
Crenshaw, Kimberlé Williams, Neil Gotanda, Gary Peller, and Kendall Thomas (eds.) (1995). *Critical Race Theory: The Key Writings That Formed the Movement*. New York: New Press.
Crivelli, Tatiana (2010). "Archiviare in rete per non archiviare il caso: note sulle poetesse d'Arcadia," *Dimensioni e Problemi della Ricerca Storica*, 43, 1, 21–29.
Croce, Benedetto (1940). "Grazia Deledda," in *La letteratura della nuova Italia. Saggi critici*, 6 vols. Bari: Laterza, VI, pp. 317–26.
Cronin, Michael (1996). *Translating Ireland: Translation, Languages, Cultures*. Cork: Cork University Press.
Crowley, John, William J. Smyth, and Mike Murphy (2012). *Atlas of the Great Irish Famine*. Cork: Cork University Press.
Crowley, Tony (2000). *The Politics of Language in Ireland, 1366–1922: A Sourcebook*. New York: Routledge.
Cunliffe, Barry (2017). *On the Ocean: The Mediterranean and the Atlantic from Prehistory to AD 1500*. Oxford: Oxford University Press.
Curtis, Lewis Perry (1968). *Anglo-Saxons and Celts: A Study of Anti-Irish Prejudice in Victorian England*. Bridgeport: Conference on British Studies.
Daimler, Morgan (2020). *A New Dictionary of Fairies: A 21st Century Exploration of Celtic and Related Western European Fairies*. Winchester and Washington: Moon Books.

Daly, Dominic (1974). *The Young Douglas Hyde: The Dawn of the Irish Revolution and Renaissance, 1874–1893*. Dublin: Irish University Press.
Dardano, Maurizio (1974). *G. I. Ascoli e la questione della lingua*. Rome: Istituto della Enciclopedia Italiana.
Darwin, Gregory (2015), "On Mermaids, Meroveus, and Mélusine: Reading the Irish Seal Woman and Mélusine as Origin Legend," *Folklore*, 126, 2, 123–41.
Davies, Anna Morpurgo (1994). "La linguistica dell'Ottocento," in *Storia della linguistica*, 3 vols., ed. Giulio C. Lepschy. Bologna: il Mulino, III, pp. 11–399.
Day, Andrea (2019). "'Almost wholly the work of Mrs. Lang': Nora Lang, Literary Labour, and the Fairy Books," *Women's Writing*, 26, 4, 400–420.
Deandrea, Pietro, and Viktoria Tchernichova (eds.) (2003). *Roots and Beginnings: Proceedings of the 2nd. AISLI Conference, Spilimbergo, Palazzo Tadea, 3–6 ottobre 2002*. Venice: Cafoscarina.
De Blécourt, Willem (2010). "Fairy Grandmothers: Images of Storytelling Events in Nineteenth-Century Germany," *Relief—Revue Électronique de Littérature Française*, 4, 2, 174–97.
de Brún, Sorcha (2024). "Island Girl, Universal Woman: *Peig: A Scéal Féin* (1998) as Narrative of Class, Labour and Femininity," *Open Library of Humanities*, 10, 1, 1–23.
Dedola, Rossana (2016). *Grazia Deledda: i luoghi, gli amori, le opere*. Rome: Avagliano Editore.
De Giovanni, Neria (1987). *L'ora di Lilith: su Grazia Deledda e la letteratura femminile del secondo Novecento*. Rome: Ellemme.
De Gubernatis, Angelo (1879). *Dizionario biografico degli scrittori contemporanei*. Florence: Le Monnier.
De Gubernatis, Angelo (1889). *Dizionario degli artisti italiani viventi: pittori, scultori, e architetti*. Florence: Tipi dei Successori Le Monnier.
De Gubernatis, Angelo (1893). "La tradizione popolare italiana," *Rivista delle tradizioni popolari italiane*, I, I, 3–19.
Delargy, James Hamilton (1945). *The Gaelic Story-Teller, with Some Notes on Gaelic Folk-Tales*. London: Geoffrey Cumberlege.
Delitala, Enrica (1992). "Grazia Deledda e la 'Rivista delle tradizioni popolari italiane,'" in Collu, I:307–12.
Delitala, Enrica (2005). "Madonne e santi nella narrativa popolare sarda," in *Fiabe di magia, leggende, racconti formulari nella narrativa popolare sarda*, ed. Anna Lecca. Cagliari: AM&D Edizioni, pp. 149–54.
Delmedico, Sara, and Elena Emma Sottilotta (2022–23). "'Le scritture rimangono': Intervista a Michela Murgia," *Chronica Mundi*, Special issue: *Women in Sardinia: Creativity and Self-Expression*, ed. Sara Delmedico and Elena Emma Sottilotta, 16/17, 278–89.
de Martino, Ernesto (1982). *Sud e magia*. Milan: Feltrinelli.
de Martino, Ernesto (2015). *Magic: A Theory from the South*, trans. Dorothy Louise Zinn. Chicago: Hau Books.
De Mauro, Tullio (1991 [1963]). *Storia linguistica dell'Italia unita*. Bari: Laterza.
De Nunzio Schilardi, Wanda (1986). *Matilde Serao giornalista*. Lecce: Milella.
De Petris, Carla (2004). "Lady Gregory and Italy: A Lasting and Profitable Relationship," *Irish University Review*, Special issue: *Lady Gregory*, ed. Anne Fogarty, 34, 1, 37–48.
De Petris, Carla, Bernard Hickey, and Francesca Romana Paci (2003). "Uniting Irish Traditions in the Sesqui-centenary of Lady Augusta Gregory's Birth: Introduction," in Deandrea and Tchernichova 2003:271–75.
De Petris, Carla, and Maria Stella (eds.) (2001). *Continente Irlanda: storia e scritture contemporanee*. Rome: Carocci.
De Sanctis Ricciardone, Paola (1987). *Il tipografo celeste: il gioco del lotto tra letteratura e demologia nell'Italia dell'Ottocento e oltre*. Bari: Dedalo.

De Sanctis Ricciardone, Paola (1990). *L'Italia di Caterina: demologia e antropologia nelle opere di Caterina Pigorini-Beri, 1845–1924*. Rome: Bagatto.
de Val, Dorothy (2011). *In Search of Song: The Life and Times of Lucy Broadwood*. Farnham: Ashgate.
Di Pilla, Francesco (1966). *Grazia Deledda premio Nobel per la letteratura 1926*. Milan: Fabbri.
Dochy, Amélie (2014). "Mr and Mrs Hall's Tour of Ireland in the 1840s, More Than a Unionist Guidebook, an Illustrated Definition of Ireland Made to Convince," *Miranda*, 9, 1–28.
Dolfi, Anna (1979). "La leggenda del reale," in *Grazia Deledda*. Milan: Mursia, pp. 41–70.
Dolfi, Anna (1992). *Del romanzesco e del romanzo: modelli di narrativa italiana tra Otto e Novecento*. Rome: Bulzoni.
Dorson, Richard (1955). "The First Group of British Folklorists," *Journal of American Folklore*, 68, 267, 1–8.
Dorson, Richard (1968). *The British Folklorists: A History*. New York: Routledge.
Dorson, Richard (1976). *Folklore and Fakelore: Essays toward a Discipline of Folk Studies*. Cambridge, MA: Harvard University Press.
Doyle, Aidan (2015). *A History of the Irish Language: From the Norman Invasion to Independence*. Oxford: Oxford University Press.
Duggan, Anne E. (2023). *The Lost Princess*. London: Reaktion Books.
Dundes, Alan (1986). "Fairy Tales from a Folkloristic Perspective," in Bottigheimer 1986:259–69.
Duse, Gina (2015). *Angela Nardo Cibele (Venezia 1850–1938). Scene di Chioggia e altri scritti*. Chioggia: Il Leggio Libreria Editrice.
Earls, Brian (1992–93). "Supernatural Legends in Nineteenth-Century Irish Writing," *Béaloideas*, Special issue: *Finscéalta agus Litríocht: Páipéir a Cuireadh i Láthair ag an Siompóisiam Nordach-Ceilteach / Legends and Fiction: Papers Presented at the Nordic-Celtic Legend Symposium*, 60/61, 93–144.
Edwards, Robert Dudley (ed.) (1960). *Ireland and the Italian Risorgimento: Three Lectures*. Dublin: Italian Institute in Dublin, Cultural Relations Committee of Ireland.
Ellmann, Richard (1988). *Oscar Wilde*. London: Penguin.
Emrich, Duncan (1946). "'Folk-Lore': William John Thoms," *California Folklore Quarterly*, 5, 4, 355–74.
Eriksen, Anne, and Torunn Selberg (2015). "The Order of Folklore: Rachel Busk and the Folk-Lore of Rome," *Folklore*, 126, 3, 301–16.
Estés, Clarissa Pinkola (1996). *The Dangerous Old Woman: Myths and Stories of the Wise Old Woman Archetype*. New York: Random House.
Fabbri, Lorenzo (2017). "Angelo De Gubernatis e la mitologia comparata," *Studi e materiali di storia delle religioni*, 83, 1, 143–69.
Faeti, Antonio (1974). "Il crepuscolo dell'orco pedagogico," introduction to Emma Perodi's *Fiabe fantastiche: Le novelle della nonna*. Turin: Einaudi, pp. vii–lxi.
Faienza, Lucia (2023). "Tra dilettantismo e scienza: la proto-etnografia di Caterina Pigorini Beri in *Costumi e superstizioni dell'Appennino marchigiano*," *Altre Modernità: Rivista di studi letterari e culturali*, Special issue: *Lo sguardo delle viaggiatrici sull'"Italia di mezzo": scrittrici, fotografe, artiste tra Otto e Novecento*, ed. Giuseppe Di Natale, Serena Guarracino, and Luca Pezzuto, 29, 69–79.
Falchi, Luigi (1937). *L'opera di Grazia Deledda, con due appendici di lettere inedite*. Milan: La Prora.
Falchi, Marcella (2000). "La figura della maestra in una rivista per giovinette: 'Cordelia,'" in *Itinerari pedagogici e culturali. Scritti in onore di Rita Vallini*, ed. Sira Serenella Macchietti. Siena: Edizioni Cantagalli, pp. 207–11.
Fanning, Ursula (2002). *Gender Meets Genre: Woman as Subject in the Fictional Universe of Matilde Serao*. Dublin: Irish Academic Press, 2002.

Fanning, Ursula (2007). "Enclosure, Escape and the Erotic: Shadows of the Self in the Writings of Grazia Deledda," in Sharon Wood 2007:215–36.
Fanning, Ursula (2017). *Italian Women's Autobiographical Writings in the Twentieth Century: Constructing Subjects*. Lanham: Fairleigh Dickinson University Press.
Fantaccini, Fiorenzo (2003). "'Dear Mariotto': Lady Gregory and Mario Manlio Rossi," in Deandrea and Tchernichova 2003:285–94.
Fantaccini, Fiorenzo (2009). *W. B. Yeats e la cultura italiana*. Florence: Florence University Press.
Farnetti, Monica (ed.) (2010). *Chi ha paura di Grazia Deledda? Traduzione, ricezione, comparazione*. Pavona: Iacobelli.
Farrer, Claire R. (1975). "Introduction: Women and Folklore: Images and Genres," *Journal of American Folklore*, Special issue: *Women and Folklore*, ed. Claire Farrer, 88, 347, v–xv.
Febvre, Lucien (1996 [1922]). *A Geographical Introduction to History*, trans. E. G. Mountford and J. H. Paxton. New York: Routledge.
Feldman, Jessica (2002). *Victorian Modernism: Pragmatism and the Varieties of Aesthetic Experience*. Cambridge: Cambridge University Press.
Ferguson, Rosaleen (2002). "Force 10 (1991)," in *The Field Day Anthology of Irish Writing: Irish Women's Writing and Traditions*, ed. Angela Bourke. New York: New York University Press, IV, pp. 1209–12.
Ferraro, Eveljn (2022). "'La tradizione è come il mare': Giuseppe Pitrè's Transnational Approach to Folk and Fairy Tales in the New Italy," *Italian Studies*, 77, 3, 1–13.
Fimi, Dimitra (2017). *Celtic Myth in Contemporary Children's Fantasy: Idealization, Identity, Ideology*. London: Palgrave Macmillan.
Fitzsimons, Eleanor (2015). *Wilde's Women: How Oscar Wilde Was Shaped by the Women He Knew*. Richmond, London: Duckworth.
Fleming, Deborah (1995). *A Man Who Does Not Exist: The Irish Peasant in the Work of W. B. Yeats and J. M. Synge*. Ann Arbor: University of Michigan Press.
Fogarty, Anne (2000). "'A Woman of the House': Gender and Nationalism in the Writings of Augusta Gregory," in *Border Crossings: Irish Women and National Identities*, ed. Kathryn Kirkpatrick. Tuscaloosa: University of Alabama Press, pp. 100–122.
Folli, Anna (1999). "Gli anni di 'Cordelia' (con una appendice)," in *Jolanda: le idee e l'opera. Atti del convegno di studi, Cento, 28–29 novembre 1997*, ed. Clemente Mazzotta. Bologna: Editografica, pp. 25–47.
Forgacs, David (2014). *Italy's Margins: Social Exclusion and Nation Formation since 1861*. Cambridge: Cambridge University Press.
Forrester, Sibelan (2020). "Translating Folktales: From National to Transnational," in *Times of Mobility: Transnational Literature and Gender in Translation*, ed. Jasmina Lukic, Sibelan Forrester, and Borbála Faragó. Budapest: Central European University Press, pp. 257–80.
Fortini, Laura (2010). "Aggiunte e mutamento. Cosa aggiunge e muta Grazia Deledda alla letteratura italiana," in Farnetti 2010:229–45.
Foster, John Wilson (1977). "Certain Set Apart: The Western Island in the Irish Renaissance," *Studies: An Irish Quarterly Review*, 66, 264, 261–74.
Foster, John Wilson (1987). *Fictions of the Irish Literary Revival: A Changeling Art*. Syracuse: Syracuse University Press.
Fowles, John (1978). *Islands, with Photographs by Fay Godwin*. London: Jonathan Cape.
Franchetti, Leopoldo, and Sidney Sonnino (1877). *La Sicilia nel 1876*, 2 vols. (vol. I Franchetti, *Condizioni politiche e amministrative della Sicilia*; vol. II Sonnino, *I contadini in Sicilia*). Florence: Vallecchi.
Frattarolo, Renzo (1989). *Per uno studio su Matilde Serao*. Florence: Olschki.
Friedman, Susan Stanford (2013). "Why Not Compare?" in *Comparison: Theories, Approaches, Uses*, ed. Rita Felski and Susan Stanford Friedman. Baltimore: Johns Hopkins University Press, pp. 34–45.

Gabbert, Lisa (2016). "Teaching Fairy Tales in Folklore Classes," in *New Approaches to Teaching Folk and Fairy Tales*, ed. Christa C. Jones and Claudia Schwabe. Boulder: University of Colorado Press, pp. 35–47.

Galanti, Bianca Maria (1956). "Le tradizioni popolari nell'opera di Evelyn Martinengo Cesaresco," *Lares*, 22, 156–63.

Gantz, Kenneth F. (1940). "Charlotte Brooke's *Reliques of Irish Poetry* and the Ossianic Controversy," *Studies in English*, 20, 137–56.

Garrigan Mattar, Sinéad (2004). *Primitivism, Science, and the Irish Revival*. Oxford: Oxford University Press.

Gavan Duffy, Charles (1898). *My Life in Two Hemispheres*, 2 vols. London: T. Fisher Unwin.

Gencarella, Stephen Olbrys (2010). "Gramsci, Good Sense, and Critical Folklore Studies," *Journal of Folklore Research*, 47, 3, 221–52.

Genette, Gérard (1997 [1987]). *Paratexts: Thresholds of Interpretation*, trans. Jane E. Lewin. Cambridge: Cambridge University Press.

Gilmartin, Elizabeth (2004). "The Anglo-Irish Dialect: Mediating Linguistic Conflict," *Victorian Literature and Culture*, 32, 1, 1–16.

Ginzburg, Carlo (1966). *I benandanti: stregoneria e culti agrari tra Cinquecento e Seicento*. Turin: Einaudi.

Ginzburg, Carlo (1989). *Storia notturna: una decifrazione del Sabba*. Turin: Einaudi.

Giuli, Paola (2003). "Women Poets and Improvisers: Cultural Assumptions and Literary Values in Arcadia," *Studies in Eighteenth-Century Culture*, 32, 69–92.

Giuli, Paola (2009). "'Monsters of Talent': Fame and Reputation of Women Improvisers in Arcadia," in *Italy's Eighteenth Century: Gender and Culture in the Age of the Grand Tour*, ed. Paula Findlen, Wendy Wassyng Roworth, and Catherine M. Sama. Stanford: Stanford University Press, pp. 303–30.

Goldring, Maurice (1975). *Irlande: idéologie d'une révolution nationale*. Paris: Éditions sociales.

Gosse, Edmund (1927). "Review of Sidonia the Sorceress," in *Leaves and Fruit*. London: William Heinemann, pp. 195–201.

Gramsci, Antonio (1966). *La questione meridionale*, ed. Franco De Felice and Valentino Parlato. Rome: Editori Riuniti.

Gramsci, Antonio (1975). *Quaderni del Carcere*, 4 vols., ed. Valentino Gerratana. Turin: Einaudi.

Gramsci, Antonio (2007). *Prison Notebooks*, 3 vols., ed. Joseph A. Buttigieg, trans. Joseph A. Buttigieg and Antonio Callari. New York: Columbia University Press.

Grant Duff, Mountstuart Elphinstone (1904). *Notes from a Diary, 1892–1895*, 2 vols. London: John Murray.

Greenhill, Pauline, and Jennifer Orme (eds.) (2024). *Just Wonder: Shifting Perspectives in Tradition*. Logan: Utah State University Press.

Gri, Gian Paolo (2008). "La reinvenzione letteraria delle tradizioni popolari," in *Caterina Percoto e l'Ottocento*, ed. Romano Vecchiet. Udine: Biblioteca Civica "Vincenzo Joppi," pp. 61–66.

Grossi, Vincenzo (1888). *Il Folk-lore nella Scienza, nella Letteratura e nell'Arte*. Milan and Turin: Fratelli Dumolard.

Grossman, Pam (2019). *Waking the Witch: Reflections on Women, Magic, and Power*. New York: Gallery Books.

Grote, Georg (1994). *Torn between Politics and Culture: The Gaelic League, 1893–1993*. New York: Waxmann Münster.

Guarracino, Serena (2023). "Sguardi della differenza: Anne MacDonell ed Estella Canziani nell'Italia di mezzo," *Altre Modernità: Rivista di studi letterari e culturali*, Special issue: *Lo sguardo delle viaggiatrici sull'"Italia di mezzo": scrittrici, fotografe, artiste tra Otto e Novecento*, ed. Giuseppe Di Natale, Serena Guarracino, and Luca Pezzuto, 29, 110–26.

Guiley, Rosemary Ellen (2008). *The Encyclopedia of Witches, Witchcraft and Wicca*. New York: Facts on File.

Guinness, Selina (1998). "'Visions and Beliefs in the West of Ireland': Irish Folklore and British Anthropology, 1898–1920," *Irish Studies Review*, 6, 1, 37–46.

Gunnell, Terry (2012). "Clerics as Collectors of Folklore in Nineteenth-Century Iceland." *Arv: Nordic Yearbook of Folklore*, 68, 45–66.

Gunnell, Terry (2022a). "Grimm Ripples: The Role of the Grimms' *Deutsche Sagen* in the Collection and Creation of National Folk Narratives in Northern Europe," in *Folklore and Nation in Britain and Ireland*, ed. Matthew Cheeseman and Carina Hart. New York: Routledge, pp. 22–47.

Gunnell, Terry (ed.) (2022b). *Grimm Ripples: The Legacy of the Grimms' Deutsche Sagen in Northern Europe*. Leiden: National Cultivation of Culture, Brill.

Gunzberg, Lynn M. (1983). "Ruralism, Folklore, and Grazia Deledda's Novels," *Modern Language Studies*, 13, 3, 112–22.

Haase, Donald (ed.) (1993). *The Reception of Grimms' Fairy Tales: Responses, Reactions, Revisions*. Detroit: Wayne State University Press.

Haase, Donald (ed.) (2004). *Fairy Tales and Feminism: New Approaches*. Detroit: Wayne State University Press.

Haase, Donald (2010). "Decolonizing Fairy-Tale Studies," *Marvels and Tales*, Special issue: *The Fairy Tale after Angela Carter*, ed. Stephen Benson and Andrew Teverson, 24, 1, 17–38.

Haase, Donald (2017). "Yours, Mine, or Ours? Perrault, the Brothers Grimm, and the Ownership of Fairy Tales," in *The Classic Fairy Tales*, ed. Maria Tatar. New York: Norton, pp. 435–46.

Haase, Donald (2019). "The Fairy-Tale Canon," in *Teaching Fairy Tales*, ed. Nancy Canepa. Detroit: Wayne State University Press, pp. 54–66.

Hafstein, Valdimar (2015). "Fairy Tales, Copyright, and the Public Domain," in *The Cambridge Companion to Fairy Tales*, ed. Maria Tatar. Cambridge: Cambridge University Press, pp. 11–38.

Hanberry, Gerard (2011). *More Lives Than One: The Remarkable Wilde Family through the Generations*. Cork: Collins.

Hancock, Ange-Marie (2016). *Intersectionality: An Intellectual History*. Oxford: Oxford University Press.

Harford, Judith (2008). *The Opening of University Education to Women in Ireland*. Dublin: Irish Academic Press.

Harries, Elizabeth Wanning (2001). *Twice upon a Time: Women Writers and the History of the Fairy Tale*. Princeton: Princeton University Press.

Harris, Daniel (1974). *Yeats: Coole Park and Ballylee*. Baltimore: Johns Hopkins University Press.

Hartwig, Otto (1870). Anonymous Translation into Italian of the preface to *Sicilianische Märchen*, *Rivista Sicula di Scienze, Letteratura ed Arti*, 2, 3, 594–601.

Harvey, Clodagh Brennan (1989). "Some Irish Women Storytellers and Reflections on the Role of Women in the Storytelling Tradition," *Western Folklore*, 48, 2, 109–28.

Heiniger, Abigail (2020). "The British Empire's Lost Slipper: Dangerous Irish Cinderellas," in *Contemporary Fairy-Tale Magic: Subverting Gender and Genre*, ed. Lydia Brugué and Auba Llompart. Leiden: Brill Rodopi, pp. 63–76.

Heiniger, Abigail (2023). *Fairy-Tale Revivals: Writing Wonder in Transatlantic Ethnic Literary Revivals, 1850–1950*, in *Fairy-Tale Revivals in the Long Nineteenth Century*, 2 vols. London: Routledge.

Hennig, John (1946). "The Brothers Grimm and T. C. Croker," *Modern Language Review*, 41, 1, 44–54.

Henningsen, Gustav (1990). "'Ladies from the Outside': An Archaic Pattern of the Witches' Sabbath," in *Early Modern European Witchcraft: Centres and Peripheries*, ed. Bengt Ankarloo and Gustav Henningsen. Oxford: Clarendon Press, pp. 191–215.

Heyer-Caput, Margherita (2008). *Grazia Deledda's Dance of Modernity*. Toronto: Toronto University Press.
Hill, Judith (2004). "Finding a Voice: Augusta Gregory, Raftery, and Cultural Nationalism, 1899–1900," *Irish University Review*, Special issue: *Lady Gregory*, ed. Anne Fogarty, 34, 1, 21–36.
Hill, Judith (2005). *Lady Gregory: An Irish Life*. Stroud: Sutton.
Hillel, Margot (2019). "Envisioning Ireland: Landscape and Longing in Children's Literature," in *Children's Literature and Imaginative Geography*, ed. Aïda Hudson. Waterloo: Wilfrid Laurier University Press, pp. 67–83.
Hiller, Jonathan R. (2012). "The Enduring Vision of Biodeterministic Sardinian Inferiority in the Works of Grazia Deledda," *Journal of Modern Italian Studies*, 17, 3, 271–87.
Hobsbawm, Eric (1962). *The Age of Revolution: 1789–1848*. London: Weidenfeld & Nicolson.
Hobsbawm, Eric (1965). *The Age of Capital: 1848–1875*. London: Weidenfeld & Nicolson.
Hobsbawm, Eric (1987). *The Age of Empire: 1875–1914*. London: Weidenfeld & Nicolson.
Holbek, Bengt (1985). "The Many Abodes of Fata Morgana or the Quest for Meaning in Fairy Tales," *Journal of Folklore Research*, 22, 1, 19–28.
Hopkin, David (2012). "Folklore beyond Nationalism: Identity Politics and Scientific Cultures in a New Discipline," in *Folklore and Nationalism in Europe During the Long Nineteenth Century*, ed. Timothy Baycroft and David Hopkin. Leiden: National Cultivation of Culture, Brill, pp. 371–401.
Hopkin, David (2017). "British Women Folklorists in Post-Unification Italy: Rachel Busk and Evelyn Martinengo-Cesaresco," *Folklore*, 128, 2, 189–97.
Hopkin, David (2018a). "'Imagine I Am the *Creatura*': Biography of Rachel Busk, a British Folklorist in Europe," *Bérose—Encyclopédie internationale des histoires de l'anthropologie*, Paris. www.berose.fr/article1473.html?lang=fr (last accessed June 30, 2024).
Hopkin, David (2018b). "An Englishwoman '*di grande dottrina e gusto*': Life and Work of Isabella Mary Anderton," *Bérose—Encyclopédie internationale des histoires de l'anthropologie*, Paris. www.berose.fr/article1549.html?lang=fr (last accessed June 30, 2024).
Hopkin, David (2018c). "The *Padrona* of Folksongs: Biography of Evelyn Carrington, Countess Martinengo-Cesaresco," *Bérose—Encyclopédie internationale des histoires de l'anthropologie*, Paris. www.berose.fr/article1480.html?lang=fr (last accessed June 30, 2024).
Hopkin, David (2019). "Regionalism and Folklore," in *Regionalism and Modern Europe: Identity Construction and Movements from 1890 to the Present Day*, ed. Xosé M. Núñez Seixas and Eric Storm. London: Bloomsbury Academic, pp. 43–64.
Howes, Marjorie (1998). "Tears and Blood: Lady Wilde and the Emergence of Irish Cultural Nationalism," in *Ideology and Ireland in the Nineteenth Century*, ed. Tadhg Foley and Seán Ryder. Dublin: Four Courts Press, pp. 151–72.
Hutchinson, John (1987). *The Dynamics of Cultural Nationalism: The Gaelic Revival and the Creation of the Irish Nation State*. London: Allen & Unwin.
Hutton, Clare (2001). "Reading *The Love Songs of Connacht*: Douglas Hyde and the Exigencies of Publication," *The Library*, 2, 4, 364–93.
Hutton, Clare (2011). "Publishing the Irish Cultural Revival, 1891–1922," in *The Oxford History of the Irish Book: The Irish Book in English 1891–2000*, ed. Clare Hutton and Patrick Walsh. Oxford: Oxford University Press, V, pp. 17–42.
Ingman, Heather, and Clíona Ó Gallchoir (eds.) (2018). *History of Modern Irish Women's Literature*. Cambridge: Cambridge University Press.
Jeckins, Richard (2007). "The Transformations of Biddy Early: From Local Reports of Magical Healing to Globalised New Age Fantasies," *Folklore*, 118, 2, 162–82.
Johnson, Colin (2010). "An 'Italian Grimm': Domenico Comparetti and the Nationalization of Italian Folktales," *Italica*, 87, 3, 462–87.

Johnston, Harry, et al. (1901). *The Living Races of Mankind: A Popular Illustrated Account of the Customs, Habits, Pursuits, Feasts and Ceremonies of the Races of Mankind Throughout the World*, 2 vols. London: Hutchinson.

Jones, Christine A. (2016). *Mother Goose Refigured: A Critical Translation of Charles Perrault's Fairy Tales*. Detroit: Wayne State University Press.

Joosen, Vanessa (2011). *Critical and Creative Perspectives on Fairy Tales: An Intertextual Dialogue between Fairy-Tale Scholarship and Postmodern Retellings*. Detroit: Wayne State University Press.

Jordan, Rosan A., and Francis A. de Caro (1986). "Women and the Study of Folklore," *Signs*, 11, 3, 500–518.

Jordan, Rosan A., and Susan J. Kalcik (1985). *Women's Folklore, Women's Culture*. Philadelphia: University of Pennsylvania Press.

Jorgensen, Jeana (2010). "Political and Theoretical Feminisms in American Folkloristics: Definition Debates, Publication Histories, and the *Folklore Feminists Communication*," *Folklore Historian*, 27, 43–73.

Jorgensen, Jeana (2014). "Strategic Silences: Voiceless Heroes in Fairy Tales," in *A Quest of Her Own: Essays on the Female Hero in Modern Fantasy*, ed. Lori M. Campbell. Jefferson, North Carolina: McFarland, pp. 15–34.

Jubber, Nicholas (2022). *The Fairy Tellers: A Journey into the Secret History of Fairy Tales*. London: John Murray.

Kalnins, Mara (2002 [1921]). Introduction to D. H. Lawrence's *Sea and Sardinia*. Cambridge: Cambridge University Press, pp. xvii–xlii.

Kiberd, Declan (1979). *Synge and the Irish Language*. London: Macmillan.

Kiberd, Declan (1995). *Inventing Ireland*. London: Cape.

Kiberd, Declan, and P. J. Mathews (eds.) (2016). *Handbook of the Irish Revival: An Anthology of Irish Cultural and Political Writings, 1891–1922*. Notre Dame: University of Notre Dame Press.

Killeen, Jarlath (2013). "Wilde, the Fairy Tales and the Oral Tradition," in *Oscar Wilde in Context*, ed. Kerry Powell and Peter Raby. Cambridge: Cambridge University Press, pp. 186–94.

Kinahan, Frank (1983). "Armchair Folklore: Yeats and the Textual Sources of *Fairy and Folk Tales of the Irish Peasantry*," *Proceedings of the Royal Irish Academy: Archaeology, Culture, History, Literature*, 83C, 255–67.

Kinealy, Christine (2002). *The Great Irish Famine: Impact, Ideology and Rebellion*. New York: Palgrave.

King, Martha (2005). *Grazia Deledda: A Legendary Life*. Leicester: Troubador.

Kinmonth, Claudia (2001). "Rags and Rushes: Art and the Irish Artefact, c. 1900," *Journal of Design History*, 14, 3, 167–85.

Knapp, James F. (1995). "Irish Primitivism and Imperial Discourse: Lady Gregory's Peasantry," in *Macropolitics of Nineteenth-Century Literature: Nationalism, Exoticism, Imperialism*, ed. Jonathan Arac and Harriet Ritvo. Durham: Duke University Press, pp. 286–301.

Koehler, Julie L. J., Shandi Lynne Wagner, Anne E. Duggan, and Adrion Dula (eds.) (2021). *Women Writing Wonder: An Anthology of Subversive Nineteenth-Century British, French, and German Fairy Tales*. Detroit: Wayne State University Press.

Kohfeldt, Mary Lou (1985). *Lady Gregory: The Woman behind the Irish Renaissance*. London: André Deutsch.

Köhler-Zülch, Ines (1997). "Who Are the Tellers? Statements by Collectors and Editors," *Fabula*, 38, 199–209.

Köhler-Zülch, Ines, and Christine Shojaei Kawan (1990). "Les Frères Grimm et leurs contemporains. Quelques réflexions sur l'adaptation des contes traditionnels dans le contexte socio-culturel du XIXe siècle," in Veronika Görög-Karady (ed.), *D'un conte... à l'autre—la variabilité dans la littérature orale*. Paris: Éditions du Centre National de la Recherche Scientifique, pp. 249–60.

Kooistra, Lorraine Janzen (2023). "'A Paper of Her Own': Pamela Colman Smith's *The Green Sheaf* (1903–1904)," *Green Sheaf Digital Edition, Yellow Nineties 2.0*, ed. Lorraine Janzen Kooistra, Ryerson University Centre for Digital Humanities, https://1890s.ca/green-sheaf-general-introduction (last accessed June 30, 2024).

Kopper, Edward A. (1976). *Lady Isabella Persse Gregory*. Boston: Twayne.

Kousaleos, Nicole (1999). "Feminist Theory and Folklore," *Folklore Forum*, 30, 1–2, 19–34.

Lambert, Eric (1967). *Mad with Much Heart: A Life of the Parents of Oscar Wilde*. London: Muller.

Lanaro, Silvio (1979). *Nazione e lavoro. Saggio sulla cultura borghese in Italia, 1870–1925*. Padua: Marsilio.

Lathey, Gillian (2010). *The Role of Translators in Children's Literature: Invisible Storytellers*. New York: Routledge.

Lathey, Gillian (2019). "By Forgotten Hands: The Role of Translation in the Emergence of the Fairy Tale," in *The Fairy Tale World*, ed. Andrew Teverson. New York: Routledge, pp. 92–101.

Laukaitis, John J. (2010). "The Politics of Language and National School Reform: The Gaelic League's Call for an Irish Ireland, 1893–1922," *American Educational History Journal*, 37, 1, 221–35.

Lavinio, Cristina (1992). "Primi appunti per una revisione critica dei giudizi sulla lingua di Grazia Deledda," in Collu 1992, I:69–82.

Lavinio, Cristina (2015). "Plurilinguismo in Sardegna tra dibattiti, politiche, ricerche e scelte d'uso," in *La Sardegna contemporanea*, ed. Luciano Marrocu, Francesco Bachis, and Valeria Deplano. Rome: Donzelli, pp. 505–29.

Lavinio, Cristina (2019). "'Era un silenzio che ascoltava'. Grazia Deledda tra leggende e fiabe," in *Oralità narrativa, cultura popolare e arte. Grazia Deledda e Dario Fo. Atti del convegno, Nuoro, 10–11 dicembre 2018*, ed. Cristina Lavinio. Nuoro: ISRE Edizioni, pp. 73–93.

Lee, Linda J. (2008). "Busk, Rachel Harriette," in *The Greenwood Encyclopedia of Folktales and Fairy Tales*, 3 vols., ed. Donald Haase. Westport: Greenwood, I, pp. 149–50.

Lee, Linda J., and Cathy Lynn Preston (2009). "Legend, Supernatural," in Locke et al. 2009, I:354–56.

Leerssen, Joep (1996). *Remembrance and Imagination: Patterns in the Historical and Literary Representation of Ireland in the Nineteenth Century*. Cork: Cork University Press.

Leino, Pentti (1989). "The Interpretation of Tales in Folkloristics," in *Studies in Oral Narrative*, ed. Anna-Leena Siikala and trans. Susan Sinisalo. Helsinki: Suomalaisen Kirjallisuuden Seura, pp. 29–44.

Lenihan, Eddie (2018). *In Search of Biddy Early*. Ennistymon: Hayes Print.

Lenihan, Eddie (2019). *Defiant Irish Women*. Cork: Mercier Press.

Lepschy, Giulio, and Helena Sanson (1991). "'(Non-)Native Speakers' and '(M)Other Tongues,'" *Anglistica*, Special issue: *English and the Other*, ed. Marie-Hélène Laforest and Jocelyne Vincent, 3, 1, 79–92.

Levy, Carl (ed.) (1996). *Italian Regionalism: History, Identity and Politics*. Oxford: Berg.

Lewis, Philip (1996). *Seeing through the Mother Goose Tales: Visual Turns in the Writings of Charles Perrault*. Stanford: Stanford University Press.

Lilliu, Giovanni (2002). *La costante resistenziale sarda*. Nuoro: Ilisso.

Linati, Carlo, et al. (1940). *Irlanda*. Rome: Edizioni Roma.

Lloyd, David (1987). *Nationalism and Minor Literature: James Clarence Mangan and the Emergence of Irish Cultural Nationalism*. Berkeley: University of California Press.

Locke, Liz, Theresa A. Vaughan, and Pauline Greenhill (eds.) (2009). *Encyclopedia of Women's Folklore and Folklife*, 2 vols. Westport: Greenwood.

Lombardi Satriani, Luigi, and Mariano Meligrana (1975). *Diritto egemone e diritto popolare. La Calabria negli studi di demologia giuridica*. Milan: Jaca Book.

Lucchitti, Irene (2010). "The Scripted Life of Peig Sayers," in *The Unsocial Sociability of Women's Lifewriting*, ed. Anne Collett and Louise D'Arcens. London: Palgrave Macmillan, pp. 71–88.

Lundell, Torborg (1986). "Gender-Related Biases in the Type and Motif Indexes of Aarne and Thompson," in Bottigheimer 1986:149–63.

Lunney, Linde (2009). "Young, Rose Maud (Ní Ó hÓgain, Róis)." *Dictionary of Irish Biography*. https://doi.org/10.3318/dib.009182.v1 (last accessed June 30, 2024).

Lynch, Taidgh (2019). "Home and Abroad: Poems." MFA thesis, University of Saskatchewan.

Lysaght, Patricia (1997 [1986]). *The Banshee: The Irish Death Messenger*. Boulder: Roberts Rinehart.

Lysaght, Patricia (1998a). "Perspectives on Narrative Communication and Gender: Lady Augusta Gregory's *Visions and Beliefs in the West of Ireland* (1920)," *Fabula*, 39, 57–94.

Lysaght, Patricia (1998b). "Seán Ó Súilleabháin (1903–1996) and the Irish Folklore Commission," *Western Folklore*, 57, 2–3, 137–51.

Lysaght, Patricia (2019). "From 'Collect the Fragments . . .' to 'Memory of the World'—Collecting the Folklore of Ireland, 1927–70: Aims, Achievement, Legacy," *Folklore*, 130, 1, 1–30.

Mac Aodha, Breandán (1972). "Was This a Social Revolution?" in *The Gaelic League Idea*, ed. Seán Ó Tuama. Cork: Mercier Press, pp. 21–23.

Macciocca, Gabriella (1991). "Alessandro D'Ancona," in *Letteratura italiana. Gli autori*, ed. Alberto Asor Rosa et al., 2 vols. Turin: Einaudi, I, p. 645.

Maddrell, Breesha (2002). "Speaking from the Shadows: Sophia Morrison and the Manx Cultural Revival," *Folklore*, 113, 2, 215–36.

Maffei, Macrina Marilena (2013). *Donne di mare. Una storia sommersa dell'arcipelago eoliano*. Messina: Pungitopo Editrice.

Maggi, Armando (2015). "Orpheus, the King of the Birds, Moves to Sicily with Cupid and Psyche: Laura Gonzenbach's 'King Cardidduˊ,'" in *Preserving the Spell: Basile's "The Tale of Tales" and Its Afterlife in the Fairy-Tale Tradition*. Chicago: University of Chicago Press, pp. 68–86.

Maguire, W. A. (2000). *A Century in Focus: Photography and Photographers in the North of Ireland, 1839–1939*. Belfast: Blackstaff.

Maier, Bernhard (2020). "The Female Quest for the Celtic Tongues of Ireland, Scotland, and Wales," in *Women in the History of Linguistics*, in Ayres-Bennett and Sanson 2020:305–18.

Mansergh, Nicholas (1965). *The Irish Question, 1840–1921: A Commentary on Anglo-Irish Relations and on Social and Political Forces in Ireland in the Age of Reform and Revolution*. Toronto: University of Toronto Press.

Manzo, Pasqualina (1999). *Storia e folklore nell'opera museografica di Giuseppe Pitrè*. Frattamaggiore, Naples: Edizioni Istituto di Studi Atellani.

Marazzini, Claudio (2018). *Breve storia della questione della lingua*. Rome: Carocci.

Marci, Giuseppe (2006). "We Looked to Ireland," trans. Francesco Marco Aresu and Máire Nic Mhaoláin, in Adamo and Marci 2006:9.

Marci, Giuseppe (2007). "'Sardo, Italiano Europeo': l'identità molteplice," in *Isola/Mondo: La Sardegna fra arcaismi e modernità (1718–1918). Atti del convegno, Sassari, 22–24 novembre 2006*, ed. Giulia Pissarello and Fiamma Lussana. Rome: Aracne, pp. 175–83.

Marett, Robert Ranulph (1935). "Obituary: Eleanor Hull," *Folklore*, 46, 1, 76–77.

Markey, Anne (2006). "The Discovery of Irish Folklore," *New Hibernia Review / Iris Éireannach Nua*, 10, 4, pp. 21–43.

Markey, Anne (2011). *Oscar Wilde's Fairy Tales: Origins and Contexts*. Dublin: Irish Academic Press.

Marren, Julie K. (1993). "From *Bean Chaointe* to *Fear Léinn*: The Lament for Art O'Leary," *Proceedings of the Harvard Celtic Colloquium*, 13, 49–53.

Masini, Roberta (ed.) (2007). *Grazia Deledda. Lettere ad Angelo De Gubernatis (1892–1909)*. Cagliari: CUEC.

Masini, Roberta (2010). "Ancora nuove e inedite lettere di Grazia Deledda ad Angelo De Gubernatis," *Bollettino di Studi Sardi*, 3, 123–34.

Masoero, Mariarosa (1990). "Donne—Spiriti—Poeti," in *Il "genio muliebre": Percorsi di donne intellettuali fra Settecento e Novecento in Piemonte*, ed. Marco Cerruti. Alessandria: Edizioni dell'Orso, pp. 63–74.

Mason, Stuart (1914). *Bibliography of Oscar Wilde*. London: T. Werner Laurie.

Massey, Doreen (1994). *Space, Place, and Gender*. Minneapolis: University of Minnesota Press.

Matvejević, Predrag (1999 [1987]). *Mediterranean: A Cultural Landscape*, trans. Michael Henry Heim. Berkeley: University of California Press.

Matvejević, Predrag (2004 [1987]). *Breviario Mediterraneo*. Milan: Garzanti.

Mazzarella, Salvatore (2008). "Nota a *Leggende del mare*," in Maria Savi-Lopez, *Leggende del mare*. Palermo: Sellerio, pp. 9–11.

Mazzoni, Cristina (2008). "'The Loving Re-Education of a Soul': Learning from Fairy Tales through Grazia Deledda and Cristina Campo," *Quaderni d'italianistica*, 24, 2, 93–110.

Mazzoni, Cristina (2019). "A Fairy Tale Madonna: Grazia Deledda's 'Our Lady of Good Counsel,'" *Spiritus: A Journal of Christian Spirituality*, 19, 1, 131–45.

McDiarmid, Lucy, and Maureen Waters (1996). *Lady Gregory: Selected Writings*. London: Penguin Twentieth Century Classics.

McGeachie, James (2016). "Wilde's Worlds: Sir William Wilde in Victorian Ireland," *Irish Journal of Medical Science*, 185, 2, 303–7.

McKee, Ruth (2006). "Grazia Deledda and Katharine Tynan: Exile and Estrangement," in Adamo and Marci 2006:122–28.

McKee, Ruth (2009). "Grazia Deledda (1871–1936) and Irish Women Writers: Nation and Transgression." PhD diss., Trinity College Dublin.

Melville, Joy (1994). *Mother of Oscar: The Life of Jane Francesca Wilde*. London: John Murray.

Mendelssohn, Michèle (2018). *Making Oscar Wilde*. Oxford: Oxford University Press.

Miele, Gina M. (2009). "Luigi Capuana: Unlikely Spinner of Fairy Tales?" *Marvels and Tales*, 23, 2, 300–324.

Migliorini, Bruno (2019). *Storia della lingua italiana*. Florence and Milan: Bompiani.

Migliorini, Bruno, and Gwynfor Griffith (1984). *The Italian Language*. London: Faber and Faber.

Mikhail, E. H. (1977). *Lady Gregory: Interviews and Recollections*. London: Macmillan.

Mitchell, Katharine, and Helena Sanson (eds.) (2013). *Women and Gender in Post-Unification Italy: Between Private and Public Spheres*. Oxford: Peter Lang.

Moe, Nelson (2002). *The View from Vesuvius: Italian Culture and the Southern Question*. Berkeley: University of California Press.

Monaghan, Charles P. (1899). "The Revival of the Gaelic Language," *PMLA: Publications of the Modern Language Association of America*, appendix I and II, proceedings, XIV, pp. xxxi–xxxix.

Morris, Lawrence P. (2010). "'Aristocracies of Thought': Social Class in the Early Folklore of Yeats and Hyde," *Irish Studies Review*, 18, 3, 299–313.

Moyle, Franny (2011). *Constance: The Tragic and Scandalous Life of Mrs Oscar Wilde*. London: John Murray.

Müller, Friedrich Max (1882). "Lettera al Dottor Giuseppe Pitrè, Oxford, 19 Ottobre 1881," *Archivio per lo studio delle tradizioni popolari*, I, 5–8.

Murgia, Michela (2008). *Viaggio in Sardegna. Undici percorsi nell'isola che non si vede*. Turin: Einaudi.
Murphy, James H. (2011). "'Two Nations on One Soil': Land, Fenians, and Politics in Fiction," in *Irish Novelists and the Victorian Age*, ed. James H. Murphy. Oxford: Oxford University Press, pp. 119–48.
Murphy, Maureen (1987). "Lady Gregory and the Gaelic League," in *Lady Gregory, Fifty Years After*, ed. Anne Saddlemyer and Colin Smythe. Gerrards Cross: Colin Smythe, pp. 143–62.
Murphy, Maureen (1991). "Lady Gregory: 'The Book of the People,'" *Colby Quarterly*, 27, 1, 40–47.
Myles, Percy (1890). "Review of Lady Wilde's *Ancient Cures, Charms, and Usages of Ireland: Contributions to Irish Lore*," *The Academy*, 960, September 27, 266.
Naithani, Sadhana (2010). *The Story-Time of the British Empire: Colonial and Postcolonial Folkloristics*. Jackson: University Press of Mississippi.
Ní Chuilleanáin, Eiléan (2003). "Speranza, an Ancestor for a Woman Poet in 2000," in *The Wilde Legacy*, ed. Eiléan Ní Chuilleanáin. Dublin: Four Courts Press, pp. 17–34.
Nic Mhaoláin, Máire (1992). "Grazia Deledda in Irlanda," in Collu 1992, II:349–52.
Nicolaisen, Wilhelm Fritz Hermann, and James Moreira (eds.) (2013). *The Ballad and the Folklorist: The Collected Papers of David Buchan*. St. John's, Newfoundland, and Labrador: Memorial University of Newfoundland.
Ní Dhuibhne, Éilís (2002). "International Folktales," in *The Field Day Anthology of Irish Writing: Irish Women's Writing and Traditions*, ed. Angela Bourke. New York: New York University Press, IV, pp. 1214–18.
Ní Fhlathúin, Máire (1999). "The Irish Oscar Wilde: Appropriations of the Artist," *Irish Studies Review*, 7, 3, 337–46.
Ní Fhrighil, Ríóna (2017). "Of Mermaids and Changelings: Human Rights, Folklore and Contemporary Irish Language Poetry," *Estudios Irlandeses*, Special issue: *New Perspectives on Irish Folklore*, ed. Audrey Robitaillié and Marjan Shokouhi, 12, 2, 107–21.
Norberg, Jakob (2022). *The Brothers Grimm and the Making of German Nationalism*. Cambridge: Cambridge University Press.
Novati, Francesco (1886). "Recensione di *Essays in the Study of Folk-Songs* di Evelyn Martinengo Cesaresco," *Archivio per lo studio delle tradizioni popolari*, V, 602–3.
Noyes, Dorothy (2003). "Review of *Fiabe e mercanti in Sicilia. La raccolta di Laura Gonzenbach. La comunità di lingua tedesca a Messina nell'Ottocento*, and *Fiabe Siciliane*, rilette da Vincenzo Consolo," *Marvels and Tales*, 17, 1, 169–75.
Noyes, Dorothy (2005). "Buried Treasure or Fairy-Tale *Verismo*? Framing Sicilian Women's Stories." Review of *Beautiful Angiola: The Great Treasury of Sicilian Folk and Fairy Tales Collected by Laura Gonzenbach*, ed. and trans. Jack Zipes, illustrated by Joellyn Rock, *Marvels and Tales*, 19, 2, 331–43.
Noyes, Dorothy (2015). "Fairy-Tale Economics: Scarcity, Risk, Choice," *Narrative Culture*, 2, 1, 1–25.
Nutt, Alfred (1903). *The Critical Study of Gaelic Literature: Indispensable for the History of the Gaelic Race*. Dublin: Corrigan & Wilson.
O'Connor, Elizabeth Foley (2021). *Pamela Colman Smith: Artist, Feminist, and Mystic*. Clemson: Clemson University Press.
O'Connor, Ulick (1985). *Celtic Dawn: A Portrait of the Irish Literary Renaissance*. London: Black Swan Books.
Ó Crualaoich, Gearóid (2005). "Reading the *Bean Feasa*," *Folklore*, 116, 1, 37–50.
Ó Giolláin, Diarmuid (2000). *Locating Irish Folklore: Tradition, Modernity, Identity*. Cork: Cork University Press.
Ó Giolláin, Diarmuid (2012). "Ireland," in Bendix and Hasan-Rokem 2012:409–25.

Ó Giolláin, Diarmuid (2022). *Exotic Dreams in the Science of* Volksgeist: *Towards a Global History of European Folklore Studies*. Helsinki: Kalevala Society.

Ó Laoire, Lillis (2017). "'Tá cuid de na mná blasta / Some Women Are Sweet Talkers': Representations of Women in Seán Ó hEochaidh's Field Diaries for the Irish Folklore Commission," *Estudios Irlandeses*, Special issue: *New Perspectives on Irish Folklore*, ed. Audrey Robitaillié and Marjan Shokouhi, 12, 2, 122–38.

O'Leary, Philip (1994). *The Prose Literature of the Gaelic Revival, 1881–1921: Ideology and Innovation*. University Park: Pennsylvania State University Press.

O'Leary, Philip (2006). "The Irish Renaissance, 1890–1940: Literature in Irish," in *The Cambridge History of Irish Literature, 1890–2000*, ed. Margaret Kelleher and Philip O'Leary. Cambridge: Cambridge University Press, II, pp. 226–69.

Olrik, Axel (1992 [1921]). *Principles for Oral Narrative Research*, trans. Kirsten Wolf and Jody Jensen. Bloomington: Indiana University Press.

O'Mahony, Patrick, and Gerard Delanty (1998). *Rethinking Irish History: Nationalism, Identity and Ideology*. New York: Palgrave.

Ó Murchú, Máirtín (1998). "Language and Society in Nineteenth-Century Ireland," in *Language and Community in the Nineteenth Century*, ed. Geraint Jenkins. Cardiff: University of Wales Press, pp. 341–68.

O'Neill, Áine (1991). "'The Fairy Hill Is on Fire' (MLSIT 6071): A Panorama of Multiple Functions," *Béaloideas*, 59, 189–96.

Ong, Walter Jackson (2002 [1982]). *Orality and Literacy: The Technologizing of the Word*. New York: Routledge.

O'Reilly, John Miles (1909). *The Native Speaker Examined Home: Two Stalking Fallacies Anatomized*. Dublin: Sealy, Bryers and Walker.

Oring, Elliott (ed.) (1986). *Folk Groups and Folklore Genres: An Introduction*. Logan: Utah State University Press.

Orioles, Vincenzo (2009). "Tra sicilianità e sicilitudine," *Linguistica*, 49, 1, 227–34.

Ortu, Leopoldo (1998). *L'Eco della Sardegna di Stefano Sampol Gandolfo*, with an introductory essay by Giuseppe Marci. Cagliari: CUEC.

Ó Súilleabháin, Seán (1970). *A Handbook of Irish Folklore*. Detroit: Singing Press.

O'Sullivan, Thomas Francis (1944). *The Young Irelanders*. Tralee: The Kerryman.

Ottaviano, Carlo, and Giulia Ottaviano (2018). "Una svizzera molto siciliana," in *I luoghi e i racconti più strani della Sicilia*. Rome: Newton Compton, pp. 69–72.

Panizza, Letizia, and Sharon Wood (eds.) (2000). *A History of Women's Writing in Italy*. Cambridge: Cambridge University Press.

Paulis, Giulio (2006). "Sardinia: The Third Ireland," trans. Francesco Marco Aresu, in Adamo and Marci 2006:144.

Pellizzi, Carlo Maria (2011). "'Ibernia fabulosa': per una storia delle immagini dell'Irlanda in Italia," *Studi Irlandesi: A Journal of Irish Studies*, 1, 1, 29–119.

Perco, Daniela (2010). "Raccogliere fiabe a fine Ottocento: la corrispondenza tra Angela Nardo Cibele e Giuseppe Pitrè," in *Tra filologia, storia e tradizioni popolari. Per Marisa Milani (1997–2007)*, ed. Luciano Morbiato and Ivano Paccagnella. Padua: Esedra, pp. 217–29.

Perricone, Rosario (ed.) (2017). *Pitrè e Salomone Marino. Atti del convegno internazionale di studi a 100 anni dalla morte*. Palermo: Edizioni Museo Pasqualino.

Perugi, Maurizio (1989). "Pascoli, Shelley, and Isabella Anderton, 'Gentle Rotskettow,'" *Modern Language Review*, 84, 51–65.

Perugi, Maurizio (1990). "The Pascoli–Anderton Correspondence," *Modern Language Review* 85, 595–608.

Perugi, Rosella (2019). "Une voyageuse en fauteuil? L'Islanda di Maria Savi Lopez," *Viaggiatori. Circolazioni scambi ed esilio*, 3, 1, 110–46.

Pethica, James (1987). "Review of Mary Lou Kohfeldt, *Lady Gregory: The Woman behind the Irish Renaissance* (London: André Deutsch, 1985)," *Yeats Annual*, 5, 257–60.
Pethica, James (1996). Introduction to *Lady Gregory's Diaries, 1892–1902*. Gerrards Cross: Colin Smythe, pp. xi–xxxvi.
Piano, Maria Giovanna (1998). *Onora la madre: autorità femminile nella narrativa di Grazia Deledda*. Turin: Rosenberg and Sellier.
Piccitto, Giorgio (1952). "Osservazioni sul linguaggio delle donne," *Orbis. Bulletin International de Documentation Linguistique*, I, 1, 14.
Pickering-Iazzi, Robin (1997). *Politics of the Visible: Writing Women, Culture and Fascism*. Minneapolis: University of Minnesota Press.
Pierantoni Mancini, Grazia (1870). "Laura Gonzenbach" in "Rivista dell'istruzione femminile," *Rivista Europea*, 1, II, III, 572–73.
Pierce, David (1995). *Yeats's Worlds: Ireland, England and the Poetic Imagination*. New Haven: Yale University Press.
Piga Martini, Maria Antonietta (2013). *Grazia Deledda: un singolare romanzo (quasi) d'amore. Dal prezioso carteggio di Grazia Deledda fanciulla con Angelo De Gubernatis dal 1 aprile 1894 a tutto il 1898*. Rome: Aletti.
Pine, Richard (1995). *The Thief of Reason: Oscar Wilde and Modern Ireland*. Dublin: Gill & Macmillan.
Piredda, Benvenuta (2010). *Le tradizioni popolari sarde in Grazia Deledda*. Sassari: Edes.
Pirodda, Giovanni (1992). *Sardegna*. Brescia: Editrice La Scuola.
Pirodda, Giovanni (1998). "L'attività letteraria tra Otto e Novecento," in *La Sardegna. Collana Storia d'Italia. Le regioni dall'unità a oggi*, ed. Luigi Berlinguer and Antonello Mattone. Turin: Einaudi, pp. 1083–1122.
Pittalis, Paola (1998). *Storia della letteratura in Sardegna*. Cagliari: Della Torre.
Plunkett, Horace Curzon (1904). *Ireland in the New Century*. London: John Murray.
Plunkett, Horace Curzon (1914). *La nuova Irlanda*, with an introduction by Gino Borgatta and a preface by Luigi Einaudi. Turin: Società tipografico-editrice nazionale.
Polezzi, Loredana (2004). "Between Gender and Genre: The Travels of Estella Canziani," in *Perspectives on Travel Writing*, ed. Glenn Hooper and Tim Youngs. Aldershot: Ashgate, pp. 121–37.
Prato, Stanislao (1895). "Una proposta," *Rivista delle tradizioni popolari italiane*, 2, V, 387.
Preston, William (1806). "Essay on the Question 'Are the Origin and Progress of the Polite Arts, in Any Country, Connected with, and Depending on, the Political State of That Country?'" in *The Transactions of the Royal Irish Academy, Vol. X, Polite Literature*. Dublin: Graisberry and Campbell, pp. 2–120.
Privat, Jean-Marie (2007). "Les Dîners de Ma Mère l'Oye: traditions populaires et sociabilité," in *Bérose—Encyclopédie internationale des histoires de l'anthropologie*, Paris. www.berose.fr/article207.html?lang=fr (last accessed June 30, 2024).
Propp, Vladimir (1984). *Theory and History of Folklore*, trans. Ariadna Y. Martin and Richard P. Martin. Minneapolis: University of Minnesota Press.
Puccini, Sandra (2005). *L'itala gente dalle molte vite. Lamberto Loria e la Mostra di Etnografia italiana del 1911*. Rome: Meltemi.
Puccini, Sandra (2011). "Una folklorista in viaggio. Caterina Pigorini Beri in Calabria (1887)," in *Se vi sono donne di genio. Appunti di viaggio nell'Antropologia dall'Unità d'Italia a oggi*, ed. Alessandro Volpone and Giovanni Destro Bisol. Rome: Università La Sapienza, pp. 59–72.
Pulido, Maria Pilar (1998). "The Incursion of the Wildes into Tír-na-nÓg," in *That Other World: The Supernatural and the Fantastic in Irish Literature and Its Contexts*, 2 vols., ed. Bruce Stewart. Gerrards Cross: Colin Smythe, II, pp. 219–27.

Quinn, James (2015). *Young Ireland and the Writing of Irish History*. Dublin: University College Dublin Press.

Rabault-Feuerhahn, Pascale (2016). "Comparative Mythology as a Transnational Enterprise: Friedrich Max Müller's Scholarly Identity through the Lens of Angelo De Gubernatis's Correspondence," *Publications of the English Goethe Society*, 85, 2–3, 145–58.

Radner, Joan Newlon (2009). "Coding," in Locke et al. 2009, I:93–97.

Radner, Joan Newlon, and Susan S. Lanser (1987). "The Feminist Voice: Strategies of Coding in Folklore and Literature," *Journal of American Folklore*, Special issue: *Folklore and Feminism*, ed. Bruce Jackson, 100, 398, 412–25.

Radner, Joan Newlon, and Susan S. Lanser (1993). "Strategies of Coding in Women's Cultures," in *Feminist Messages: Coding in Women's Folk Culture*, ed. Joan N. Radner. Urbana: University of Illinois Press, pp. 1–29.

Raftery, Deirdre, Judith Harford, and Susan M. Parkes (2010). "Mapping the Terrain of Female Education in Ireland, 1830–1910," *Gender and Education*, 22, 5, 565–78.

Raftery, Deirdre, and Susan M. Parkes (2007). *Female Education in Ireland, 1700–1900: Minerva or Madonna?* Dublin: Irish Academic Press.

Ragan, Kathleen (2009). "What Happened to the Heroines in Folktales? An Analysis by Gender of a Multicultural Sample of Published Folktales Collected from Storytellers," *Marvels and Tales*, 23, 2, 227–47.

Remport, Eglantina (2018). *Lady Gregory and the Irish National Theatre: Art, Drama, Politics*. Basingstoke: Palgrave Macmillan.

Reynolds, Paige (2018). "Poetry, Drama and Prose, 1891–1920," in *History of Modern Irish Women's Literature*, ed. Heather Ingman and Clíona Ó Gallchoir. Cambridge: Cambridge University Press, pp. 131–48.

Riall, Lucy (1994). *Italian Risorgimento: State, Society and National Unification*. New York: Routledge.

Ricaldone, Luisa (2010). "La montagna di Maria Savi Lopez (1846–1940) nelle lettere ad Antonio Fogazzaro," in Bani 2010:66–71.

Ritchie, Susan (1993). "Ventriloquist Folklore: Who Speaks for Representation?" *Western Folklore*, Special issue: *Theorizing Folklore: Toward New Perspectives on the Politics of Culture*, ed. Amy Shuman and Charles L. Briggs, 52, 2/4, 365–78.

Rizzo, Ester (2022). "Il cortile delle sette fate," *Vitamine Vaganti. Toponomastica femminile*. https://vitaminevaganti.com/2022/12/17/il-cortile-delle-sette-fate (last accessed June 30, 2024).

Robinson, Tim (1992). "Place/Person/Book: Synge's *The Aran Islands*," introduction to J. M. Synge's *The Aran Islands*. London: Penguin, pp. vii–l.

Romani, Gabriella, Ursula Fanning, and Katharine Mitchell (2022). *Matilde Serao: International Profile, Reception, and Networks*. Paris: Classiques Garnier.

Rosati, Claudio (2001). *Beatrice Bugelli di Pian degli Ontani. Poetessa, Pastora*. Pistoia: Brigata del Leoncino.

Rouse, Paul (2009). "Borthwick, Mariella Norma," *Dictionary of Irish Biography*. https://doi.org/10.3318/dib.000791.v1 (last accessed June 30, 2024).

Roversi Monaco, Francesca (2013). "Il 'Medioevo contraffatto' di Emma Perodi. L'ombra del Sire di Narbona," *Storicamente*, 9, 11, 1–12.

Rowe, Karen E. (1986). "To Spin a Yarn: The Female Voice in Folklore and Fairy Tale," in Bottigheimer 1986:53–74.

Rubini, Luisa (1996). "Della 'traducibilità' del folklore. Figure e aspetti della mediazione culturale tra Italia e Germania nell'Ottocento," *La Ricerca folklorica*, 33, pp. 51–57.

Rubini, Luisa (1998). *Fiabe e mercanti in Sicilia. La raccolta di Laura Gonzenbach. La comunità di lingua tedesca a Messina nell'Ottocento*. Florence: Leo S. Olschki.

Rubini, Luisa (2006). "'Che bella sta signora, che me l'ha fatta dire'. La raccolta di Laura Gonzenbach," in *La fiaba e altri frammenti di narrazione popolare. Convegno internazionale di studio sulla narrazione popolare, Padova, 1–2 aprile 2004*, ed. Luciano Morbiato. Florence: Leo S. Olschki, pp. 77–96.

Rudas, Nereide (2004 [1997]). *L'isola dei coralli. Itinerari dell'identità*. Rome: Carocci.

Ruffino, Giovanni (2017). "La linguistica siciliana di fine Ottocento," in Perricone 2017: 333–40.

Ryan, Meda (1978). *Biddy Early: The Wise Woman of Clare*. Dublin and Cork: Mercier Press.

Ryder, Sean (2013). "Son and Parents: Speranza and Sir William Wilde," in *Oscar Wilde in Context*, ed. Kerry Powell and Peter Raby. Cambridge: Cambridge University Press, pp. 7–16.

Said, Edward (1977). "Imaginative Geography and Its Representations: Orientalizing the Oriental," in *Orientalism*. London: Penguin, pp. 49–71.

Said, Edward (1986). "Yeats and Decolonization," in *Nationalism, Colonialism, and Literature*, ed. Terry Eagleton, Fredric Jameson, and Edward Said. Minneapolis: University of Minnesota Press, pp. 69–95.

Saltzman, Rachelle H. (1987). "Folklore, Feminism, and the Folk: Whose Lore Is It?" *Journal of American Folklore*, Special issue: *Folklore and Feminism*, ed. Bruce Jackson, 100, 398, 548–62.

Salvadori Lonergan, Corinna (1970). "Yeats e Castiglione: poeta e cortigiano," in *Il pensiero italiano del Rinascimento e il tempo nostro. Atti del V convegno internazionale del centro di studi umanistici, Montepulciano, Palazzo Tarugi, 8–13 agosto 1968*, ed. Giovannangiola Tarugi. Florence: L. S. Olschki, pp. 195–209.

Sanfilippo, Marina (2020a). "Libri, lettere, scritte e testamenti: magia e pericoli della scrittura nelle raccolte di racconti popolari siciliani dell'Ottocento," *Cuadernos de Filología Italiana*, 27, 199–219.

Sanfilippo, Marina (2020b). "Elisabetta Sanfratello da Vallelunga: la fulminante simplicitas di una narratrice," *Zibaldone. Estudios italianos*, 8, 1–2, 129–45.

Sanson, Helena (2007). *Donne, precettistica e lingua nell'Italia del Cinquecento: un contributo alla storia del pensiero linguistico*. Florence: Accademia della Crusca.

Sanson, Helena (2010). "Women Writers and the Questione della Lingua in Ottocento Italy: The Cases of Caterina Percoto, La Marchesa Colombi, and Matilde Serao," *Modern Language Review*, 105, 4, 1028–1052.

Sanson, Helena (2011). *Women, Language and Grammar in Italy, 1500–1900*. Oxford: Oxford University Press.

Sanson, Helena (2013a). "The Romance Languages in the Renaissance and After," in *The Cambridge History of the Romance Languages*, 2 vols., ed. Adam Ledgeway, Martin Maiden, and John Charles Smith. Cambridge: Cambridge University Press, II, pp. 237–82.

Sanson, Helena (2013b). "'La madre educatrice' in the Family and in Society in Post-Unification Italy: The Question of Language," in Mitchell and Sanson 2013:39–63.

Sanson, Helena (2020). "Women and Language Codification in Italy: Marginalized Voices, Forgotten Contributions," in *Women in the History of Linguistics*, in Ayres-Bennett and Sanson 2020:59–90.

Santoro, Anna (1987). "Maria Savi Lopez," in *Narratrici italiane dell'Ottocento*. Naples: Federico & Ardia, pp. 67–68.

Sarti, Luca (2023a). "Voci differenti, differenti corpi. Il caso delle fiabe femministe di Deirdre Sullivan," *De Genere—Rivista di Studi Letterari, Postcoloniali e di Genere*, 8, 65–84. www.degenere-journal.it/index.php/degenere/article/view/178 (last accessed June 30, 2024).

Sarti, Luca (2023b). "Tra rispetto per la natura e *fairy faith*: i racconti *(ever)green* di Eddie Lenihan." *Studi Irlandesi. A Journal of Irish Studies*, 13, 201–14.

Sawin, Patricia (2004). *Listening for a Life: A Dialogic Ethnography of Bessie Eldreth through her Songs and Stories*. Logan: Utah State University Press.

Scancarello, Walter (ed.) (2014). *Su Emma Perodi: nuovi saggi critici. Atti delle giornate di studio "Emma Perodi: non solo novelle," Firenze, Biblioteca Nazionale Centrale, 9 maggio 2013, e "Raccontar fiabe oggi: rileggendo Emma Perodi," Verona, Teatro Camploy, 10 dicembre 2013*. Pontedera: Bibliografia e Informazione.

Scapecchi, Pietro (1993). *Una donna tra le fate. Ricerca sulla vita e sulle opere di Emma Perodi*. Poppi: Edizioni della Biblioteca Rilliana.

Scappaticci, Tommaso (1995). *Introduzione a Serao*. Bari: Laterza.

Scappaticci, Tommaso (1997). *La contessa e i contadini. Studio su Caterina Percoto*. Naples: Edizioni Scientifiche Italiane.

Scatasta, Gino (1998). "Introduzione," in Lady Francesca Speranza Wilde's *Leggende Irlandesi*, ed. Gino Scatasta, trans. Micaela Tarquinio. Bologna: Re Enzo, pp. 3–22.

Schacker, Jennifer (2003). *National Dreams: The Remaking of Fairy Tales in Nineteenth-Century England*. Philadelphia: University of Pennsylvania Press.

Schenda, Rudolf (1986). *Folklore e letteratura popolare: Italia—Germania—Francia*, trans. Maria Chiara Figliozzi and Ingeborg Walter. Rome: Istituto della Enciclopedia Italiana.

Schram-Pighi, Laura (2003). *La narrativa italiana di utopia dal 1750 al 1915*. Ravenna: Longo.

Schubert, Clara (1888). "La pastorella poetessa. Beatrice di Pian degli Ontani," in *L'Illustrazione Italiana*, 31, pp. 51–52; 32, p. 71, p. 74; 34, pp. 108–9, p. 112.

Sciascia, Leonardo (1970). "Sicilia e Sicilitudine," in *La corda pazza: scrittori e cose della Sicilia*. Turin: Einaudi, pp. 11–17.

Sébillot, Paul (1892). "Les Femmes et les traditions populaires," *Revue des traditions populaires*, VII, 8–9, 449–56.

Secci, Lia (1988). "Viaggio italiano di Fanny Lewald," in *Viaggio e scrittura. Le straniere nell'Italia dell'Ottocento*, ed. Liana Borghi, Nicoletta Livi Bacci, and Uta Treder. Geneva: Slatkine, pp. 101–8.

Secci, Maria Giovanna (1966). "I sardismi nella lingua di Grazia Deledda," *Annali della Facoltà di Lettere e Filosofia dell'Università di Cagliari*, 30, 125–83.

Senehi, Jessica, and Marcie G. Hawranik (2009). "Politics," in Locke et al. 2009, II:463–69.

Serianni, Luca (1989). *Il primo Ottocento*. Bologna: Il Mulino.

Serianni, Luca (1990). *Il secondo Ottocento*. Bologna: Il Mulino.

Serra, Valentina (2017). "Island Geopoetics and the Postcolonial Discourse of Sardinia in German-Language Literature," *Island Studies Journal*, 12, 2, 281–90.

Soldi, Manuela (2015). "Esporre il femminile. L'Esposizione Beatrice (Firenze, 1890)," *Ricerche di S/Confine: Oggetti e pratiche artistico/culturali*, 4, 1, 24–26.

Solinas Donghi, Beatrice (2022). *La fiaba come racconto e altri scritti sul fiabesco*, ed. and with a preface by Pino Boero. Milan: Topipittori.

Sottile, Roberto (2017), "Aspetti della variabilità in 'Fiabe novelle e racconti popolari siciliani,'" in Perricone 2017:373–90.

Sottilotta, Elena Emma (2021). "From Avalon to Southern Italy: The Afterlife of Fata Morgana in Laura Gonzenbach's *Sicilianische Märchen* (1870)," *Women Language Literature in Italy / Donne Lingua Letteratura in Italia*, 3, 103–21.

Sottilotta, Elena Emma (2022). "Maria Savi-Lopez: The Portrait of a Neglected Woman Writer and Folklorist in Post-Unification Italy," *P.R.I.S.M.I. Revue d'études italiennes*, Nouvelle série, 3, 141–63.

Sottilotta, Elena Emma (2023). "(Re)Collections of a 'Piccola Streghina' from the Heart of the Mediterranean: Gender and Class Consciousness in Grazia Deledda's Folkloric Writings," *I.S. MED.—Interdisciplinary Studies on the Mediterranean*, 1, 109–29.

Sottilotta, Elena Emma (2024). "'Miniere di fiabe': Poetics of Space and Performance within and outside Angela Nardo Cibele's Folk and Fairy-Tale Writings," *Women Language Literature in Italy / Donne Lingua Letteratura in Italia*, 6.
Spivak, Gayatri Chakravorty (1988). "Can the Subaltern Speak?" in *Marxism and the Interpretation of Culture*, ed. Lawrence Grossberg and Cary Nelson. Urbana: University of Illinois Press, pp. 271–313.
Stampa, Stefano (1885). *Alessandro Manzoni: la sua famiglia, i suoi amici. Appunti e memorie*, 2 vols. Milan: Hoepli.
Stapleton-Corcoran, Erin (2009). "Banshee," in Locke et al. 2009, I:31–32.
Stein, Arnold (1949). "Yeats: A Study in Recklessness," *Sewanee Review*, 57, 4, 603–26.
Stone, Kay (2008). *Some Day Your Witch Will Come*. Detroit: Wayne State University Press.
Sulis, Gigliola (2001). "Introduzione," in *Trovare racconti mai narrati, dirli con gioia. Convegno di studi su Sergio Atzeni, Cagliari, 25–26 novembre 1996*, ed. Giuseppe Marci and Gigliola Sulis. Cagliari: CUEC, pp. 7–32.
Sulis, Gigliola (2011). Review of Grazia Deledda's *Dance of Modernity* by Margherita Heyer-Caput and *The Challenge of Modernity: Essays on Grazia Deledda*, ed. Sharon Wood, *Modern Language Review*, 106, 4, 1174–76.
Sulis, Gigliola (2017). "Sardinian Fiction at End of the Twentieth and Beginning of the Twenty-first Century: An Overview and First Assessment," *Incontri: Rivista europea di studi italiani*, 32, 2, 69–79.
Sulis, Gigliola (2022–23). "Lungo il filo delle *janas*. La scrittura al femminile in Sardegna oltre la categoria dell'eccezionalità," *Chronica Mundi*, Special issue: *Women in Sardinia: Creativity and Self-Expression*, ed. Sara Delmedico and Elena Emma Sottilotta, 16/17, 13–64.
Tanda, Nicola (1992). *Dal mito dell'isola all'isola del mito: Deledda e dintorni*. Rome: Bulzoni.
Tasca, Luisa (2003). "Cordelia," in *Giornali di donne in Toscana. Un catalogo, molte storie (1770–1945)*, 2 vols., ed. Silvia Franchini, Monica Pacini, and Simonetta Soldani. Florence: Olschki, I, pp. 278–86.
Tatar, Maria (2003). *The Hard Facts of the Grimms' Fairy Tales*. Princeton: Princeton University Press.
Tatar, Maria (2021). *The Heroine with 1001 Faces*. New York: Liveright.
Tedlock, Barbara (1995). "Works and Wives: On the Sexual Division of Textual Labor," in *Women Writing Culture*, ed. Ruth Behar and Deborah A. Gordon. Berkeley: University of California Press, pp. 267–86.
Teza, Emilio (1870). "Recensione di *Sicilianische Märchen. Aus dem Volksmund gesammelt von Laura Gonzenbach*, Leipzig 1870 (I.° LIII 368. II.° 263). Novelline siciliane raccolte da L. Gonzenbach, con note di R. Köhler e pubblicate con una introduzione da Ottone Hartwig," *Rivista Bolognese di Scienze e Lettere diretta e compilata dai professori Albicini, Fiorentino e Tocco*, IV, II, 212–22.
Thompson, Stith (1946). *The Folktale*. New York: Dryden Press.
Thompson, Stith (1956). *Motif-Index of Folk-Literature: A Classification of Narrative Elements in Folktales, Ballads, Myths, Fables, Mediaeval Romances, Exempla, Fabliaux, Jest-Books, and Local Legends*, vol. III F–H. Bloomington: Indiana University Press.
Thuente, Mary Helen (1981). *W. B. Yeats and Irish Folklore*. Totowa: Barnes & Noble Books.
Tipper, Karen Sasha Anthony (2002). *A Critical Biography of Lady Jane Wilde, 1821?–1896: Irish Revolutionist, Humanist, Scholar and Poet*. Lewiston: Edwin Mellen Press.
Tipper, Karen Sasha Anthony (2008) (ed.). *Lady Jane Wilde's Letters to Fröken Lotten von Kræmer, 1857–1885*. Lewiston: Edwin Mellen Press.
Tipper, Karen Sasha Anthony (2013) (ed.). *Lady Wilde's Letters to Constance Wilde, Friends and Acquaintances, with Selected Correspondence Received*. Lewiston: Edwin Mellen Press.

Tóibín, Colm (2002). *Lady Gregory's Toothbrush*. Dublin: Lilliput Press.
Tóibín, Colm (2019). *Mad, Bad, Dangerous to Know: The Fathers of Wilde, Yeats and Joyce*. London: Penguin Books.
Tolkien, John Ronald Reuel (2014 [1939]). *On Fairy-Stories*. London: HarperCollins.
Tomasi di Lampedusa, Giuseppe (1926). "W. B. Yeats e il risorgimento irlandese," *Le opere e i giorni. Rassegna mensile di politica, lettere, arti*, V, 11, 36–46.
Tommaseo, Niccolò (1832). "Gita nel Pistojese," *Antologia. Giornale di Scienze, Lettere e Arti*, 48, 12–33.
Toomey, Deirdre (1998). "The Story-Teller at Fault: Oscar Wilde and Irish Orality," in *Wilde the Irishman*, ed. Jerusha McCormack. New Haven: Yale University Press, pp. 24–35.
Toschi, Paolo (1964). "Presentazione," in *Tradizione popolare nelle fiabe siciliane di Laura von Gonzenbach*, ed. and trans. Renata La Racine. Messina: D'Anna, pp. 7–9.
Tosi, Arturo (2020). "Women Travellers and Gender Issues," in *Language and the Grand Tour: Linguistic Experiences of Travelling in Early Modern Europe*. Cambridge: Cambridge University Press, pp. 240–59.
Trapani, Eleonora (2010). "Profilo biografico di un'improvvisatrice toscana del Settecento: Fortunata Sulgher Fantastici," *Archivio per la memoria e la scrittura delle donne, Archivio di Stato di Firenze*, 1–11.
Trombatore, Ignazio Arturo (1894a). "Ancora delle 'donne di casa,'" *Rivista delle tradizioni popolari italiane*, 1, X, 764.
Trombatore, Ignazio Arturo (1894b). "Le donne di casa," *Rivista delle tradizioni popolari italiane*, 1, XII, 930–32.
Trombatore, Ignazio Arturo (1896). *Folk-lore catanese*. Turin: Carlo Clausen.
Turchi, Dolores (1995). Introduction to Grazia Deledda's *Tradizioni popolari di Sardegna: credenze magiche, antiche feste, superstizioni e riti di una volta nei più significativi scritti etnografici dell'autrice sarda*, ed. Dolores Turchi. Rome: Newton Compton, pp. 7–63.
Turtas, Gloria (2022–23). "Maria Elena Sini. Una voce allo scoppio del primo conflitto mondiale. Con un'introduzione sulla poesia femminile cantata e 'a tavolino' nelle fonti," *Chronica Mundi*, Special issue: *Women in Sardinia: Creativity and Self-Expression*, ed. Sara Delmedico and Elena Emma Sottilotta, 16/17, 158–79.
Upchurch, David A. (1992). *Wilde's Use of Irish Celtic Elements in* The Picture of Dorian Gray. New York: Peter Lang.
Uther, Hans-Jörg (2004). *The Types of International Folktales: A Classification and Bibliography Based on the System of Antti Aarne and Stith Thompson*, 3 vols. Helsinki: Suomalainen Tiedeakatemia, Academia Scientiarum Fennica.
Valisa, Silvia (2018). "Cosa scrivevano le donne di fine Ottocento? Il contributo italiano alla *Woman's Building Library* della World Fair di Chicago (1893)," *gender/sexuality/Italy*, 5, 236–56.
Varty, Anne (1998). *A Preface to Oscar Wilde*. London: Longman.
Vejvoda, Kathleen (2004). "'Too Much Knowledge of the Other World': Women and Nineteenth-Century Irish Folktales," *Victorian Literature and Culture*, 32, 1, 41–61.
Vicente, Filipa Lowndes (2012). *Altri Orientalismi. L'India a Firenze, 1860–1900*. Florence: Florence University Press.
von Franz, Marie-Louise (2001 [1977]). *The Feminine in Fairy Tales*. Boston: Shambhala.
Wagner, Birgit (2011). "La questione sarda. La sfida dell'alterità," in *Aut aut: il postcoloniale in Italia*, 349, ed. Giovanni Leghissa. Milan: il Saggiatore, pp. 10–29.
Wagner, Max Leopold (1997 [1951]). *La lingua sarda*. Nuoro: Ilisso.
Walker, Brian Mercer (1977). "Rose Shaw: Women of Clogher," in *Shadows on Glass: A Portfolio of Early Ulster Photography*. Belfast: Appletree Press, pp. 56–65.
Walshe, Eibhear (2020). *Selected Writings of Speranza and William Wilde*. Clemson: Clemson University Press.

Walshe, Eibhear (2023a). *Jane Wilde*. Brighton: Edward Everett Root.
Walshe, Eibhear (2023b). "The Silencing of Speranza," in *Narratives of the Unspoken in Contemporary Irish Fiction: Silences That Speak*, ed. M. Teresa Caneda-Cabrera and José Carregal-Romero. Cham: Palgrave Macmillan, pp. 131–48.
Warner, Marina (1994). *From the Beast to the Blonde: On Fairy Tales and Their Tellers*. London: Vintage.
Warner, Marina (ed.) (1996). *Wonder Tales: Six Stories of Enchantment*, illustrated by Sophie Herxheimer. London: Vintage.
Warner, Marina (2013 [1976]). *Alone of All her Sex: The Myth and the Cult of the Virgin Mary*. Oxford: Oxford University Press.
Warner, Marina (2018). *Fairy Tale: A Very Short Introduction*. Oxford: Oxford University Press.
Waters, Maureen (1995). "Lady Gregory's 'Grania': A Feminist Voice," *Irish University Review*, 25, 1, 11–24.
White, Timothy J. (2004). "Myth-Making and the Creation of Irish Nationalism in the 19th Century," *Studi Celtici. Rivista internazionale di storia, linguistica e antropologia culturale. An International Journal of History, Linguistics and Cultural Anthropology*, 3, 325–39.
Wilde, Oscar (1886). "'The Poetry of the People': Review of Evelyn Martinengo-Cesaresco, *Essays in the Study of Folk-Songs*," *Pall Mall Gazette*, May 13, 5.
Wilson, Thomas George (1942). *Victorian Doctor: Being the Life of Sir William Wilde*. London: Methuen.
Winston, Greg (2001). "Redefining Coole: Lady Gregory, Class Politics, and the Land War," *Colby Quarterly*, 37, 3, 205–22.
Winter, Susanne (2019). "Performatività e improvvisazione: l'artista Teresa Bandettini Landucci," *Italica Wratislaviensia*, 10, 161–74.
Wood, Juliette (1999). "Folklore Studies at the Celtic Dawn: The Role of Alfred Nutt as Publisher and Scholar," *Folklore*, 110, 1–2, 3–12.
Wood, Juliette (2000). "A Welsh Triad: Charlotte Guest (1812–1895), Marie Trevelyan (1853–1922), Mary Williams (1883–1977)," in Blacker and Davidson 2000:259–76.
Wood, Sharon (ed.) (2007). *The Challenge of the Modern: Essays on Grazia Deledda*. Leicester: Troubador.
Woodham-Smith, Cecil (1962). *The Great Hunger*. New York: Harper & Row.
Wright, Thomas (2008). *Oscar's Books*. London: Chatto & Windus.
Wyndham, Horace (1951). *Speranza: A Biography of Lady Wilde*. London: T. V. Boardman.
Yeats, William Butler (1890). "Poetry and Science in Folk-lore," *The Academy*, October 11, 320.
Yeats, William Butler (1999 [1893]). "The Message of the Folk-Lorist," in *International Folkloristics: Classic Contributions by the Founders of Folklore*, ed. Alan Dundes. Blue Ridge Summit: Rowman & Littlefield, pp. 47–53.
Yeats, William Butler (2004 [1890]). "'Tales from the Twilight': Review of Lady Wilde's *Ancient Cures, The Scots Observer*, 1 March 1890," in *The Collected Works of W. B. Yeats: Uncollected Articles and Reviews Written between 1886 and 1900*, 14 vols., ed. John P. Frayne and Madeleine Marchaterre. New York: Scribner, IX, pp. 113–16.
Young, Ella (1951). "Autobiographical Sketch," in *The Junior Book of Authors*, ed. Stanley J. Kunitz and Howard Haycraft. New York: H. W. Wilson, pp. 304–6.
Zimmermann, Georges Denis (2001). *The Irish Storyteller*. Dublin: Four Courts Press.
Zipes, Jack (ed.) (1986). *Don't Bet on the Prince: Contemporary Feminist Fairy Tales in North America and England*. New York: Routledge.
Zipes, Jack (2002a). *The Brothers Grimm: From Enchanted Forests to the Modern World*. New York: Palgrave Macmillan.
Zipes, Jack (2002b). *Breaking the Magic Spell: Radical Theories of Folk and Fairy Tales*. Lexington: University Press of Kentucky.

Zipes, Jack (2006a). "Laura Gonzenbach's Buried Treasure," in *Beautiful Angiola: The Lost Sicilian Folk and Fairy Tales of Laura Gonzenbach*, ed. and trans. Jack Zipes. New York: Routledge, pp. xi–xxvii.

Zipes, Jack (2006b). *Fairy Tales and the Art of Subversion: The Classical Genre for Children and the Process of Civilization*. New York: Routledge.

Zipes, Jack (2009a). "The Indomitable Giuseppe Pitrè," *Folklore*, 120, 1, 1–18.

Zipes, Jack (2009b). "Luigi Capuana's Search for the New Fairy Tale," *Marvels and Tales*, 23, 2, 367–90.

Zipes, Jack (2012). *The Irresistible Fairy Tale: The Cultural and Social History of a Genre*. Princeton: Princeton University Press.

Zipes, Jack (ed.) (2013). *The Golden Age of Folk and Fairy Tales from the Brothers Grimm to Andrew Lang*. Indianapolis: Hackett.

Zipes, Jack (2015). *Grimm Legacies: The Magic Spell of the Grimms' Folk and Fairy Tales*. Princeton: Princeton University Press.

Zipes, Jack (2019). *Ernst Bloch: The Pugnacious Philosopher of Hope*. Cham: Palgrave Macmillan.

Zipes, Jack (2023). *Buried Treasures: The Power of Political Fairy Tales*. Princeton: Princeton University Press.

Zuccala, Brian (2020). *A Self-Reflexive* Verista*: Metareference and Autofiction in Luigi Capuana's Narrative*. Venice: Edizioni Ca' Foscari Digital.

Zumthor, Paul (1983). *Introduction à la poésie orale*. Paris: Éditions du Seuil.

INDEX

Page numbers in italics indicate illustrations.

Aarne-Thompson-Uther Index (ATU), 94; *The Animal as Bridegroom*, 216n80; *The Black and White Bride*, 229; *Girl's Riddling Answer Betrays a Theft*, 182; *Goldener*, 203n62; *The Magic Flight*, 216n80; *The Maiden without Hands*, 212; *The Serpent's Crown*, 199–200; *The Three Old Spinning Women*, 194n52
Abbey Theatre, 148
Adamo, Giuliana, 126
Aders, Julie, 90
Aeolian Islands, 236
Alexander, Francesca (née Esther Frances), 54–59
Andersen, Hans Christian, 14, 75, 229
Anderson, Benedict, 162
Anderton, Isabella, 53–54, 59
animal fables, 146
Aprile, Renato, 203
Apuleius, Lucius, 216
Aran Islands, 7, 34; Gregory's visits to, 156, 159, 211; Synge on, 36
Archivio per l'Antropologia e la Etnologia, 43
Archivio per lo studio delle tradizioni popolari (*ASTP*), 39, 42, 44n62, 45, 47, 114n73, 144n124
Arlia, Costantino, 22n3
Arnold, Matthew, 143
Arthurian legends, 203, 234
Ascoli, Graziadio Isaia, 37–38, 41
Atlantis myth, 6
ATU. *See* Aarne-Thompson-Uther Index
authority, 14, 71, 84–85, 142, 170
authorship, 60–61, 171, 239; collective, 9, 173–74; editorial redactions and, 140, 144, 231

Bacchilega, Cristina, 3, 14, 104, 170, 235
Balázs, Béla, 1, 20
ballads, 69, 133, 136–37, 149, 156
Ballero, Antonio, 192
bandits, 80, 111n64
banshee, 225–27, 235
Barlow, Jane, 80–82, 156
Basile, Giambattista, 176
Bassi, Ugo, 133n111
Battaglia, Salvatore, 22n3
Battle, Mary, 177–78
Bauman, Richard, 88
Bayne, Marie, 79
Béaloideas (journal), 82
béaloideas ("oral teaching"), 22n3
bean feasa ("woman of knowledge"), 214
bean sí. *See* banshee
Beatrice di Pian degli Ontani (Beatrice Bugelli), 54–59, *57*, *58*, 174
Beccari, Gualberta Alaide, 46
Beiner, Guy, 83n144
Bellorini, Egidio, 114, 124
benandanti ("people who go out to do good"), 218n84
Benfey, Theodor, 146
Beranger, Gabriel, 135, 138
Bergin, Osborn, 75
Bibbò, Antonio, 28–30, 34n34, 151
Blacker, Carmen, 11
Blackie, Sharon, 17n22
Blasket Islands, 34
Bloch, Ernst, 181
Boccaccio, Giovanni, 176
Böhl de Faber, Cecilia (Fernán Caballero), 118–19
Borgatta, Gino, 30
Bork (or Borcke), Sidonia von, 131

279

Borthwick, Norma, 75, 150
Bottiglioni, Gino, 114n72, 231
Bourdieu, Pierre, 86
Bourke, Angela, 8, 12, 83
Briggs, Katharine, 221n95, 224
Broadwood, Lucy, 77
Brooke, Charlotte, 67
Brothers Grimm, 14, 20, 25–26, 33; informants of, 175–76, 176; Sicilian fairy tales and, 102; Zipes on, 175n7. Works of: *Deutsche Sagen*, 26; *Kinder- und Hausmärchen*, 26
Brusca, Rosa, 179–80
Buckley, Ned, 212
Bugelli, Beatrice. *See* Beatrice di Pian degli Ontani
Burne, Charlotte, 74n134
Burne-Jones, Edward, 131
Busk, Rachel H., 11, 41, 52–53; Pitrè on, 119n81; *The Folk-Lore of Rome*, 95, 104

Caballero, Fernán (Cecilia Böhl de Faber), 118–19n81
Caico, Louisa Hamilton, 51
Calvia, Giuseppe, 114
Calvino, Italo, 39n46; on Percoto, 43; on Sardinian folklore, 113. Works of: *Collezione di sabbia*, 21, 23; *Fiabe italiane*, 104, 170, 178–79
Campbell, Joseph, 16
Campbell, Matthew, 26
Cane, Crescenzio, 161n150
Canepa, Nancy, 102, 108, 199n55; *The Enchanted Boot*, 16, 213n76
Cantù, Cesare, 27–28, 41, 56–59
Canz, Wilhelmine, 131
Canziani, Estella, 51–52, 74
"Caoineadh Airt Uí Laoghaire" (lament), 68
Cappelletti, Licurgo, 94n16, 96
Capuana, Luigi, 60–61, 88, 216n80, 221n92
Carducci, Giosuè, 49
Carleton, William, 34, 80
Carrassi, Vito, 24
Carrington, Henry, 64
Carroll, Hannah Elizabeth, 52
Carter, Angela, 17n22, 173
Castellana, Riccardo, 220
Castiglione, Baldassare, 155
Cattaneo, Carlo, 31
Cavazza, Stefano, 28, 88n1

Cavour, Camillo Benso di, 31–32
Celtic peoples, 146–47; Anglo-Saxons versus, 70n129, 143, 147; languages of, 65–66; mythology of, 78. *See also* Ireland
Certo, Caterina, 182, *183*, 185, 186
Ceylon, 150
Chambers, Iain, 31
changelings, 206, 219–25
children, 127; evil eye and, 210; fairy abduction of, 206, 211, 219–25; games of, 74, 110; *janas* and, 231; mortality rates among, 224
Chini, Chiara, 30
Chiostri, Carlo, 59, *60*, *61*
Christiansen, Reidar, 194n52, 228n105
Cian, Vittorio, 114n73
Cinderella, 44, 101, 120–21, 232
Cirese, Alberto Mario, 101
Ciusa, Francesco, 192
class awareness, 19, 209, 219, 239–40; Busk and, 52–53; De Gubernatis and, 189; Deledda and, 107, 187, 190; educational opportunities and, 66, 88; folklore collectors and, 23–24, 62, 86–87, 127; Gonzenbach and, 167, 168, 187, 200; Gregory and, 147, 151, 156–57, 161; Halls and, 70, 71; Nardo Cibele and, 46–47; Wilde and, 129, 137, 147, 160, 164–65. *See also* identity politics
Cleary, Bridget (née Boland), 224n100
Clementina (Anderton's informant), 53–54, 174
Cocchiara, Giuseppe, 12, 65, 102, 113
Collins, Michael, 154
Colman Smith, Pamela "Pixie," 75
Colum, Mary (née Maguire), 70n130
Colum, Padraic, 70n130
Comparetti, Domenico, 39n46, 100–101
Conkling, Philip, 209–10
Connacht insurrection (1798), 83n144
Consolo, Vincenzo, 2, 103
conteuses, 16, 174. *See also* fairy tales
Cook, Keningale, 139
Coppola, Maurizio, 40, 54–55
Coronedi Berti, Carolina, 47–48
Costello, Eileen (née Edith Drury), 77, 78
Coxhead, Elizabeth, 150
Crane, Thomas Frederick, 47n77, 103
Crialese, Francesca, 182, *184*
criminology, 110–11

Crivelli, Tatiana, 55n102
Croce, Benedetto, 49
Croker, Thomas Crofton, 221–22, 226; *Fairy Legends*, 33, 143, 228n105
crones, 175n8, 176, 186, 195, 221, 226. *See also* witches
Cruciani, Veronica, 233
Cú Chulainn (Ulster hero), 148
cultural appropriation, 24, 102–4, 113
cultural identity, 5, 162, 165, 170. *See also* identity politics
Curatolo, Maria, 180
Curtin, Jeremiah, 228n105
Curtis, Lewis Perry, 147

D'Ancona, Alessandro, 42, 62
Dante Alighieri, 40, 129
d'Arborea, Eleonora, 190, 232
Darwin, Charles, 127
d'Aulnoy, Marie-Catherine, 16
Davidson, Hilda Ellis, 11
Davis, Thomas Osborn, 127
Day, Andrea, 11n14
"daydream religion" (Henningsen), 219
Deae Matres, 226n102. *See also* banshee
de Caro, Francis A., 15
De Gubernatis, Angelo, 19, 40–44; Busk and, 53; Deledda and, 112, 116–25, *117*, *122*, 187; Laura Gonzenbach and, 98–99, 101; Magdalena Gonzenbach and, 91–92; in *Natura ed Arte*, 40n51, 189; Savi-Lopez and, 50
de la Motte Fouqué, Friedrich, 229
Delargy, James H. (Séamus Ó Duilearga), 82–83
Deledda, Andrea, 124
Deledda, Giovanni Antonio, 107
Deledda, Grazia, 2–4, 17–19, 32, 106–26; Cocchiara on, 113; as cultural intermediary, 87; on curses, 206–7; De Gubernatis and, 112, 116–25, *117*, *122*, 187; ethnographic studies of, 41; films about, 107n50; gender norms and, 109, 113, 124–25; on *gosos*, 108n54; on healers, 214–15; informants of, 186; on *janas*, 231–35; legacy of, 237–39; in *Natura ed Arte*, 110, 118, 120, 186–89, *188*; as Nobel laureate, 106, 238. Works of, 109–10; *Canne al vento*, 186, 234; *Cenere*, 111n63; *Cosima*, 107–9, 232–33; "La donna in Sardegna," 189–94, 204; *La madre*, 31, 115; "Nostra Signora del Buon Consiglio," 213; "Ricordi di Sardegna," 108; "Tipi e paesaggi sardi", 190–92, *191*; *Tradizioni popolari di Nuoro*, 110–14, 163–64, 206–7; *La via del male*, 110, 111n63

Delitala, Enrica, 178n14
de Martino, Ernesto, 208–9
De Roberto, Federico, 88
De Rosa, Francesco, 114
de Valera, Éamon, 79n139
de Valera, Sinéad, 79n139
Diana (Roman deity), 231n109
Di Francia, Letterio, 121n88, 178
Dillon, John Blake, 127
Disney, Walt, 14
Dolfi, Anna, 109n60
domestic violence, 204–6
doñas de fuera (*donne di fuori*), 217–21, 225n102, 231, 235
Dracula figure, 197
Drury, Edith (Eileen Costello), 77, 78
Duggan, Anne, 16
Dumas, Alexandre, 131
Dundes, Alan, 10

Early, Biddy, 214
Easter Rising (1916), 35, 76, 78
education, female, 66, 76–77, 88, 129, 205
Egerton, George, 32
Einaudi, Luigi, 30
Eldreth, Bessie, 10n13
Elgee, Charles, 129
Elgee, Jane. *See* Wilde, Jane Francesca
Enclosures, Edict of (1820), 111
Eriksen, Anne, 52
evil eye, 73, 208, 210–12

fairy cults, 219
fairy godmothers, 213
"Fairy Justice," 181, 200, 204–6
fairy tales: Calvino on, 145; Cinderella, 44, 101, 120, 121, 232; folktales and, 174; hopeful themes in, 181, 193, 204, 219, 235, 240; of *janas*, 231–35; Lathey on, 87; Manx, 77n138; perspectives of, 172–73; "realistic," 93; Snow-White, 54; wonder tales versus, 3n3. *See also individual folklorists*
"fakelore" (Dorson), 145, 230n106

Falchi, Luigi, 114, 123
Fanfani, Pietro, 22n3
Fata Morgana (Morgan le Fay), 203–4, 234
Fates (Parche), 45–46
Febvre, Lucien, 5
Feis na nGleann festival, 78
feminism, 7–9, 11–17; protofeminism and, 90–91, 127–28, 132–33; Wilde on, 205. *See also* gender dynamics
femme fatale, 131
Ferraro, Giuseppe, 114
Ferri, Enrico, 111n63
Fienga, Dino, 30
Fitzsimons, Eleanor, 129
Fogazzaro, Antonio, 49, 51
Fois, Marcello, 233
"folk," 3, 21–22, 173
folk healers, 171, 214–15
folklore, 174, 181, 235, 239; animal fables and, 146; "fakelore" and, 145, 230n106; folksongs and, 178–79; "gaelicization" of, 38; genres of, 49, 83; Hawaiian, 71n130; of highwaymen, 80; inbetweenness of, 161–69; Irish word for, 22n3; as lingua franca, 239; magical creatures of, 215–35; "meridionalization" of, 39; as "minor history," 2; negative connotation of, 109; old wives' tales as, 14, 223; spinning women and, 195–97, *196*; utopian potential of, 181. *See also* fairy tales
folklore studies, 3, 22, 39; dialectology and, 46–47; Gramsci on, 23; strategies of, 161–69
folk revivals, 21–22, 26
folksongs, 62–63, 77n138, 108
Forgacs, David, 37
Franchetti, Leopoldo, 105
Friedman, Susan Stanford, 6

Gaelic League, 34–35, 36, 163n152; Costello and, 78; educational reforms of, 163; Gregory and, 150; Rossi and, 153. *See also* Irish Revival
Gaeltacht, 38–39, 126–27, 197–98. *See also* Irish language
Garibaldi, Giuseppe, 63n115
Garrigan Mattar, Sinéad, 151n139, 160
Gavan Duffy, Charles, 74, 127, 130
gender dynamics, 7–9, 24, 199, 237; in Deledda, 109, 113, 124–25; educational opportunities and, 66, 76–77, 129, 205; of folktale classification, 94n15; geopolitics of place and, 86, 127; in Gonzenbach, 199–200; of informants, 175–77; of Irish Folklore Commission, 82–83; language and, 44n63, 46n73; property rights and, 205; in Sayers, 84–85; of suffrage, 75–76, 78, 205. *See also* feminism; identity politics
Genette, Gérard, 9, 141
Ginzburg, Carlo, 218n84
Gomme, Alice Bertha (née Merck), 74
Gonne, Maud, 79
Gonzenbach, Laura, 2–4, 17–19, 88–106, 167–68; as cultural intermediary, 87; daughters of, 92–93; De Gubernatis on, 98–99, 101; Deledda and, 166; informants of, 182–86, *183*, *184*; legacy of, 237–39; on *mammadraga*, 216–17; Martinengo-Cesaresco on, 95; Pitrè and, 19, 99–102; women characters of, 199–201; Zipes on, 11, 102, 103. Works of: "La figlia della Madonna," 212–13; "La serpe che testimoniò in favore di una ragazza," 199–200; *Sicilianische Märchen*, 2, 89, 181–87, 203–4, 216; "La storia della Fata Morgana," 203–4; "La storia di Sorfarina," 200–202
Gonzenbach, Magdalena, 90–93, 205
Gonzenbach, Peter Viktor, 90
Goodwin, Edmund, 77n138
Gore-Booth, Constance (Countess Markievicz), 76
Gore-Booth, Eva, 75–76
Gosse, Edmund, 131
Gower Chapman, Charlotte, 168n163
Gramsci, Antonio, 15, 23–24
Grant Duff, Mountstuart Elphinstone, 156
Great Irish Famine (1845–52), 7, 134–35, 209; educational reforms after, 163; linguistic implications of, 35
Greenhill, Pauline, 3
Gregory, Augusta (née Persse), 2–4, 17–19, 147–63, 237–39; Aran Islands visits by, 156, 159, 211; on banshees, 226–27; Borthwick and, 75; on changelings, 221; Coole Park estate of, 238; as cultural intermediary, 87; on evil eye, 210, 212; on folklore's importance, 157–58; on healers, 214; informants of, 197–98, 210, 212; as Irish

language learner, 149–50, 159–60, 162–63; Irish Revival and, 148, 151, 152, 155, 160; Italy visits by, 150; on mermaids, 227–29; as playwright, 147–48; portrait of, 153; Rossi and, 151–52; translations of, 148n134, 162–63; Wilde and, 147; Yeats and, 34–35, 151, 154–55. Works of: "The Continuity of Folklore," 157, 162; *Coole*, 155n145; *Cuchulain of Muirthemne*, 148, 149; *Gods and Fighting Men*, 148; Kiltartan books, 148, 154, 158, 162–63, 228; "The Man That Served the Sea," 228; *Poets and Dreamers*, 148, 156–57, 198, 219; *Seventy Years*, 153–54; *Visions and Beliefs*, 148, 158–60, 197, 198, 214, 227
Gregory, Margaret, 158
Gregory, Robert, 150
Gregory, William, 150
Grierson, Elizabeth W., 79
Grimm, Jacob, 25–26. *See also* Brothers Grimm
Grimm, Ludwig Emil, 176
Grimm, Wilhelm, 25–26, 33n33
"Grimm Ripples," 26
Grossi, Vincenzo, 22n3
Guest, Charlotte, 77n138
Gunnell, Terry, 26

Haase, Donald, 16
habitus, 86
Hall, Anna Maria (née Fielding), 70–72, 226n104
Hall, Samuel Carter, 70–72, 226n104
Harlem Renaissance, 167
harps, 69
Harries, Elizabeth Wanning, 172
Hart, Biddy, 177
Hartwig, Otto, 94, 96, 101, 167, 182–83, 186
Hawaiian folklore, 71n130
Hebrides Islands, 63, 77n138
Heiniger, Abigail, 121
Henningsen, Gustave, 219
Hiberno-English, 162, 163. *See also* Irish language
Higginson, Agnes (Moira O'Neill), 79
Hill, Judith, 148
Hobsbawm, Eric, 18n24
Holbek, Bengt, 172–73, 184
Holland, Ann, 80
Hone, Joseph Maunsell, 151

hopeful themes in fairy tales, 181, 193, 204, 219, 235, 240
horned women, 194–95. *See also* witches
Hull, Eleanor, 74–75
Hunt, Margaret (née Raine), 11n14
Hunt, Violet, 11n14
Hurston, Zora Neale, 167
Hyde, Douglas, 33, 35, 74; on folklore collecting, 159, 166; Irish song collections of, 35; McClintock and, 72; Wilde and, 142–43, 164

identity politics, 5, 86, 129, 170; language and, 162; Massey on, 127; race and, 146–47, 165; self-representation and, 112. *See also* class awareness; gender dynamics
Imbriani, Vittorio, 42
"insularity," 4n4
intersectionality, 3–4, 10, 24, 127, 173
intertextuality, 3, 9, 16, 49, 88
Invernizio, Carolina, 40n52
Ireland, 5–8; Calvino on, 145; Connacht insurrection in, 83n144; cultural nationalism in, 7; Easter Rising in, 76, 78; rural revolts in, 160–61; Sardinia and, 32, 121, 126; Sicily and, 31–32; women's folklore of, 65–85. *See also* Celtic peoples
"Ireland of Italy," 29–32
Irish Folklore Commission, 82–83
Irish Great Famine. *See* Great Irish Famine
Irish language, 7, 35, 65–66, 78; in Gaeltacht, 38–39, 126–27, 197–98; Gregory and, 149–50, 159–60, 162–63; revitalization of, 38, 75; William Wilde on, 163n153
Irishness, 161–62
Irish Question, 35n37, 121n89
Irish Revival, 7, 38, 78, 221; Gregory and, 148, 151, 152, 155, 160; Yeats and, 160, 198. *See also* Gaelic League
Irish Texts Society, 74–75
Irish War of Independence (1919–21), 29, 78
Irish Women's Franchise League, 76–77
islandness, 4–6, 161, 169, 209–10, 240

Jackson, Kenneth, 83
Jaeger, Wilhelm, 93
Jamaica, 75
janas (Sardinian fairies), 231–35
jettatura, 208. *See also* evil eye

Jordan, Rosan, 15
Journal of American Folklore, 14–15
Joyce, James, 71n130, 160
Joynt, Maud, 76–77
Jubber, Nicholas, 174
Jungian archetypes, 175n8
justice. *See* "Fairy Justice"
Juta, Jan, 115

Kalcik, Susan, 15
Kane, Colman, 197, 198
keening, 68, 227
Keightley, Thomas, 230n106
Kendall, May, 11n14
Kennedy, Patrick, 34
Kennedy-Fraser, Marjory, 77
Kiberd, Declan, 35, 178
Killala, French landing at (1798), 83n144, 149
Killeen, Jarlath, 166
"Kiltartanese," 162–63
King, Martha, 116
Kingsbury, Sarah, 129
Kinsella, Thomas, 68n127
Knapp, James, 28
Knust, Hermann, 100n32
Koehler, Julie, 16, 128n102
Köhler, Reinhold, 94, 101
Kooistra, Lorraine Janzen, 75

Laboulaye, Édouard, 201n58
La Force, Charlotte-Rose Caumont de, 16
Lai, Maria, 233
Lamartine, Alphonse de, 131
Lang, Andrew, 11
Lang, Leonora Blanche, 11
language, 239; dialects of, 37–38, 46–47, 87, 101–2, 166; gender dynamics of, 44n63, 46n73; identity politics and, 162; Manx, 77n138; Sanskrit, 146. *See also individual countries*
Lanser, Susan, 15, 113
La Racine, Renata, 103
Lathey, Gillian, 87
Lavinio, Cristina, 213
Lawrence, D. H., 115
Lazzaro, Bianca, 16–17
Lee, Kate, 77
Leerssen, Joep, 38n45
Lenihan, Eddie, 17, 224n99

Leslie, Shane, 80
Lévesque, Nannette, 11
Levi, Eugenia, 48–49, 62
L'Héritier, Marie-Jeanne, 16
Lilliu, Giovanni, 165
literacy, 54, 109. *See also* oral traditions
Lloyd, Constance. *See* Wilde, Constance Lloyd
Lloyd, David, 130n105
Lombardi Satriani, Luigi, 39
Lombroso, Cesare, 111
"long nineteenth century" (Hobsbawm), 18n24, 65–85
Loria, Lamberto, 42n55
Loriga, Francesco, 114n72
Lover, Samuel, 34
Lutzu, Pietro, 114n72
Lyall, Juanita, 64
Lydis, Mariette, 20n26
Lysaght, Patricia, 8

Mabinogion, 77n138
MacDonald, George, 76
Macpherson, James, 67
Madesani, Palmiro, 107
Maeve, Queen of Connacht, 76
Maffei, Macrina Marilena, 236
Maggi, Armando, 102, 216
Maier, Bernhard, 65–66, 67, 77
Mameli, Goffredo, 29
mammadraga figure, 215–16, 222, 235
Manca, Maria, 231n108
Mancini, Antonio, 152, 153
Mango, Francesco, 114n72
Manx language, 77n138
Manzoni, Alessandro, 37, 59
Marci, Giuseppe, 31–32
Marcucci, Regina, 59–62, 60, 61
Marett, Robert Ranulph, 74
Margherita of Savoy, 41
Marian worship, 211–14
Markey, Anne, 138, 141, 195, 229n106
Markievicz, Countess (Constance Gore-Booth), 76
Martinengo-Cesaresco, Evelyn Carrington, 12–13, 41, 63–64, 94–95, 182
Masini, Roberta, 116
Massey, Doreen, 86, 127, 237
Mathews, P. J., 35, 178
Maturin, Charles, 127

Matvejević, Predrag, 4–5
Mazzini, Giuseppe, 29, 31, 35n37
Mazzoni, Cristina, 16, 213n76
McClintock, Letitia, 72–74
McKee, Ruth, 32
Meinhold, Wilhelm, 131
Meligrana, Mariano, 39
mermaids, 215, 227–29, 235
Merton, Ambrose (William Thoms), 22n3
Messia, Agatuzza, 178, 179, 200n58
Mikhail, E. H., 155
Mill, John Stuart, 91
Moe, Nelson, 5
Molesworth, Mary Louisa, 174n6
Monaci, Ernesto, 179
Moore, George Augustus, 155, 160
Moore, Thomas, 33, 149
Morelli, Maria Maddalena, 55n102
Morgan, Charles, 68–69
Morgan, Lady (Sydney Owenson), 68–69
Morgan le Fay (Fata Morgana), 203–4, 234
Morganti, Salvatore, 94–96
Morrison, Sophia, 77n138
Mother Goose, 175–76
Müller, Max, 144n124
Murgia, Michela, 233
Myles, Percy, 144, 145
myth-making, 78, 127, 157–58; Atlantis, 6; Norse, 49n84, 228; Ossian, 67; political, 7n10

Naithani, Sadhana, 27
Narayan, Kirin, 167
Nardo Cibele, Angela, 45–46, 48, 56
Natura ed Arte (journal): De Gubernatis in, 40n51, 189; Deledda in, 110, 118, 120, 186–87, *188*
Němcová, Božena, 11
Neumann, Adolf, 183n28
Niceforo, Alfredo, 110–11, 126
Ní Chonaill, Eibhlín Dubh, 68
Ní Chuilleanáin, Eiléan, 142, 195
Nic Mhaoláin, Máire, 31
Nigra, Costantino, 42
Ní Shíndile, Nóra (Norrie Singleton), 68
noble savage myth, 127
Nogelmeier, Puakea, 104
Novati, Francesco, 12–13
Nurra, Pietro, 114
Nutt, Alfred, 28, 121

O'Connell, Mary Anne, 68n127
O'Connor, Frank, 68n127
O'Connor, Ulick, 135n114
O'Donoghue, David James, 132
Ó Duilearga, Séamus (James H. Delargy), 82–83
Ó Gaoithin, Micheál, 84
Ó Giolláin, Diarmuid, 7, 26, 67
O'Growney, Eugene, 150
O'Holland, Cormic, 80
Ó Laoghaire, Peadar, 75
old wives' tales, 14, 223
O'Neill, Moira (Agnes Higginson), 79
Ong, Walter, 4
oral traditions, 9–10, 97–98, 227; Deledda on, 110, 213; from Gaeltacht, 126–27; keening in, 68, 227; literacy and, 54, 109; performativity of, 7–8, 178–79; Sébillot on, 13; Thompson on, 172. *See also* storytelling
Orano, Paolo, 110–11
orientalism, 5, 173
Oring, Elliott, 37
Orme, Jennifer, 3
Ortu, Leopoldo, 32
Ossian controversy, 67
Ó Súilleabháin, Seán, 82, 194n52
"otherwise stories" (Bacchilega), 235
Ovid, 174, 195
Owenson, Sydney (Lady Morgan), 68–69

pagan beliefs, 115, 136, 208–15
"pancake tossing," 72, 73
paratexts, 4, 9, 140–41
Parche (the Fates), 45–46
Pearse, Patrick, 35
Percoto, Caterina, 42–43
Perodi, Emma, 59–61
Perraudin, Michael, 26
Perrault, Charles, 14, 20, 175–76
Persia, 146
Persse, Isabella Augusta. *See* Gregory, Augusta
Piccitto, Giorgio, 46n73
Pierantoni Mancini, Grazia, 93
Piga Martini, Maria Antonietta, 116–17
Pigorini, Luigi, 44
Pigorini Beri, Caterina, 43–45, 48
Pirandello, Luigi, 220–21

Pirodda, Andrea, 114
Pitrè, Giuseppe, 2, 42; Busk and, 53n97, 119n81; Coronedi Berti and, 48; Crane and, 47n77; on *doñas de fuera*, 217–19; Gonzenbach and, 19, 99–102; informants of, 178–81; Levi and, 49; on *mammadraga*, 215; Martinengo-Cesaresco on, 63; medical practice of, 135n114; Müller and, 144n124; Nardo Cibele and, 45–46; Perodi and, 59; Pigorini Beri and, 44–45; on Sicilian dialect, 101–2, 166; on spitting, 212. Works of: *Biblioteca delle tradizioni popolari siciliane*, 39; *Canti popolari siciliani*, 62; "Catarina la Sapienti," 200n58; *Costumi siciliani*, 185–86; "Lu cuntu di 'Si raccunta,'" 180n18; *Fiabe novelle e racconti popolari siciliani*, 119n81, 180, 200n58; *Medicina popolare siciliana*, 212; *Novelle popolari toscane*, 180–81
Plunkett, Horace, 30
Pollexfen, George, 178
Pooka (shape-shifter), 71
Popert, Carlotta Ida, 190n38
positivism, 88
Potato Famine. *See* Great Irish Famine
Prato, Stanislao, 175
Pre-Raphaelite artists, 131
Preston, William, 69–70
"prison-isles" (Febvre), 5
protofeminism, 90–91, 127–28, 132–33. *See also* gender dynamics
Puccini, Mario, 49

racial theories, 146–47, 165
Radner, Joan, 15, 113
Raftery, Anthony, 156
Ragan, Kathleen, 12
Rajna, Pio, 49
Renan, Ernest, 143
Reynolds, Paige, 238
Riall, Lucy, 111
riddles, 83, 110, 182
Risorgimento, 7, 29, 63, 91, 111
Ritchie, Anne Thackeray, 174n6
Ritchie, Susan, 166
Rivista delle tradizioni popolari italiane (RTPI), 42; De Gubernatis's work in, 40, 45, 118; Deledda's work in, 107, 108n54, 110–14, 163–64, 186–87; Manca's work in, 231n108; Trombatore's work in, 220
Rivista Sicula di Scienze, Letteratura ed Arti, 95, 182
Rizzo, Ester, 218n86
Roeder, Charles, 77n138
Rolleston, Thomas William, 74
Romanticism, 25, 34, 88
Roper, Esther, 76
Rossetti, Dante Gabriel, 131
Rossi, Mario Manlio, 151–53
Rubieri, Ermolao, 42, 62
Rubini, Luisa, 2, 8, 89, 168n163; Gonzenbach and, 103, 106, 203
Ruskin, John, 55, 56

Said, Edward, 5, 173
Salomone-Marino, Salvatore, 39
Sampol Gandolfo, Stefano, 32n30
Sanfratello, Elisabetta, 179–80
Sanskrit, 146
Sardinia, 5–6, 31, 190–91, *191*; "barbarism" of, 115, 116, 125–26; Enclosures Edict and, 111; folklore of, 87, 106–26, 163–66, *188*; Ireland and, 32, 121, 126; *janas* of, 231–35; language of, 109, 115, 163–64; law code of, 190
Sardinianness, 161–62
Sardinian Question, 31, 192. *See also* Southern Question
Sarti, Luca, 224n99
Satta, Giuseppe, 118–19
Satta, Sebastiano, 192
Savi-Lopez, Maria, 18n23, 49–51
Sawin, Patricia, 10n13
Sayers, Peig, 83–85, *84*, 174
Scano, Antonio, 118–19
Scatasta, Gino, 164
Schacker, Jennifer, 9, 175, 195n53
Schenda, Rudolph, 89, 98
Schneller, Christian, 100n32
Schubert, Clara, 55–56
Sciascia, Leonardo, 161n150
Sébillot, Paul, 13, 64, 94
Selberg, Torunn, 52
selkies, 228. *See also* mermaids
Serao, Matilde, 64
Shakespeare, William, 33, 73
shape-shifters, 71, 218
Shaw, Rose, 79–80, *81*

Shedden-Ralston, William, 101–2
Shelley, Mary, 147n131
Sheridan, Mary, 149, 162n151
Siciliano, Giovanni, 180–81
Sicily, 5–6, 31, 161–62; Brothers Grimm and, 102; Curtigghiu di li setti Fati in, 218; earthquake in, 89–90; Gonzenbach and, 2, 89, 181–87, 203–4, 216; language of, 95–96, 101–2, 163, 166–67, 179; Martinengo-Cesaresco and, 94–95; Vigo and, 99; wonder tales of, 94–106
Singleton, Norrie (Nóra Ní Shíndile), 68
síscéalta (fairy tales), 139
síthe (*Sidhe*), 221–25, 227, 231
Snow-White, 54
Società Nazionale per le Tradizioni Popolari Italiane, 40–41, 92, 118–19
Solinas Donghi, Beatrice, 240–41
Sonnino, Sidney, 105
Southern Question, 30–32, 39, 105–6, 192
Sparling, Henry Halliday, 136–37
spinning women, 195–97, 196; ATU Index on, 194n52; banshees and, 227
spitting, 211–13
Spivak, Gayatri, 9, 173, 236
Stewart Murray, Evelyn, 77n138
Stoker, Bram, 75, 197
storytelling, 83, 159, 174–80, 187, 237; anonymity of, 174; Calvino on, 178–79; Holbek on, 172–73; performativity of, 9–10, 98, 179; Sébillot on, 13; Thompson on, 172. *See also* oral traditions
subversive narratives, 171, 181, 200
suffrage, 75–76, 78, 205
Sullivan, Deirdre, 17n22
Swedenborg, Emanuel, 131, 159
Synge, J. M., 35–36, 160

tarot cards, 75
Tatar, Maria, 16, 175n7
Taylor, Edgar, 175
Tenniel, John, 147n131
Terranova, Nadia, 218
Teza, Emilio, 96
Thiselton-Dyer, T. F., 33
Thompson, Stith, 94, 172. *See also* Aarne-Thompson-Uther Index
Thoms, William (Ambrose Merton), 22n3

Thousand and One Nights, 104, 174
Thuente, Mary Helen, 72
Tipper, Karen, 131
Tír inna mBan (Land of Women), 5n7
Tír na nÓg (Land of the Young), 34
Tóibín, Colm, 160
Tolkien, J. R. R., 171–72
Tolmie, Frances, 77
Tomasi di Lampedusa, Giuseppe, 29
Tommaseo, Niccolò, 41, 43; Bugelli and, 54–55; folksong collection of, 108; as lexicographer, 181n22; Nardo Cibele and, 46n72
Toponomastica femminile (organization), 218n86
Toschi, Paolo, 168, 177
Travers, Mary, 140n120
Tre-Pi (wizard), 60–62
Trevelyan, Marie, 77n138
Turati, Vittorio, 185
Turchi, Dolores, 231
Tylor, Edward Burnett, 127
Tynan, Katharine, 32

Umberto I of Italy, 41
Uther, Hans-Jörg, 94n15. *See also* Aarne-Thompson-Uther Index
utopian thinking, 181

Valla, Filippo, 114n73
Verga, Giovanni, 88, 163
verismo literature, 88, 93
Viehmann, Dorothea, 175, 176
Vigo, Lionardo, 99
Vita Sarda (journal), 118, 120
Vittorio Amedeo II of Savoy, 111
von Franz, Marie-Louise, 175n8
von Kræmer, Lotten, 225

Wagner, Birgit, 31
Wagner, Max Leopold, 115
Wales, 77n138
Wall, Thomas, 160
Walsh, Angela, 17n22
Walshe, Eibhear, 129, 134, 140n120
Warner, Marina, 3, 14, 186
Warrack, Grace, 62–63
Wentrup, Christian Friedrich, 102n38
Widter, Georg, 100n32
Wilde, Constance Lloyd, 139, 225

Wilde, Isola Francesca Emily, 225
Wilde, Jane Francesca "Speranza," 2–4, 17–19, 126–47, 164–66; on banshees, 225–26; on changelings, 223–25; on child mortality, 224; death of, 225–26; education of, 129–30; on evil eye, 211–12; family of, 127, 129, 139, 160; on folk healers, 214; Gregory and, 147; husband of, 19, 87, 134; Hyde on, 142–43; legacy of, 237–39; Markey on, 141; on mermaids, 230–31; as polyglot, 130, 131; portrait of, *128*; racial theories of, 146–47; salons of, 134; on *síthe*, 221–25; Stoker and, 197; on women's rights, 205; writing style of, 164; Yeats and, 134n113, 137, 143–45, 166. Works of: *Ancient Cures*, 137–44, 147, 165, 214, 223, 235; *Ancient Legends*, 137–46, 165, 194–95, 204–5, 214, 223; "The Bondage of Woman," 132; "The Dead Soldier," 229, 230; *Driftwood from Scandinavia*, 132–34; "The Fairy Child," 205–6; "Fairy Justice," 204, 205; "The Fisherman," 230; "The Horned Women," 194–97; *Notes on Men, Women, and Books*, 132, 140; *Poems by Speranza*, 130; *Social Studies*, 132; *Ugo Bassi*, 133n111
Wilde, Oscar, 64, 138, 139, 225; fairy-tale collections of, 138–39; family of, 127, 138–39; as *Woman's World* editor, 140n121. Works of: *De Profundis*, 138; "The Fisherman and His Soul," 229
Wilde, William, 19, 87, 134–36; scandal of, 140n120. Works of: "The Ancient Races of Ireland," 139; *Irish Popular Superstitions*, 163n153; *Memoir of Gabriel Beranger*, 135, 138

William of Orange, 230
Williams, Maria Jane, 77
Williams, Mary, 77n138
witches, 215; crones and, 176, 186, 221, 226; *doñas de fuera* as, 218; fairies and, 217–19, 234; horned women as, 194–95; *síthe* and, 221
Wolf, Adam, 100n32
Women Writing Wonder (Koehler et al.), 16, 128n102
wonder tales, 3, 17, 26, 52, 208, 227; Celtic, 78; definition of, 3n3; Sicilian, 94–106
Wood, Sharon, 109

Yeats, W. B., 75; Carrassi on, 24; on folklore, 33, 34, 158–59, 170; Gregory and, 34–35, 151, 154–55; informants of, 177–78; Irish Revival and, 160, 198; as Nobel laureate, 155; Swedenborg and, 159; Thuente and, 72; Wilde and, 134n113, 137, 143–45, 166. Works of: *The Celtic Twilight*, 154, 177, 178; *Fairy and Folk Tales of the Irish Peasantry*, 170; *Irish Fairy Tales*, 177–78
Young, Ella, 78
Young, Rose Maud, 77, 78
Young Ireland movement, 127, 129, 130

Zambrini, Francesco, 47n75
Zanetti, Ombretta, 47n77
Zinn, Dorothy Louise, 208n73
Zipes, Jack, 2, 8, 16, 24; on *benandanti*, 218n84; on fairy tales, 11–12, 102, 103; on folktales' utopian potential, 181; on nationalistic movements, 77; on "romantic regionalism," 25
Zumthor, Paul, 9

A NOTE ON THE TYPE

This book has been composed in Arno, an Old-style serif typeface in the classic Venetian tradition, designed by Robert Slimbach at Adobe.

GPSR Authorized Representative: Easy Access System Europe - Mustamäe tee
50, 10621 Tallinn, Estonia, gpsr.requests@easproject.com

www.ingramcontent.com/pod-product-compliance
Lightning Source LLC
Chambersburg PA
CBHW030609230426
43661CB00053B/1906